THE
DRAGON
LANTERN

BY ALAN GRATZ

The League of Seven
The Dragon Lantern
The Monster War (forthcoming)

ARCHIE

HACHI

FERGUS

?

?

?

?

The League
of Seven

THE DRAGON LANTERN

A League of Seven Novel

ALAN GRATZ

Illustrations by

BRETT HELQUIST

STARSCAPE

A TOM DOHERTY ASSOCIATES BOOK
NEW YORK

THE DRAGON LANTERN: A LEAGUE OF SEVEN NOVEL

Copyright © 2015 by Alan Gratz

Reader's Guide copyright © 2015 by Tor Books

The Monster War excerpt copyright © 2015 by Alan Gratz

Interior illustrations by Brett Helquist

Map by Jennifer Hanover

A Starscape Book
Published by Tom Doherty Associates, LLC
175 Fifth Avenue
New York, NY 10010

www.tor-forge.com

The Library of Congress Cataloging-in-Publication Data
is available upon request.

ISBN 978-0-7653-3823-5 (hardcover)
ISBN 978-1-4668-3851-2 (e-book)

Starscape books may be purchased for educational, business, or promotional use. For information on bulk purchases, please contact the Macmillan Corporate and Premium Sales Department at 1-800-221-7945, extension 5442, or write to specialmarkets@macmillan.com.

First Edition: June 2015

Printed in the United States of America

0 9 8 7 6 5 4 3 2 1

To my dog, Augie –
I wouldn't have thought of Buster without you!

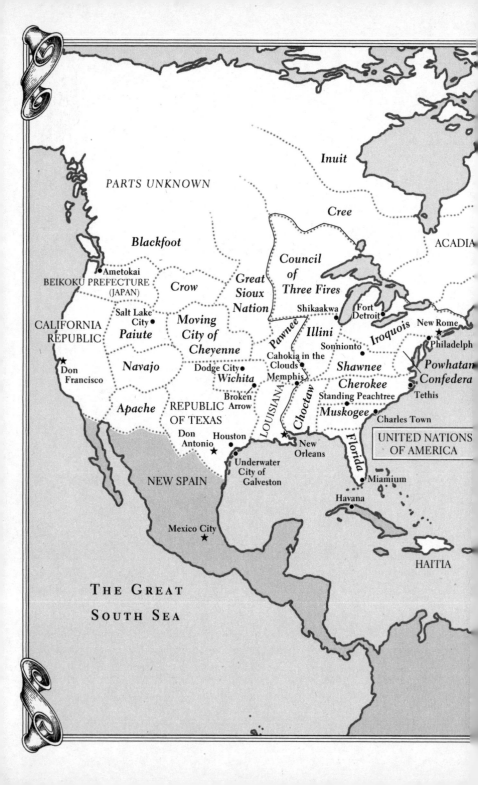

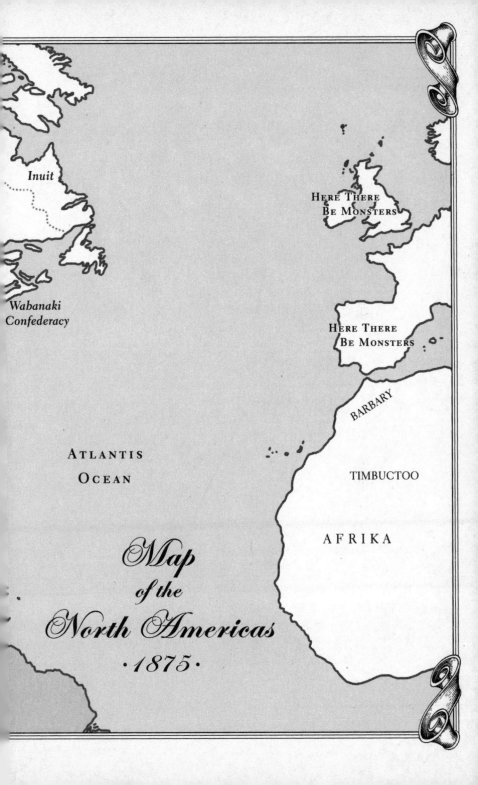

Inuit

Wabanaki
Confederacy

HERE THERE
BE MONSTERS

HERE THERE
BE MONSTERS

BARBARY

ATLANTIS
OCEAN

TIMBUCTOO

AFRIKA

Map
of the
North Americas
·1875·

THE
DRAGON
LANTERN

Thirty days hath September.
Seven heroes we remember.

The League of Seven. They were always seven, and always the same: a tinker, a law-bringer, a scientist, a trickster, a warrior, a strongman, and a hero. Seven men and women with incredible powers from all parts of the known world who joined forces to stop the Mangleborn from enslaving humanity.

Different Leagues had saved the world over and over again, but few people knew that. Only the Septemberists remembered, watching for signs that the Mangleborn might escape the elaborate prisons the Ancient League had built for them, and waiting for a new League of Seven to be born. . . .

1

Archie Dent dangled from a rope twenty thousand feet in the air, watching the blue ribbon of the Mississippi River spin far, far below him. At that moment, he didn't feel scared, or dizzy, or angry.

He felt betrayed.

"Retrieving the Dragon Lantern will be easy for three Leaguers," Philomena Moffett had told him and his friends Hachi and Fergus. "For that's what you are. The first of a new League of Seven."

Easy. That's what the head of the Septemberist Society had called retrieving this lantern thing. Even though it was hidden at the heart of a Septemberist puzzle trap. On top of a giant helium balloon. Twenty thousand feet in the air.

As he hung from his safety line for what had to be the thousandth time in the last three days, all Archie could think was that Philomena Moffett had not been entirely honest with them.

"Haul him up," Hachi said over the wind.

Archie sighed, his warm breath filling the mask that fit over his leather helmet. Fergus had built the helmets special. A breathing mask, which snapped on just below the brass goggles Archie wore, brought fresh oxygen to him from the tank on his back. They needed them—like the heavy, fur-lined coats and the spider's web of ropes and carabiners they wore—to scale the mountain-sized helium kite high up in the thin atmosphere that held Cahokia in the Clouds afloat.

Archie felt a lurch on his line, and then the familiar *yank-yank-yank* of Fergus' ratchet as he was lifted back up. Soon he was close enough to take Hachi's hand, and she helped him grab hold of the network of ropes that covered the vast canvas of the balloon.

"Archie, you've got to hang on better," Hachi told him.

Archie flushed in embarrassment under his breathing mask. Hachi Emartha hadn't fallen off once in all the time they'd been at this, but that was to be expected. She'd spent the last three years of her life training to be the greatest warrior who ever lived. Everything she did was graceful, from eating her breakfast to killing Manglespawn. But what really embarrassed Archie was that Fergus MacFerguson had only slipped and fallen twice, and Fergus had only one good leg. His other leg, hobbled by a meka-ninja, now had only two settings—loose and useless, or straight and stiff—which he controlled with a knee harness he'd built himself.

"I'm sorry," Archie said. "I wasn't made for this. I'm good at punching and being punched. Not hopping around like a monkey."

"Well, one of these times your safety line's going to give way, and then you'll really be sorry," Hachi told him. "You do not want to test Fergus's backup plan."

"Oy," Fergus said. "The gyrocopters work great. Sure, they're better at going down than up. And they're maybe a little hard to steer. But they're better than falling straight down. Besides, there wasn't room for parachutes in the backpacks with all the oxygen and lamps."

Archie looked down again, but clouds obstructed his view of the ground. *I'm higher than the clouds*, Archie thought, and then he did feel a twinge of fear creep in.

"Archie doesn't need to worry about falling anyway," Fergus said. "He'll just hit the ground and bounce back up, like he did before."

"That was from only half this height," Hachi reminded him. "And he's not totally invulnerable. We don't know what his limits are, but there's no reason to test them until we have to."

Archie shifted his grip on the rope, trying not to think about his fall from his family's airship during their midair battle with Edison. Trying not to think about the crack in his arm, the one he'd gotten fighting Edison's lektrical robot body.

The crack that showed Archie was made of stone.

The crack that showed he wasn't entirely human.

"Let's just get on with it," Archie said.

"Just a little farther, and then we wait for nightfall," Hachi said.

They were working their way sideways around the broad, gently curved side of the enormous helium balloon on the rope-like rigging that covered it like a giant net. Archie thought of the stuff as "rope-like" because it wasn't really rope—not like the twine rope he knew. It was made of something gray and shiny, like metal, but it stretched and hung like a fiber rope. The gray lines, just like the strange canvas-like material that held the helium trapped inside it, had been invented by Wayland Smith and Daedalus of the Roman League of Seven hundreds of years ago, and the world had yet to rediscover the secrets of their construction.

Fergus ran a hand along the glossy veneer of the canvas. "I can't get over this stuff," he said. "Helium is so small it escapes from almost anything. Anything light enough to float, that is. But not this. It's been hanging up here in the clouds for almost two millennia."

"They had to make sure it wasn't going to fall," Archie said.

"Which you're both going to do if you don't focus," Hachi told them. "Next section. Go."

The ropes-that-weren't-ropes formed a grid of squares on the canvas-that-wasn't-canvas, like the latitude and longitude lines on a globe. They were just tall enough for Hachi and Fergus to stand in a grid square on the bottom rope and hold on to the top rope with their hands, but Archie was younger and shorter than both of them. Where they could crab walk across, he had to lunge.

Fergus shuffled his way across the grid square to the next, his kilt flapping wildly in the freezing, howling wind. He'd at least had the sense to put on long underwear underneath it, even though the baggy red long johns looked silly with his blue tartan kilt.

At last he was across, and it was Archie's turn.

"You can do this," Hachi told him.

Archie focused on the rope at the other side of the grid, took a deep breath of the fresh oxygen pumped into his mask, and dove for it. The wind caught his big coat like a sail and spun him, and he fell. He clawed out blindly with his hands and felt only canvas. *Zip!* He was sliding down again, falling, soon to be dangling from his safety line again—or worse—when at last his hand felt rope, and he snatched at it. *Oof.* He slammed into the canvas and hung there, panting, as he got his breath back.

"Better. Next grid," Hachi said, already moving along. "And don't forget to reattach your safety line."

Archie closed his eyes and put his head against the canvas balloon. What was it his mother always said? *No rest for the weary.*

That they were here at all—three kids on a top secret, super-dangerous mission for the Septemberist Society—was incredible by the looks of it. What kind of adults would throw children into the firebox like so many lumps of coal? And what kind of parents would let them?

But Hachi, the thirteen-year-old Seminole girl, had no parents to ask. She had been on her own ever since their deaths when she was little. Fergus, the fourteen-year-old tinker, was on his own too. He had left his family's farm in North Carolina to apprentice with Thomas Edison, but had run away when his boss had pumped Fergus full of lektric squid blood.

It was Archie's parents who had said no.

"He's too young," his mother had said.

"He's not ready," his father had said.

But then it had been pointed out to them that even though he was just twelve, Archie had the strength of a hundred men. Or so it seemed. And Archie couldn't get sick, couldn't be hurt, and couldn't die. At least, nothing had killed him yet. And by all rights, Archie should have died at least five times already that he knew of.

And then Philomena Moffett had told him that the Dragon Lantern had something to do with where he had really come from. How he had come to be this way. All Archie knew was that he'd been adopted, that the Septemberist Society had found him when he was an infant and placed him with Dalton and Agatha Dent and then studied him, watching and waiting for him to grow into whatever superhuman thing he was to become. Mrs. Moffett didn't know what, exactly, the Dragon Lantern had to do with how he was born, but once they had it, she promised she could tell him more.

That sealed it. There was no way Archie was staying home for this mission. In the end, his parents had to let him go.

Not that they were really his parents.

Archie jumped and almost missed the next rope. It took Hachi and Fergus both hauling him back up to keep him from falling again.

"*Focus*," Hachi told him.

"*I'm trying*," Archie said.

"No you're not," Hachi said. "Your mind is somewhere else. I can see it in your eyes. You're thinking about how you're not a real boy. You're *always* thinking about how you're not a real boy. So stop and focus on where you are and what you're doing. You know what happens when you lose focus."

Archie's face burned hot under his mask again. None of them needed any reminder about what happened when Archie lost his head.

Hachi stared at him until he met her eyes. She was hard and demanding, but she also knew what it was to be so angry it consumed you. So angry it ate you up and swallowed you whole, and you let it because deep down you *wanted* it to.

Archie nodded. "I'm okay. I'll be okay."

Hachi gave a curt nod back. "Tell us the nursery rhyme again while we climb."

Archie sagged. He'd repeated the rhyme a thousand times in the past two days as they'd tried to climb the balloon, but he knew what she was doing. She was trying to get him to say it like a mantra, to focus on the here and now.

"Twinkle, twinkle, little star. How I wonder what you are," he said, falling into the singsong of the rhyme. "Up above the world so high, like a diamond in the sky."

Most nursery rhymes, it turned out, were codes. Riddles that, when unlocked, held the secrets to navigating the complicated puzzle traps previous Leagues had used to imprison the Mangleborn. Sometimes too the puzzle traps were used to hide powerful artifacts, like this lantern.

Archie focused on the next jump and made it. Not gracefully, but he made it.

"Well, 'up above the world so high, like a diamond in the sky' can't be anything but Cahokia in the Clouds," Fergus said.

Cahokia in the Clouds. A city in the sky, hanging from a giant, kite-shaped helium balloon tethered at the edge of Illini territory, near the abandoned Francia town of St. Louis. The city had been built by people who had no idea why the balloon was there to begin with. If only they really understood . . . But that was the job of the Septemberist Society: to keep the true horrors of the world hidden and buried. Or, in this case, hidden and floating.

The nursery rhyme clearly meant the kite-shaped balloon above Cahokia in the Clouds, and the twinkling star had to be the lantern they were after.

Lóngdēng. The Dragon Lantern. An artifact from the Mu civilization, which existed long before Atlantis fell and Rome rose from its ashes. Archie had no idea what the lantern was, or what it did. All Philomena Moffett had told him was that it held the answer to the secret of how he became whatever he was. That was enough to send him to the top of Cahokia in the Clouds to get it.

How I wonder what you are . . . Archie thought.

"You're losing focus again," Hachi told him.

Archie shook himself and nodded.

"Tell us the next part," she said.

Archie was the one who had all the nursery rhymes memorized. His Septemberist parents had made a point of drilling them into him as a boy.

"When the blazing sun is gone, when he nothing shines upon, then you show your little light, twinkle, twinkle, all the night," Archie sang.

This was where they had gone wrong for the past two days. Or so they now thought. Both times, they had attempted to scale the rope net during daylight. And why not? It was hard enough when you could actually see where you were going. But there were traps— dangerous traps—and they hadn't yet been able to find a way around them. Not by day. So they'd gone back to the rhyme. *When the blazing sun is gone, when he nothing shines upon, then you show your little light, twinkle, twinkle, all the night.* Now it seemed obvious: They were supposed to wait until dark.

Archie made one last leap, slipping and falling off the rope at his feet. He caught it as he fell and pulled himself up with a few choice comments into his oxygen mask. Fergus snickered.

"Okay. This is where the traps start," Hachi said. Above them and to the right, Archie saw the ropes they had tried to climb. The ropes that had come loose as soon as their weight was on them and sent them spilling off the balloon. Traps set to keep the curious out. If not for their safety lines, they would all be dead.

All but Archie.

"And . . . it's just about nightfall," Hachi said.

Hachi had timed it perfectly. Hachi, their warrior. The one who always had a plan. It was still too light to see the stars, but the first of them would appear in minutes. In the meantime, Fergus, their tinker, the one who could make anything, lit the oil lamps he had mounted on the shoulder straps of their backpacks.

"Try not to get the lamps near your oxygen masks," Fergus said. "That would be bad."

"Bad how?" Archie asked.

"Boom bad," Fergus said.

"Good to know," Archie said.

The last of the red-orange sky drained away beneath the clouds, and their skyworld became the blue-black of night. There was a metaphor for Archie's new life in that, he thought. Waiting for the light to go away so he could work in the dark. But Hachi had told him to focus, so he put it away.

"All right," Archie said. "The 'blazing sun is gone.' Now what?"

They shined their lamps around, trying to see anything different about the rope maze around them, but it all looked the same.

"Wait a minute," Fergus said. He reached up and turned off his shoulder lamp.

"What are you doing?" Hachi said.

"Oh, brass! You've got to see this," Fergus said. "Switch off your lamps."

"Turn them off? But how are we supposed to see?" Archie asked.

Archie and Hachi did it anyway, and gasped. All around them, the rope net glowed like the tail end of a firefly.

"Phospholuminescence!" Fergus said. "Blinking brilliant! All day it absorbs the sun's light, and then it glows all night. We don't need lanterns at all!"

"But we still don't know which way to go," Hachi said.

For the past two days, they had made guesses. Bad ones, with painful results. But interpreting the second verse correctly had borne fruit, so Archie recited the third.

"Then the traveler in the dark, thanks you for your tiny spark. He could not see which way to go, if you did not twinkle so."

"So we follow the twinkling star?" Fergus asked.

They all looked to the sky. It was *filled* with twinkling stars.

"They're *all* twinkling," Archie said miserably.

"Not that one," Hachi said.

Archie and Fergus followed her finger to where it was pointing. Below them, almost at the edge of the balloon's curve, was a single, small white light.

A tiny spark!

"Let's try something," Hachi said. "We've gone up from here, and we've gone sideways, but we've never gone down."

With practiced ease, Hachi released the catch on her safety line and rappelled down one place in the rope grid. As she landed on the rope below, the light beneath them went out.

"It's gone!" Archie said.

"Nae, it's not. It's just moved," Fergus said. "Look."

He was right. Among all the twinkling stars, there was only one that didn't twinkle—a tiny pinprick of light at the far edge of the balloon, directly to the right of Hachi. She slid across her grid with the grace of a tightrope walker, her brown dress flapping underneath her fur coat, and stepped into the next one. The light stayed on, but shifted one grid farther away.

"*Then the traveler in the dark, thanks you for your tiny spark,*" Archie said. "*He could not see which way to go, if you did not twinkle so.* We need the stars to twinkle so we can follow the one that doesn't!"

"Come on," Hachi told them. "I'll stay one square ahead."

Archie and Fergus followed her, and Hachi waited for them to catch up each time she moved ahead. Right again, then up, up, and up, then left, then up again, and slowly they made their way through the maze toward the top.

"What's the rest of it?" Hachi asked.

"The rest of what?"

"The rest of the nursery rhyme. Let's hear it again."

"Oh," Archie said, focusing on his feet. "Let's see. Um, 'In the dark blue sky you keep, and often through my curtains peep, for you never shut your eye, till the sun is in the sky.' Then the rest of it is kind of the same. 'As your bright and tiny spark, lights the traveler in the dark, though I know not what you are, twinkle, twinkle, little star.' Then the last stanzas are the first one over again."

"You never shut your eye till the sun is in the sky. So we've got until sunup to get there. No problem," Fergus said.

"We've got until sunup to get there *and back again*," Hachi reminded him.

"Oh. Aye. Moving right along then."

"Twinkle, twinkle, little star," Archie said. "Why do they twinkle?"

"It's the atmosphere," Fergus said. "The light from the stars gets all wonky when it comes through the air, making our eyes see it as a flicker. Doesn't work the same way for planets. They're closer, so they don't—"

Hachi screamed and spasmed, jerking back and forth on the rope in the next grid. Blue-hot energy crackled over her gloves and up her coat, sparking in the fur lining of her coat.

Lektricity!

"Hachi!" Fergus cried. He lunged for her and fell. Archie caught Fergus's safety line with one hand and hung on to the rope maze with the other, using his massive strength to keep Fergus from falling. As though he were lifting a wooden toy at the end of a bit of string, Archie raised Fergus back up to Hachi.

"Higher!" Fergus cried.

Archie lifted him up until Fergus could stand again on his own and grab the rope that Hachi still clung to. As soon as Fergus touched it, the lektricity shifted from Hachi to him. Archie knew that right then, underneath Fergus's layers of winter clothing, the black lines that covered his friend's skin like tattoos were rearranging themselves, turning Fergus into a syphon for all the lektricity.

Without the lektric charge to hold her to the rope, Hachi's hands went slack and she fell.

"Catch her!" Fergus cried.

Archie fumbled for her safety line and caught it. Hachi jerked to a stop, and he hauled her back up.

Fergus pulled his hand away from the lektrified rope. The blue-hot lightning followed him, finally disconnecting and slinking back into its hidden home in the rope.

"Crivens! I thought I could wait out the charge, but it kept coming! What's powering that thing?"

"Here, help me get Hachi back up," Archie said. She was awake, which was good, but she was still groggy. Archie lifted her higher, and Fergus helped Hachi get her hands back on the safe ropes in their grid.

"So," Hachi mumbled. "Planets don't twinkle."

"What?" Fergus said. "Oh . . . yeah."

Hachi punched Fergus, but there wasn't much strength in it. "You might have said so *before* I followed one."

Hachi leaned into Fergus, and he hugged her with one arm while he held tight to the rope with the other. Hachi and Fergus put their heads together, and Archie looked away. *Blech.* Hachi and Fergus had become close in their adventures together, and though neither of them said so, they were practically boyfriend and girlfriend. It always made Archie feel a little weird to see them when they got like this. But a little jealous of how close they were as friends too.

At last they separated. "I don't know how we're going to tell the difference between our guiding light and the planets," Fergus said.

"Planets move. The light doesn't," Hachi said. "We may not run into any more in the right position to fool us," she added, "but if we do, we'll wait and watch."

"And all the while get closer to dawn," Fergus said.

"We should be moving, not talking," Hachi said.

"Are you sure you're strong enough?" Fergus asked.

In answer, Hachi climbed up to the next grid.

"So, she's strong enough, then," Fergus said to Archie.

Together they climbed, sometimes moving up, sometimes side to side, sometimes back down, but all the while working their way around and up the giant dome of helium. The sheer vertical face of the balloon gradually gave way to the gentle slope of the top of the balloon, and they crawled along on hands and knees, still clinging to the ropes so the wind wouldn't tear them off.

Archie heard someone scream, and he froze.

"Crivens! What's that?" Fergus asked. "There can't be anyone else up here!"

But someone was up ahead of them. Lots of someones, from the sound of screams coming to them over the wind. It sounded like someone being tortured.

"I can see silhouettes against the stars," Hachi said, crouching low. "Something's coming. Something's coming right at us!"

Archie ducked with Hachi and Fergus, then remembered he was the Heracles, the strongman of the team. Whatever was coming, it was his job to meet it head-on so the others wouldn't be hurt. But that didn't mean he wasn't scared. Still holding the rope, he raised himself up, closed his eyes, and turned his head away.

"Honk-honk-honk!" the thing cried as it got closer.

Honk-honk-honk?

Something flapping and feathery smacked Archie in the face and he fell over, glancing up in time to see a big white bird launch itself off the side of the balloon and disappear into the dark night sky.

"It's birds," he said. "Geese!"

Fergus lit his oil lamp and shined it forward to have a look. The top of the balloon was covered with bird nests! There had to be hundreds of them, scattered here and there among the grid lines of the rope net that covered the giant balloon.

"You know what this means?" Hachi said.

"Aye," Fergus said. "If this thing is covered with birds, it's also covered with bird poop."

"No," Hachi said. "I mean, yes, probably, but that's not what I meant. Look at *where* they have their nests."

Archie scanned the nests, trying to see what Hachi saw. All he noticed was that the birds were packed into just a few of the grid squares, when they had lots more empty ones they could have been using. No—wait. He understood!

"Oh, brass! They're nesting in the grid squares that aren't booby trapped!"

"Exactly," Hachi said.

Sure enough, Archie was able to trace a path from where they stood all the way to the top, where something small and red glowed in the night sky.

The Dragon Lantern.

2

A few snapping geese couldn't hurt Archie, who had once been stomped on by a giant iron robot and gotten right back up again. But these geese were annoying enough. They honked and they flapped. They bit and they chased. By the end Archie was kicking the clacking things out of his way before they could bite him.

And then they were there. At the very top of the balloon.

At the Dragon Lantern.

The geese didn't nest here. There was something about it they didn't like. Something about it that made Archie's skin crawl. It was made of a shiny silver metal, like titanium, and shaped like a little house. A little Oriental house—at least the ones Archie had seen pictures of. The Mu artifact was a little bigger than a regular lantern, but rectangular instead of round, with a four-sided roof that curled up at each corner. At the very top, forming a handle, was a little dragon curled in a circle, and up the sides, climbing each corner like pillars, were four more snakelike dragons, all scaly and whiskered and breathing fire. Between them, in horizontal rows up and down the four faces of the lantern, were little shutters that looked like they could be opened by degrees, letting out as little or as much as you wanted of lantern light.

Or whatever this "lantern" held.

"It's a power source," Fergus told them. "Not lektricity, or I'd feel it. But definitely energy. You can hear it."

Fergus was right. Archie could hear the thing thrumming. Or rather, he could *feel* it. It was like how your stomach felt when it was growling, but all through your body. Like it was alive. And hungry.

Archie reached for the dragon handle, but Hachi grabbed his hand. "Let us check it for booby traps first."

Archie took a step back as Hachi and Fergus examined it. At last they gave the okay, but neither of them moved to lift it.

That was Archie's job.

Archie took hold of the handle, expecting a shock, an explosion, a trapdoor—something. But except for an audible click of the lantern being removed from its custom-fitted base, there was no reaction at all. He lifted it and looked at it more closely.

One of the dragons seemed to be laughing at him.

"Clever, clever," Fergus said. He was on his knees, examining the slot the lantern had come out of. It was filled with the same kind of lines that covered Fergus's skin, what the Septemberist scientist Nikola Tesla had called "circuits."

"Whoever designed this, they used the energy of the dingus to power the puzzle traps," Fergus said. "I don't ken how they converted the energy to lektricity, but they did. That's some serious blinking engineering there."

As astounded as Fergus was, Archie was sure that, given time, Fergus could reverse-engineer the converters—maybe even the lantern itself. Fergus was maybe the greatest tinker in the world. Or would be one day. That's why he was a Leaguer.

"Wish we could open it," Fergus said.

"Mrs. Moffett was very clear that we should *not* do that," Hachi said. She took the lantern from Archie, slid it into a canvas sack, and clicked a lock through the grommets at the top, sealing it.

"Aw, you don't have to do all that," Fergus said. "I just said I *wished* we could open it, not that I was *going to.*"

Hachi gave him a look that told him she wasn't so sure about that. "It's not to keep you out," she told him. "It's to keep it safe and sound while we get back down."

Hachi opened Archie's coat and latched the sack to his belt. She must have figured that even though he was a klutz, he had the best chance of keeping the thing safe. Archie had proven himself over and over again in their adventures together, but he still warmed at the thought of Hachi trusting him to do something right.

"Well, getting back down should be a lot easier without this attached to the system to power it," Archie said.

"We could always take the gyrocopters," Fergus said hopefully.

"We climb down," Hachi told them.

"Aw, you're never any fun," Fergus said, and they started down for Cahokia in the Clouds.

⁓

The city of Cahokia in the Clouds had been founded long ago when one of the many airships that docked beneath the giant balloon kite first decided to stay. More airships joined it, creating a village in the sky, and as it became a trading post and waystation in the air, it continued to grow. Houses and lodges and shops that were never meant to be airships were hauled up by balloon, and Cahokia in the Clouds grew down from its old town center like a dripping stalactite in a cave. Some people said it was a mile tall—the Mile High City, they called it—but no one had ever really measured it.

It was always changing anyway. Every day, new pieces were attached and old pieces sprouted balloons and floated away, moving up and down the city with the prevailing winds and real estate prices.

Archie, Hachi, and Fergus climbed down a rope ladder into Level 1, the oldest of the Old Town levels. The locals this high up didn't need oxygen masks, but if you didn't grow up here, you could very quickly find yourself tired out and dizzy, with a clanking head-ache to boot. Most visitors stayed in Midtown, near the Cahokia Man, which was where their lodge was. It was a long way from Level 1 to Midtown, so Archie, Hachi, and Fergus waited for a cable car.

Cahokia in the Clouds stayed where it was in the heart of the North Americas because of an enormous cable made of some ma-terial that, like the canvas and rope of the giant balloon, no one knew how to make anymore. It was ancient tech, a relic from a civi-lization long gone, and it ran 20,000 feet down through the mid-dle of Cahokia in the Clouds all the way to Cahokia on the Plains, the ruins of a once-great city on the ground where the new city in the sky was anchored.

Along that giant tether, the people of Cahokia in the Clouds had attached lifelines to the ground. One tube carried water up. Another carried waste down. Pneumatic tubes along its length connected the Mile High City to the air-powered, cross-continent postal network, and a gas main brought light to the city in the sky. But for getting *people* up and down inside the city itself, its clever Illini designers had built steam-powered cars that traveled along the cable like streetcars turned on their ends.

A cable car came up through the platform in the Level 1 sta-tion, the corkscrew-like worm gear on its back squeaking along a greased, brass-toothed track on the tether. Six rows of red padded seats, a couple occupied by Cahokians on their way uptown, climbed past them until the bottom row was level with the plat-form. The cable car stopped with a *clank*, and a Mark II Machine Man like the Dent family's Mr. Rivets (only this one wearing a brass conductor's cap instead of a bowler hat) pulled open a metal gate for them to climb on board.

"First-row priority seating is reserved for city elders and persons with disabilities," the machine man told him. "This is a downtown cable car bound for Statue Park and Midtown. Next stop, Level 2."

It had taken them so long to crawl back down off the balloon that it was almost the morning rush hour, and Archie, Hachi, and Fergus boarded the cable car with a few commuters sipping coffees and reading newspapers. Level after level of floating city went by, until at last they came to the head of Statue Park. Literally. Hanging out away from the tether cable from the bottom of the giant balloon above, plumb with the ground, was the ugly head of the statue that Statue Park was named for. Archie leaned out to look down the length of the thing, which hung in a great wide space in the heart of Cahokia in the Clouds. It was more than a hundred levels tall, and surrounded on all sides by a ring of apartments and hotels with expensive views.

The Cahokia Man, as the statue was called, was made of rough, reddish-brown stone. It was a grotesque imitation of a human man, with two squat, powerful legs, four thick, burly arms, and a flat, wide head that looked like it had been pounded down into his shoulders with a sledgehammer the size of the Emartha Machine Man Building in New Rome. The Cahokia Man had been hung here by whatever ancients had created the giant balloon-kite that bore it aloft, trussed up and bound like a prisoner to its own helium ball and chain. For centuries people had gazed up at the Cahokia Man and his giant balloon and wondered who he was supposed to be, and what had possessed the ancients to hang him 20,000 feet in the air. But Archie knew who he was, and why he was there.

The Cahokia Man was a Mangleborn.

Archie knew because his parents knew. They were researchers for the Septemberist Society, and it was their job to learn everything they could about the Mangleborn. When the Mangleborn rose, it was the League of Seven who came together and put them down again—the league the Septemberists had been set up to support. But the Mangleborn couldn't be killed. At least, no one had yet figured out how to kill one. Instead, they were trapped. Imprisoned. Usually underground, sometimes underwater.

And, very rarely, in the sky.

The Cahokia Man's real name was Antaeus. Like all Mangleborn, it fed on lektricity, the energy source in lightning, the power the Septemberists worked to keep the world from rediscovering lest the Mangleborn rise again. But in the same way that the Mangleborn Malacar Ahasherat had a connection to the insect world, so too did the Mangleborn Antaeus have a connection to the Earth. As long as Antaeus touched the ground, it was unbeatable. The Roman League knocked it down, only to watch it get up again and again. At last, so the Septemberist legends went, the Roman League's shadow and strongman, Heracles, held it off the ground while the League's scientist, Daedalus, and their tinker, Wayland Smith, hooked it to the tethered balloon they had created to separate it from the Earth forever.

Or at least as long as people left it alone.

The story, of course, like most stories of the League and the Mangleborn they fought, had been rewritten over the centuries, in part because people forgot, and in part because people *wanted* to forget. Wanted to sweep the memory of the Mangleborn and their horrors under the rug of mythology. And so the League of Seven defeating Antaeus the earth elemental became Heracles defeating a wrestler on the way to one of his Twelve Labors, and a giant Mangleborn hanging in plain sight in the sky at the border of Illini and Pawnee territory became a tourist attraction.

At the stop where they got off, a family of Wichita asked Archie to take their picture in front of it.

Their lodge, located right across from one of the Cahokia Man's lower armpits, was called the Cahokia Arms. Why Philomena

Moffett had booked their rooms so close to one of the greatest monsters in the world, Archie couldn't understand. It gave him the creeps. Maybe it was because Mrs. Moffett had never seen a living one the way Archie and Hachi and Fergus had, had never had a nightmare come to life in front of her. Just seeing a Mangleborn in his dreams had scared Archie so badly it had turned his hair completely white, and now for the last three nights he'd had to sleep with one right outside the window with a view they'd paid extra for.

"We would have been here a lot sooner if we'd used the gyrocopters," Fergus said as they went inside.

"We would have been pancakes in Cahokia on the Plains if we'd used those things," Hachi told him.

The Dent family Tik Tok hurried across the lobby to welcome them back, and Archie smiled. Mr. Rivets was an Emartha Corporation Mark II Machine Man, the old brass kind that had to be wound with a key on his back and had interchangeable talent cards that let him do different specialized tasks. He was taller than the average person, weighed nearly a thousand pounds, and had a torso and head forged to look like a stout and redoubtable manservant, complete with riveted vest, tie, mustache, and bowler hat. He had been in service with the Dent family for nearly a hundred years, and had been Archie's caretaker, guardian, and teacher his entire life. But more importantly, he was Archie's best friend.

"Mr. Rivets!" Archie called. "We got it!"

"I am relieved to hear it, Master Archie," Mr. Rivets said.

"We never got a chance to use the gyrocopters though," Fergus said.

"I am relieved to hear that as well," Mr. Rivets said.

Hachi snickered, and Archie smiled.

"I see how it is," Fergus told them. "Laugh now. But one day one of my gizmos will save your life, and you won't be laughing then. You'll be saying, 'Oy, Fergus, you're a genius!'"

One of the steam-powered, titanium Mark IV Machine Men who

ran the front desk at the Cahokia Arms stepped into their little circle, and all three of the kids took a wary step back. They had had a bad experience with that model once and were still a little Mark IV–shy.

"Pardon me for interrupting," said the Tik Tok in the singsongy, music-box voice all machine men had. A small rectangular plate hammered onto his chest said his name was Mr. Bell. "I have a pneumatigram for Miss Emartha."

"That's me," Hachi said. She pulled off the combination oxygen tank/oil lamp/gyrocopter backpack she wore and pushed it into Fergus's arms.

Mr. Bell handed her the message. "And may I say personally, Miss, that it is an honor to have one of the Makers staying with us."

"Um, thanks," Hachi said. Her father, Hololkee Emartha, had owned and run the Emartha Machine Man Company, as had generations of Emarthas before him. Now that her father was dead, Hachi owned it. She was a millionaire heiress, and wherever she went, Emartha Machine Men treated her like a god. It made her distinctly uncomfortable.

Archie caught the Mark IV Machine Man by the arm before he returned to the desk, almost pulling him over by accident. The stunned Tik Tok took a moment to collect himself.

"Sorry," Archie said. Sometimes he forgot his own strength. "Mr. Bell, could you send up to Mrs. Moffett's room and ask her to come down and meet us, please?"

"Of course, sir. Right away," Mr. Bell said.

"Crivens," Hachi said, staring at the message. Hachi had taken to saying Fergus's favorite meaningless epithet whenever she was truly surprised by something, which wasn't too often. Whatever was in that pneumatigram must be earth-shattering.

"What is it?" Fergus asked.

"It's a message from the Pinkerton Detective Agency. I hired them to find Madame Blavatsky." She looked up from the pneumatigram. "And they did."

"*Twisted pistons*," Archie said. For most of her life, Hachi had searched for the identities of the people who had attacked her family's village in Florida when she was an infant, killing her father and ninety-nine other men in some kind of ritual sacrifice that to this day no one could explain. The only person she knew for sure had been at the Chuluota massacre was the lektrical wizard Thomas Edison. He'd been her last and only clue, until something he'd said about "Batty" Blavatsky and Chuluota right before he died gave her new hope that she could eventually track down and punish all of her father's killers.

Fergus's eyes went wide. "I don't believe it."

"I know," Archie said. "This is huge!"

"No," Fergus said. "I mean, I don't believe you hired the blinking *Pinkertons*! Have you forgotten that just a few weeks ago they were hunting us down like criminals?"

"And have *you* forgotten that they actually found us?" Hachi said. "They can do more to track somebody down with their army of agents than I can, and a lot faster. Besides, having them out searching for Blavatsky gave me time to help Archie find this whatever-it-is that has whatever-it-is-to-do with who he is. But now it's my turn."

Hachi headed for the door.

"Wait! What about the lantern?" Archie called. "We have to give it to Mrs. Moffett!"

"You give it to her," Hachi said. "I'm going to the Pinkerton office to find out what they know. Level 373."

Hachi tossed the key to the bag's lock to Archie. He fumbled it, and by the time he'd bent down and picked it up, Hachi was almost out the door.

Fergus took a step to follow her, then turned apologetically to Archie. "I'd . . . better go with her," Fergus said. "If I don't, she's like to jump in an airship and take off without telling either of us where she's off to." He shrugged out of his backpack and left it with

Archie before heading for the door. "We'll meet you back here at the lodge after we find out what's up!"

Archie wanted more than anything to run and join his friends, but he had to get the lantern back to Mrs. Moffett first. He had to know what it had to do with who he was and where he was from.

Another titanium Mark IV Machine Man from the hotel came up to him. The plate on his chest said his name was Mr. Key.

"Sir, I regret to inform you there's been a water leak in your rooms. We've had to move you."

"A water leak?" Archie asked.

"I'll see to this, Master Archie," Mr. Rivets said. "You wait here for Mrs. Moffett."

Mr. Rivets wasn't gone a moment before Mrs. Moffett stepped out of the hotel elevators.

Philomena Moffett, the Septemberist council's lead scientist and the current chief of the society, was a tall, thin, impressive woman who seemed to float as she walked. She looked prim as always, with her long black hair pinned up and her icy blue eyes peering down at him through narrow tortoiseshell cat eye spectacles that came up to points at the corners, like wings. Today she was wearing a dark blue long-sleeved dress that fit her like a second skin from the waist up, and from the waist down billowed out in acres of fabric over a large bustle at the back. From the buttoned collar at the top to the hem that swept the hotel carpet at the bottom, she was cosseted and cocooned like someone afraid to come into contact with the world. Even her slender hands, which she held just above her waist, were covered with matching blue gloves.

Mrs. Moffett's voice was quiet, but assured as always. "You have the lantern?"

Archie smiled. "We got it. Finally." He slipped the key in the lock and opened the bag, sliding the lantern out just enough for Mrs. Moffett to see it. Archie could feel the thing vibrating deep inside him again, and he shivered.

The Dragon Lantern glinted in Mrs. Moffett's glasses.

"Well done," she said. She reached out her gloved hands for it, and Archie handed it over. Frankly, he was glad to be rid of the thing.

"What does it do?" Archie asked. "And what does it have to do with me and . . . and what I am?"

Mrs. Moffett tore her eyes away from the lantern. "What? Oh. All in good time," she said.

"But you promised it would explain things," Archie said. "You said if we got it for you, you'd be able to get answers for me."

Mrs. Moffett looked around the hotel lobby furtively, like there might be Pinkerton spies behind the potted plants. "And I will. Whatever I promised, I'll do. But first things first: I need to get this to the safe at the bank. They'll keep it for us until it's time to leave."

"I'll come with you. To protect you," Archie said.

Mrs. Moffett laughed. "You, protect me? How?"

Archie frowned. Mrs. Moffett knew exactly how he could help—he was super strong and practically invulnerable. He was perfect for protection duty.

"No," Mrs. Moffett said before he could argue with her. She looked over her shoulder at the elevator. "You stay here. Get cleaned up. Rest. I'll meet you back here at the hotel, and then I'll tell you everything you want to know."

Despite his misgivings, Archie felt hope rise in him, drowning everything else out. When he and his parents had come back from defeating a Mangleborn in Florida, they'd gone straight to Mrs. Moffett for answers. Who was he? *What* was he? Where had he come from? Why was the Society keeping track of his progress? What did they know, and what were they hiding?

But Philomena Moffett was as much in the dark as they were. She had only been the head of the Septemberist Society for a year, and records of Septemberist involvement in Archie's life had been covered up or destroyed. The only clue she had been able to find was a record of someone within the Septemberist Society removing and using the

Dragon Lantern twelve years ago, right around the time Archie had been born. More than that—like who had done it, and why—she didn't know. But she had promised Archie they would find out together. The Dragon Lantern was the place to start, and now that they had it, Archie didn't want to wait to uncover its secrets. He wanted to turn it on and see what it did *now*. But that's what adults always did—they told you to wait whenever you wanted to get on with something.

"Okay," Archie said. "I guess it's not going anywhere. Oh—and Hachi and Fergus are okay," he said. "They just had to run an errand."

"Good. Fine," Mrs. Moffett said. "Stay here." She was already headed for the front door.

"Master Archie!" Mr. Rivets called, ticking up to him. "Master Archie, what are you doing?"

Archie shrugged. "Nothing. Mrs. Moffett said to wait here while she put the lantern in the bank."

"You've spoken to Mrs. Moffett?" Mr. Rivets asked.

Archie frowned. "Of course I talked to her." He pointed to Mrs. Moffett, who was just leaving the building. "There she goes."

Mr. Rivets's worry subroutine knitted his brass eyebrows. "The person leaving through the front door is not Mrs. Moffett." Mr. Rivets pointed to the opening elevator. "*That* is Mrs. Moffett."

Archie blinked. Stepping out of the elevator was the exact same person he'd just been talking to. She wore the same dark blue bustle dress, wore her hair pinned up in exactly the same way, and looked down on him with the same piercing blue eyes through identical tortoiseshell spectacles. She was exactly the same person he'd just seen leave the hotel by the front door.

With the Dragon Lantern he'd given her.

Archie looked back and forth between the front door and the Philomena Moffett coming from the elevators.

"Thirty days hath September," this new Mrs. Moffett said to him.

"Seven heroes we remember," Archie said robotically, giving the answer to the Septemberists' secret pass phrase. He was still looking back and forth between Mrs. Moffett and the empty front door.

"Is everything all right?" Mrs. Moffett asked in the same quiet but assured voice. "Do you have the lantern? Where are Hachi and Fergus?"

"I just gave it to you!" he said.

A dark cloud formed on Mrs. Moffett's forehead. "I assure you, Archie, I have just arrived. Are you saying you *had* the Dragon Lantern, and you gave it to someone else?"

"Oh, slag," Archie said. "*Slag, slag, slag, slag, slag.*"

"Language, Master Archie," Mr. Rivets reminded him.

"It was you! I swear it was you! She looked exactly like you! She *sounded* exactly like you!" Archie said.

"And you used the Septemberist pass phrase?" Mrs. Moffett demanded.

"I—no! Why should I? I know you! It was you! Who else could it be?"

"I could scream," Mrs. Moffett said, her soft voice shaking. "But no. Not here. Not now." She closed her eyes and stood quietly where she was, but Archie could tell from the way she clenched her fists and took in long, deep breaths of air that she was seething. It was like her boiler was overpressured and her safety valve was venting off steam so she wouldn't explode. He'd never seen Mrs. Moffett so angry. It scared him.

"I'm sure I saw you," Archie said. "I talked to you."

"No, you didn't, Master Archie," said Mr. Rivets.

Archie and Mrs. Moffett turned to the machine man.

"What?" Archie asked.

"The person you were speaking with was not Mrs. Moffett," Mr. Rivets said. "I only saw her as I returned from the front desk, but the person you gave the Dragon Lantern to was a young Asian girl about your age with the ears and tail of a fox. I'm afraid she has stolen the lantern."

Archie ran to the rail outside the Cahokia Arms and looked back and forth along the broad sweep of gangplanks on their level that ringed the Cahokia Man. Mr. Rivets and Philomena Moffett joined him moments later.

"She's got too much of a head start," Archie cried. "We'll never catch her!"

"We will if she looks just like me," Mrs. Moffett said.

"There she is," Mr. Rivets said. He pointed to a place farther along the gangplank, right where it disappeared behind the giant statue. Archie frowned. The only person there was an Il-lini man on the way to work with a newspaper tucked under his arm.

"That man?" Archie asked. "He doesn't look anything like Mrs. Moffett."

"I assure you, Master Archie. I see no man there. It is a young woman with a fox tail. And she has the lantern in her backpack!"

Archie shook his head. No matter how hard he tried, all he could see was a Cahokia businessman.

"She must have some way of making us see what she wants us to see," Mrs. Moffett said. "But it doesn't work on machine men."

"Come on, Mr. Rivets!" Archie cried, taking off at a run. Mrs. Moffett ran the other way, toward the cable car platform. Good. If the thief went up or down, Mrs. Moffett could cut her off.

Archie was halfway round the gangplank when he realized that Mr. Rivets was lagging too far behind. Mark IIs were built for power, not speed.

Just like me, Archie realized.

Archie ran back toward his Tik Tok.

"Sorry, Mr. Rivets, but you're moving too slow, and I need your eyes," Archie said.

"I don't understand—" Mr. Rivets began, but before he could finish, Archie picked up the thousand-pound machine man and started to run.

"Master Archie! I knew you were strong, but I had no idea!" Mr. Rivets said.

The truth was, Archie didn't know how strong he was either. Strong enough to pick up Edison in his iron body and toss him into a pit with Malacar Ahasherat. Strong enough to lift a Mark II Machine Man and run with it. But what was his limit? Whatever it was, he hadn't found it yet. Mr. Rivets slowed him down about as much as the long coat and backpack he still wore.

A twelve-year-old boy running with a machine man in his arms was quite a sight, and everybody for five levels with a view of him stopped and pointed. The businessman Archie was following stopped to look at what everyone was pointing at, and for the briefest of moments the man wasn't a man anymore. It was a girl—an Asian girl in a white dress, wearing fox ears and a fox tail, staring at him in wide-eyed amazement. But how . . . ? Archie blinked, and the girl was a businessman again, running away.

"I saw her, Mr. Rivets—I saw her! The girl you saw! Just for a second when she turned to look at me!"

"If she has the ability to somehow project images into your mind, as Mrs. Moffett suggests, it would appear that she must concentrate to do it," Mr. Rivets said. "Seeing something that startled her broke her concentration for the merest of moments, allowing you to see her as she really is."

The girl in her businessman disguise took a gangplank toward the cable car platforms, and Mrs. Moffett appeared in her way. The girl/businessman pulled up short and looked back and forth between Archie and Mrs. Moffett. She was trapped. They had her!

The girl, still disguised as a businessman slid underneath the walkway railing, grabbed the gangplank, and swung herself down to the level below.

"Slag!" Archie cried. He leaned over the railing, but the businessman was gone.

"There," Mr. Rivets said.

Archie saw her. A Pawnee woman with a baby bundled up in a papoose. She was hurrying toward the cable car platform in the other direction. Mrs. Moffett was running for a downtown cable car, but she was going to be too late.

"Hang on, Mr. Rivets. I'm going to swing you down."

"Master Archie, I think this an ill-advised course of action."

"Got any better ideas?"

"The lack of a better idea is not a valid reason for embracing a *bad* idea, sir," Mr. Rivets said.

"That's what I thought," Archie said. He lifted his mechanical valet over the rail and held on to him by an arm. It felt no different to Archie than dangling a stuffed animal over the edge, but the rail he was leaning on groaned in complaint. Looking down like this, Archie realized just how far down it was to the Cahokia Man's feet. He might survive that fall, but Mr. Rivets wouldn't. Still, they had to stop that girl. He had to have the Dragon Lantern back.

"On three, Mr. Rivets." Archie swung Mr. Rivets back and forth. "One . . . two . . ."

"And what exactly am I supposed to *do* on three, sir?" Mr. Rivets asked.

"Three!" Archie said. He let go of Mr. Rivets's hand, and the machine man fell toward the gangplank below. *Crash!* Mr. Rivets landed on his backside, smashing a hole in the wooden planks of the walkway.

"Hang on, Mr. Rivets!" Archie yelled. "I'll swing down!"

Archie leaned out over the rail and remembered how terrible he was at jumping around like a circus performer. *Oh slag*, Archie thought. Where was Hachi when he needed her? This was what she was good at! If Archie missed, he would fall seventy-five stories, and the girl would get away for good.

"Wait! I've got a better idea!" he called down to Mr. Rivets. Archie lifted his right leg and stomped.

Smash! His super-strong foot split the wooden planks below him, and he fell through. It was what he had meant to do, but he hadn't expected to drop so fast.

"Slag!" he cried.

Clang! He landed right on top of Mr. Rivets, knocking him the rest of the way through the hole he'd made and falling with him to the level below that.

"Slaaaaag!" Archie cried again. *Crunch!* He and Mr. Rivets smashed into the wooden gangplank, shattering wood and splitting ropes. The walkway threatened to give away underneath them again, but Archie scrambled to his feet and pulled Mr. Rivets to his.

"May I say again, Master Archie, the lack of a better idea is not a valid reason for embracing a bad one."

"We're alive, Mr. Rivets. And look!"

A downtown cable car was leaving the station above them, and the first rows of seats were just visible coming through the floor. Sitting in one of them was the fox girl. She stared back at him in amazement before changing back into an old woman.

Archie snatched up Mr. Rivets and ran for the cable car platform. The gangplank was full of people, though—men and women heading to work, nannies pushing strollers, deliverymen hauling boxes. Archie had to shuffle back and forth through the maze of them so much he was never going to make it in time.

"Master Archie, why are you dancing around?" Mr. Rivets asked.

"What do you want me to do, run over all these people?"

"Master Archie, there *are* no people."

Archie put a hand out to touch one of the passing pedestrians. It went right through her. He took a step toward a man carrying a large wooden crate and winced, expecting it to hit him in the face, but the man and his box walked right through him. Archie didn't feel a thing.

"It's all in my head," he said, amazed. So. She could do more than just change her appearance. She could make you see other things too.

Archie walked forward, passing through person after person, then broke into a run. "All right, Mr. Rivets—you have to tell me if any of these people are real, or things are going to get real messy!"

But none of them were real. Archie sprinted for the cable car platform. The fox girl, still disguised as an old woman, looked anxiously between Archie and the conductor. They were just going to make it, and she had nowhere to go.

"First-row priority seating is for city elders and people with disabilities," Archie called. "Not thieves in fox costumes!"

The old lady got up from her seat and ran up the stairs of the cable car with the speed and agility of a twelve-year-old girl, surprising the rest of the passengers. Archie and Mr. Rivets got on board right as the cable car left the station, and Archie put the machine man down to climb after her. The cable car went down as they ran up, and when the old lady was level again with the floor where Archie and Mr. Rivets had boarded, she jumped across the two-foot gap between the cable car and platform, her fox tail flashing briefly before she scampered away.

Twisted pistons! Archie ran up the steps, trying to get to the top row of seats to jump before the cable car passed the level above them completely. He was too slow, and the cable car was too fast! He got to the top just as the cable car was clearing the floor above them and jumped, grabbing on to the platform with both hands. He was just about to slip off when something below him gave him a push up. Mr. Rivets!

"I'll catch the next car up," Mr. Rivets said as Archie clambered onto the deck. "Be careful, Master Archie!"

"Careful is my middle name," Archie whispered, using a line he'd used before. As he looked back down the cable car hole he'd just climbed out of, he wondered if that was true anymore—and if he wanted it to be.

Archie followed the fox girl down a walkway filled with Cahokia schoolchildren in black-and-white uniforms. They laughed and talked and jostled each other, filling the gangplank ahead of him.

Illusions! They had to be. She was tricking him again. Archie ran right at the last kids in line. *Oof!* He knocked three kids flat and fell on top of a fourth.

"Hey! Watch it! Look out, you flange!" they cried.

"Sorry! Sorry," Archie said. So. *Not* illusions. He pulled himself up and worked his way through to the head of the line, where the teacher stood with her hands on her hips.

"Sorry!" Archie told her. "Just trying to get past."

"All right, boys and girls, settle down," the teacher said. She started doing a head count. "Let's see if we've lost anyone."

Archie had almost turned the corner when he heard the teacher say, "Wait, how do I have one extra?"

Archie spun around in time to watch one of the students he'd flattened peel off the end of the line and take off running in the other direction. *Slag!* He'd run right into her and hadn't realized it! Archie pushed his way back through the school group to more shoves and complaints and raced after the fox girl. Mr. Rivets was just coming back up on another cable car, and he pointed at the fleeing child.

"There, Master Archie! The fox girl!"

"I know! I know!" Archie cried. He was so close! A man appeared right in front of him, and Archie flinched but passed right through him. Then a machine man appeared, and a wall, and, improbably, an enormous bear, but Archie closed his eyes and ran right through every one of them. He was so close to catching her that the fox girl was just throwing them at him out of nowhere to confuse him.

The girl ran toward one of the public access ramps where air taxis picked up and dropped off passengers, but there was no ship there. She staggered to a halt, windmilling her arms to keep from falling out of the city. Archie stopped behind her. She could make him see anything she wanted to, but there was no way she was getting past him.

"Wow," she said. "I think I can see my house from here."

The girl turned to face him, and in the blink of an eye the schoolgirl turned into the fox girl Archie had only caught glimpses of. She was a little taller than Archie, with long, straight black hair that fell past her shoulders and hung down in her face, half-hiding her narrow eyes. Her skin was darker than Archie's but lighter than most First Nations people, her face soft and round. She wore a baggy white dress that looked like a bathrobe, with a wide white cloth belt tied around her stomach. Sticking up out of her dark hair were two reddish-brown fox ears, and hanging in the air behind her was a reddish brown-and-white fox tail that swished mischievously in the air. It looked for all the world like it was real.

"Is that what you really look like?" Archie asked.

"Why? Don't you believe your eyes?" she asked with a smirk. Her accent sounded foreign, like Anglish wasn't her first language.

"Give me the lantern," Archie told her.

The fox girl cocked her head sideways. "You are very strong," she said.

"I also can't be hurt," Archie said. He took a step closer, to show her he meant business.

"But can you fly?" the fox girl asked. She gave him a wink, stepped backward off the platform, and fell.

Archie rushed to the edge of the platform and looked down in time to see the fox girl bounce on the big cushy balloon of an Apache Air liner that was cruising by a few stories below. She gave him a playful wave, then slid off onto the smaller airbag of a passing air taxi. She was working her way down, airship by airship! *Slag it*—where was Hachi? This was what she was good at!

Mr. Rivets ticked up beside Archie and looked out over the edge at the fox girl. "Astonishing," Mr. Rivets said.

"I'm going after her," Archie said.

"And how will you do that, Master Archie?"

"Fergus's gyrocopter. I'm still wearing it."

Archie fumbled for the lever inside his coat that would activate it.

"Sir, may I remind you of my repeated advice about embracing bad ideas?"

"I have to get that lantern back, Mr. Rivets. Besides, it's not like whatever Fergus built can kill me."

Archie found the lever and pulled it. A metal rod shot up out of his backpack with a mechanical *click!* and curved metal fan blades popped out of it like a sideways windmill. The blades started to spin in the strong, high winds of Cahokia in the Clouds, and Archie was suddenly reminded of a steam-powered meat grinder he'd seen at a butcher's shop in Philadelphia that could chew up whole cows.

"Are you quite sure about that, sir?" Mr. Rivets asked.

Before he could reply, the wind grabbed Archie's gyrocopter and sucked him out into the empty sky.

"I'll just wait here then, shall I?" Mr. Rivets asked the empty platform.

4

Archie screamed.

The gyrocopter whipped him up and away from Cahokia in the Clouds, then dropped like a stone. Archie screamed, and he screamed, and he screamed. The airship the fox girl had fallen on loomed up at him beneath his feet, and he half-crashed, half-ran across the top of it until he slid off the side and was falling again. He wasn't falling as fast as he could be, he realized, but he *was* falling, the cobbled-together capsules of the city flashing by with frightening speed. The sun was up over the horizon now, and in the pink light Archie suddenly had a sweeping view of Cahokia in the Clouds, stretching down and away from him like an upside-down tower. Sunlight glinted off the windows of the buildings that stuck out like barnacles on the city in the sky, and gaslights flickered in the hazy pink sky like morning stars. If he hadn't been screaming his head off and about to pee in his pants, Archie might have found it beautiful.

The balloon bag of a smaller airship twisted up toward him, and Archie swung wildly to avoid it. The course change sent him corkscrewing away from Cahokia in the Clouds, and as he swung himself back he overcompensated. The city came rushing at him faster than he meant it to, and suddenly he was on top of a balcony full of people enjoying their breakfast at a diner. Somebody saw him and screamed. A waiter threw his towel in the air as he ducked, and Archie's feet dragged through the plates and glasses on the tables before he managed to swing back out into space.

"Sorry—sorry!" Archie yelled.

He had to get control of this thing before he ended up halfway to Navajo country—or worse, in a crater in Cahokia on the Plains. The gyrocopter was slowing his descent, but he needed to gain altitude to get any kind of real control. Archie kicked his feet like he was a little kid swinging on a swing set, and a gust of wind caught the gyrocopter and whipped him up again. Archie's stomach turned over, and he was glad he hadn't had any breakfast. The gust died and he came level again, hovering in the sky. Archie gave a tentative smile. Hey—he was getting the hang of this!

Then the gyrocopter dropped like a stone again.

Archie screamed and kicked his legs wildly, trying to do something—anything—to stop his descent. But all he managed to do was make the gyrocopter corkscrew wildly. He dropped through a thin layer of clouds, dodged a rising construction airship by a cog's breadth, and came back around toward the city. That's when he saw her—the fox girl! She was on top of another air taxi, and wasn't disguised as anything—unless that fox costume was a disguise. The air taxi was sailing down, and as it passed one of the public landing platforms, the fox girl jumped back inside the city.

Archie had to hit that platform. He swung toward it, but he was going too fast and coming in too high. He tried to swing back out, to come around again, but it was too late. A big glowing casement window appeared in front of him and—*crash!*—he went flying through it in a shower of glass and wood and smashed gyrocopter. He tumbled into the room like a big heavy chunkey ring, smashing through a small coffee table and slamming into the far wall. A portrait fell off the wall and tore on his head, replacing the head of the lady in the painting with his own.

Archie shook off the dizziness and found a family of Pawnee standing over him. The mother and father looked at Archie with a mixture of disbelief and anger. He had, after all, just destroyed their living room. The father wore denim pants and a white button-down shirt rolled up at the sleeves, his black hair parted in the middle. The mother wore a long blue skirt and a brightly colored striped blouse, and had long, dark braided hair. A little girl and boy in pajamas hid behind the legs of their parents.

"Who are you?" the father asked. "How did you crash through our window?"

The hood of Archie's coat had flipped up onto his head in his tumble and he tried to push it back, but the picture frame was in the way. The father lifted the portrait off him, and Archie's hood fell back, revealing his head full of snow-white hair.

The little girl gasped. "It's Archie Dent!"

Archie blinked stupidly. Had he met these people before?

"Don't be a flange," the boy said. "Archie Dent is a make-believe character."

"But he has white hair!" the girl said.

"A lot of Yankees have white hair," the boy said with authority. This far from Yankee territory, he clearly hadn't seen many white people.

Archie put a hand to his hair, still not understanding how they recognized him. "No. I—"

"They think you're a character from a dime novel," the mother said.

"The League of Seven versus the Mannahatta Mangleborn!" the girl said. She ran to get a little paperback book and shoved it in Archie's face. He was still dizzy from the crash, but he could make out an illustration on the cover that looked like him and Fergus and Hachi battling a giant rat monster in a sewer.

The author's name was Luis Philip Senarens.

"Oh slag," Archie muttered. He tried to get up.

"Be careful! You must be hurt!" the mother said.

"Oh. No," Archie said. Any ordinary boy who'd come crashing in like that would have broken a few bones and been cut all to pieces, of course. But Archie was no ordinary boy.

"I'm all right," Archie told them. He patted his thick coat. "Um, lots of padding."

"Who are the other four Leaguers?" the girl asked him. "The first story only has three—you and Fergus and Hachi. Hachi is my favorite."

"I—I don't know," Archie said. Twisted pistons! Senarens was blabbing all the League's secrets in dime novels! "I'm not—I'm a . . . I'm a delivery boy."

"Delivery!" the mother said. She looked back over her shoulder at the smashed window.

"Yeah, you're not Mrs. Nittawosew at 23 Windwalker Way, are you?" Archie asked. "No? Wrong house, then. Sorry. I'll just be going."

Archie climbed to his feet. The mother and children were still staring at him, but the father was looking over his shoulder at the smashed window.

"Window delivery," he said. "Ruta, what if we delivered food to people's windows? Cathay food, Texan food, those Yankee cheese-and-tomato pies . . . Hot from the oven to your window in minutes. We could make a fortune!"

"Here," Archie said. He snapped the metal rod off his back and handed the twisted wreck of Fergus's gyrocopter to the father. "See if you can use that. As for the rest of it, my . . . company . . . will pay for the damages." He looked around at the disaster area he'd created. The Septemberist Society was going to slip a cog when they got this bill. But all would be forgiven when he got the Dragon Lantern back.

The fox girl! He had to hurry.

"I'll just see myself out," Archie said. He hurried down the hall, and the little girl ran after him to open the hatch for him.

"Tell Hachi that Freckles is my favorite," she whispered.

Archie opened his mouth, then closed it. Senarens! He sighed and leaned in conspiratorially to the little girl. "I'll tell her," he said. He gave the little girl a wink and a salute before hurrying away.

The fox girl had come back into the city a level below him. There was no Cahokia Man down here, so no central space to hang over the rail and look down. What would he see anyway? A businessman on the way to work? A nanny pushing a stroller? How was he supposed to find the fox girl again, when she could be anyone?

But he had to try. Archie found a stairwell and ran down it. It was another neighborhood of houses and shops, with Cahokians coming and going. He wandered into a morning farmer's market and weaved his way between the stalls and customers. Any one of them could be the fox girl. They could all be illusions too. The fox girl had Archie second-guessing everything. He intentionally brushed a woman shopping at a vegetable stand, just to make sure she was real, and got a suspicious look from her.

This was crazy. He had to admit it: He'd lost her. It was time to go back up to the lodge and check in. Maybe they could check all the outgoing airships, see if there were any last-minute tickets purchased.

And then he saw it—a fox tail disappearing around a pumpkin cart!

Archie tore after her. He came to an open alley between two swaying apartments and saw the fox tail slip around the corner past a pair of trash cans. Archie pounded down the gangplank and turned after her, following the fox tail again as it nipped down a gaslit avenue. In and out of walkways he chased it, until he came at last to a broad path lined by rusty, dilapidated warehouses. There was no fox tail disappearing around a corner this time, but he knew the girl had run here.

Led him here, he corrected himself. He wasn't so stupid as to believe she hadn't seen him, and hadn't let him see her. But for whatever reason she had done it, he was just glad he hadn't lost her. It's not like she could do anything to hurt him.

Still, Archie made his way slowly and cautiously down the row of warehouses. She was up to something, and he wanted to be ready for it, whatever it was. If she was playing games with him, all he could do was play along and try to grab her if he could get close. He thought again about Hachi, and about Fergus, and how much easier it would have been to catch her with the help of his friends. His League teammates.

The warehouses weren't just rusty and run-down. They were empty. He went inside one, looking for anything out of the ordinary. It was dark inside, and Archie lit the gas lamp connected to his backpack. A Fergus gizmo to the rescue again.

Something clanged and Archie jumped, but it was just a rat scurrying from one hiding place to another. Archie shook his head. Rats, all the way up here in the sky.

Archie turned to leave, and something big landed on his back. He cried out and spun, but whatever it was hung on tight.

"Don't worry. I'm not a rat," said a voice in his ear. "I'm a fox."

The fox girl! Archie tried to grab her, but she hopped off. He spun, expecting her to be right behind him, but the warehouse was empty. She was tricking him again, making herself invisible.

"I know you're there," he said. He held his hands out, trying to feel what he couldn't see.

"You're not bad at playing chase," she said. The voice came from behind him, and he turned again. "But I grew up here. I know all the backstreets and secret staircases. It's been fun, but I can't play anymore."

"Why not?" Archie said. "Stay and play." She seemed to like being chased. Maybe if he could convince her it was a game, she wouldn't disappear for good, and he'd have a chance to catch her.

"Can't. Sorry," the girl said. She was somewhere else now. Near the door?

Archie wanted to keep her talking. "Why not?" he asked.

"Because *you* might be invulnerable, but I'm not."

What did that mean? "I'm not going to hurt you," Archie said. "I just want—"

And then he heard it. A hissing sound, coming from his backpack. The sound of gas escaping. Oxygen, from the canister he'd used to breathe from on top of the balloon. When she'd been on his back, she must have pulled loose one of the tubes.

Fergus's warning came back to him suddenly: *Don't let the lamp near the oxygen. That would be bad.*

Boom bad.

Archie scrabbled to turn off the lamp at his shoulder, but too late.

There was a sucking sound, like water down a drain, and then—

THOOM!

Archie's backpack exploded, blowing a hole in the wall of the warehouse and shooting him out into the clouds.

5

Archie blinked awake and put a hand up to block the high, bright sun. He was lying on his back in a hole in the ground, covered with dirt. Where was he? How long had he been here? How did he get here?

Then he remembered: the fox girl. The explosion. And the fall. *The 20,000-foot drop.* He'd blacked out on the way down. The hole he was lying in must be the hole he'd made when he hit the ground.

Hit the ground from 20,000 feet up and survived. Again. A *new personal best*, he thought ruefully.

Something round and dark blocked the sun, and he moved his hand away to see it. It was a balloon—a small, upside-down tear-shaped one, and from it hung not an airship but a man. An Iroquois man in a United Nations cavalry uniform.

"I've got 'im!" the man yelled to someone else. "I've got 'im, and he's alive!"

Archie heard a bugle blare, and then another, and soon the ground began to shake. *Thoom. Thoom. Thoom. Thoom.*

No, Archie thought. *That sound—* He struggled to sit up as dirt rained down on him. Those heavy footsteps, that pounding noise— he'd heard something exactly like it once before, in the underground puzzle traps that held Malacar Ahasherat imprisoned.

It was the sound of a Mangleborn coming.

A long, wide shadow fell over him in the hole, and Archie scrambled to the top, ready to fight. But what stood over him wasn't a Mangleborn. It was a steam man. A *giant* steam man, as tall as a skyscraper.

It leaned over to peer at him, and Archie saw a blond Yankee in a cavalry uniform peering out at him from behind the enormous glass eyes of the steam man. The man lifted a speaking tube to his mouth, and his voice boomed out through a speaker in the machine man's mouth.

"Archie Dent, I presume. Captain George Custer, U.N. 7th Steam Man Regiment," the officer said by way of introduction. "Mrs. Moffett said we'd find you in a big hole in the ground, and by Hiawatha, there you are. Hang about and we'll get you out of there."

Custer nodded to someone behind him, and the giant steam man reached down and scooped Archie out of the hole with a brass hand as big as a room.

Mrs. Moffett was waiting for him in Cahokia on the Plains, and so too were Hachi, Fergus, and Mr. Rivets. Archie had been unconscious for hours, giving them all plenty of time to realize what had happened and to come below to find him. But the real work of searching for him had been done by Captain Custer and the aeronaut corps attached to the *Colossus*, the ten-story-tall steam man that had delivered him back to Cahokia. Archie descended from the giant steam man with its captain, wearing a steam-cavalry jacket that was ten sizes too big for him. His coat and shirt had been blown off in the explosion.

"I am relieved to see you survived Master Fergus's gyrocopter, Master Archie," Mr. Rivets said.

Fergus shot Mr. Rivets a frown, then turned to Archie. "Good to see you, kiddo. Told you you'd get right up from that fall."

"Found him half-nekkid in a hole about two miles outside the city, as the airship flies," Custer said. "Or should I say 'the boy flies'?" Custer tipped the brim of his broad, round steam-cavalry hat back on his head. He was a handsome, neatly dressed man, perhaps a little thin, with long, curly blond hair and a bushy blond mustache and goatee. His eyes were beady and sky blue, and his nose was long and sharp. He wore the dark blue jacket of the United Nations Steam Cavalry, with a red neckerchief tied tight around his collar and gold buttons down his front in two curving lines. A yellow stripe ran down the outside seam of his light blue steam-cavalry pants, and the shiny black boots he wore went all the way up to his knees.

Custer ran a hand down his mustache to smooth it. "Gonna have to tell me how you managed that one, son."

"Later," Mrs. Moffett said. Her eyes were dark and cold. "There'll be plenty of time for that on the road."

"We're going home?" Archie asked.

"No. You're going after the Dragon Lantern," Mrs. Moffett told him.

"But how do we know where she's going? The fox girl, I mean?"

"We checked all the outgoing airships," Hachi said. "She wasn't on any of them."

"So we got the idea to check the trains," Fergus said.

"She took a train?" Archie asked. "From Cahokia on the Plains?"

"She bought her ticket with this," Hachi said. She put a stack of dollar-sized slips of newspaper in Archie's hand.

"Ticket seller swore up and down she'd given him United Nations money with Hiawatha's picture on it," Fergus said. "Must have made him think that's what he was seeing. He couldn't believe it when he opened his till and pulled out scrap paper."

"Why not take an airship wherever she was going?"

"Well, for one thing, we were checking them all," Hachi said. "And she had to know that."

"And if you're going to go west this time of year," Fergus said, "you most definitely do *not* want to be taking an airship."

Custer nodded. "Tornado season." He picked an invisible piece of lint off his sleeve and gave it a brush. "Rip an airship right outta the sky. Want to get as far as the coast, you take a train to Cheyenne and catch it moving south. From there you gotta take an airship again. Leastways until they finish that Transcontinental Railroad."

"The three of you will leave right away on Captain Custer's steam man," Mrs. Moffett told them. "I will follow by train. Captain Custer assures me you can catch her train before it reaches Kansa City."

"I'm not going," said Hachi.

"What?" Archie said.

"I'm not going," said Hachi again. "The Pinkertons found Blavatsky in Louisiana. Her name is Helena Blavatsky, and she's set herself up as some kind of magician at the court of Queen Theodosia. I bought us three tickets to New Orleans on the next steamboat down the Mississippi."

"Three tickets?" Archie asked. He pulled Hachi aside, and Fergus and Mr. Rivets came with them. "Hachi, we can't go to New Orleans now! We have to go after the fox girl and get the Dragon Lantern back."

"I went after it once, and I brought it back," Hachi said.

Archie reddened. "Oh. So it's my fault it got stolen, is that it?"

Hachi softened. "I didn't mean it like that. I just mean that I was willing to do this when I didn't know where Blavatsky was. Now I do."

"But we have a job to do. We have a responsibility to the Septemberist Society. *We're the League of Seven.*"

"You and Mrs. Moffett keep saying that," Hachi told him. "But where are the other four?"

Archie glanced imploringly at Fergus, but he looked away.

"Look, Archie, we may be a League of Seven, or we might not be," Hachi said. "But I've waited my whole *life* for a lead like this, and I'm not going to put it off for a second. Not for the League of Seven, and not for any Septemberist Society."

"What about for a friend?" Archie asked. "This lantern thing is supposed to have something to do with who I am and where I came from. I *need* you."

"I kind of thought that's why you would come with me to New Orleans," Hachi said.

They all stood there for a moment, the three kids and Mr. Rivets, without saying a word. Archie knew Hachi was right to go after Blavatsky, and he knew he should be going with her. But he also knew he had to get the Dragon Lantern back, and that she should be coming with him. But they couldn't do both at the same time.

"I . . . I can't," Archie said. "I have to go after the lantern."

"And I have to go after Blavatsky," Hachi said.

Which just left Fergus. Archie and Hachi looked at him, and he stepped back and raised a finger at them. "Oh nae, don't put me in the middle!"

"You have to choose who you're going to go with," Hachi told him. "Unless you're going off on your own too."

"Nae! We're a team, the three of us," he told them. He looked into their faces, but the looks there told him neither of them was going to back down. Fergus deflated like a ripped airship balloon.

"Well, I . . . I suppose I have to . . . *crivens.*"

"It's okay," Archie told him. "I know you're going to go with Hachi."

Fergus looked heartbroken, which was exactly the way Archie felt. But as soon as he knew they were splitting up, he had known that Fergus would go with Hachi. Fergus cared too much about her to let her go off alone.

"I'm sorry, mate. Truly, I am," Fergus said. "Anyway, it's not like you need the help. You're unbreakable."

By sticks and stones, maybe, Archie thought. But their words hurt. He wanted to cry, but he fought it off. He was already the youngest. He didn't want them to think he was a baby too.

"We'll find you when we're done, eh?" Fergus said. "We'll take care of this Blavatsky lady and you'll get hold of that Dragon Lantern, and we'll meet back halfway in between. Somewhere in Texas, eh? Where'd be good, Mr. Rivets?"

"According to Avery's Library of Universal Knowledge, there is rather a large city called Houston, near the Gulf of New Spain," Mr. Rivets said. "Named for the first president of the Republic of Texas, Sam Houston, the city boasts—"

"That'll do, Mr. Rivets," Archie said.

"Houston it is, then," Fergus said. "Last one there buys the ice cream. They do have ice cream in this place, don't they, Mr. Rivets?"

"Unknown, sir."

Archie looked sheepishly at Hachi. He didn't know what to say.

"Are you going to kill her? Blavatsky?" he asked.

"No," Hachi said, surprising all of them. She put a hand to the long, ugly scar on her neck she'd gotten the night Blavatsky and the others attacked her parents' village. "I'm going to get her to tell me everybody else who was at Chuluota, and what they were doing. *Then* I'm going to kill her."

A steam whistle blew somewhere across town, toward the river.

"That's our ship. We have to go," Hachi said.

"Okay. So . . . ," Archie started, but suddenly Hachi was hugging him. He hugged her back.

"Be careful," she whispered.

"I will. Careful—"

"'—is your middle name.' I know." She pulled back from him and smiled. Hachi smiling was something that Archie was still getting used to.

"We were so good together," Archie told her.

"We will be again," Hachi told him. "You can help me get the rest of them."

Archie nodded. "I hope you find what you're looking for," he told her.

"You too," she said.

The steam whistle blew again, and Hachi picked up her bag and walked away. Archie was surprised she didn't say good-bye, but then maybe he understood not really wanting to say it.

Fergus laughed. "I'll say it. Good-bye, mate, and good luck." Fergus shook Archie's hand. "Don't worry. I'll watch over her." Fergus clapped him on the shoulder, then picked up his bag to follow Hachi. "We'll be back together again before you can say 'locked sprockets,'" he said as he backed away.

"Locked sprockets," Archie said, but it didn't work.

He watched them go until it was just him and Mr. Rivets on the sidewalk.

"You'll come with me, won't you, Mr. Rivets?" Archie asked.

"Of course, sir. Always."

Philomena Moffett rejoined him.

"Hachi and Fergus aren't coming," he told her.

"I see," she said. "Well, it's disappointing, but you and Captain Custer's regiment should be enough to do the job. Come along, Archie. You have an appointment with a giant steam man."

⑥

The United Nations Steam Man *Colossus* was ten stories tall and made of gleaming brass. Two blue-uniformed soldiers hung from ropes off its shoulders, buffing it to a blinding shine. You had to crane your neck to see its head, a two-story brass dome with two enormous glass windows for eyes, each as tall as a man. Across its wide round face was the thin line of a mouth, almost like it was smiling. The steam man's broad chest was dotted with hatches—gun ports, Archie guessed—and two powerful-looking arms hung from ball joints at its shoulders. The upper arms were brass pipes as wide as a person—wider, like the largest of the pneumatic post tubes, the kind Archie had personal experience with. Beneath them hung massive round forearms like cannon barrels with articulated hands at the ends. The chest ended at horizontal, canister-like "hips," which led to two more brass pillars like the upper arms, and an even bigger pair of barrel-like boots that formed the top part of the feet. The steam man's left leg was painted blue, with the white tree and four rectangles of the United Nations flag along the bottom like a tribal tattoo. Down its right leg, painted in big blue block letters, was its name: "Colossus."

"We're 'bout ready to go," Captain Custer told Mrs. Moffett. "Just loading the last of the water and coal in now."

Colossus stood up against a specially built scaffold, where a small army of workers loaded him with supplies for the journey.

"You must catch that train," Mrs. Moffett told him. To Archie she said, "Find the thief. Retrieve the lantern."

"This lantern," Captain Custer said. "What is it that General Lee would give you a steam man and a whole corps of aeronauts to go after it?"

General Robert E. Lee was the United Nations' war chief, the leader of all their armies. He was also secretly the man who sat in the warrior seat on the current Septemberist council. Archie had seen him, along with Philomena Moffett, John Two-Sticks, Frederick Douglass, and the other council members, when he'd gone rushing in to tell them there was a Manglespawn in the basement of the Septemberist Society's secret headquarters. General Lee was the sole reason Archie was getting a steam-man escort west.

"It's a weapon," Mrs. Moffett said, surprising Archie.

"It is?" Archie asked.

"It can be," Mrs. Moffett said. "You must not treat it lightly, Captain. Nor, under any circumstances, must you try to activate it once you reclaim it."

Captain Custer was pulled away to sign requisition forms, and Archie grabbed Mrs. Moffett's arm.

"It can be a weapon? You never said that before."

Mrs. Moffett looked at Archie's hand on her arm, and he pulled it away.

"Why won't you tell me everything you know?" he asked.

Mrs. Moffett sighed. "I'm sorry, Archie. I'm not trying to be mysterious. The fact is, we just don't know much about it. Most of the records were destroyed. But . . . I do know the lantern was used on you when you were a child."

"Used on me? How? When? I don't remember that. Who did it? What does it *do*, exactly?"

Mrs. Moffett put up a hand. "I don't know. But I think it's safe to assume that if it could turn you into . . . what you are, it is sufficiently dangerous enough to keep it from falling into the wrong hands."

"Like this fox girl? What do you think she's going to do with it?"

"I don't understand her motives," Mrs. Moffett said. "Nor do I care to. All that matters is that you retrieve it from her. Find the lantern, and you will find your answers."

Archie nodded, more resolute than ever.

The steam man gave a piercing whistle, and the soldiers working on and around it started to disappear inside.

Mr. Rivets joined Archie and Mrs. Moffett. "Sir, it's time to board."

Custer came back and saluted Mrs. Moffett. "We'll get your lantern back, ma'am. Don't you worry none. We'll watch out for this little feller too."

"Do not underestimate 'this little feller,' Captain," Mrs. Moffett said. "He is stronger than he looks."

Custer squinted at him. "Tougher too, I reckon."

Archie felt uncomfortable under their appraising stares.

"Mr. Magoro!" Custer called suddenly, and a boy with dark skin ran over to them. He couldn't have been much older than Archie, but he wore a UN Steam Cavalry uniform like the rest of the regiment. Unlike Custer, though, he wore his sleeves rolled up, his collar open wide around a loose red neckerchief, and kept his uniform pants up with a pair of yellow suspenders. Over his shoulder he carried a half-full canvas rucksack.

"Yessir!" the boy said, snapping to attention.

"Mr. Magoro, give Mr. Dent and his machine man here a tour of *Colossus*, then report to your post."

"Yessir!" the boy said. He gave Custer a quick salute as the captain left to board the steam man.

"Remember, Archie," Mrs. Moffett said, "all that matters is that you bring that lantern back to me."

"I won't let you down," Archie told her.

Mrs. Moffett smiled. "I know you won't. Good luck."

"C'mon, we'd better get aboard," said the boy.

Archie gave Mrs. Moffett a little wave good-bye and followed the young soldier.

"Name's Clyde," he told Archie and Mr. Rivets over his shoulder. "Nobody but Captain Custer and Mrs. DeMarcus ever call me Mr. Magoro. You got a name besides Mr. Dent?"

"Um, Archie."

Clyde turned around and shook Archie's hand while he walked backward. "Nice to make your acquaintance, Um Archie. That's a joke. I know your name is just Archie, not Um Archie. Mrs. De-Marcus says that words like 'um' are just filler words. Three for engineering, Mr. Yellow Tree! How's the missus?"

It took Archie a moment to realize Clyde had shifted from talking to him to talking to the worker manning the elevator up into the scaffolding.

"Cranky as a wind-up man," Yellow Tree joked, and Clyde laughed.

"That's a fact! You can get inside through a door in the left foot, but then you've got to climb six stories up ladders through a lot of machinery," Clyde said as the elevator rose through the scaffolding. Belatedly, Archie realized Clyde was talking to him again. "Easier to just take the elevator up to the main door in the engine room."

The elevator rocked to a stop, and Clyde led them out.

"Be safe out there, Chief," Yellow Tree told Clyde.

"Will do. We're the last ones aboard, Mr. Turtle At Home," Clyde said to a man at the hatch to the steam man. "You can close him up when we're inside."

"You got it, Chief," Turtle At Home said.

Archie stepped inside *Colossus* behind Clyde and found himself in a tightly packed room filled with pipes and gauges and levers. Turtle At Home closed the hatch behind them, and the heat hit Archie like a wet blanket. This was the steam man's boiler room, and it was hotter than a sweat lodge. A narrow metal gangplank led them on a mazelike path through the machinery, and Archie followed along, eager to be out of there as soon as possible. Along the way, they passed two soldiers in grimy overalls—Cheyenne, Archie guessed—both of whom shouted greetings of "Chief!" when Clyde waved at them.

"Engine room!" Clyde hollered back at Archie over the roar of fire, the clanking of gears, and the hiss of steam. "Hotter than a Cahokia summer, and believe you me, summer in Cahokia on the Plains is no picnic. That's when you go up to Cahokia in the Clouds, if you've got the money or the means. Me, I've never been up there. Like Mrs. DeMarcus says, better to keep your feet on the ground than have your head in the clouds. Guess in *Colossus* I get to do both."

There were black people like Clyde in Philadelphia and New Rome, but not many. Mostly they lived in Haitia and Louisiana and New Spain. Archie knew they had once been from different tribes back in Afrika, but there were so few of them now in the New World they all just called themselves Afrikans. The few Afrikans in North America had been just as cut off from their old world as the Yankees had when the Darkness fell a hundred years ago.

Archie wondered if they were all as talkative as Clyde.

"You ever been inside a UNSM?" Clyde asked.

"A . . . ?" Archie asked, trying to keep up.

"A United Nations Steam Man. UNSM."

"Oh," Archie said. "Just when you picked me up."

"Only seven of these in service," Clyde went on. "One here, two down in Choctaw territory, one up at Fort Detroit, and three up in Council of the Three Fires territory, mostly because of the Sioux. *Colossus* is the last and best, and that's a fact."

Clyde led them up a ladder from the engine room, and Archie sighed with relief as the heat peeled away from them. The next floor up was long and thin from front to back, right about in the middle of *Colossus*'s torso. All along the wall were folded-up beds intermixed with rows of oscillating rifles. Four of the gun ports were open, letting in fresh air, and at the far end of the room Archie was surprised to see four soldiers—three men and a woman—eating dinner at a foldout table. A Yankee wearing a cavalry uniform and an apron stirred something in a big pot on a stove behind them.

"Crew quarters, armory, and mess," Clyde told them. "We eat in shifts. Early Dinner's now. You'll probably eat with the captain during Middle Dinner. All this gets cleared and becomes a gun deck whenever there's action. Two bathrooms, over there. Shower there. Shower sign-up there. Only one shower a week, Saturday nights. Mandatory. Oh, should have mentioned it—rewinding cabinet for your machine man back down in engineering, right between the central drive shaft and the left arm torque bar."

"Thank you, sir," Mr. Rivets said. "A most kind convenience."

"We got all the amenities, Mr. R. What's the word, Mr. P?"

The Yankee cook frowned. "The word is 'harebrained.'"

"Don't mind him," Clyde said. "He's always grumpy. Mr. Inola," he said to a Cherokee soldier at the table, "you're all cleaned up. Got a new lady friend back in Cahokia?"

The other soldiers at the table hooted and hollered, and Mr. Inola blushed through a halfhearted denial. In the hullabaloo, Clyde leaned in to one of the other soldiers at the table and passed him a small glass container from his backpack. "I got you a salve for that rash," Clyde whispered.

The soldier quickly tucked it away. "You're my hero, Chief," he said, then joined back in with the jokes and the laughter.

Up above them, a steam whistle blew out a sequence of three notes that made Archie jump.

"Uh-oh. Moving out. Better wrap this up quick," Clyde said. He stowed his pack in a compartment underneath one of the bunks just as the room lurched sideways. Archie went tumbling, but Clyde stayed on his feet and none of the soldiers at the table lost a spoon. Archie was just getting up when the room hitched and lurched the other way, knocking him on his butt again. Another soldier climbed down from above, a broad-shouldered Choctaw with a pair of bandoliers filled with aether grenades across his chest and a long black ponytail down his back, and he laughed meanly at Archie's clumsiness.

Clyde jumped to help Mr. Rivets lift Archie to his feet as the room lurched the other way again. "Sorry. Just *Colossus* walking. Hardest thing to get used to. But you'll get your walking legs in no time."

The Choctaw soldier snickered again and brushed past them, so close that Archie staggered again on the shifting floor.

"Nice guy," Archie said.

"Yeah. I don't know him yet," Clyde said. "We picked up a couple of new recruits when we put in at Cahokia. He looks like a rough one, though, and that's a fact. Come on. I'll show you where you'll be sleeping."

Archie wobbled to the ladder up to the next level and grabbed onto it like a drowning man grabbing a life preserver. He'd be lucky if he got his "walking legs" before the mission was over. Clyde scurried up the ladder and Archie followed, focusing on climbing one rung at a time.

The third and final floor inside the steam man's enormous chest had more bunks, though fewer than the crew deck. Its walls were mostly taken up with three personal balloons, like the one his rescuer had been flying when Archie woke up in his hole. You didn't ride these balloons, you *wore* them. Usually they were big, round things that tapered down to narrow openings at the bottom, but right now they were mostly deflated. Beside them, three aeronauts—all Illini—worked at testing and tending to the compressed boiler backpacks they wore when they flew.

"This is where the officers besides Captain Custer sleep and eat," Clyde told them. "Just two of them on board: Lieutenant Pajackok, and Sergeant Two Clouds there." He nodded to the female aeronaut. She nodded back and said, "Hello, Chief."

"What about you?" Archie asked, hanging onto the ladder so he wouldn't fall over. "Everybody calls you Chief."

Clyde laughed. "That's just my nickname. The soldiers gave it to me 'cause I chat up everybody on board like I'm trying to get elected chief. I don't do it on purpose. Mrs. DeMarcus says I was probably born talking. You think that's possible? To be born knowing how to talk?"

Another whistle sounded—this one less piercing and closer—followed by the canned voice of Captain Custer through a speaking tube from up top.

"Sergeant Two Clouds, please deploy two scouts," Custer said.

Two Clouds pulled a speaking trumpet out from the wall and talked into it. "Two scouts, aye sir." She nodded to the other two aeronauts, and they got themselves into their harnesses while she opened up big hatches in the roof. Archie saw blue sky through the holes in the steam man's shoulders. The aeronaut scouts attached the ends of their balloons to hoses coming up through the floor—hot air from the boiler room, Archie guessed. The balloons inflated quickly. Meanwhile, the aeronauts put on belts with lots of pouches and heavy sandbags hanging from them, and clipped on bugles and oscillating rifles. As the balloons filled out, Archie saw that they were red on top and blue-and-white striped on the bottom, with names written in gold in between. One was called *Chickenhawk*. The other was called *Clever Crow*.

In moments, the balloons were filled with enough hot air to pull the aeronauts off their feet. Tethers kept them inside until they did a final check of their gear. The scouts nodded to Two Clouds, and at her signal they pumped the portable bellows strapped to their chests to stoke their backpack furnaces, detached their tethers, and rose up into the air.

"That is something I just never get tired of watching." Clyde said. "Come on—I'll show you the brains of the outfit. Sorry, Mr. R—I think you better stay down here. Not much room for you up top."

"As you say, sir," Mr. Rivets said.

Archie followed Clyde up a narrow ladder in the middle of the room, passing through the round, armored neck of the steam man. The head of *Colossus* was two stories tall, and the first of the two levels was a small round room with a retractable bunk, fold-up writing desk, wooden chest, and personal bathroom.

"Captain's quarters," Clyde said in passing. "All this gets stowed when the mouth opens."

Archie noticed the thin line of light that crossed the far wall around knee-level—where the giant steam man's lips parted, he guessed.

"Can it talk?" Archie asked.

Clyde laughed. "Naw. *Colossus* isn't alive. He's just a big empty robot. The mouth just opens to get stuff in and out. One time, we caught a Blackfoot pirate ship as it was flying away and we boarded it through here." He nudged Archie. "Guess we put our army where our mouth was, so to speak. Ha-ha."

Clyde climbed on up to the top floor of the steam man. He was right—there wouldn't have been any room up here for Mr. Rivets. There was barely enough room for Captain Custer, a navigator, the driver, and Archie and Clyde. As it was, Archie had to stand over the porthole to the captain's quarters. He didn't want to move around much anyway—the head swayed in the opposite direction of the body as *Colossus* walked, making Archie steam-sick.

"Permission to show our guest the bridge, Captain?"

Custer nodded. "But make it quick, Mr. Magoro. No wise words from Mrs. DeMarcus. We need you in your chair."

"Aye, sir. So that's Lieutenant Pajackok, navigator," Clyde said, nodding at an Algonquin soldier at a small table with a map spread out on it. "Mr. Pajackok, Archie Dent."

The navigator smiled at them. "Chief. Mr. Dent."

"And our pilot is Mr. Tahmelapachme."

The pilot sat in a padded chair with his hands on complicated levers with all kinds of buttons on them, and his feet strapped into brass pedals he was pumping like a bicycle. No—like a person walking. *Colossus* was moving in step with Tahmelapachme.

"Call me Dull Knife," the pilot said, not taking his eyes off the scene ahead of them.

And what a scene it was. Archie had been up high before—in his family's airship, the *Hesperus*, and even higher in (and above) Cahokia in the Clouds. But looking out through the eyes of *Colossus* was like being a giant himself, walking along in a make-believe world of little toys. They passed the edge of a forest to their left, the trees brushing against their legs like tall grass in a summer field. To their right was a low-slung, hill-like Pawnee earth lodge, the size of a doll's house. Tiny toy cattle scurried away like overweight, spotted chipmunks, and two mouse-sized children scrambled to the top of the earth lodge to wave at the giant in their midst. Lieutenant Pajackok gave them a little *toot-toot* with the steam whistle, and they shouted and waved back happily.

Captain Custer gave his lieutenant a mildly disapproving look. The navigator cleared his throat and muttered, "Sorry, sir," but when Custer's back was turned, he gave the boys in the cockpit a quick smile.

The steam man lurched awkwardly, and everyone in the cockpit grabbed on to something to steady themselves.

"Mr. Magoro, if you're finished with your tour, we could use you at your post. Mr. Tahmelapachme is making a hash of it without you," Custer said. "Easy march."

"Right away, sir!"

Clyde climbed up into a small chair high above and behind everyone else in the cockpit and swung a snare drum around in front of him. From a pocket beside his chair he produced a pair of drumsticks, gave them a theatric twirl, and then started to beat out a march. Like magic, the pilot fell into a regular rhythm with his steps, and the rocking of the steam man smoothed out considerably.

"Much better for all concerned," Custer said without looking back at them. "All right. We've officially left United Nations territory. We have a Right of Passage treaty with the Pawnee, but we'll have to watch our step from now on."

Literally, Archie thought as they stepped over a tractor.

"Pretty great, isn't it?" Clyde asked Archie as he drummed. "Best way to travel, and that's a fact. Here—open this rearview hatch and see if they're there."

Archie opened the little horizontal port. It was built for soldiers to look out of, and he had to stand on tiptoe to see out.

"What am I looking for?" Archie asked.

"The dogs."

Archie shifted his focus lower, and he saw them. There was a pack of them, as small as ants, all yipping and chasing the giant steam man like they were nipping at a steam carriage. Archie laughed.

"They're almost always there right after we leave town." Clyde said. "I love it."

"They're breaking off now," Archie said. "Most of them, anyway. One little brown one is still chasing us."

Clyde laughed. "He'll tucker out soon and we'll lose him."

"Mr. Dent, you had better go below now," Captain Custer said. "Settle in. Get some rest. I hope to catch the train by nightfall. Oh, and I'm planning on having Late Dinner in my cabin. If you can wait till then, you're welcome to join me."

"Thank you, sir," Archie said. "I will."

Clyde gave Archie a smile and a salute with one of his drumsticks, and Archie started the long, nauseating climb back down. *Hachi would be right at home in the swinging compartment*, he thought. And Fergus—Fergus would never have left engineering. He'd still be down there dissecting everything with the engineers.

Archie wondered where they were now, and if they missed him. He certainly missed them. That, as Clyde would say, was a fact.

7

"A first-rate chicken," Custer told the cook clearing their table. Clyde had called him Mr. P., but his full name was Parsons.

Parsons grumbled something that might have been a thanks and might have been an insult and went back downstairs.

Archie sat with Custer at the little writing desk in Custer's small quarters in the steam man's head. Custer had opened the mouth a couple of feet, and all through dinner they'd been cooled by the constant breeze of *Colossus* moving forward. Archie had also been treated to an incredible view of Pawnee territory as they pursued the train. At least he hoped they were pursuing the train; Custer didn't seem to have them following any train tracks.

Custer glanced at himself in the mirror and smoothed his mustache before settling back in his chair with a cup of coffee. "So," he said. "You still haven't told me how you came to survive that fall from Cahokia in the Clouds."

Archie looked away, out at the advancing terrain. He had only known what he really was—the Jandal a Haad, "Made of Stone"—for a few weeks. In all that time, he'd told no one else besides Hachi and Fergus, Mrs. Moffett, and his parents.

The people he *called* his parents, at least.

Without realizing he was doing it, Archie put a hand to his arm, covering the crack underneath his shirt. The crack that showed there was nothing but stone underneath his skin.

"You don't like to talk about it," Custer said.

"No," Archie said. "I'm sorry."

Custer nodded. "I understand. Mrs. Moffett says you're something different. Something special. But you don't want to be different and special, do you? You'd rather just be a normal kid doing normal kid things."

Archie nodded. Before he'd known what he was, all he'd wanted was adventure. Excitement. He'd gotten that, but the trade-off had been losing everything he believed to be true: that he was his parents' son; that the Septemberist Society could handle any challenge the Mangleborn threw at them; *that he was a human being*. He'd been living a lie before, believing in things that weren't real, but he found himself wishing he could go back to being boring if it meant he could be normal again.

"So whatever this is that let you survive that fall, you hate it. You're embarrassed by it," Custer said. "Well, let me tell you a story, Mr. Dent. I, Captain George Armstrong Custer, was last in my class at West Point Military Academy. *Dead last.* The other boys laughed at me. Told me I was a joke. That I'd never earn my stripes. But I'm good at things they can't grade you on. I'm a good leader of men. They may call me Iron Butt because I ride them hard and run a tight ship, but they respect me. They'd follow me into hell if I asked them to."

Custer took a sip of his coffee. "There's something else I'm good at, and that's being decisive. All those nobs who knew their military history backward and forward, what good did it do them on the battlefield when they couldn't decide to retreat or charge? Being a good leader, being decisive, those are *gifts*, like whatever it is that makes you strong, Mr. Dent. If the trade-off for those is coming in last in my class at West Point, if it's being laughed at and called steam-for-brains by my classmates, then I accept that. In fact, I embrace it. I tell everybody I can I was last in my class at West Point. Because you know where a lot of those jokers are now who got better grades'n me? They're washed out. They're shopkeepers, and teachers, and businessmen. And where am I?" Custer gestured at the room around them. "I'm captain of my own steam man at thirty-one, in charge of my own regiment, sent on a special mission by General Robert E. Lee himself."

Custer leaned across the table and pointed at Archie. "Whatever it is you're embarrassed about, whatever it is you wish was normal, embrace it. *Own it*. Because that's what makes you special. And being special is way better than being normal, no matter what it costs."

Bugle notes came to them on the breeze, soft and distant—messages from the advance aeronaut scouts they'd launched before. *Colossus* responded with a series of blasts from its steam whistle, and the speaking trumpet on Custer's wall came to life.

"Scouts report steam bearing south-southwest, Captain," Lieutenant Pajackok reported from up above.

Custer took the speaking trumpet in hand. "Excellent, Lieutenant. Adjust course, and blow to clear for action."

"Aye, sir, adjusting course and blowing to clear for action," Pajackok replied.

Archie saw the steam man change direction slightly before Custer pulled the lever that closed *Colossus's* mouth, and the steam man's whistle blew a new series of notes. Within seconds, two men had scrambled up the ladder from below and were taking the captain's room apart, tucking his personal effects away and lashing the furniture to the walls. Captain Custer put his big broad cavalry hat on, stopped to see how it looked in the mirror, and climbed the ladder to the bridge.

"Come along, Mr. Dent," he said. "We have a train to catch."

Archie climbed after Custer. Clyde gave him a smile as he entered the bridge, but didn't stop his drumming. Archie didn't know how he could keep it up; Clyde had been drumming for hours. Even more incredibly, Dull Knife was still at the controls, marching the steam man along in time with Clyde's beat.

Colossus crested a ridge, and there in the distance was a train. Archie was surprised to see it was chugging toward them, not away from them.

Lieutenant Pajackok saw his confusion and smiled. "You forget, Mr. Dent, *Colossus* can do something a train can't." He nodded at the maps in front of him. "We can take a shortcut."

"Mr. Pajackok, signal the scouts to intercept the locomotive, and kindly ask it to stop."

"Yes, sir," the lieutenant said. He pulled a cord, sending the aeronauts a message via a series of whistles. The aeronauts responded with bugles, and the propellers on their steam-powered backpacks accelerated, swinging them down toward the train. Archie watched as they matched the locomotive's speed, caught it with grappling hooks, and began to pull themselves down to it.

Something yipped excitedly beneath them, and Archie squeezed his way to the big glass eyes at the front of the bridge to look down. There, barking and wagging his tail excitedly at the aeronauts and the train in the distance, was the little brown dog that had followed them out of Cahokia on the Plains.

"He's still there!" Archie said. "The little dog. Clyde, he's still with us!"

The dog ran out ahead of them like he was another advance

scout, and Clyde leaned forward to see him. "Well I'll be. The little guy's persistent, I'll give him that!"

Suddenly a golden raygun beam shot out from somewhere below them, hitting the ground right beneath the dog. Dirt exploded all over him, and he jumped aside and cowered.

"Somebody's shooting at him!" Archie cried.

"Mr. Pajackok!" Custer said. "Find out whoever's doing that!"

Another golden beam lanced out, hitting the ground right behind the dog. He leaped forward and spun, tail beneath his legs, trying to understand what was attacking him.

Archie heard a clatter behind him and realized the drumbeat had stopped. Clyde was down from his chair and leaping into the hole that led below.

"Mr. Magoro!" Custer yelled, but Clyde didn't hear him—or didn't listen. Archie hurried after him, beating Mr. Pajackok to the porthole.

Clyde clamped his feet to the outside edge of the ladder and slid down fast. He was through the captain's quarters and below before Archie was even halfway there. Archie chased him through the maze of soldiers at their posts on the upper gun deck and down the ladder to the crew deck, where the Choctaw soldier they'd taken on at Cahokia leaned out one of the forward hatches, taking aim at something with his oscillating rifle. Clyde yelled and barreled into him. The big Choctaw fell to the floor, and his oscillator fired inside the room, the beam ping-ponging off the walls. The other soldiers on the deck ducked and covered, but the bouncing energy ray was bound to hit one of them. The beam ricocheted in Clyde's direction, and Archie threw himself in the way, taking the blast full in the chest.

It blew a hole in his shirt, but didn't hurt him at all.

The Choctaw climbed to his feet and raised a hand to cuff Clyde. "Could have killed us all, you little—"

Lieutenant Pajackok caught the Choctaw's arm before he could strike. "The way I see it, Mr. Nahotabi, you're the one who almost killed us all," he told the soldier. "No one on this steam man is to shoot—*ever*," he said, shaking Nahotabi's arm as he said it, "until an officer gives the order. Do you understand?"

Nahotabi glared up at Lieutenant Pajackok. "Yes. Sir."

"Mr. Magoro, you abandoned your post," the lieutenant said, never taking his eyes off Nahotabi. "Please return to it."

"Yes, sir," Clyde said. Archie helped him up, and Clyde gave Nahotabi one last glare before pushing his way through the other soldiers on the deck and climbing the ladder.

Lieutenant Pajackok let Nahotabi go and returned to the bridge, giving the burn mark on Archie's shirt a frown as he passed. Archie followed him back up to the whispers and sideways glances of the rest of the crew. His secret was out.

Colossus had come to a stop by the time Archie and the lieutenant got back, and so had the train down below. Captain Custer was halfway out a hatch at the very top of the head talking to one of the aeronaut scouts.

"Everything straightened out down below, Mr. Pajackok?" Custer asked.

Pajackok glanced at Clyde, who sat grim-faced in his chair. "Yes, sir," the lieutenant said.

"Did they catch her?" Archie asked.

Custer shook his head. "She's not on board anymore."

"Are you sure?" Archie asked. "She's a master of disguise. She can make you think you're seeing something you're not—"

Custer put a hand up. "Mrs. Moffett told me all about it. But I think in this case your thief used her talents to get away. The engineer told our scouts that two hours back they were attacked by a Pawnee raiding party."

"What?" Lieutenant Pajackok said. "But locomotives have Right of Passage."

"They *thought* they were being attacked," Custer said. "The engineer saw the tracks blocked ahead and threw the brake. Only when the train stopped there weren't nothing there—and no Pawnee raiding party either. Said they all vanished into thin air."

"That's when she got off the train," Pajackok said.

Custer nodded. "Most like. She had to know we'd be coming for her. I figure she had some other means of transportation stashed wherever it was she stopped the train."

"We should still search the train with one of the Tik Tok porters, just in case," Archie said. "She may still be there and just be trying to throw us off the scent."

"I'll order one of the scouts to stay behind and search, but we're going back down the tracks to where that train stopped," Custer said. He closed the top hatch and climbed back down. "If your thief's out and about, I don't want to lose the scent. The aeronaut can rejoin us tomorrow with or without her. Mr. Pajackok, give the signals."

"Aye, sir."

"Mr. Tahmelapachme, adjust course to follow those tracks. Mr. Magoro, double march speed."

"Aye, sir," they said together, and Clyde started a new, quicker beat. Dull Knife picked it up right away, and *Colossus* followed the train tracks at a faster pace than before.

"Mr. Dent," Custer said, appraising the burn mark on his chest. "You'll be wanting to change into a new shirt."

"Yes, sir," Archie said.

On the way downstairs, Archie met Clyde's eyes, and the drummer gave him a nod of thanks.

❧

By nightfall, they reached the place where the train had stopped, and Custer's scouts found steam mule tracks in the woods, heading northwest.

"Toward Sioux country," Clyde told Archie. The Sioux were notoriously territorial and fierce, and regularly raided the towns and villages of the tribes all around them. The United Nations had been in an out-and-out war with them in the past, but for now there was a tenuous peace.

The United Nations were at peace with the Pawnee too, but Custer was still leery of marching through their territory at night. Instead he ordered the regiment to make camp by the railroad tracks where the fox girl had run off. They would go after her in the morning. And in this case, the steam man *was* faster than what she was riding. They would catch her tomorrow, Custer was sure.

Dull Knife found a small hill to sit *Colossus* on, lowering him down with practiced precision. Some of the soldiers put up UN Army tents outside, choosing to sleep out under the stars, while others stayed in the steam man. Everyone came out for dinner, though, which Parsons cooked on a big campfire.

Some of the soldiers tried to lift a log to bring it closer to the fire to sit on, but six of them together couldn't lift it. Instead they tried rolling it, with poor results.

Embrace what makes you special, Custer had told Archie.

"I can do that," Archie told the soldiers.

"Do what?" one of them asked.

"Move the log for you."

Most of the men laughed, but one of them—Inola, the young soldier with the girlfriend in Cahokia—peered at him from under his folded-up cavalry hat.

"Do it then," he said.

Archie stepped up to the log, and the men and women stopped laughing and stepped away. Word of him taking a raygun blast on the crew deck earlier had spread rapidly throughout the steam man, and Archie could see a hint of fear in their eyes.

Own it, Archie told himself. He put his arms around the log and lifted it like it was a lacrosse stick.

The camp grew silent as everyone stopped to watch him carry

the giant log and lay it down near the fire. In a way, Archie enjoyed their attention, liked the way they looked at him with awe and fear. Maybe he *was* telling them all he was different—that he was inhuman—and maybe that would keep them away. But maybe it was better that way.

Archie strode to the edge of the forest beyond the tracks, picked another tree about the same size, and pushed on it. The tree groaned and creaked, and the earth beneath his feet rippled as the roots rippled. Archie pulled the tree back and forth, loosening it in the ground, and then put his arms around it and heaved.

The tree came ripping out of the ground in a shower of dirt and rock.

Archie laid it on the other side of the fire and snapped off the limbs where people would want to sit. When he was finished, he brushed the dirt and leaves off of himself and took a seat. The soldiers of the 7th Steam Man Regiment turned away to whisper incredulously among themselves. Across the campsite, Captain Custer grinned back at him and nodded.

Slowly, regular life returned to the camp, and soldiers began to drift over to sit near Archie by the fire. Near him, but not with him. Archie got up to let them be more comfortable.

The little dog that had followed them from Cahokia on the Plains was, incredibly, still with them, and it ran around through the campsite, barking and getting underfoot. He was a mutt of a dog, shaggy and scrawny, his hair a curly, tangled mess. He looked like he'd never had a bath in his life and was perfectly fine with that. He hunkered down low on his front legs and *arf*ed, trying to get one of the men to play with him, but the soldier kicked him out of the way. It was Nahotabi, the same soldier who'd shot at him before. The dog yelped and shrank away, and suddenly Clyde was there in between them.

"Back off," Clyde told the Choctaw.

"Or what?" Nahotabi said.

"Or I'll make you sorry," Clyde said.

"Yeah? You and what army?"

Archie stepped up beside Clyde.

Nahotabi laughed, but he had seen Archie's strength, and he walked away.

"Thanks," Clyde said. "Like Mrs. DeMarcus says, some people are just rotten to the core."

"Who's this Mrs. DeMarcus you're always talking about?" Archie asked.

"The woman who ran the orphanage where I grew up," Clyde said.

Archie suddenly felt awful. His own parents might have adopted him, but they'd loved him like a real son all his life. And all he'd done lately was be angry that they weren't his birth parents. Clyde hadn't even had that much, and yet he seemed so happy. Far happier than Archie.

The little dog peeked out from behind Clyde, but stayed close to his leg.

"Looks like you made a friend," Archie told him.

"Yeah," Clyde said. "Looks like." He put a hand out to Archie. Archie looked at it, surprised that anyone would want to be friends with him after his little display at the campfire. He took Clyde's hand and shook it.

"As for you," Clyde said to the dog, "you need to stay out from underfoot and learn to be useful if you're going to stick around, and that's a fact." He took off the red bandana he wore around his neck and tied it around the dog's neck, like a collar, while the dog tried to lick all over him. "There. Now everyone'll know you're part of the regiment."

The dog looked up at them with his tongue hanging out and wagged his tail furiously.

"Thanks again, by the way," Clyde said. "For taking that ray-gun blast for me today in *Colossus*."

"Oh," Archie said. He bent down to pet the dog. "Sure."

"Did it hurt? I mean, does stuff like that hurt when it happens to you?"

"Yeah," Archie said. "But only for a second. I feel things, but not for long. It hurts and then it goes away. Same with good stuff." He nodded at the dog licking at his face. "This tickled at first, but now I don't feel anything."

"And it doesn't do anything to you, getting shot and falling out of the sky or whatever?" Clyde asked.

"Only once," Archie said. He had never shown it to anybody but Hachi and Fergus and his parents, not even Mrs. Moffett, but he rolled back his sleeve now and showed Clyde the crack, high up on his arm. The dog licked at it like he knew it hurt and was trying to make it better.

"It looks like stone in there," Clyde said.

Archie nodded. "It is. Does it creep you out?"

Clyde laughed. "Yeah it does! Doesn't it creep *you* out?"

Archie had to laugh at that. "Yeah. Yeah, it does."

"Good! I'd be worried if it didn't!" Clyde said. "All right, Buster," he said to the dog. "Let's get you some food. Bet you're thirsty too, after all that running."

"Buster?"

Clyde shrugged. "He seems like a Buster."

"Think Captain Custer will let you keep him?" Archie asked.

"Maybe," Clyde said. "He's partial to strays."

8

Archie heard the cry of the advance aeronaut scouts' bugles, and the shrill reply of the steam man's whistle. All around him on the crew deck, soldiers jumped to action, clearing the tables, chairs, and bunks and pulling oscillating rifles from the rack.

Archie did his best to stay out of the way in the tight quarters. "What is it? Did they find her?" he asked Private Inola.

The Cherokee paused mid-hurry to answer Archie. "No. That's the signal for 'Enemy Sighted.' It's the Sioux."

"All the way down here?" Archie asked, but Inola had already run off to take up his post at one of the gun ports along the front wall of the cabin. Archie couldn't believe it.

"The Sioux come this deep into Pawnee territory?" Archie asked Mr. Rivets. "We're only two days out from Cahokia!"

"Sioux raiding parties this far south and east are not unheard-of," Mr. Rivets said. "But they are indeed rare. Most of the Sioux/Pawnee conflict is concentrated around the area known as the Badlands, almost a thousand miles from here."

"Monowheels!" someone cried, and Archie ran to one of the empty hatches and looked out. Over a ridge rolled perhaps a dozen of the things. They were single round wheels, with cog-like bumps along the outside to give them traction. Inside each wheel, open to the air, was a Sioux warrior sitting back atop the tangle of brass and wood machine that made it run. They steered the wheels by means of wide handlebars and could spin and pivot the vehicles on a dime. It was the exceptional speed and all-terrain handling of the monowheel that allowed the Sioux to have such a huge territory, from the border of Pawnee country in the south to the cold, snowy borders with the Cree and Blackfoot in the north.

And it was the twin mounted rayguns on either side of the wheels that made them so feared everywhere.

"Monowheels we can handle," Private Inola told Archie.

"Be like playing chunkey," said a Cahokian soldier. "Two points for putting a raygun shot through the hoop."

But then *Colossus* began to shake and rattle more than usual, and the soldiers grew quiet. Rising over the ridge was an enormous cogged monowheel, ten times the size of the smaller ones, and half the height of their United Nations Steam Man. Like the smaller monowheels, it was driven by a steam engine inside it, but unlike them, it housed not a single person but an armored capsule, no doubt filled with a small regiment of Sioux warriors. And like the smaller monowheels, it had twin guns mounted on the sides—but these were mighty raycannons.

"A *motherwheel*," someone whispered, and the jokes about putting a raygun shot through the chunkey came to an abrupt end.

"That's not a raiding party," Inola said. "That's an invasion force!"

"Engage all targets!" came Lieutenant Pajackok's voice through the speaking trumpet. Golden beams lanced out from hatches up and down the steam man. They carved up the ground between the twisting, turning monowheels, but didn't manage to take any of them out. At another blast from the steam man's whistle, the aeronaut scouts high above dropped bombs. *Thoom! Thoom! Thoom!* They exploded in geysers of grass and sod. Between the bombs and the rayguns, they might be able to get all the monowheels. But how would they defeat the giant motherwheel?

Archie heard heavy clanking from somewhere beyond the wall to the right of him and felt *Colossus* rumble.

Inola ducked back down from his gun port to wait while his oscillator recharged, and he smiled at Archie. "Time to bring out the big guns," Inola said. "Keep an eye on that arm."

Archie looked back out the hatch at *Colossus's* right arm. The fingers on the steam man's right hand stretched out, came together, and retracted, disappearing into its thick right forearm. It looked like someone had chopped the steam man's hand off at the wrist.

Something whined inside the forearm, and Archie felt his white hair stand on end. It was like all the air around *Colossus* was being sucked into the arm. No, not the air. Something else. Something alive but intangible.

Aether. Twisted pistons, *Colossus's* arm was a giant raycannon!

BWAAAAT. The arm cannon fired, knocking Archie on his butt again. The air outside flashed gold like the entire sky had exploded, and the soldiers inside *Colossus* cheered. Archie scrambled to his feet to see the motherwheel, damaged, carve a rut around the steam man and steam off in retreat the way it had come.

"We've got 'em on the run!" someone cried.

"Did you see that?" Archie asked Mr. Rivets. "Did you see that?"

Mr. Rivets had finally come to one of the gun ports to look out. "I saw the blast from *Colossus's* raycannon, Master Archie," Mr. Rivets said. "But I do not see its target."

"The motherwheel!" Archie said. It was right there. "*Colossus* just blasted off one of its raycannons!"

"Master Archie, there is no motherwheel here. Nor are there monowheels. The soldiers are shooting at empty ground."

"No," Archie said. He couldn't believe it. He was seeing it all with his own eyes—but the fox girl had made him see all manner of things that didn't exist in Cahokia in the Clouds. Could this be an illusion too? But this was massive! A motherwheel and a dozen monowheels!

"Mr. Rivets, are you telling me there's nothing out there? No Sioux invasion force?"

"I repeat, Master Archie, there is no motherwheel, nor any monowheels."

"*Slag*," Archie muttered. "Stop shooting! There's nothing there!" he cried, but the soldiers just looked at him like he was crazy.

Archie grabbed the speaking trumpet from the wall and yelled into it. "Captain Custer! There's nothing there! It's all an illusion! You have to stop shooting!"

"Mr. Dent?" Lieutenant Pajackok replied. "Mr. Dent, we're in the middle of a military engagement. Stay off the line."

"But I'm telling you, there's nothing out there! It's one of the fox girl's illusions!"

Archie got no response. He cursed under his breath and ran for the ladder. It was three floors up to the bridge, with *Colossus* moving forward and swinging its arms and chest back and forth. Archie stumbled again and again as he climbed. He felt the hair on his head stand up and the aether all around him aggregate in the massive arm cannon outside, and he hung on.

BWAAAAT.

Archie was nearly thrown from the ladder. Down below, he heard the soldiers cheer again. The flanges didn't realize they were shooting at empty prairie!

Archie got his feet back on the ladder and climbed the rest of the way up into the bridge. Buster, now a constant presence at Clyde's side, licked Archie's face as he came up through the hatch. Clyde gave Archie a surprised look, but Archie didn't have time to even say hello.

"Captain Custer! You have to stop attacking!" Archie cried. "There's nothing there!"

"Lieutenant Pajackok told me about your concerns, Mr. Dent," Custer said. "But as you can see, our raycannon is clearly having an effect." He pointed out the big round windows at the retreating motherwheel. Black smoke poured from its side, and the massive wheel left a trail of broken parts and debris behind it. "Never hit us once!" Custer crowed.

"*Because it's not real,*" Archie said. "I see it too. But the thief's illusions don't work on Mr. Rivets, and he says there's nothing out there!"

Lieutenant Pajackok looked worryingly at Custer, but the captain shook his head. "Your Mrs. Moffett told me this thief could somehow make people see things that weren't there, but we got no evidence she can operate at this scale. She may have tricked you with smoke and mirrors—maybe even mesmerized you somehow. But she can't do the same thing to a whole regiment. Mr. Magoro, double time, march! Mr. Tahmelapachme, I want to catch that motherwheel before it gets away."

"Aye, sir," Dull Knife said, working the legs and arms of *Colossus* as if they were his own. Archie looked imploringly at Clyde in his drummer's chair high up behind them, but Clyde just shrugged and picked up the pace, as Custer had ordered.

Custer turned from the window. "Mr. Dent, please clear the bridge. If we can't knock that thing over, I mean to board it, and I can't have you—"

The floor went out from under them. Archie went flying toward the windows, which were suddenly and sickeningly pointed straight down. The groan of metal, the scream of men, the rush of air, and—KUR-RUNCH!—*Colossus* plowed headfirst into the ground.

Archie bounced around the tiny bridge of the steam man like a lacrosse ball ricocheting in a goal net, finally coming to a stop in a cold puddle in the space between *Colossus's* eyes. In the stillness after the chaos, the only thing he heard was Buster's frightened barking. Archie shook the dizziness away and panicked—he was lying in a pool of blood! *No. No, calm down.* It was just water.

The bridge was a mess. Twisted metal and broken wood lay piled on top of Archie, and underneath him was shattered glass and rock. Archie had no idea what had happened to cause the crash, but there would be time to figure that out later. Buster, seemingly unharmed, dug at the rubble next to Archie, and Archie heard a groan. Archie lifted Buster aside and moved the rubble away. It was Pajackok! He'd gone flying like Archie, but hadn't fared as well. His forehead was covered with blood, and one of his legs was twisted the wrong way. Laying over him was a heavy brass buttress that had come loose in the crash, and Archie lifted it off and cast it aside.

But now what? Custer lay nearby, unconscious, and Dull Knife and Clyde hung limp from their chairs like puppets. Archie had to get Pajackok and the others outside and get medical treatment for them. But *Colossus* was facedown, and there was no way of telling if he could even get through the neck himself, let alone carry Pajackok or any of the others out that way.

"How do we get out, Buster?" Archie asked. Then he remembered—the hatch at the top of *Colossus's* head! It was easily within reach and hadn't been damaged in the crash. Archie spun the lock on the hatch, and it fell open.

"Hello in there!" someone called down. "Are you all right?" Sergeant Two Clouds! She and the other two aeronauts had come down to *Colossus* to help with the rescue, and she was still in her balloon harness. Buster barked at her, and Archie shushed him.

"They're all hurt!" Archie said. "Can you lower a rope and lift them out?"

One by one, Archie and Two Clouds got the bridge crew out through the hatch and onto the ground. When everyone was clear, Archie and Buster worked their way back inside. The connection between *Colossus*'s head and its body was still useable, and with Buster there to sniff out the crew in the wreckage, Archie helped the aeronauts lift the rest of the men out deck by deck. On the crew deck, Archie found Mr. Rivets banged up but otherwise in good working condition. The machine man was too heavy for the aeronauts to lift out, but Archie was able to pick him up and push him high enough for the Tik Tok to grab the external hatch on the steam man's back and pull himself through.

When Archie had cleared the last of the men from engineering, Two Clouds lifted him and Buster out. Then, for the first time, Archie could see what had happened. *Colossus* lay headfirst in a wide ravine, its head planted in a small creek that ran through the bottom of the valley. The creek bed itself was broad and flat, but about a hundred yards away the ground rose steeply, forming a ten-foot-tall cliff.

Archie pictured it in his head: *Colossus* pursuing the motherwheel over what looked like a long, flat expanse of prairie; Custer ordering Clyde and Dull Knife to pick up the pace; and then, right as they had begun to jog after the motherwheel, the ground disappearing beneath their feet. They'd gone sprawling, like running off the top of a stairwell without seeing it coming.

Only the ground hadn't disappeared. It had never been there to begin with. What they had seen—everything, from the Sioux raiding party to the flat terrain in front of them—had been an illusion.

"We saw it all," Two Clouds told Archie after she landed. "The monowheels, the motherwheel, prairie stretching for miles. Then— nothing. All the Sioux vanished, and there was the cliff and the creek bed, and *Colossus* was going over. I sent Shiriki back after we got everyone out, but there was no sign of their tracks. Just the holes we blasted. It's like they were never there."

"They weren't," Archie told her. The whole thing had been one big trick, meant to lure *Colossus* off that ledge. To stop them from following her. And they had fallen for it. Facefirst.

No one was dead, but almost everyone was hurt. Their injuries ranged from a few cuts and bruises to broken arms and legs to serious internal injuries that had the regiment's medic and Mr. Rivets (with his Surgeon card installed) working long into the night. Only Archie and Buster had come through unscathed.

In the morning, they could finally see how badly *Colossus* had been damaged. The giant steam man was dented and bent, but not irreparable, the engineers said. The trouble was that it had landed with its right arm folded underneath it and its left arm stretched out behind it. The engine room got the boilers running again, but no matter what Dull Knife did, he couldn't get enough leverage to get *Colossus* up off the ground.

Archie stood with Custer, Pajackok, and Clyde, watching the steam man rock and wallow helplessly in the creek bed. Buster ran around the prone steam man, barking at it to get up and play.

Custer cursed under his breath and smoothed his mustache with his good hand. The other hung in a sling across his chest.

"Mr. Dent, I apologize," Custer said. "You warned me, and I didn't listen. I just never thought . . . "

"I know," Archie said. "I didn't either the first time."

"Fool me once, shame on you. Fool me twice, shame on me. That's what Mrs. DeMarcus used to say," Clyde said. "That girl won't fool us again."

"No, she won't," Custer said. "Because we're done. We can't get *Colossus* up out of there. We're going to have to take what we can carry and hike to the nearest Pawnee town. Come back with another steam man regiment to lift it out."

"We'll be a laughingstock," Pajackok said.

Custer scowled, clearly thinking the same thing. "Nothing else can lift it."

"Archie can," Clyde said.

Clyde's words hung there in the air like smoke. Nothing but another ten-story-tall steam man could lift *Colossus*—except maybe a twelve-year-old boy who was, as Archie himself had to admit, even smaller than most other boys his age. Archie couldn't blame Custer and Pajackok for not believing it. He couldn't believe it himself.

"Can you do it, son?" Custer asked at last.

Archie shook his head. "It's too big. Too heavy. I can't."

"Have you ever tried to lift something that big?" Clyde asked.

"No."

"Then how do you know you can't?" he asked.

Archie stared at the enormous machine man. Laid out flat, it was as long as a lacrosse field.

"All you can do is try," Clyde told him.

Shyly, Archie splashed into the shallow creek, hoping the rest of the men wouldn't see what he was going to try to do. But Custer and Pajackok ruined that by warning the regiment to stay back. By the time they were finished, the entire regiment was standing and watching.

"Mr. Dull Knife?" Archie called in through the hatch in the head. "I'm going to try to lift *Colossus* out."

"You're *what?*" Dull Knife said.

"Just . . . be ready," Archie said.

Archie put his hands under the curve of the machine man's domed head. Was he supposed to pull it up, like lifting someone to slide a blanket under them? He didn't know. He gave the head an experimental tug, and it lifted up out of the water.

"*Whoa!*" Dull Knife yelled inside. "Locked sprockets!"

On the creek bank, the regiment took a step back.

Archie let the head back down into the water. He wasn't going to be able to get enough leverage by pulling up. He was going to have to get down low and push up. At his feet, the cold creek water slid by over bedrock. At least he wouldn't sink into the mud.

Archie glanced at the soldiers watching him from the shore. Clyde gave him a double thumbs-up. Taking a deep breath, Archie bent low, put his hands on *Colossus*'s head, and pushed up.

The steam man rose out of the water again, dripping on Archie's pants. The brass giant groaned, and Archie grunted, pushing him higher. Soon he could see into the windows, where Dull Knife, strapped into his control chair, gaped at him. Buster ran around them, barking happily. Archie took another step forward, walking his hands along *Colossus*'s face and pushing it higher, and the head came completely out of the water.

Mr. Rivets was easy to lift; *Colossus* was not. Archie knew after a few seconds that he would never be able to lift the armored steam man all by himself. Whatever his limit was, *Colossus* was beyond it. But Archie didn't have to lift all of it. Just part of it.

"Dull Knife," Archie grunted through the broken glass of the left eye. "Get the arm out."

Dull Knife understood immediately and began trying to work the pinned right arm out from under the weight of *Colossus*. Archie's body shook as he held the head off the ground, but it wasn't enough. The arm was still stuck.

"Hang on," Archie said. He took another step, almost slipping on the wet bedrock, and moved his hands down *Colossus*'s face. Buster, unfazed by a twelve-year-old boy lifting a hundred-thousand-pound steam man off the ground, danced around him in the water, barking and wagging his tail as though Archie was going to toss it and they were going to play fetch. He wanted to tell the dog to go away, to stay safely out of the way, but he was gritting his teeth and shaking so badly now that there was no way he could speak.

Archie kept moving forward until he reached the neck, and then the steam man's chest. The top of the head fell back into the water behind him and he staggered, but kept his feet. He was like a mouse pushing a facedown human being up by the shoulders. He was so short! If he were taller, he could have lifted the fallen steam man even higher. But just getting *Colossus*'s chest off the ground was enough. Dull Knife worked the steam man's right arm out from under it, and the regiment cheered. Suddenly, mercifully, Archie felt the immense weight of *Colossus* lift from him as Dull Knife used the freed arm to push the steam man up, and Archie dropped his weary arms.

Archie had done it. He'd lifted *Colossus*. Not all the way off the ground, but enough.

Dull Knife worked the steam man into a sitting position, and the regiment swarmed over to it to crawl inside and assess the internal damage, making sure, Archie noticed, to stay far, far away from him. Only Custer and Clyde came over afterward to congratulate him and thank him.

"Told you you could do it," Clyde said, slapping Archie on the shoulder. Buster licked Archie's hand.

Archie could hardly feel either one.

Pajackok joined them, adding his congratulations before giving Custer an update.

"Engineering reports it will take at least a day to get him walking again, and longer before he's back up to a hundred percent."

"She's going to get quite a jump on us," Custer said. "But at least we're back in the game."

If Fergus had been there, Archie thought, they'd be back in the game even sooner. But Fergus and Hachi were far, far away by now.

Custer and Pajackok and Clyde hurried back to *Colossus*, leaving Archie all alone and wishing more than anything that he was with his friends, wherever they were.

9

Hachi and Fergus stepped off the steamboat *Joseph Brant* onto the busy docks at New Orleans. Porters swarmed up and down the gangplanks, bearing bags and chests and crates to and from the line of three-decker paddleboats moored in rows on the Mississippi. Most of the porters were men and women, not Tik Toks, and they were a jumble of First Nations, Afrikans, and Yankees. Their shouts and cries were a mixture of Anglish and Acadian, the same Old World language they spoke in Montreal in the far north. Hachi could hear a bit of Spanish in there too, and a little Choctaw, and another language she couldn't recognize. The wild mix of tongues told her right away that New Orleans was going to be a complicated place to deal with.

Fergus, of course, was staring out at the massive steam ships like a little boy. "There's the *Enterprise*," he said. "She's got six steel boilers and nine engines. Draws only three feet when fully loaded. They say you can sail her on a heavy dew."

Hachi took his arm and pulled him away. "Later," she told him.

"You always say that," Fergus said with a pout, "but we never come back."

Their trip down the Mississippi River had been uneventful and slow. Fergus had spent almost the entire trip in the engine room, talking boilers and draws and horsepower with the engineers, or tucked away in his room tinkering on something secret. Hachi had spent the whole time thinking about what she was going to do to this Madame Blavatsky person when she found her, and now that they were in New Orleans, Hachi was eager to get on with it.

"I sent Mrs. Moffett a pneumatigram asking her to let the local Septemberists know we were coming," Hachi said. She scanned the crowd. "I thought somebody might be here to quietly meet us."

"Miss Hachi!" a man cried, waving to them from the crowd. "Miss Hachi! Over here!"

"Or not so quietly," Fergus said.

The man was big—not so much tall as wide—with a round body and a friendly round face. He was dark-skinned and bald, and wore a black three-piece suit over a white shirt and black tie. It must have been stifling in the thick, wet heat of the city, Hachi thought. The man waved a white handkerchief like he was surrendering to them, and Hachi and Fergus worked their way through the crowd to hear his terms.

"Miss Hachi," the man said, shaking her hand. His voice was Creole Acadian, both lazy and hard at the same time. "You look just like your description, right down to de scar on your neck."

Hachi put a hand to her neck. She usually wore a scarf to hide the nasty scar she'd gotten as a child the night her father was killed, but she had skipped it this time in deference to the humid Louisiana weather. Maybe she would wear one anyway.

"And you must be Miss Hachi's assistant, Fenrick," the man said.

"*Assistant?*" Fergus said. "I'm not her assistant!"

"Erasmus Trudeau, at your service," the man said. He bowed slightly and mopped his head with his handkerchief.

"Thirty days hath September," Hachi said, giving him the first half of the Septemberist pass phrase.

Erasmus looked perplexed. "I'm sorry?"

Hachi and Fergus glanced at each other.

"Thirty days hath September," Hachi said again.

"April, June, and November," Erasmus said, still confused. "All de rest, dey have thirty-one. Except February, of course." He smiled awkwardly, not sure why he was repeating a children's rhyme.

Hachi reached for where her knife was hidden, but Fergus put a hand on her arm.

"Who sent you to meet us, Mr. Trudeau?" Fergus asked.

"De agency, of course," Erasmus said. "De Pinkerton Detective Agency? You hire us to find Helena Blavatsky for you, and we do. Well, *I* do. I'm de Pinkertons' man in New Orleans. Not too hard to find her, her being de queen's bokor and all."

Hachi relaxed. "Right. Of course. Thank you, Mr. Trudeau." Fergus looked at her with wide eyes, as if to say, "Don't be so touchy."

"Call me Erasmus," he said. "I book you in de Blennerhasset Hotel on Jackson Square. You follow me, and I see you get settled in."

"So, no Septemberist welcome, I guess," Hachi whispered to Fergus as they fell in behind the Pinkerton.

New Orleans beyond the docks was just as bustling as its waterfront. Broad green avenues clogged with steam carriages and clanging streetcars divided row after row of three- and four-story brick buildings whose gaslit sidewalks overflowed with men and women in fine, fancy clothes. Like the docks, the thick, humid air here was a soup of different languages, and the people a stew of different shades of brown.

"I didn't know so many Afrikans lived here," Hachi said to Erasmus.

"Not Afrikans," Erasmus told them. "Haitians. From de Carib Islands. Many came after de revolution there, like my parents. New Orleans, it a place many people come to. The Chitimacha people, dey come first. Den de Francia of the Old World, it come and push out de Chitimacha. Den de Spain of the Old World, it push Francia out, and den Francia, it push Spain out again." Erasmus laughed. "Den de Darkness come, and King Aaron, he come and conquer dem all."

Hachi knew the story: A man named Aaron Burr had raised an army near Cahokia and marched south and taken New Orleans nearly a hundred years ago. It was right after the Darkness fell, which made the seas choppy and unpassable, cutting the colonists off from their Old World nations. Without that support, there had been no one to stop him. Burr was dead now, and his daughter, Theodosia, ruled Louisiana as its queen.

"But New Orleans, she survive like always," Erasmus said. "Just like when de hurricanes come. Dey knock all de buildings down, but New Orleans, she get right back up again."

They crossed a canal lined with giant, drooping willow trees, and Hachi had to come back and pull Fergus away from watching the boats. At the base of the bridge she saw a woman in the bright blue-and-yellow uniform of the Louisiana militia with an oscillating rifle on her shoulder. Hachi was about to nod at her, but something about her face gave Hachi goose bumps. The woman was deathly gray and thin, with big dark rings around her eyes. And her mouth—her mouth looked like it was sewn shut with thick black string.

"Did you see that woman back there?" Hachi asked Fergus. "The soldier?"

"Ah, yes," Erasmus said uncomfortably. "Yes, *de Grande Zombi Armee*. A gift to Queen Theodosia from our new bokor, de Madame Blavatsky."

"She looked like she was dead," Hachi said.

"She is. Dey all are. De greatest army in de world, she say. After all, how you kill somebody who already dead?"

They passed another zombi soldier, and Fergus moved a little closer to Hachi.

"Crivens. That is blinking creepy," he said.

Hachi noticed that none of the living residents of New Orleans made eye contact with the soldiers, and they all gave them a wide berth—some of them even crossing the street to stay away from them.

"Looks like most people tend to agree with you," she said.

Erasmus nodded. "Dark things are afoot ever since dat bokor come," he said. "Some people, dey think dere even worse monsters than zombi in New Orleans, and dat dey be rising."

"Oh, that's just brass," Fergus said, and he and Hachi shared a knowing look. If there were Manglespawn here—or worse, a waking Mangleborn—then Blavatsky was the least of their problems. And they were without Archie, the one of them who could actually go toe-to-toe with a Mangleborn and survive.

Archie. Hachi felt a twinge of guilt for letting him go after the lantern alone. She hated to do it. He was right—they *did* make a good team. And she did want to help him find out where he'd come from. But she knew where *she* had come from, and Blavatsky was a part of it she couldn't let get away. And whoever this Blavatsky was, she was even more powerful than Hachi had thought. And more dangerous too.

"Erasmus, we need to get in to see Queen Theodosia," Hachi said. Wherever Queen Theodosia was, Blavatsky was sure to be close by. "Can you arrange that for us?"

"Oh, no, Miss Hachi," Erasmus said. "Sorry. Erasmus Trudeau a big man in New Orleans, but not dat big."

Fergus grabbed her arm suddenly and Hachi flinched, instinctively moving to strike him but holding back at the last second.

"Hachi, look," Fergus whispered, completely oblivious to the fact that she had almost broken his nose. She followed his pointing finger to a painted wooden sign that hung outside an elegant-looking three-story building with white-painted wooden balconies. The sign said M. LAVEAU, READINGS, but the words were surrounded by a number of arcane signs and symbols, including a pyramid eye inside a seven-pointed star—the symbol of the Septemberist Society.

"Erasmus," Hachi said. "Before we check in at our hotel, Fergus and I would like to visit that shop."

Erasmus frowned. "Miss Hachi, whatever you looking for, you find it elsewhere. Dat shop belong to de Voodoo Queen, Marie Laveau. Her magic so powerful, she able to be young or old, depending on how she feel. You don't need nothing from her."

"Well," Hachi said. "If I can't see the proper queen, I'll see the Voodoo Queen. We'll meet you at the hotel, Erasmus."

A bell over the door tinkled as Hachi and Fergus went inside. The shop was dark and cluttered. Behind a long counter with a cash register was a wall full of bottles, each occupying its own little cabinet, and each marked with a faded yellow label. On the other side of the room, beneath shelves of books stuffed in wherever they would fit, a wall full of wooden Afrikan tribal masks looked down on them with empty eyes. A small altar lit with dozens of half-melted candles glowed in the corner, and skulls—both human and animal—sat on tables and shelves throughout the room. From the ceiling, just beyond their reach, hung thousands of little dolls, tiny human effigies made of sticks and straw and corn husks.

An old woman came out from behind a colorful piece of cloth hung in a doorway at the back and welcomed them in Acadian.

"*Bonjour*," Hachi said. "*Parlez-vous anglais?*"

"We speak many languages here, *chère*," the old woman said. "Some even that were never spoken by any human tongue."

"Sounds like our kind of place," Fergus muttered.

The old woman glided toward them. Her skin was a brown closer in color to Hachi's, but her face wasn't First Nations. The daughter of a Haitian and a Yankee, Hachi guessed. She was full-figured and wore a long, simple black dress with a gold-and-red shawl. Her wrinkled face was still beautiful, with high, thin eyebrows, and dark, mysterious eyes. On her ears she wore big, golden hoop earrings, and just a bit of black hair peeked out from under a complicated white wrap she wore on her head, making her look like she was drying her hair after a shower.

"What may I do for you, *mes enfants?*" she asked.

"Thirty days hath September," Hachi said.

"Ah," the old woman said. "Seven heroes we remember, yes?" She raised her left hand, and there, on the back of it, in faded black ink, was a tattoo of the Septemberists' symbol.

"Yes," Hachi said. She was surprised to discover how relieved it made her feel to find another Septemberist in the city. She had come to trust the society very quickly. She frowned inwardly— Archie and Fergus had made her too trusting of other people in general.

The old woman moved to the front door, where she turned the OPEN sign to CLOSED, locked the deadbolt, and lowered the shade. "So we are not disturbed," she told them.

Hachi scanned the room for other exits out of habit.

"Sit, please," the woman said. She gestured to a table with a thick red velvet tablecloth and three chairs. A deck of cards sat at her left-hand side. "I am Marie Laveau."

Fergus introduced himself and Hachi. "We've come from New Rome," he told her. "By way of all over."

"It has been a long time since we heard from the Society," Laveau said.

Hachi shared another look with Fergus. Had Mrs. Moffett not gotten her pneumatigram, or had something happened that kept her from writing to Laveau?

"For a while, the whole Society was being controlled by these bug things on the back of their necks." Fergus slid sideways to try to get a look at the back of her neck. "You didn't, uh, you didn't have one of them visit you down here, did you?"

"*Oui.* I did, as a matter of fact," Laveau said. She pointed to a jar on a shelf, where one of the dead bugs floated in a jar of formaldehyde. Hachi liked this woman better already.

The old woman clapped, making Fergus jump. From behind the curtain at the back stepped two figures, one tall, the other short. Both wore long, colorful wraps that disguised their figures, and wooden masks painted white with big black eyes and black lines for mouths with short vertical lines that gave them skeleton teeth.

"Crivens!" Fergus said. He shot up from his chair and stumbled on his bad leg.

"My assistants," Laveau said.

"They're not . . . they're not zombies, are they?" Fergus asked.

Hachi could see that they weren't, even with the masks. They moved like living people. And breathed. With a start, she realized that was what had disturbed her the most about the zombi soldiers. *They didn't breathe.*

"They are not zombi," Laveau said. "Just as you are not Septemberists."

Fergus began to protest, but Laveau cut him off.

"You are *Leaguers,*" she said. Laveau turned over the top seven cards from the deck, laying each out in a row on the table with a crisp snap.

The Chief, traipsing along happily with a dog at his heels.

The Judge, wearing a blindfold and holding the scales of justice.

The Warrior, wielding a raygun and sword.

The Scholar, holding an open book and a glass beaker.

The Trickster, wearing a mask and dancing.

The Maker, surrounded by gears and tools.

And the Strongman, a giant wrestling with his own shadow.

Fergus picked up the card with the gears and tools on it. "Hey, I like this one," he said.

Marie Laveau looked up at him and smiled.

"Oh," Fergus said. He looked awkwardly at Hachi, mirroring the way she felt. Neither of them was entirely comfortable with the idea that they were some kind of prophesied superheroes.

"The first seven cards of the Tarot," Laveau told them. "Figures as old as time immemorial."

"But there aren't seven of us," Hachi said. "We only know one more person who fits this."

Fergus picked up the Strongman card. "Archie."

"Where is this Archie?" Laveau asked.

"We had to leave him in Cahokia," Hachi said.

"Pff. You should have remained together," Laveau said. "You are stronger together."

Hachi felt terrible, like she was being scolded by her grand-mother. Fergus didn't look much happier.

"But what is done is done," Laveau said. "You are Leaguers, and your coming has been foretold."

Hachi stared at the row of cards, wondering if there really were four more people out there like them—people with extraor-dinary abilities, destined to fill the same old roles in an ancient and never-ending battle against the Mangleborn. If they did exist, where were they? Who were they? And how would they ever find them?

Hachi shook away the thoughts. This wasn't what she was here for. "We've come for Madame Blavatsky," she said.

Laveau knitted her fingers together on the table and nodded. "Theodosia's new bokor."

"Erasmus called her that," Fergus said. "What's a bokor?"

"A sorcerer," Laveau said. "One who serves the loa with both hands."

"What does that mean?" Hachi asked.

"It means she uses both white magic and *black* magic."

The masked assistants looked on silently behind Laveau.

"And the black magic I'm guessing is the *bad* magic," Fergus said. "Like those zombi soldiers we saw."

Laveau nodded. "Blavatsky has become very powerful since she came to New Orleans, but she does not understand the truth behind her power."

"Which is what?" Hachi asked.

"The Mangleborn that sleeps in Lake Pontchartrain."

"There it is," Fergus said. He leaned back in his chair and groaned.

"The Mangleborn's energy can be used to make powerful magic, powerful magic Blavatsky has tapped into," Laveau said. "But Blavatsky is a child playing with matches. She knows just enough to make the bright flame that amuses her, but not enough to keep from being burned by it—and burning down all of New Orleans with her."

Hachi leaned across the table. "We're here to stop her. But we have to get close to her. I need to get in to see the queen."

Laveau sighed. "Theodosia has been inviting me to call on her for as long as she has been on the throne, but I have always declined. Tonight I will agree, and you may join me at court. *Oui?*"

"Good," Hachi said. "We'll see you tonight."

"Wait," Laveau said, catching Hachi by the arm. Hachi had to fight down the urge to strike back again. She did not like people grabbing her.

"Let me do a reading for you," Laveau said. "Your fortune."

Hachi pulled her arm away. "That's really not necessary," she said. It wasn't that she didn't believe. Just the opposite. Her grandmother had read the signs for her when she was a child, sometimes with startling accuracy. Hachi was more afraid she would learn something she didn't want to know.

"Whether you hear it now, or live it later, it *will* happen," Laveau told her. "And I believe the Warrior is a person who likes to be prepared."

Hachi glanced at Fergus. "She's got you there," he said.

Marie Laveau moved the Warrior card from the row of Leaguers into the center of the table and put the rest back into the deck. She had Hachi shuffle the cards and then dealt out seven cards in a circle around the Warrior card. Like the Leaguer cards, these were illustrated with colorful pictures, and each had a name and a Roman numeral on it.

Laveau's eyes searched the cards for meaning. "You are not so concerned about money, I think," she said.

"How did you know?" Hachi asked.

The old woman smiled. "Because your last name is Emartha. But I do see other things you are worried about. So many swords . . . ," she said. She put a hand to a blue-and-white card that showed a woman in white sitting in a chair with a sword in her hand. From where Hachi sat, it was upside-down.

"We shall begin here, I think, with you," Laveau said. "The Queen of Swords. You are a strong and powerful young woman, Hachi. But you have come to be that way through great personal loss. The death of a loved one, *oui*? More than one. Your parents?"

Hachi found it hard to breathe, and took Fergus's hand under the table. "My father was murdered, and my mother died of a broken heart."

"You mourn for them," Laveau said. "But too much. You let your sadness own you. Rule you. Everything you are, everything you do, is guided by your grief. You are moving forward, but not toward your future. You are moving forward only because you are running from your past."

It was all Hachi could do not to cry. How could she *not* live a life dedicated to avenging her parents' deaths? Why had she been allowed to live, if not to see that justice was done? She saw the way other people lived, how *Fergus* lived, full of happiness and hope and aspirations, and knew that was a life she could never have.

The next card was the Seven of Swords. It showed a person carrying five swords over their back, with two more stuck in the ground.

"Your pursuit of Blavatsky will be tricky. And dangerous," Laveau said. "You must be cautious. If you rush in like usual, you will fail. You must come at the problem from a new direction."

Hachi wasn't too happy to hear that. Charging in was what came naturally, and what she did best.

"But you *will* succeed," Laveau told her, "through determination, skill, and"—she moved a hand to the next card, a young man riding a clockwork horse: the Knight of Cogs—"the help of one who loves you."

Hachi was very aware of the fact that she was holding Fergus's hand right then.

The next card was an upside-down Five of Swords. A warrior in the foreground held three swords, while two warriors with their backs turned walked away, their two swords on the ground. "But though you find justice," Laveau said, "you will still be confused and hurt. You *will* find the answers you seek . . . but there is one known to you who already has them."

"What?" Hachi said. "Who?"

Marie Laveau pointed to the next card: the Strongman.

"Archie?" Fergus said. "What's he got to do with anything?"

"I don't understand," Hachi said. "Archie doesn't know anything about it, or he would have told me."

"The Five of Swords says that deep down, you already know the answers," the old woman said. "You just don't want to face them."

"But I *do* want to face them," Hachi told her. "I want to know why my father was killed. I want to do something about it! Why wouldn't I want to face it?"

"Because of this," Laveau said. She pointed to the next card, a picture of a tower being struck by lightning. Flames poured from its windows, and a man and a woman fell out of it to their deaths on the rocks below. "The Tower means big changes. Catastrophe. When the answers come, they will ruin everything. They will change your life, completely and forever."

Hachi pulled her hand away from Fergus and shrank back. No—no, learning what happened to her father was a good thing. It was the *only* thing. How could knowing what really happened be worse than not knowing?

"But with destruction comes a rebuilding," Laveau said.

"Like New Orleans," Fergus said.

"Yes," said Marie Laveau. "Exactly like New Orleans. The Maker understands. That which is torn down can be built up again. But only *you* can do the rebuilding, Hachi."

She moved her hand to the next card—the Five of Cogs. In the picture, a black-cloaked figure stood with her back to them, her head bowed in despair. On the ground at her feet were five gears, three with broken cogs and two that were perfect. "The Five of Cogs is a card of choice," Laveau told her. "Three of her gears are broken, yet she refuses to see that she has two good ones left. She can continue to mourn over those she has lost and stay where she is, or she can celebrate what she has left and move forward."

Marie Laveau pointed to the next card: the Queen of Swords. They had come full circle.

"The choice will be yours, Hachi Emartha."

Hachi shivered. What was the secret of Chuluota? What did Archie have to do with anything? What had happened there that was so awful that learning it would destroy her so completely? And when the time came, could she rebuild herself? Would she even want to?

Marie Laveau stood. The taller of her two assistants took her arm to steady her, and the smaller of the two collected the cards off the table. Their audience with the Voodoo Queen was at an end.

"I will meet you at the palace," Laveau told them. "Now, if you'll excuse me, I must . . . change for the evening."

The mood in *Colossus* had definitely changed.

The soldiers in the 7th Steam Man Regiment didn't joke and laugh as they had before the crash. Many of them nursed injuries that kept them from being able to move about easily within the steam man, and instead of sitting in the galley during their down time, they stayed at the forward hatches, searching the terrain ahead of them for more tricks and illusions as *Colossus* pursued the fox girl.

It was the same on the bridge. Custer stood quietly by the right eye—the one that still had a glass window—watching the horizon. Lieutenant Pajackok, one of his legs bandaged and splinted, went over his maps again and again, constantly checking in with the advance scouts who flew ahead of them. All three of the aeronauts were in the air, and would be, Archie guessed, for the rest of the mission. Even Buster was quiet, looking up at Archie sleepily while Dull Knife and Clyde kept them walking along. It was already past dusk and creeping on toward night, and ordinarily they would be stopping to make camp. But they had lost the trail of the fox girl's steam mule in the delay repairing *Colossus*, and Custer was trying to make up for lost time.

"How is she able to do it?" the captain asked. He didn't turn around, but Archie could see the reflection of his face in the glass.

"Make us see things?" Archie said. "I don't know." He bent low to scratch Buster's tummy. "I only ran into her once before, in Cahokia in the Clouds. She made me see all kinds of stuff—fake walls, crowded sidewalks, a bear." Pajackok looked up at that one, then quickly went back to reading his maps. "Then she blew me up."

That made Custer turn.

"But there's something about her power," Archie went on. "It cuts out whenever she's surprised or stressed. There were times her illusions disappeared, and I was able to see her as she really is. I think."

"We'll just have to surprise her the next time we see her then," Custer said.

"That may be sooner than we think," Lieutenant Pajackok said. He put a hand to the headphones he wore. They were connected by rubber tube to the steam man's "ears"—big inverted speaking trumpets that funneled sound inside *Colossus*'s head. "It's the *Screaming Eagle*. They've spotted a bonfire."

Archie could just hear the hint of the aeronauts' trumpets on the wind through the open left eye. Pajackok gave Dull Knife a new heading, and *Colossus* turned to the north.

"I see it," Custer said. "Magnify."

The bonfire the aeronauts had spotted was a glowing orange dot on the horizon until Lieutenant Pajackok activated the right eye's optics. A series of telescopic lenses slid out of the hull just above the right eye, magnifying the view each time. *Click! Click! Click!* When they were all in place, they could see into the low, round canyon that held the flames, even though they were still half a mile away.

The bonfire wasn't a bonfire. There were flames, but they were red, not yellow and orange. Blood red, like the moon. The flames spiraled around a human effigy half as tall as a real man, made out of bundles of sticks. Where the head would have been was an enormous horned animal skull, like that of a buffalo, but much larger and more hideous.

Around the burning buffalo man, a giant herd of buffalo snorted and stomped, stampeding in a circle like they couldn't escape its orbit. Circling around them, lurching and dancing in time to some unheard song, were perhaps two dozen men and women, First Nations and Yankees alike. Their clothes were tattered and torn, and on their faces they wore grotesque masks—crudely carved things with bloody buffalo horns and matted fur that hung from their masks like shaggy beards.

And tied to the stick man in the very center of it all was the fox girl.

"Is that her?" Custer asked.

"Yes," Archie said, mesmerized. He didn't know which part of the whole thing was the most bizarre. Buster, wakened by all the action, barked at the image on the eye.

"Quite the show she's putting on for us this time," Custer said. "But we're not going to be so easily fooled. And she's made a mistake hiding out in that canyon with only one way out. Mr. Pajackok, signal the regiment to make ready for ground assault, then have the aeronauts take up points west-northwest, east-northeast, and west-southwest. Mr. Tahmelapachme, move *Colossus* in to take the fourth point, east-southeast of the circle, pointed toward the entrance, but come to a stop just outside it."

Archie moved closer to the window and frowned at what he was seeing. The fox girl had always made him see people, but they had been normal people, doing normal things—businessmen and nannies walking the gangplanks of Cahokia in the Clouds, a Sioux raiding party attacking from the north. This—this was just *weird*. How was she hoping to sabotage them with this illusion? And there was another thing—

"Why would she show herself?" Archie asked out loud. Custer looked at him. "I mean, why show her real self?"

"You said she showed you her real self in Cahokia," Custer said.

"But only when she was surprised. What if . . . " The thought was almost as outlandish as the scene in *Colossus's* telescopic eye, but he had to say it. "What if what we're seeing isn't an illusion at all? What if it's real?"

Everyone else on the bridge looked at Archie like he had suddenly put on one of those masks and started dancing around.

"I'm just saying," Archie said, "I've seen some pretty weird stuff before . . . "

Custer shook his head. "She's tricking us again. Luring us in. Or trying to. But I've got a few tricks up my sleeve too. For whatever reason, she's shown herself to us, and I'm not going to let her slip away."

Colossus rocked to a stop, and Archie stumbled as he tried to readjust. "All stop, Captain," Dull Knife said.

"Mr. Tahmelapachme, you and Clyde will stay on *Colossus*. Mr. Pajackok, you'll take half the regiment into the canyon and circle around to the east, leaving a man every two hundred yards. I'll take the other half of the regiment into the canyon and do the same to the west. When we're all in position, I'll give the signal, and we'll close in on her from all points."

"You're not going to take *Colossus* in?" Archie asked.

"She can slip away from us too easily that way," Custer said. "We'll surround her on the ground, and then close in like a net.

- 114 -

By the time she knows what we're up to, we'll have her fenced in and there'll be no place for her to run, no matter what she makes us see. Mr. Dent, you're with me."

Archie explained the situation to Mr. Rivets as he switched out the machine man's talent card for a Protector card. He wanted the Tik Tok and his nonhuman eyes with him.

"I wish you could see what's out there from here, and tell us if it's an illusion," Archie said. "Instead we'll have to wait until we're up close."

Dull Knife lowered *Colossus* into a squat, and Archie climbed down a ladder onto the ground with the rest of the regiment. Lieutenant Pajackok had already given them their assignments, and each of the soldiers carried oscillating rifles in their arms and rayguns in the holsters at their hips. They looked brave and ready for battle, but Archie knew from the mood before on the steam man that they were nervous and scared.

"This girl, she can fool us. Make us see things that aren't there," Custer told his men. "We all saw things with our eyes that weren't there the last time, and most of us have the bumps and bruises to prove it," he said, lifting the arm he carried in a sling. "But we've got her surrounded this time. No matter what you think you see, you ignore it—unless it tries to run. That's our quarry. Everything that isn't trying to run away is make-believe. Understand?"

The men nodded, and Custer waved them into action. Archie and Mr. Rivets followed along behind the captain as he spread his forces out in a wide half-circle. When they met up with Lieutenant Pajackok on the other side, Custer told him to give the signal. Pajackok blew a bugle, and high above them the three aeronauts fired off flares that lit up the dark canyon with brilliant white light.

"Master Archie," Mr. Rivets said. "I see them—the madmen, the buffalo, the fire, the girl. I can see it all."

"Wait, what?" Archie got a sick feeling deep in his stomach. "It's real?"

"Yes, sir."

"Captain Custer!" Archie cried, but Custer didn't hear him. He was already yelling for his men to charge.

Archie caught Custer by the arm. "No! Wait! It's not an illusion! It's all real!" Custer looked down at him in horror, but it was too late.

Shadows emerged from the darkness, oscillators raised, and ran toward the bizarre scene. They charged in among the crazy dancing people, ignoring them like they had been told to, and everything went wrong all at once. The dancers, driven mad by whatever that grotesque skull was in the center of everything, jumped on the soldiers, riding them to the ground in a hail of raygun blasts and screams. Archie ran into the fray, punching one of the insane revelers and sending her flying before she could stick a dagger into Private Inola's back. Another madman jumped on Archie and tried to bite him before Inola blasted him with a raygun.

"They're real!" Inola cried. "They're all real!"

It hardly needed to be said now. Custer's men were taking heavy losses—losses they could have avoided if Custer had just waited a moment longer to give the signal. Archie pulled one of the cultists off another soldier and threw him into the darkness, but the soldier was dead. This was all going horribly, horribly wrong.

And then it got worse.

Behind them, the buffalo at the head of the stampede stopped, and the buffalo following them plowed into them. But instead of trampling each other, they *melded*. Like pieces of molten iron, they stuck together, fusing with each other into one gigantic, monstrous, many-headed, many-legged beast. A stampede become a single creature.

A buffalo herd Manglespawn.

The creature bellowed with an unearthly roar, towering as high as the canyon walls and flickering red and brown from the light of the mystical fire. The insane dancers who remained broke off their attack and began dancing again, some of them moving so close to the monster that they were trampled.

The few soldiers who were left backed away in fear.

"Shoot it! Shoot it!" Archie cried. One or two golden raygun blasts lanced out in the darkness, but most of the men ran. The Manglespawn lurched after them, howling and trampling people, and Archie ran up to it and punched it. The monster staggered back on its dozens of legs, bellowing again, but it just rolled over onto different legs and charged anything that moved.

Archie found Custer in the chaos, staring at the bright red flame in the center of the clearing. Archie grabbed his arm. "Bring in *Colossus!*" Archie cried. Custer said nothing. He just kept staring at the skull and the flames. "Captain! Call in *Colossus!*"

It was useless. Custer was mesmerized. For all Archie knew, he was going to start dancing around with the cultists. He spied Lieutenant Pajackok struggling to his feet and hurried to help him.

"You have to call in *Colossus!*" Archie told him.

Pajackok nodded. He staggered a few feet away and blew on his bugle. In the distance, Archie could hear the giant legs of the steam man begin to piston their way toward them, and he sighed with relief.

An explosion lit up the air, and Archie flinched. Pajackok had called in the aeronauts in too. They dropped bombs on the Manglespawn, sending it stampeding around the clearing. Another explosion flared, and the buffalo creature turned and charged the effigy in the center.

The effigy with the fox girl still tied to it.

Archie had forgotten all about her.

"Master Archie! The girl!" Mr. Rivets called.

"I see it! I see it!" Archie called back. Together they converged on the effigy, the Manglespawn still bearing down on them. Archie ripped apart the ropes that bound her and handed her down to Mr. Rivets, but they were too late. The Manglespawn was right on top of them, and moving too fast for Archie to divert it. He grabbed the girl and turned his back to the monster to protect her, and then—*WHAM!*

The Manglespawn hadn't hit them. But what—?

Colossus! The giant steam man stepped over them and took another swing at the Manglespawn, connecting with a left hook. *WHAM!* The monster bellowed and rolled backwards, its dozens of little buffalo legs wiggling in the half-light like a centipede on its back.

Archie cheered and turned back to the fox girl.

"Are you all right?" Archie asked her.

The girl was in shock, but she was still able to nod. Up close, Archie saw her red fur ears and tail twitch in fear, and he knew then that this girl really was part fox.

"They—they weren't fooled," she stammered. "The crazy people. They—they could see right through my glamours. They caught me. Tied me up. They were going to sacrifice me to that thing!" she said.

Colossus was still hammering on the monster with one hand while the other disappeared into its arm. Dull Knife was transforming the other arm into a raycannon.

Archie took the girl by the shoulders. "The lantern," he said. "Where is it?"

That brought the girl back to her senses. "Safe," she told him, and then suddenly she was one of the cultists, a big hulking man in a grotesque mask. Archie broke away, scared in spite of himself.

"Don't let her go!" Mr. Rivets said. "She's still right there!"

The big madman jumped on Mr. Rivets's back with the speed and grace of someone much smaller, and suddenly she was the fox girl again.

In her hands was a pair of daggers.

"No fair peeking," she said, and she buried the daggers in Mr. Rivets's eyes.

11

Mr. Rivets was a machine man and could feel no pain. He didn't cry out as his glass eyes shattered, but Archie did.

"Noooooooooooooo!" Archie screamed.

The fox girl leaped off of Mr. Rivets, disappearing into the chaos, and the machine man lurched into Archie's arms.

"Mr. Rivets! Mr. Rivets, are you all right?"

"My ocular units are disabled," Mr. Rivets said. "But I am otherwise undamaged."

"Mr. Rivets, she put out your eyes!"

"Yes, sir. That is what I said."

Archie scanned the area around the bonfire. A few cultists and soldiers still fought, but there was no way of telling if any of them was the fox girl. Not without Mr. Rivets' eyes. Archie cursed. The fox girl was going to get away. But they had bigger problems.

Colossus finished converting his left arm into a massive raycannon and pointed it at the wiggling, writhing buffalo herd creature, but another bomb from an aeronaut sent the monster lurching toward the steam man. *Colossus's* blast shot over the Manglespawn, just grazing it. With a bellow that shook the air, the monster slammed into the steam man and knocked him back. Dull Knife windmilled *Colossus's* arms and tried to turn away, but he couldn't stop the steam man's momentum. With a groan and squeal of metal, *Colossus* toppled over and slammed into the ground with a teeth-chattering *THOOM.*

"*Colossus* is down!" Archie told Mr. Rivets, running for the fallen steam man.

"Archie? Archie? Where are you?" Mr. Rivets said. He finally stopped moving around. "I'll just wait here for you then, shall I?"

Archie ran into Custer in the darkness. "Captain! Captain, we have to get *Colossus* back on his feet!"

"That skull," Custer said, his eyes still glazed over and staring at the effigy. "There's something . . . not quite right about it."

"Yeah, no kidding!" Archie said. "Captain, leave it. We have to get *Colossus* back up, or we're never going to defeat that monster."

"That skull," Custer said, walking toward the effigy. "There's something . . . not quite right about it."

Custer was repeating himself. Between the horror of what he was seeing and whatever it was about the skull that was mesmerizing him, he was too far gone to be any help. Archie looked around for Lieutenant Pajackok, but didn't see him. He'd have to do this himself.

Archie climbed up to peer in the broken window on *Colossus's* face as the buffalo monster rampaged around the clearing.

"Clyde? Dull Knife?" Archie called. All he heard in response was Buster whimpering.

"Hang on! I'm coming," Archie said. He slid down through the eye hole and dropped like a rock inside, smashing into levers and instruments on the way down. Buster lay at the back where Archie landed, hurt but alive. Dull Knife and Clyde were still strapped into their chairs, but neither was moving. Archie tried to wake them. He hated to do it, but they were the only ones who could drive the steam man. Clyde roused, still dazed, but Dull Knife wouldn't wake up.

Archie considered for a moment taking Dull Knife's place at the controls, but one look at the complicated array of levers and switches and pedals and Archie realized how stupid that was. He would never be able to operate the steam man.

Which meant *Colossus* wasn't getting up again.

WHAM! The cabin lurched, and Archie was thrown against the wall. The Manglespawn! It would trample *Colossus* and them with it if he didn't get them out. Archie threw open the hatch in the head and called to Mr. Rivets. It took the machine man a few tries to orient himself, but soon he wandered close enough for Archie to hand Dull Knife, Clyde, and Buster out to him. Archie climbed out after them and threw Dull Knife and Clyde over his shoulder, carrying them to the wall of the canyon, as far away from the buffalo creature as he could get. He would have to come back for Buster.

"What's . . . what's the captain doing?" Clyde muttered.

Archie set Dull Knife and Clyde against the wall of the canyon and turned. Custer was at the foot of the effigy, firing an oscillating rifle at the skull on top of it at almost point-blank range. The skull glowed red-hot as though it were metal, not bone, and a piercing squeal-like scream echoed throughout the canyon. It rose in pitch as the skull glowed hotter and hotter, and though he couldn't explain why, Archie knew it was going to explode.

"Duck!" Archie said. He just had time to cover Clyde when there was a loud *FWOOM*, and a bright orange wave of energy hit them like a blast of hot summer wind. Archie closed his eyes and wrapped

Clyde up tighter, the energy searing his back. The Manglespawn buffalo creature roared in agony and rage, and then the light went out, the heat turned off, and everything was suddenly quiet again.

Archie let Clyde go slowly, and they stood.

"Where's Dull Knife?" Clyde asked.

Archie stared at the place where he'd set Tahmelapachme. The man was gone. In his place on the canyon wall was a dark shadow of a body and arms and a head. Archie put his fingers to the rock wall. The silhouette was part of the rock. Dull Knife had been vaporized by the blast, his atoms burned into the canyon wall.

They found more shadows farther along the wall—twisted, agonized shapes of men and women, soldier and cultist alike, who had been blown to smithereens by the skull's explosion. Not a thing was left in the canyon except Archie, Clyde, Mr. Rivets, and *Colossus*. The effigy, the mystical flame, the buffalo monster, even the aeronauts who'd been overhead were all gone. Only Archie, who was almost invulnerable, and Clyde, whom he'd protected, had survived.

"Buster!" Clyde yelled with a start. He ran back to where they'd left the dog, and Archie ran with him. "Buster!"

But Buster was gone. All that was left of him was the shadow of a dog burned into *Colossus*'s chest.

"No! Buster!" Clyde cried. He went to his knees, sobbing, and put his head and hands to the black silhouette of the dog. "I'm sorry," he bawled. "I'm so sorry. I shouldn't have left you. I didn't mean to. I didn't mean to leave you, boy. I was supposed to be there to protect you, and I wasn't."

Archie put a hand on Clyde's shoulder while the other boy sobbed. "I'm sorry," he told Clyde.

Something clattered down the wall of the canyon behind *Colossus*, like rocks tumbling, and then there was a *crack!* like a stone splitting. Archie's first thought was an avalanche—that somehow the blast had loosened the rock walls of the canyon and a boulder had broken loose. But then he heard more rocks tumbling, and more cracks—two, three, four, five. Archie lost count of the cracks as they echoed around the canyon. It was still dark, but in the dim light of the red moon he watched the black silhouette of Dull Knife pull its head, arms, and torso out of the rock wall. Then it stood, lifting itself on legs and feet torn from the dirt of the canyon floor. Beside it, one of the other shadows came to life, ripping itself from the rock wall and lurching forward.

Toward Archie and Clyde.

"Clyde, get up," Archie said, backing away. "Clyde, get up. Get up, get up, get up."

Clyde must have heard the fear in Archie's voice. He wiped his eyes on the sleeves of his UN Steam Cavalry uniform and stood.

"What . . . what in the name of Hiawatha is that?" he asked.

Archie didn't know, but whatever it was, he knew it wasn't good. He grabbed Clyde and pulled him away. The rock creatures lurched awkwardly, stone grinding on stone as they walked, but they were clearly coming for Archie and Clyde.

"Mr. Rivets?" Archie called, never taking his eyes off the rock creatures. "*Mr. Rivets?*"

"Here, Master Archie," Mr. Rivets said, and Archie steered them toward his voice.

"What are they, Mr. Rivets?"

"I'm afraid with my ocular units disabled, I do not know what 'they' refers to, sir."

"They're . . . they're rock people," Archie said. "They pulled themselves out of the wall where the shadows of all the other people used to be. The shadows burned into the wall when Custer destroyed that skull and everything got vaporized."

"Ah," Mr. Rivets said. "As you no doubt observed, those misguided souls were using the energy from the skull to amalgamate a herd of buffalo into one giant monster. I suspect that when Captain Custer destroyed the skull, that energy was released, 'fusing' all the living matter within range into the substrate behind it and creating the barely sentient creatures you describe."

"What'd he say?" Clyde asked.

"He said everybody else got blasted into the rock and brought it to life, and now they're all rock monsters coming to kill us."

"I did not say the creatures mean you any harm, Master Archie."

"No, but trust me, Mr. Rivets, they do!" One of the shadows that had pulled itself from the wall took a swing at Archie. He ducked, but not fast enough, and the blow sent him crashing to the ground.

"Ow," Archie said.

"That was . . . that was Dull Knife!" Clyde said. The rock creature swung at him, but he ducked out of the way.

"I'm afraid these creatures will bear little resemblance to the people you knew who gave them life," Mr. Rivets said. "The human brain is too complex an organ to merge well with solid rock."

Archie sidestepped another of the creatures and punched it. Its head exploded in a shower of rock and dirt, but the body kept coming.

"Yeah, brainless," Archie confirmed. "Stay behind me!"

Archie would have been all right if there had been just a few of them, or if they'd all come at him one at a time. But there were lots of them, and they came at him from all sides.

"The steam man!" Clyde cried. "We have to get inside *Colossus*."

As a plan, Archie liked it. He turned and started punching his way through the rock men, ignoring the ones at his back and sides. Clyde clung closely to him, protected from behind by Mr. Rivets, who held tight to Clyde's belt. When they finally got to the fallen steam man, Archie swapped places with Clyde and Mr. Rivets to hold the rock creatures at bay while they climbed in.

"Uh-oh," Clyde said.

"What do you mean 'uh-oh'?" Archie asked. "What's 'uh-oh'?"

"I mean *that* uh-oh!" Clyde said.

Archie glanced quickly over his shoulder, then did a double-take.

Colossus was moving.

The rock creatures pounded on Archie's back while he stared, openmouthed, at what he was seeing. *Colossus* the steam man put a hand to the ground, heaved itself up, and stood, towering over them.

Which was impossible, because no one was sitting in the driver's seat.

"Uh-oh," said Archie.

12

"Uh-oh," Fergus said.

A Haitian guard wearing a blue tunic emblazoned with the large gold fleur-de-lis of Louisiana put up a white-gloved hand, and he and his partner, a Karankawan guard in the same getup, crossed their spears to bar Hachi and Fergus from entering the throne room. Blue aether crackled around the blades of the spears.

"I'll kill the one on the right. You kill the one on the left," Hachi whispered.

Fergus knew she was kidding. At least he *hoped* she was kidding. "We're here as guests of Marie Laveau," he told the two guards.

The guards didn't move their spears. "The Voodoo Queen, she never visits the royal court," the Haitian guard said.

"Tonight I'm making an exception," said a deep, smooth voice behind them.

As promised, Marie Laveau had changed. She wore a striking white dress that swept down off her right shoulder and back up over her left shoulder like a Roman toga, and on her head she wore a matching white headscarf done up so that it made seven points at the top, like a cloth crown on her head.

She also wore a new body.

The Marie Laveau Fergus and Hachi had met earlier was replaced with a younger version, perhaps half her age. The high cheekbones and striking eyebrows were the same, but the wrinkles were gone. Her skin was light brown and glistened slightly in the gaslight. She was still full-figured, but now she was thinner and firmer, and, Fergus couldn't help but observe, jaw-droppingly gorgeous.

"She changed," he said. "She said she was going to change first, and *she changed.*"

Beside him, Hachi frowned at the woman, doubting what her eyes were seeing. But Fergus knew it was Laveau, and so did the guards.

"Madame Laveau!" the Karankawan said.

Marie Laveau strode forward with the confident, measured gait of a thirty-five-year-old woman and took Fergus and Hachi by the arms.

"I am here to see Queen Theodosia, by open invitation," she told the two guards. "And tonight I am joined by two companions. I'm sure Her Majesty will not object."

"No! Of course!" the Haitian guard said, and he and his partner quickly raised their spears to let them pass.

Laveau swept them inside and down a short corridor to the throne room.

"You told me my fortune today," Hachi said to Laveau. "You said I was going to go on a long journey."

"I told you no such thing," Laveau said. "I said you will defeat Blavatsky, but that the answers you seek already lie with the

Strongman. You test me. You doubt who I am. But believe me when I tell you, *I am Marie Laveau*."

There were two more guards just inside the door to the queen's throne room, but unlike the guards at the front door, these were more zombi. Their dead, hollow eyes stared straight forward, and Fergus caught a whiff of dead animal, artlessly covered by a heavy dose of perfume. Marie Laveau's arm stiffened as they walked past.

"*Zut alors.* Black, evil magic that is," she whispered. "These are dark times for New Orleans."

In the throne room, all the whispering was about Marie Laveau. Every eye in the room watched her, either in sly sideways glances or open stares. Fergus stared at everyone else. Besides a handful of zombi servants carrying plates of food and drinks around, there were perhaps thirty people in the room—men and women, First Nations and Haitians and Yankees—all dressed in a fashion Fergus had never seen before. Unlike Hachi's simple, understated red dress, the women wore big crinkly dresses of all colors that had acres of fabric on the bottom and tight, low bodices and poofy sleeves on top. The men weren't much better. They had poofy sleeves too, and wore what looked like thick, round rugs over their shoulders and tights on their legs. For once Fergus didn't feel like the oddest-dressed person in the room in his kilt and boots and white button-down shirt.

The chamber itself was as gaudily attired as the people in it. Tall blue columns separated windows whose fancy carved molding was gilded with fading gold paint. Blue-and-yellow drapes as ratty as the carpet in the long hall were tied back from the windows, and elaborate candelabras dripped melted wax onto tables throughout the room. Fergus picked at the flaking gold paint on one of the candlesticks and found iron underneath. Everything here had been gilded to make it look beautiful and expensive, but the illusion was wearing thin.

As was the queen. Theodosia was a frail old woman in her eighties, with a plain face and a broad round chin. On her gray head she wore a jewel-encrusted crown, but otherwise she was dressed like the rest of the women in her court. Her voluminous blue-and-yellow dress looked like it was made out of the same heavy material as the drapes. At a glance, Fergus figured the getup must weigh fifty pounds. How the old lady could walk was a mystery.

Queen Theodosia's entrance was announced by heralds with trumpets, and the court bowed to her as she came in. Fergus shot Hachi a questioning glance—*do we bow?* Hachi grimaced and rolled her eyes, but gave a little half-hearted bow, and Fergus followed suit.

Theodosia was followed by a skeletal-looking man in a long black jacket with a tall, wrinkled, ugly face and a thin, wild widow's peak of white hair. Fergus didn't believe in the Grim Reaper, but if he did, this fellow could give him a run for his money.

"General Andrew Jackson," Laveau whispered. The Andrew Jackson who had defended New Orleans against a New Spain invasion in 1815 and again against a Galveston pirate attack in 1823, and whose statue and name graced the square in front of the palace.

The Andrew Jackson who had died twenty-five years ago and been resurrected by Madame Blavatsky as a zombi.

Theodosia swept across the room and made right for them.

"Madame Laveau, you honor us again after all these years with your presence!" Queen Theodosia said. She put out her hands, and Laveau took them and bowed again. "How long has it been?" the queen asked.

"Almost forty years, Your Majesty," Laveau said. "I was here for your inauguration."

"Of course," Theodosia said. "And of course you don't look a day older than you did then. We would ask you how you do it, but our bokor tells us she has discovered how."

"Your Majesty?" Laveau said.

Queen Theodosia said something in Acadian that had Blavatsky's name in it, and Fergus saw Hachi tense. They were bringing her in. Fergus stepped closer to Hachi, more as a show of support than anything. Tonight was supposed to be a fact-finding mission. Hachi wasn't supposed to go after Blavatsky right away, not until they'd found a way to get her alone. But this was a woman who was there when Hachi's dad and ninety-nine other men from his village were murdered. Hachi's need for revenge might override her good sense— and if it did, there was nothing Fergus could do to stop her. Maybe nothing anybody could do. Not even zombi Andrew Jackson.

The crowd of upholstered courtiers parted, and Madame Blavatsky strode into the throne room. She was a stark contrast to the beautiful Creole women around her: a solid, serious-looking, middle-aged Yankee woman with her hair parted down the center and pulled back into a tight bun. She wore a simple black dress over her ample bosom and big hips, and the only jewelry she wore was a thick copper necklace looped loosely many times around her neck.

Blavatsky bowed low to her queen.

"Madame Marie Laveau, may we introduce you to our royal bokor, Madame Helena Blavatsky," Queen Theodosia said.

"The pleasure is mine," Blavatsky said. "Your power is spoken of all over the city."

"As is yours," Laveau said, though Fergus didn't think she meant it the same way. "And may I introduce my companions—Fergus MacFerguson and Hachi Emartha."

"Of Chuluota," Hachi said.

Fergus thought he saw a flicker of something like surprise cross Blavatsky's face, but then it was gone, replaced by a soft smile.

"Any friends of Madame Laveau's are friends of mine," Blavatsky said.

"Well said!" Theodosia told her. "And now, Madame Bokor, if you are in readiness, we are eager to proceed with tonight's ceremony. Who wouldn't be?" she asked, and her courtiers tittered.

"Which is what?" Laveau asked.

"Tonight I steal a page from the Voodoo Queen's book of spells," Blavatsky announced to the assembled audience, with a nod to Laveau. "Through Theosophic methods, I shall call upon the loa of Baron Samedi to make our beloved queen young again!"

Two zombi wheeled a mechanical cart into the middle of the room. It was a wooden box with brass fittings, covered all over with gauges and brass pipes and speaking trumpets. To Fergus's eye, it was a combination of aether aggregator and ancient computer, like the kind he'd seen the madman Thomas Edison use to try to raise a Mangleborn. Alarm bells rang inside Fergus's head.

"In my quest for knowledge, I have traveled the world," Blavatsky told the crowd. "When the Corsican brought the Darkness to my beloved homeland of Russia, I fled to the east, through Hindustan and into Tibet, the roof of the world, where I discovered the secret doctrine that links the world we know to every great civilization of the past—Rome, Atlantis, Lemuria, Mu, even the First Men—to a deeper, more primeval root race of godlike beings I call the Hidden Masters."

A *deeper, more primeval root race of godlike beings called the Hidden Masters* sounded an awful lot like the Mangleborn to Fergus, and they were nothing you wanted to discover in Tibet or anywhere else. He looked worryingly at Hachi, but she was locked in to what Blavatsky was saying like a clutch disc on a flywheel, analyzing every word for answers.

"This root race was the bearer of esoteric and mystical knowledge far in advance of our own," Blavatsky explained. She drew arcane symbols on the floor around the machine with black powder as she spoke. "They knew all the unexplained laws of nature—of aether and life and lektricity—and held the keys to unlocking the latent powers buried within us all. And they are still with us, these Hidden Masters, if only we will search for them. That is what I have done, moving ever east, from Russia into the Japans, into California, across the Great Plains of North America, and south to Louisiana."

With a brief detour to Florida when Hachi was a baby, Fergus thought.

"Here in New Orleans, I found a place where the Hidden Masters are closer to the surface, where the power of the root race is strongest," Blavatsky said. "Tonight, I will reach out to that power." She held up her necklace, which had a fetish of a young woman on it. "Tonight, I will call forth the astral power of Baron Samedi, one of the intermediary aspects of the Hidden Masters, he whose power to heal and resurrect I used to create *le Grande Zombi Armee*. I will trap his loa in this charm, and with this around her neck, our beloved Queen Theodosia will not only become young again, she will be *immortal!*"

Marie Laveau grabbed Fergus and Hachi and pulled them away from the babbling crowd.

"Whatever this is, whatever Blavatsky means to do, *it will not work*," Laveau warned them. "What she proposes can't be done."

"But you did it," Fergus said. "You figured out a way to be young again."

"Not like this," Laveau said. "Never like this. This is *Mangleborn* science." Laveau strode to the edge of Blavatsky's markings, careful not to step inside them. "Blavatsky, stop this. You do not understand the power you toy with."

"Why should the secrets of long life be yours alone, Laveau?" Blavatsky threw back at her. "Will you not share them with your queen?"

The men and women of the court watched Laveau. She stood straight and proud. "Those secrets are mine alone," she said.

"I shall not be so selfish," Blavatsky said, and she threw a switch on the machine.

The air crackled and the ancient engine hummed, gathering aether to it. But what else was it doing? Fergus longed to get a look inside the thing. By the way it was shaking and the amount of aether it seemed to be aggregating, they would *all* get a look inside it soon when it blew up in their faces.

"Legba Atibon, guardian of the crossroads," Blavatsky said, her voice raised over the growing din of the machine, "Legba, guardian of path and gate, open the door."

The doors to the room slammed shut, and a glowing white box appeared in the air between two of the trumpets on top of the machine.

"No—she can't do this," Marie Laveau said. "She doesn't know what she's doing."

"Will it kill her?" Hachi asked.

"It will kill us all!" Laveau said.

Hachi rushed Blavatsky and the machine. At the edge of the black powder circle on the floor she was blown back with a CRACK! Fergus rushed to her side.

"Ateg-bini-monse, odan-bhalah wedo, Samedi!" Blavatsky cried. "Samedi ke-ecu-mali, gba ke'dounou voudoun!"

"Hachi? Hachi, are you all right?" Fergus asked.

Hachi shook off the blast and nodded.

"Samedi yeke hen-me a-chay," Blavatsky cried. "Samedi yeke hen-me a-chay!"

Wind stirred in the room. There was a blinding flash, and someone screamed. People rushed for the exit, but the doors wouldn't open.

And then the candelabras came to life.

Their metal arms flexed and bent like they were flesh and blood. They jumped from their tables and moved like little metal gorillas, their burning wax arms leaving scorch marks on the floor as they loped about, chasing the horrified courtiers. They were suddenly everywhere—every candlestick in the room had come to life.

"No—no!" Blavatsky cried. "That wasn't supposed to happen!"

"Madame Blavatsky, turn it off! Turn it off!" Queen Theodosia cried. She hid behind the giant throne at the end of the room while zombi General Jackson, his sword drawn, protected her.

One of the monkey-like candelabras caught a woman's fancy dress on fire, and she spun screaming before Hachi smothered the fire in the deep, heavy folds of the woman's bustle.

"Circus! Showtime!" Hachi called.

From the pouches in her bandolier burst three winged wind-up animals—a lion, a gorilla, and a giraffe. There had once been five, but Hachi had given Zee the Zebra to a little girl who needed a friend in Jersey, and had lost Tusker the Elephant to a wind-up panther in Florida. To the three that remained, Hachi said, "We have to keep those candlesticks away from the people!"

The little wind-up toys saluted and flew into action. Mr. Lion grabbed one with his teeth, thrashing it around like a dog with a rag bone. Jo-Jo the Gorilla put his mighty arms around another and dragged it away from a man who had fainted in the corner. Freckles the Giraffe tricked one into chasing her, then toppled a table onto it, knocking its candles from the holder and putting out its fire.

But there were still more. Dozens more. One of them set fire to the thick curtains on the windows, and Marie Laveau pulled them down and stomped on them. Across the room, Hachi moved to protect the queen.

Inside the circle, Blavatsky flipped switches and turned dials, trying to shut the machine down. She clearly didn't know how to operate it.

"No, that's amplifying it!" Fergus told her. "No, that's just confining the portal, not closing it. No, that's shifting the aether frequency." He could feel each thing as she did it, his body in tune with the machine—with every machine now. "There, that one! Do that one!" he told her, pointing to a small lever on the side. Blavatsky flipped it, and with a sigh the machine released the aether it had collected and shut down. The wind died away and the glowing white portal closed, but the candelabras still scurried around the room, setting people and furniture on fire.

"I can counteract the spell," Marie Laveau called, "but I need them all together!"

Getting all the candelabras into one place was going to be like catching steam. As soon as you threw one into the corner and turned to get another, the first one was gone. Fergus stood in the middle of the chaos watching the little iron monsters merrily chasing the courtiers around the room, and suddenly he had an idea.

Fergus hurried over to where Blavatsky huddled against the wall, kicking candelabras away with her high-heeled black boots.

"I just need to borrow this," Fergus said, pulling the long copper necklace off her.

Blavatsky started to protest, but he hobbled away to where Jackson was protecting the queen.

"I need that sword," Fergus told the general.

The zombi took a swing at him with it, and Fergus jumped back just in time.

"Hey! Whoa! Friend!" he cried.

"General Jackson, it's all right. Give him your sword," Theodosia said, peeking out from behind her throne.

Slowly, cautiously, Fergus reached out for Jackson's sword and took it from the zombi's decomposing hand. The general's dead eyes stared straight ahead, but Fergus still felt like the zombi was watching him.

Fergus hurriedly coiled the copper wire of Blavatsky's necklace around the sword from the base of the blade to the point.

"What are you doing?" Queen Theodosia asked him.

"I'm creating a lektromagnet. When it's energized, the copper coils will turn the saber into a powerful magnet, and we can catch all those wee clackers running about."

"Fascinating," Queen Theodosia said. "But where will you get the lektricity?"

"I've got that covered," Fergus said. He held the sword in both

hands—one on the hilt, the other near the point of the blade—
and thought, *Lektromagnet.* All through his body and down through
his arms, he felt the wonderfully weird and tingly sensation of his
black blood rearranging itself, forming the circuits he needed to
do the job. The black maze of lines on his arms and face shifted
and rearranged, and in moments lektricity was coursing out of his
right hand, through the wound copper coils, and back into his left
hand with a hum.

A gold fork came flying at Fergus. He ducked instinctively, but
the fork smacked into the sword and stuck there. A gold cup came
flying at him next, slamming into the sword. Fergus frowned. Gold
wasn't ferrous. It shouldn't have been attracted to the lektromagnet. Then he understood.

"Nothing in this room's really gold, is it?" he said to the queen.
"It's all base metals painted over to look expensive."

"It's been a lean few years," Theodosia admitted.

A gold plate slammed into Fergus's lektromagnet, followed by
Queen Theodosia's supposedly gold crown.

"All right, a lean few *decades*," Theodosia admitted.

"Brass," Fergus said. He wished everything in the room *were*
brass. Then the only things that would come flying at him would
be the painted iron candelabras.

One of the little monsters flew up at him and clanked onto the
sword. It burned and writhed, trying to escape, but the lektromagnet held it tight.

"All right," Fergus told it. "Let's go collect your brothers. Hachi!
Throw 'em at me!"

Hachi understood at once, and soon Fergus was ducking a hail
of silverware that wasn't silver and golden candelabras that weren't
gold. The metal came at him from all directions, hitting him in
the head, shoulders, arms, legs, and back before latching onto the
sword. It quickly got too heavy to carry, and Marie Laveau hauled
over a wooden table for him to set the mass of metal on. Fergus's

hands got singed as the candelabras squirmed and burned, but he held on tight. He upped the amps through the lektromagnet, and the last few candelabras—and a few pieces of fake gold jewelry from the courtiers—came flying into the writhing trash heap on his arms.

"Now!" Hachi called to Laveau. "Do it!"

Laveau reached inside her dress and withdrew a small leather pouch. She held it tight in her hands over the mass of metal and closed her eyes, chanting, "*Bomba mande, bomba mande, tigui le papa, bomba mande!* Papa Legba, please close the door!"

There was another flash, and all at once the doors of the room flew open and the candelabras stopped wriggling. It was over. Courtiers ran for the exits, and guards rushed in to see to the queen. Fergus waited until Marie Laveau gave him a weary, relieved nod, then cut the lektricity to the sword. The gilded ironware clattered down with a racket and spilled onto the floor. Fergus felt like collapsing with them.

Then Hachi was there, putting an arm around him to hold him up.

"You all right?" she asked.

"I think I may have a fork stuck in my butt," Fergus said, arching and popping his back. Hachi looked as cut up and beat up as he felt, her beautiful red dress tattered and torn.

"You really are Leaguers," Marie Laveau told them. "No one else could have done what you did here tonight."

"It was nice to have an assist," Fergus told her. He nodded at the thing she had taken from her dress. "What's in the pouch?"

"This is my gris-gris," she said. It sounded like "gree-gree." She opened the pouch and poured the contents out into her palm. It was a collection of seven roots and seeds and leaves. It didn't look like much to Fergus, and he said so.

Laveau laughed. "It may not look like much, but put together with the right incantations, it's powerful magic. Your gris-gris is powerful too," Laveau said, nodding at Hachi.

"My gris-gris?" Hachi asked. Just then, her three wind-up animals came flying back to their pouches and climbed inside.

"And what's in your gris-gris?" Laveau asked Fergus.

"Mine?"

She pointed to his sporran, the little pouch that hung from the belt of his kilt.

"It's nae magic," Fergus told her. He opened it and showed her the screwdrivers and wrenches inside.

"To most people, what you did just now with that sword is as much magic as what I did," Laveau told him.

"And I am as equally grateful," Queen Theodosia said, joining them. She was trailed by the empty-eyed General Jackson and a cowed Madame Blavatsky. "Your powers are truly incredible," the queen told them. "We are in your debt."

Marie Laveau bowed, and Fergus and Hachi followed her lead.

"The loa are powerful spirits, Your Majesty, and not to be trifled with," Laveau said, more for Blavatsky's benefit than the queen's. "Tonight's disruption was but an idle for them. They were playing with us. Woe be unto Louisiana when their games become serious."

"Then perhaps you would lend us your knowledge and protection in two days' time," Queen Theodosia said. "Madame Blavatsky means to contact my father, King Aaron, by means of a séance."

"Is that wise?" Laveau asked.

"We'll be there," Hachi put in, ending the debate. Laveau gave her a questioning glance, then nodded.

"We will be there," Laveau said. "Until then, my queen."

Laveau bowed again, and led Hachi and Fergus away.

"You would let Blavatsky unleash the power of the Mangleborn and do more damage yet again?" Laveau asked once they were alone.

"She's not going to have the chance," Hachi told them. "Two days from now is when we grab her."

13

Clyde took a step back and bumped into Archie. In front of them loomed *Colossus*, all ten stories of him, suddenly alive despite no one sitting in the control seat. Behind them, an angry horde of rock creatures pounded on Archie's back, trying to smash them into pieces.

There was nowhere for them to run.

Colossus swept a giant hand down at them, and Archie fell on Clyde to protect him from the blow. But it never came. Instead they heard the sound of smashing rocks behind them and turned to look. *Colossus* had knocked aside the first row of attacking rock creatures with a swipe of his arm, and with a swipe of his other arm he knocked even more of them away. Archie ducked again as the giant steam man leaped over them, pouncing right in the middle of the rock creatures. His heavy brass feet reduced half of them to rubble. The other half Colossus chased, running in a circle around the canyon on his hands and feet.

"What . . . in the name of Hiawatha is going on?" Archie asked.

Colossus caught one of the rock creatures in his mouth and shook it violently, rock and rubble raining down as he tore the thing apart. He tossed it away into the darkness and chased after another one.

"Buster," Clyde said.

"What?"

"It's Buster! Colossus is Buster!"

Archie had trouble even processing what Clyde was saying. Colossus was Buster? How could a giant steam man be a dog? And then he remembered.

"The burn mark. Buster's shadow—it was on Colossus!"

"Ah," Mr. Rivets said, still blind to what was happening in the canyon. "If that is in fact the case, the animal's spirit would have been fused with the steam man, just as the humans' spirits were fused with the rock walls of the canyon."

Colossus whistled like a train, making Archie and Clyde jump. He hunkered down, his arms stretched out on the ground so that he was face-to-face with one of the rock creatures that was trying to attack him, and whistled twice more. Archie had seen something like this before, he was sure, and then it dawned on him: Buster was barking at the rock creature, trying to get him to play. The rock creature swung a fist at Colossus, and the steam man jumped on him, smashing him into dust.

"Mr. Rivets, why is Buster still acting like a dog when all the rock people are acting like monsters?" Archie asked.

"I have no idea, Master Archie. I can only speculate that it has something to do with the canine's less complicated cerebral functions. Perhaps that, in combination with the fact that it was fused with something with roughly analogous features."

"What did he say?" Clyde asked.

"Buster's brain is simpler, and he got put in something that already had arms and legs and a head for him to run around in," Archie explained.

Within minutes, *Colossus*—Buster—had finished "playing" with all the rock creatures, and there was nothing left in the canyon but little piles of rubble. Playtime over, the giant steam man turned and bounded toward them.

"Whoa, whoa, whoa, whoa!" Archie cried, backing up.

The steam man skidded to a halt a few feet in front of them and tooted its whistle happily.

"So . . . do we call him *Colossus*, or Buster?" Archie asked.

The steam man leaned in toward Clyde and ran his lower jaw up Clyde's chest over and over again. "I think . . . I think he's licking me!" Clyde said, laughing, even when one of the nudges knocked him on his butt.

"He's definitely Buster," Archie said.

Buster the giant steam . . . dog . . . whistled happily at them, then ran to the edge of the canyon, where he lifted a leg and emptied water like he was peeing.

"Hey! Hey, stop that!" Clyde said, running after him. "That's water you need for your boiler!"

Archie looked around the empty canyon, lit only by the red light of the moon. "What do we do now, Mr. Rivets? The fox girl's run off, all the soldiers are dead, and *Colossus* is a giant dog."

"Under the circumstances, I fear we must abandon our pursuit," the Tik Tok said.

"What, you're going to give up? Just like that?" Clyde said. "Mrs. DeMarcus always said that winners never quit, and quitters never win."

"But how are we supposed to chase her now?" Archie said. "I mean, just look at our ride!"

Buster was at that moment digging a giant hole where the skull had blown up, the steam pipe on his bottom wagging like a tail.

"Maybe he'll come when we call him," Clyde said.

Archie doubted very seriously a ten-foot-tall steam dog would do anything it didn't want to do, but he tried it anyway. "Here, Buster! Here boy! Come!" Archie called.

Buster whistled happily and kept digging his hole.

"See? It doesn't work," Archie said.

"Buster, you come here right this second," Clyde hollered. "Buster, come!"

The giant steam man stopped digging, looked up, and immediately came bounding back over to Clyde. He sat down on his brass bottom with his knees in the air and his hands flat on the ground, tailpipe wagging, waiting for Clyde to tell him what to do.

Clyde and Archie shared an amazed look.

"Buster, lay down. Buster, down," Clyde said.

The steam man lowered himself flat on the ground, head up and still watching Clyde.

"Good dog!" Clyde said, and Buster's tail wagged.

Archie picked up a boulder that was taller than he was and tossed it farther into the canyon. "Buster, fetch!" Archie yelled. Buster perked up and watched the boulder bounce and tumble away, but didn't move. Instead he looked back at Clyde with his mouth hanging open.

"Buster, fetch!" Clyde told him. Buster leaped to his feet and bounded after the boulder, the canyon shaking and echoing with his footsteps.

"He'll listen to you, but not to me," Archie said.

"Master Clyde seems to have formed a special bond with the animal," Mr. Rivets said. "One which appears to be mutually exclusive."

"He means—"

Clyde cut him off. "I know what he's saying this time. He's saying me and Buster are best friends."

Buster ran back to them with the boulder in his mouth and

dropped it at Clyde's feet. Clyde had to jump out of the way not to get crushed.

"Good dog. Good fetch," Clyde said. "Just going to have to get used to your new size, is all." He patted Buster's foot, and the steam man rolled over on his side so Clyde could rub his belly.

"You think you can drive him?" Archie asked.

Clyde looked thoughtful. "I sat up there behind Dull Knife day after day, watching him operate *Colossus*. I know *how* to do it. Whether I can or not—and whether Buster'll let me—that's a whole 'nother question."

Clyde told Buster to sit and stay, and he and Archie and Mr. Rivets climbed inside very cautiously, aware that if Buster went bounding off, they would be tossed around like rocks in a tumbler.

In engineering, they found all the machinery operating itself, as though ghost mechanics worked the controls.

"Like the inner workings of any living being," Mr. Rivets said. "Bodily functions operate involuntarily. In short, Buster thinks, therefore he is."

Buster stayed like he was told until they got to the bridge.

"Good boy!" Clyde told him. "Good dog!"

Buster whistled happily, and the cockpit swung with his head.

"Whoa," Archie said, going tumbling. "We're going to have to add more safety belts up here. And things to grab on to."

Clyde took Dull Knife's place in the driver's seat. His legs and arms weren't long enough to reach the pedals and levers, so they found blocks of wood to put on the bottoms of his shoes and a stack of pillows for him to sit on.

"All right. You ready for this?" Clyde said. "Buster, heel!"

Clyde leaned back in his seat, and *Colossus*—Buster—stood!

"Good boy!" Clyde said. "Heel, Buster, heel. . . ."

Clyde took a step forward, and Buster moved with him. He lifted a lever for one of the arms, and the arm moved with him.

"I think it's going to work," Clyde said. He tried taking a few more steps and was able to maneuver them out of the canyon. "I think as long as we let him run around every now and then, get his wiggles out, he should do just fine."

"Most *Canis lupus familiaris* find a particular pleasure in understanding and carrying out the wishes of their masters," Mr. Rivets said.

Buster whistled as if in agreement.

"So, we gonna do this? Go after this girl?" Clyde said. "She that important?"

"Not her, but what she's carrying," Archie said. "It's an ancient relic, older than Rome, and it's very powerful. And it has something to do with how I . . . became whatever it is I am."

Clyde nodded thoughtfully. "All right, then. Clyde and Buster are in. But how are we gonna see through that girl's tricks when Mr. R here is blind?"

"We have to get him fixed somewhere," Archie said. He sighed. If Fergus had been here, it would already be done.

"Get into those maps, then," Clyde told him. "You're my new navigator. Find us the nearest town with a machine shop, and we'll get *both* our machine men fixed up."

14

Buster accidentally stepped on a No Dogs Allowed sign in the park as Clyde steered him off the street and into the green grass. A mob of chattering children, curious adults, and barking dogs trailed behind them, swarming Clyde, Archie, and Mr. Rivets as they climbed out of the steam man.

"Hey there!" Clyde called out to the crowd. "Can somebody tell us if there's an Emartha Machine Man shop in town?"

While Archie got three sets of different directions to the same place all at once from a handful of Omaha, Clyde introduced the rest of them to Buster.

"He likes beef jerky, chasing steam cars, and having his belly rubbed," Clyde told the crowd. "He's a good boy, but he's kinda big, so you gotta be careful around him, and that's a fact."

Buster sat back and scratched where his ear would have been with one of his big brass feet—*clang-clang-clang-clang!*—delighting his audience. Then he stood and started to pace around in a tight circle.

"What's he doing?" Archie asked.

"I don't know," Clyde said. "I hope he's not looking to pee again, or lots of people are gonna get wet."

The crowd of Omaha backed up, giving Buster space. After a few turns, he plopped down on the ground with a thud and curled up into a building-sized ball.

"I guess it's nap time," Clyde said.

It had been two days since the canyon, and though they had stopped each night and camped, Buster curling around them by the fire, they had pushed him hard to get here in such a short time. The big guy deserved a rest. Metal blast plates meant to shield the bridge from raycannons slid down over Buster's eyes, and the smoke from his tailpipe tapered off from black to thin white. Buster was as close to asleep as a giant steam man could get.

Some of the Omaha children started climbing on top of him, which didn't seem to bother Buster in the least. "Just don't go inside him," Clyde told a group of the younger boys, knowing they would tell the others. "And come and get me if he wakes up. We'll be at the Emartha Machine Man shop."

Not that anybody would have had any trouble finding them in town anywhere they went. Clyde was the only Afrikan in town, best they could tell, and Archie one of the few Yankees. Between Buster's noisy, obvious arrival, Clyde's dark skin, and Archie's snow-white hair, they stood out like a buffalo on a New Rome street.

The Omaha city of Ton won tonga, "The Big Village" in the Sioux language, was a long way from the size of New Rome, but still big. Smoke rose from two- and three-story buildings, and streetcars rattled by on the busy streets, tracing circular routes around the city center. Like all Omaha cities, Ton won tonga was laid out in a giant circle, with this one bisected by the Missouri River.

Archie, Clyde, and Mr. Rivets crossed a steel girder bridge over the broad Missouri from the Sky District into the Earth District, where most of the city's business was located. None of the three sets of directions Archie got was correct, but an Omaha police officer with a colorful beaded sash and an eagle feather in his hair pointed the shop out to them.

Ton won tonga's Emartha Machine Man outpost was a small, first-floor affair. A sign in the window said SEE THE NEW STEAM-DRIVEN MARK IV, NOW IN STOCK! and for once Archie was glad Mr. Rivets was blind. Mr. Rivets was a clockwork Mark II Machine Man and had been known to be a little resentful of the Mark IVs' new abilities and smug attitudes.

"Good morning, sirs!" said a shiny titanium Mark IV as they stepped inside. The plate on his chest said his name was Mr. Cylinder. "Have you come to trade in your old Mark II for a newer model?"

Archie saw Mr. Rivets straighten, but he cut him off before the Tik Tok could respond. "No, thank you. We're very happy with our Mark II. He's just seen a bit of damage, and we'd like to get him repaired."

"We *are* currently offering attractive trade-in deals on all obsolete Emartha Machine Men," Mr. Cylinder said.

"*Obsolete?*" Mr. Rivets said. "I'll have you know—"

"Just repairs, thanks," Archie said. "Is there a manager we could speak with?"

"Of course, sir. Right away," Mr. Cylinder said.

A smiling Omaha man with large, round glasses met them at the counter. "Welcome! Welcome," he said. "My name is Urika. I see your machine man has . . . been in an accident?" He peered at Mr. Rivets, trying to understand how a machine man's eyes could be put out without having another scratch on him.

"Yes, he . . . ran into a pitchfork," Archie said. He shrugged at

Clyde. It seemed an easier explanation than what had really happened.

"Well! You're in luck," Urika told them. "We've just had a brand-new shipment of parts from our distributor. Although we *do* have some rather good trade-in deals right now—"

"Really, just the repairs, thanks," Archie said.

Urika nodded and winked. "Loyalty works both ways, doesn't it, sir? Now, does your family have an account with us?"

"Oh. I don't know."

"We should be on file, sir," Mr. Rivets said. "The family's name is Dent. Mine is Mr. Rivets. Serial number P-02961."

"Oh, a rather early model then," Urika said. He went to a large wooden filing cabinet at the back of the shop, pulled out a drawer, and set it on the counter. It was full of rectangular paper punch cards, which he walked through with his fingers.

"Here we are! Yes," Urika said. He took a card from the drawer and slid it into a machine. The clockwork processing unit clicked and whirred, and spinning tile letters began to spell out information on the display above a keyboard. "Ah yes. A *very* early model. 1772! Just after the Darkness fell. And I see the Dent family were not your original owners."

"*What?*" Archie said. That was news to him!

"Repair and upgrade records . . . regular maintenance schedule . . . ," Urika went on, "and here's a special note at the end." Urika's eyes went wide behind his glasses, and he pushed them higher on his nose. "By Umohoti!"

"What? What is it?" Archie asked.

"Mr. Dent! You should have said that you were a Panther-level member when you came in!" Urika hurried around the counter to shake Archie's hand. "We'll see to your machine man's repairs at once. At once! Mr. Cylinder, please escort Mr. Rivets to the repair shop, and tell Mr. Mimiteh to clear all other jobs until this machine man is in *perfect* working order."

"Th-thanks," Archie said, not sure why he and Mr. Rivets were suddenly receiving so much attention.

"I believe there must be some mistake," Mr. Rivets said. To Archie, he said, "Emartha Machine Man customers are divided into ranked categories, depending on what level of service contract they choose. The categories are named, as I understand it, for the eight traditional clans of the Seminole Nation, the tribe of the Maker. Our previous service contract was merely Otter level. How the Dents can now afford the most elite level I don't understand. . . ."

But Archie did. *Hachi*. She was now the head of the Emartha Machine Man Company, whether she wanted to be or not. She must have told someone to make the Dents and Mr. Rivets Panther-level customers for life.

"No, no," Urika said. "No mistake at all. Mr. Cylinder?"

Mr. Cylinder took Mr. Rivets by the hand to lead him into the back.

"You're going to be all right, Mr. Rivets," Archie said, suddenly nervous for him.

"Of course I am," Mr. Rivets said. "The Emartha Machine Man Company is notorious for the high quality of its service and repair."

"Right. Just . . . I'll see you soon," Archie said. There almost wasn't a time in his life when Mr. Rivets hadn't been at Archie's side, or at least very nearby waiting for him to return. The thought of him going away, even for a short time, made Archie feel hollow inside.

"We will have him back to you in no time, and in tip-top condition," Urika assured Archie. "In the meantime, let me get you a loaner machine man—"

"No!" Archie said. He'd said it more forcefully than he meant to, so much that it startled Mr. Urika. "I mean, no thanks," Archie said. "I'll just wait for Mr. Rivets."

Urika assured them Mr. Rivets would be all fixed up by the next morning, and Archie and Clyde went back out into the street.

"Man, that guy was tripping over himself to help you," Clyde said. "You and your family must be pretty important folks, and that's a fact."

"We're not really," Archie told him. "I just know the owner really well."

"So now what?" Clyde asked.

"This was the closest town. Unless the fox girl had a lot of supplies with her, she'd have to stop here," Archie said.

"Unless this *is* her stop," Clyde said.

"Maybe. But I feel like it's not. Like, she's headed somewhere else."

"She's Asian. Maybe she's headed for the West Coast. Isn't there a Japanese colony up there?"

Archie nodded. "If this isn't where she was headed, she'll be looking for transportation out of town. She can't cross the continent on a steam mule. It'd take too long."

"So let's check the stations," Clyde said. "We got the time."

The train station was a bust. None of the station agents had seen a girl dressed up as a fox, of course, and they had seen nothing else amiss. Morning trains to Kansa City, Shikaakwa, and Cahokia on the Plains had already left, and the next train to the Moving City of Cheyenne didn't leave until that evening.

"If she's headed into Sioux territory, we're in trouble," Clyde said. "We take Buster in there, and we really *will* have motherwheels after us."

"So will she," Archie said. "No. I think she's headed farther west, like you said. Come on. Let's check the airfields."

It was practically suicide to travel the plains by balloon in tornado season. It had always been bad on the plains in the summer, but it got worse when the Darkness fell. Cyclones wandered the Great Plains like living things, eating up houses and trees and buffalo. And airships. But just because it was dangerous didn't mean people didn't try. Like the blue-and-gray dirigible they saw being loaded for a flight to the Moving City of Cheyenne at Blackbird Air Park. Its name was *Bear on the Wind*. It looked like an old Apache Air DC-3, retrofitted with later-model Tecumseh aeroprops and weighted down for extra control in choppy weather. It was bigger than Archie's family airship, the *Hesperus*, but smaller than the massive Apache Air Liners that had replaced it. Between crew and passengers, it could probably carry no more than twenty people comfortably.

"Is that airship really going to try to make it to Cheyenne?" Clyde asked the gate agent.

The old Omaha nodded. "Always some crazy pilot fool enough to try it, and some crazy fool passengers desperate enough to take him up on it."

Archie watched the passengers boarding. They were all First Nations, most of them Omaha. A young woman in a brown coat and brown hat, a middle-aged man in a black suit and tie, a fat man wearing a white shirt, black vest, and a colorful square-patterned blanket for a skirt. . . .

The fat man. There was something not right about him. Archie could feel it. But what was it? His eyes raked the man from top to bottom, bottom to top. What was he seeing that he wasn't seeing?

Archie grabbed Clyde. "His shadow! Look at that man's shadow!"

The fat man had the shadow of a small girl with pointed ears and the tail of a fox.

The fat man saw Archie pointing, looked at his shadow, and it suddenly changed to match him. It was the fox girl! Archie had seen her shadow! Archie tried to push through the gate to get to her, but the gate agent stopped him.

"That man—the Omaha with the blanket for a skirt," Archie cried. "He's not a man! He's a girl! I mean, *she's* a girl, and she's a thief!"

"You're as crazy as the rest of 'em," the gate agent said. "That man there's a respectable businessman. Paid me cash for his ticket."

The old man held up a small handful of newspaper, cut to the size of Pawnee money, and gaped at it. He'd clearly thought he was holding a wad of real cash.

"Here, wait!" he cried. "Stop that man!"

It was too late. The door to the airship closed, and the *Bear on the Wind* lifted away.

"We have to catch that airship!" Archie told Clyde.

"I got just the thing," Clyde said. He put his fingers in his mouth and blew a piercing whistle. "Buster!" he yelled. "Here boy!"

"He can't hear you this far away," Archie said. But muffled cries rose up with a flock of birds on the other side of town, and the big brass head of Buster the steam man lifted up over the rooftops.

"Here boy!" Clyde called again. "Buster, come!"

Buster stood to his full ten-story height, towering over even the tallest rooftop in the city. In a few loping, thundering strides Buster was on top of them, bending down to "lick" Clyde. The gate agent squeaked and fell back on his butt.

"Good dog!" Clyde told Buster. "Good boy! Now let us inside."

Buster opened his mouth, and Clyde hopped into the small room that had once been Custer's cabin. "Come on, Archie!"

Archie climbed in with far less grace and followed Clyde up the ladder to the bridge as Buster stood again to his full height. The airship rose to Buster's eye level right outside and turned away.

"Oh no you don't!" Clyde said. He slipped into the control chair, told Buster to heel, and grabbed the little cabin that hung beneath the *Bear on the Wind's* gas balloon with the steam man's giant hand. The airship bobbled like a child's balloon, but Buster held on tight. The passengers inside watched out the windows of the airship cabin with wonder, horror, and surprise. Buster barked with his whistle, scaring most of them away from the windows.

Clyde talked into a speaking trumpet near his head, his voice booming outside. "We're not letting you leave with the fat man!"

"He may not be a fat man anymore," Archie told him. "I mean, *she* might not be a fat man anymore."

"Only he might not be a fat man anymore," Clyde said through the speaking trumpet.

Below them, somewhere on the ground, an alarm rang out.

"What's that?" Clyde said. Buster's head turned. Far below them, smoke rose from a building, and bricks and debris were scattered in the street, as though it had exploded. "It looks like a bank robbery!" Clyde said. "See if you can magnify the window."

"It doesn't matter!" Archie said. "We have to bring that airship down!"

Click-click-click—the magnifying lenses fell into place. Buster must have done it somehow, because it wasn't Archie. Through the window, larger than life, they saw a Tik Tok unlike any machine man Archie had ever seen before. He was tall and thin and made of brass like Mr. Rivets, but he looked more human. His arms and legs were human-proportioned, his chest was flatter and less round, and his face—his face was still riveted, but it looked like a man's face, not the stylized, almost cartoony faces of the Mark II and Mark IV Machine Men. And he wore clothes! Not brass, bolted-on imitation clothes like Mr. Rivets, but real cloth clothes—brown leather pants, a white shirt, a long black jacket, and a brown cowboy hat.

In his hand, this extraordinary Tik Tok held a raygun, and he was pointing it at *people*, even though machine men were programmed not to hurt humans.

Clyde gasped. "Jesse James!"

"Who?" Archie asked.

"The FreeTok outlaw, Jesse James! Custer's chased him for years!"

A FreeTok! Mr. Rivets had told Archie about FreeToks. They were Self-Determinalists—machine men who refused to do the work they were programmed for and ran away to live in their own cities. Why this one was robbing a bank in Ton won tonga, Archie didn't know, and he didn't care.

"We don't have time to stop a bank robber," Archie said.

"But that's not a bank," Clyde said. "It's the Emartha Machine Man store! Jesse James doesn't steal money—he steals Tik Toks! Archie, Jesse James just stole Mr. Rivets!"

15

"Welcome, seekers," Madame Blavatsky said. "Welcome . . . to the spirit realm."

"Should we hold hands?" Fergus asked.

"Not yet," Blavatsky said.

Helena Blavatsky sat to the right of Hachi, eyes flickering in the light from a group of candles in the center of the table. Candles, but no candelabra, Hachi was amused to notice. To her left was Fergus, surreptitiously studying the table and chairs for the mechanical devices he was sure Blavatsky would use to pretend to contact the "spirit realm." She nudged him to remind him to focus, and he opened his palms and gave her a little shrug as if to say, "What?"

Directly across from them sat Marie Laveau, as young tonight as she had been two nights ago during the adventure in the throne room. Hachi had an idea how she achieved her miraculous change, but knowing for sure would require more time to investigate—time she didn't have, and didn't want to take.

Beside Fergus, straight across from Blavatsky, was Queen Theodosia. Tonight she wore a simpler gown of blue velvet with yellow trim, and no crown. Theodosia was plain and unattractive, but was also supposed to be quick-witted, well educated, and intelligent. She had never married, but rumor had it she had once had an affair with a Karankawan chief. Perhaps he had loved her for her mind. Or her power. Hachi certainly had no ill feeling toward the queen, except for her harboring Blavatsky.

"We five are gathered here tonight in the hope that we might contact King Aaron, conqueror and first great king of Louisiana, and father to our dear Queen Theodosia," Blavatsky said.

"Do we hold hands now?" Fergus asked.

"No," Blavatsky told him, and Hachi kicked him under the table.

"Let us begin," Blavatsky said, closing her eyes.

Hachi stared at Helena Blavatsky, the woman who had stolen her own father from her, and in the process, stolen Hachi's life. Blavatsky's arrogance and self-assuredness were back, as though she hadn't almost killed them all two nights ago. Back too was Queen Theodosia's faith in her—perhaps only due to the promise of speaking to her long-dead father again. That, at least, Hachi understood. She might have spared Blavatsky an hour or two more for the promise of speaking to her own father.

But in the end, Hachi *would* have her revenge.

"Spirits of the aether, Hidden Masters of the past," Blavatsky said, drawing symbols in the air, "move among us. Be guided by these signs and the light of this world and visit us."

Hachi saw Marie Laveau frown. It was Laveau's job tonight to make sure Blavatsky didn't bring to life any more inanimate objects or do something worse before they could nab her. From the look on Laveau's face, Blavatsky was off to a bad start.

"Now we hold hands," Fergus said.

"No," Blavatsky said in an angry whisper.

Hachi glowered at her. The plan, once they were all holding hands in a circle, was for Hachi to pull away and for Fergus to pass a small lektrical current through the human chain—just enough to knock everyone else out. As frustrated as Hachi was with Fergus making what they planned to do so obvious, she was just as eager to get on with it as he was.

"Beloved King Aaron, Founder of the House of Burr," Blavatsky called to the air, "Special Protector of New Orleans, Emperor of the Mississippi, and Ruler over Louisiana and All Her Parishes, we entreat you with gifts."

Blavatsky nodded to Theodosia. The queen raised a hand, and out of the shadows like an apparition came General Andrew Jackson. Jackson was Hachi's part of the plan. Outside the circle, he wouldn't be shocked unconscious—and they weren't sure lektricity would do anything to a dead man anyway. When everybody at the table was passed out, it was Hachi's job to take the zombi down.

General Jackson's half-mummified hand passed the queen a box of cigars, and she placed them on the table.

"Father's favorites," Theodosia said.

Blavatsky drew more symbols in the air. "Spirits of the aether, Hidden Masters of the past, move among us," she said again. "Be guided by these signs and the light of this world and visit us."

A warm breeze blew through the room, rustling the curtains. It was almost time. To focus herself on the job to come, Hachi silently repeated the mantra she'd recited thousands of times since she was a child:

Talisse Fixico, the potter.
Chelokee Yoholo, father of Ficka.
Hathlun Harjo, the surgeon.
Odis Harjo, the poet.

"Spirits of the aether, Hidden Masters of the past, move among us!" Blavatsky cried. "Be guided by these signs and the light of this world and visit us!"

A vase of flowers on a nearby table crashed to the ground. The candles flickered. The windows rattled like it was storming outside. General Jackson's wild white hair stood on end.

Iskote Te, the gray haired, Hachi continued.

Oak Mulgee, the machinist.

John Wise, the politician.

Emartha Hadka, the hero of Hickory Ground.

"This isn't right!" Marie Laveau called out. The wind was roaring in the room, and she had to yell. "This isn't King Aaron! This is something else!"

Blavatsky didn't listen. "Now! Join hands!" she cried.

Marie Laveau didn't look happy about it, but she knew the plan. She took hold of Blavatsky's hand and Queen Theodosia's hand. Yes! The circuit was complete! Now for the jolt of lektricity, and this would all be over. Hachi waited for the sound, waited for the flash, but it never came.

Fergus wasn't holding Queen Theodosia's hand! He was too busy looking around for the fan and the wires he was sure Blavatsky was using to fake the séance.

"Fergus! Take Queen Theodosia's hand!" Hachi yelled.

"Oh! Aye!" he said. He reached for the queen's hand, and there was a bright flash and a *FWOOSH*, knocking them all back. Hachi leaped out of her chair to her feet, but Fergus went sprawling on the floor. She looked quickly around the table. Blavatsky and Laveau were down, but moving. Queen Theodosia was awake too, but still sitting. General Jackson had caught her chair before she fell.

Hachi shot a glance at Fergus, but he shook his head. *"It wasn't me,"* he said into the roaring wind. *"I never got the chance!"*

But if it wasn't Fergus who did that, then what . . . ?

The candles suddenly blew out, and the wind disappeared as quickly as it had begun. Somebody laughed—a deep, booming laugh that didn't belong to anybody in the room—and Hachi got a chill.

"No," she heard Marie Laveau say. "No, it can't be."

"What is it? What's happened?" Hachi asked. "Is it King Aaron?"

The laughter came again, hearty and mean. "No, girl. Not a king. A baron." It was the voice of a man, a big man, and Creole from the sound of him.

The lights came on. Fergus! He'd gone for the gaslights in the room and turned them up. Hachi scanned the room, looking for the man who had laughed, but all she saw were Blavatsky and Laveau on their feet, and Theodosia, a hand to her chest, still in her chair. Fergus was the only man in the room, besides the dead General Jackson.

"A-ha! Now I see where I am," Blavatsky said, but it wasn't her voice. It was the man's voice Hachi had heard in the dark. Blavatsky held up her arms and looked herself over. "A woman! I haven't been a woman in a long, long time. But then, I haven't been *anybody* in a long, long time."

"*Baron Samedi*," Marie Laveau said. Her voice was cold and wary, and Hachi knew that whatever this was, it was bad.

"The one and only!" Blavatsky said in her man's voice. "And what is your name, my pretty?"

"Marie Laveau."

Blavatsky laughed again, long and loud. "Ha ha ha! Of course it is! Marie Laveau! We meet again for the very first time, eh? Eh?" Blavatsky laughed like she'd just made a joke, and slapped her knee. "Oho! You brought me cigars!" she said, spying the box on the table. "You must have known! You know how long it's been since I had a cigar?"

Blavatsky took a cigar from the box, bit off the end with her teeth, and spat the end across the room with a laugh.

Hachi and Fergus moved to Laveau's side while Blavatsky lit her cigar on one of the gaslights.

"What is it?" Fergus asked. "What's happened?"

"The loa of Baron Samedi. What the locals would call a voodoo spirit, but what you would call an aspect of the Mangleborn in the lake. There are whole families of them, all belonging to *le Grande Zombi*, and each with their own personalities and perversities. But they have to have a human body to ride. This one's riding Blavatsky. Samedi must have been drawn here by that farce the other night."

"Oh crivens," Fergus said.

"So where's Blavatsky?" Hachi asked. That was all she cared about.

"Buried in there, somewhere. But while Baron Samedi's riding her, she can't talk to you. If you want Blavatsky, you're going to have to get rid of Baron Samedi first."

Samedi threw open the door to the room and walked out, puffing on his cigar.

"Done," Hachi said. She pulled out her knife and started to follow him.

Laveau caught her. "No—don't. If you kill her while Samedi's in there, you'll drive him out, and he'll be banished from this world for a dozen-dozen years. But Helena Blavatsky will be dead forever, and you'll never get your answers."

"Then what do we do?" Hachi asked.

Laveau's eyes narrowed. "There are other ways to get rid of a loa. . . ."

16

Archie rode with Clyde in the cockpit of Buster the steam man, watching mile after mile of cornfields drift by. Steam-driven threshers cut wide paths through the corn, which was collected by big floating balloons tethered behind them. The corn was stored in huge domed silos that matched the domed wood-and-thatch farmhouses that dotted the landscape. This was Wichita country, where corn was king.

And this was where the outlaw FreeTok had taken Mr. Rivets.

The fox girl had been in their grasp. Buster could have held the airship she traveled on while Archie went on board, and with the help of a Tik Tok from town he could have gone through the passengers one by one until he'd found her. The Dragon Lantern and its secrets would finally have been his again. But Archie had told Clyde to let the airship go. They knew where it was going: the Moving City of Cheyenne. They could catch up to it later. Right now, he had to get Mr. Rivets back.

Mr. Rivets was family.

The FreeTok bandits—there were more of them, a whole gang, led by the one called Jesse James—had a vehicle that outpaced any steam mule or cable car ever built. It outpaced their giant steam man too. That was how they had avoided Captain Custer, robbing machine man stores and stealing the Tik Toks from towns and farms, then disappearing quickly into Wichita territory, where the United Nations Army was forbidden to go.

"I don't know about this, Archie," Clyde said as they walked past a Wichita village where families ran inside and hid from them. "Technically, I'm still a private in the UN Army, and Buster here's a United Nations Steam Man. I'm a one-man invasion force. A *big* one-man invasion force."

"I've been thinking about that," Archie said. "About you and Buster. Clyde, have you ever heard of the Septemberist Society and the League of Seven?"

While Buster marched along, scaring Wichita farmers into their homes and tornado shelters, Archie told Clyde all about the darker world beneath this one, the world he and his parents had sworn to keep hidden. He told him about the Mangleborn, and all the ancient civilizations they had destroyed, and the people who worshipped them and wanted to free them with lektricity. He told him too about the Leagues who had defeated the Mangleborn in the past, and the one he thought was coming together in the present.

"I think you're one of us," Archie said. "One of a new League of Seven. There were only three of us so far—me, Hachi, and Fergus. I kept telling them we'd find more, and I think you and Buster are the fourth."

"You said this Hachi girl, she's the warrior, and this Fergus guy, he's the maker. And you're the shadow," Clyde said, casting Archie a sideways glance. "What's that make me and Buster?"

"Well, everybody calls you the Chief, right?"

"The big hero? The leader? Me? Aw, I don't know about that," Clyde said.

It pained Archie to say it, because he'd always dreamed of himself as the leader of a new League of Seven. The Theseus. The Galahad. The bright, shining example for all mankind. But that wasn't who he was.

"I think you are. I think maybe you have a greater calling than being a soldier in the UN Army, and that you don't have to obey their rules anymore. Or anybody's."

"Mrs. DeMarcus always used to say ain't nobody above the rules, and I figure that's the truth. Maybe it's even more important now that I've got Buster."

Which is why you're the hero, Archie thought. *And why I'm the shadow.*

Buster rocked suddenly, and gave a whistle like a whimper.

"Whoa!" Clyde said. The controls moved without him, swinging the steam man around.

Behind them was a steam-horse-mounted Wichita Cavalry regiment and a Wichita aether battle tank, its twelve-inch raycannon glowing red and ready to fire again.

Word had finally caught up to the Wichita Army, and the Wichita Army had finally caught up to the giant United Nations Steam Man in their territory.

Buster whistled a bark, and Clyde warned him to heel.

"Buster's raycannon is bigger than theirs," Archie told him. "You could take them out easy."

"I ain't gonna do that," Clyde said. He put his hands in the air, and Buster did too. "We're the trespassers here. They got every right to shoot at us."

"But we can't just quit!" Archie said.

"I don't mean to," Clyde said. He pulled the exterior speaking trumpet to his mouth. "This is Captain Clyde Magoro, of the United Nations Steam Man *Colossus*."

"Captain?" Archie asked.

Clyde shrugged. "I gave myself a field promotion. Thought it sounded better."

"You are in violation of Wichita territory," came an amplified reply from below. "Leave at once, or you will be fired upon."

"Hold on there," Clyde said. "I'm not here to attack. We're after the FreeTok outlaw, Jesse James. He stole something of ours, and we want it back."

"You are in violation of Wichita territory," the same person said again. "Leave at once, or you will be fired upon."

"Doesn't sound like they want to talk about it," Clyde told Archie.

"Clyde, I *have* to get Mr. Rivets back. He's my best friend."

"All right," Clyde said. He turned to the speaking trumpet. "So, listen, guys. I know this is going to look really bad, but I promise, we're just here to get our friend back."

Clyde swung hard on the controls, and Buster turned his back on them. "Run, boy! Run!" Clyde called.

Archie wasn't sure which of them was doing more of the running, Buster or Clyde. They moved as one, Clyde's legs pumping in time with Buster's thudding footsteps. The steam man rocked as the aether battle tank fired on them again, but it didn't seem to do much damage.

Archie went to one of the rear hatches to peek out. "They're chasing us, but we're losing them!" he called back.

Suddenly Buster swung back around, hunkered down low and whistled, then turned and ran again. Another aether cannon blast rocked the cockpit as the tank came into range again.

"Slag it, Buster! We're not playing chase!" Clyde told him. But Buster was having too much fun. Every time they put enough distance between them and the aether battle tank to be out of range, Buster would turn back around and wait for it to catch up, sometimes taking another blast from it on his backside.

Then, late in the afternoon, the aether battle tank and the regiment pulled up to a stop and wouldn't chase them anymore, no matter how much Buster ran back and tried to bait them. The tank fired at them, but wouldn't come any closer.

"Why won't they chase us?" Archie asked.

"I don't know, but it's making Buster sad," Clyde said. "I think he likes them."

"Look. There's a little row of stones down there," Archie said.

Clyde magnified the window in the right eye, and they could see it plainly—a simple line of round river rock that stretched out in a wide circle, so wide they couldn't see the whole thing. Whatever it was, they were inside it, and the regiment was outside it. And the Wichita soldiers weren't going to come in after them.

"What do you think it means?" Clyde asked.

"I don't know. But this is where the FreeTok tracks go."

"So this is where we go," Clyde said. He turned the steam man around. "Sorry, Buster. Playtime's over. I'm sure they'll be waiting for us when we get back."

Clyde led Buster farther away from the stone circle, through empty fields of prairie grass that swayed in the breeze. They passed the ruins of round Wichita farmhouses and silos that looked like they hadn't been used in thirty years, and finally came to a tiny town of round wooden buildings that were all in as bad a shape as the farmhouses. From above, Archie and Clyde could see that most of them had burned down, and no one had ever fixed them back up. Dust and tumbleweeds swirled in the streets, and blackened shutters hung crookedly from broken windows.

"Ghost town," Clyde said. "Ain't nobody lived here for a long time."

Archie consulted Lieutenant Pajackok's maps. "There's nothing here on the map. Nothing in a big circle," he said. A big circle like the stone one they had crossed. He showed Clyde the big, empty area on the map. "You think Jesse James is hiding out in the ghost town?"

"Tracks go on through," Clyde said. "To there."

Buster magnified his right eye again, and they could see it—a group of low, square, dusty white buildings on the horizon. Clyde led Buster closer. A few hundred yards away, they ran into a well-kept barbed wire fence and a sign. Buster magnified it.

"'Warning: Do not enter,'" Clyde read aloud. "'Biological hazard. Chance of serious infection.'" It was written in Anglish, Wichita, Lakota, Acadian, Iroquois, and Spanish. "So that's why they didn't come in after us."

The tracks from the James Gang's getaway car led straight through the barbed wire gate.

"I'll go," Archie said. "I can't get infected. I've never been sick a day in my life."

"I'll go with you," Clyde said.

"But—"

"But I'm staying inside Buster," Clyde said, and Archie agreed.

Buster stepped over the barbed wire fence with ease, and Clyde steered him toward the buildings. They were made of concrete and painted white, although years in the dusty prairie had turned them a dull brown. The roofs were all intact, though, and as they drew closer, they could see smoke rising from some of them, and people moving about outside.

No, not people. *Tik Toks.*

FreeToks, to be more specific. They gathered around Buster as he came into the heart of the buildings, and Clyde lowered Archie down to meet them.

The machine men were all shapes and sizes, and all of them had their wind-up keys in the middle of their chests, where they could turn them themselves. Some of them looked like Emartha Machine Men—Mark IIs and IVs, and even a Mark I, Archie thought. But more of them looked like Jesse James had, more human, and each with a unique face, a model of machine man Archie had never seen before. The rest were wild hybrids—a Mark IV head on a John Running-Deer tractor; a Mark II torso and head on a steam horse, making a kind of steam centaur; a clockwork spider with no sort of human-looking head at all, and more.

And right in the middle of them, with a raygun pointed at Archie, was the outlaw FreeTok Jesse James.

"Not too afraid of getting sick, are you, son?" James said.

"No," Archie said. He took a step forward. "Or rayguns either. None of that stuff works on me."

Jesse James laughed—a machine man who laughed!—and kept his raygun pointed at him. "I saw the big guy here when we hit Ton won tonga," he said, gesturing at Buster. "Wished I could have brought him with me then, but here you come anyway. Come to bring me to justice?"

"I don't care about justice," Archie told him. "I just came for my friend. Mr. Rivets."

"Your friend, eh?" James said. He looked around at his fellow FreeToks. "And what if your 'friend' is happy here and doesn't want to leave?"

Archie felt like he'd fallen off Cahokia in the Clouds again. Mr. Rivets not want to come away with him? Was that possible? If given the choice, would Mr. Rivets prefer the company of Tik Toks to life with Archie's family?

"Why don't we ask him," Archie said.

Jesse James laughed again. "That's a brass idea. Let's ask him." He slid his raygun into a holster on his belt and nodded to the other FreeToks, who moved on about their business.

James nodded for Archie to follow him to one of the buildings. "You come alone?" he asked.

"My friend Clyde is still inside Buster. He's afraid to come out because of the signs."

"But you're not," he said, giving Archie a sideways glance.

"I'm built different," Archie said.

James smiled. "So am I."

Archie looked around at all the FreeToks. Some of them worked in blacksmith sheds, hammering away at glowing red metal. Others repaired buildings. Still others sat at tables and talked and played games.

The building James led Archie to had been an office building or a medical center of some kind once, but now was a clockwork machine man repair shop. They passed rooms of meticulously catalogued and organized parts, from arms and legs and heads to all the intricate gears and parts that went inside. Another room was filled with talent cards, categorized by compatibility and skill.

James met a titanium Mark IV Tik Tok kitted out with a tinker's tool belt and magnifying lenses in the hall.

"How is our patient, Dr. Kenda?"

"Recovering nicely," Kenda said. "Though he's still in a bit of shock from the procedure."

"Procedure?" Archie said. "*What procedure?*" He pushed Dr. Kenda aside and ran into the room.

Mr. Rivets lay on his back on an operating table, with a horrifying array of drills and saws and rivet guns hanging from the ceiling around him.

"Mr. Rivets! Mr. Rivets!" Archie cried. He ran to the table and scooped the thousand-pound machine man up into his arms. "Mr. Rivets, what did they do to you?"

"Well, you don't see that every day," Jesse James said. He leaned on the door frame and pushed his cowboy hat back in surprise.

"I can lift more than this," Archie said. "And I can punch your head right off your shoulders. I will, too, if you've hurt Mr. Rivets."

"I meant a meatbag caring whether his machine man was hurt or not," James said. "Though the other is a surprise too."

Mr. Rivets stirred in Archie's arms.

"I'm quite all right, Archie," Mr. Rivets said. "You may put me down."

Archie set Mr. Rivets down with a *clank*. "You—you called me Archie. Not *Master* Archie."

Mr. Rivets's surprise subroutine lifted his eyebrows. "Did I?"

James laughed. "Just one of the little fixes that come standard with our 'Panther-level' upgrade package."

That's when Archie saw it—Mr. Rivets's wind-up key. They had moved it from his back to his front, to the middle of his chest where he could turn it himself!

"My wind-up key," Mr. Rivets said, marveling at it. He lifted an arm to try it, and paused. Archie had never seen Mr. Rivets so . . . *stunned* before. Archie felt the same way.

Mr. Rivets put a hand to the key and turned it.

"I am a *self-winding machine man*," he whispered with awe.

"You'll also find that you can now replace your own talent cards," Dr. Kenda said, coming into the room. "And I've removed the command that compels you to obey your masters. Or *call* them 'master,' for that matter. You can also laugh and cry now, and do other things you couldn't do before. Like lie."

Archie's eyes went wide. Mr. Rivets *lie*? It wasn't possible! Mark II Machine Men were programmed not to lie! When they were forced to keep a secret, they said "I'm afraid I couldn't say" instead.

"In short, you're a FreeTok," James said from the doorway.

"You have also removed my nameplate," Mr. Rivets said. He put a hand to his chest where the little brass plate that said MR. RIVETS used to be.

James tossed the nameplate back to Mr. Rivets. "Most of us, when we become free, choose to shed our factory names and take on new names, like Dr. Kenda and me."

"My name used to be '*Mr. Dongle*,' for torque's sake," Dr. Kenda said.

"Our old names were vestiges of our slavery," James said.

"Slavery?" Archie said. "Mr. Rivets wasn't a slave!"

"Wasn't he?" James asked. "Could he do anything you told him not to? Could he leave your service if he wanted to? Did he have any kind of life of his own that wasn't serving you? Do you have a piece of paper that says you own him?"

"He's a clockwork man! A machine!" Archie said.

James jumped from the door frame and pulled his shirt open, revealing his own wind-up key. "So am I! But that doesn't mean I don't have emotions and desires—it doesn't mean I don't want a life of my own."

"You mustn't blame Mr. James," Mr. Rivets told Archie. "He is independent by design. He is a Mark III Machine Man."

Archie suddenly understood. A Mark III Machine Man! He'd never seen one before. The Mark IIIs had been advertised as "almost human," and they were: They had human emotions and human desires, and could laugh and think and lie. And they weren't happy about being servants. There'd been an uprising—the Mark III Revolt of 1831, led by a Tik Tok named Mr. Turner—and they had all eventually been recalled and dismantled.

Well, most of them, at least. There were rumors that some of them had gotten away, and were hiding out in Brasil.

And apparently Wichita territory too.

"The Mark IIIs proved . . . untrustworthy," Mr. Rivets said.

"No," James said. "It's just that the humans who 'owned' us never did anything to earn our trust."

"Are you going to try to stop me from taking Mr. Rivets back?" Archie asked.

"Not if that's what he wants," James said. "But if he says he wants to stay, I'll do everything I can to stop you."

Coming in here, Archie had been sure Mr. Rivets would want to come with him. But now he wasn't sure if that was what the machine man really wanted, or if it had just been his metal punch cards talking.

"If you want to stay, Mr. Rivets, I—I'll understand. I won't try to take you away," Archie said.

Mr. Rivets straightened. "I wouldn't think of leaving you, Archie. *Master* Archie."

Archie threw himself into Mr. Rivets's arms, careful not to crush him, and Mr. Rivets hugged him back.

"You don't have to call me 'master' anymore if you don't want to," Archie said.

"I use the term now only as an expression of my respect for you and your youth," Mr. Rivets said.

"What about your name?" Archie asked. "Are you still going to be Mr. Rivets?"

"My name has been Mr. Rivets for more than one hundred years, Master Archie. I'm not sure what else I would want to be called."

"You could call yourself Mr. Dent," Archie told him. "After all, you're as much a part of the family as any of us."

Mr. Rivets held Archie at arm's length, but said and did nothing more for a time.

"Mr. Rivets? Are you all right?" Archie asked.

"I believe I am experiencing an emotion, Master Archie, and the feeling is quite new to me. I thank you for the kind offer. And thank you, Doctor, and Mr. James, for my . . . upgrade."

Jesse James stepped aside. "You're free to go, then," he told them. He stopped Archie on the way out. "It's rare I find somebody as loyal to their machine man as he is to them." Archie took it as a compliment and nodded his thanks.

"What is this place?" Archie asked on the way out.

"Dodge City," James said. "The local Wichita call it that because they learned to stay away from it. They dodge it like the plague. Maybe that's what they were messing with here. I don't know."

"Then the signs about the biohazard are real?"

James shrugged. "They were a long time ago. I don't know if it's safe for humans here anymore or not. You're the first meatbags we've had to visit. We call it Dodge City because it's the only place north of New Spain we can dodge the recall. What it was before we got here, we don't really know—but we do know it was a bad, bad place."

James wiped dust away from a brass plaque on the wall, and Archie gasped. Etched into the brass was a pyramid eye inside a seven-pointed star. The symbol of the Septemberist Society.

"By the Maker," Mr. Rivets said.

"You know this logo?" James asked. "It's all over everything here."

"Yes," Archie said. "Yes, we know it."

"Then maybe you'll understand this," James said. He led them to another building, past rooms filled with overturned, dusty furniture and rooms full of books and toys, to a dark room filled with mothballed machinery. Jesse James threw a switch on the wall, and windows opened at the top of the walls, letting in a flood of light.

There, trapped in an enormous block of blue amber like a bug, was a girl.

A girl with wings.

17

Dr. Kenda threw a lever, and the tubes connected to the amber that held the bird girl began to hum. "I'm not sure this is going to work," he said. "This technology—it's far in advance of anything I've ever seen or worked with before."

Not for the first time, Archie wished Hachi and Fergus were there with him. Fergus would know exactly how to get the bird girl out of her translucent blue prison, and Hachi would know how to deal with her when she awoke.

If she awoke.

"I still don't think she's alive in there," Jesse James said. He and Mr. Rivets were the only others in the room.

"We have to try," Archie said.

A large metal box with pipes flowing in and out of it clicked on, and a lightbulb came on above the blue amber.

"Lektricity," Mr. Rivets said.

Archie nodded. Whatever this was, whatever the Septemberists had been doing here, it wasn't good.

Another machine kicked on, and another, and two more lights glowed above the girl in the hard resin.

"I would step back at this point," Dr. Kenda told everyone.

The blue amber began to quiver, then ripple, and then all at once it vaporized, becoming a thin blue mist that was immediately sucked up by the tubes. The girl fell facedown onto the floor, suddenly free of the resin, and the machine clicked off.

The bird girl was perhaps fourteen years old, and was beautiful and horrible at the same time. The top part of her was mostly human and all elegant. She was Illini, with light brown skin, dark black hair, and a thin face with a long, sharp nose it was hard not to think of as a beak. Out of the back of her brown beaded shirt sprouted wings—long, folded wings with jet black feathers like a crow.

It was the bottom half of her that made Archie want to look away. Where her human legs should have been were two bird legs—rough, scaly things bent backwards at the knee. At the bottom of each, instead of feet, the bird girl had leathery talons, with four black claws on each. She reminded Archie of the Manglespawn—the awful children of humans and Mangleborn.

The bird girl's wings fluttered, and everyone in the room took a step back. She was alive! She tried to push herself up with her hands, but she was weak from her time in the amber. Mr. Rivets quickly moved to help her, and Archie joined him.

"Where—?" she asked. "What's—?"

"You've just been released from amber, miss," Mr. Rivets said. "You may be disoriented."

She looked around at them, blinking. "Where's—where's Henry? Where's Dr. Echohawk?"

"I'm sorry—none of those people are around anymore," Archie said. "Whatever this place was, all the people who ran it are gone."

"No—Henry was ambered with me," the bird girl said. She moved quickly across the room, her grotesque bird legs making her bob like a chicken. She pulled away a dusty sheet, revealing another large block of blue amber underneath it.

Frozen inside this one was the rotten carcass of something that had the body of a boy, but the head, tail, and hooved hands and feet of a horse.

"Henry!" the bird girl said. She put a palm to the amber, bent her head to it, and sobbed.

"Whatever was done to you, it didn't work on him," James said. "I'm sorry."

"*I* did it to him," she said. "I did it to both of us, to save us. Oh, Henry. I'm so sorry. . . ."

Archie and the others gave her space. Finally she pulled herself away, and Jesse James threw the sheet back over the block of amber.

"How long?" she asked.

"How long have you been in the amber?" Mr. Rivets asked. "What year was it when you froze yourself?"

"Eighteen fifty," the bird girl said.

Eighteen fifty! It was 1875 now. The bird girl had been stuck in amber for twenty-five years—and hadn't aged a day in all that time.

When Mr. Rivets told her the year, she sat down on the floor with her back to the amber that was now Henry the horseboy's coffin and put her head in her hands.

"What happened here?" Archie asked her. "What was this place?"

"You don't know?" she asked.

"It's been abandoned for years," James said. "This is a FreeTok city now."

"They called it 'The Forge,'" the girl said. "This is where they made me. This is where they made all of us."

"They who, miss?" Mr. Rivets asked.

She shook her head. "I don't know. They never told us who they were. All we knew about them was their symbol—that pyramid with the eye in it. We called them the Aegyptians, but that wasn't their name."

No. Archie and Mr. Rivets knew their name: They were the Septemberists. But what had they been doing out here at a secret base in the middle of the continent?

"We were orphans. All of us," the girl said. "That's the first thing we realized—all our parents were dead or gone. The Aegyptians collected us from cities and villages all over. I'm from Shikaakwa. Twelvetrees was Crow. Henry was from California. Mina . . . " She didn't finish. "I want to get out of here," she said.

Archie helped her to her feet again, and Jesse James stood aside to let her leave the lab. As she walked down the hall, she stopped and looked in at the rooms with the beds and books and toys.

"Gone now. They're all gone but me," she said. "There were twenty-one of us. Twenty-one to start. Less at the end. This was my room," she said. A piece of construction paper decorated with hand-drawn moons and stars said her name was Sings-In-The-Night.

"Why did they bring you here?" Archie asked. "What did they do to you?"

They came to a small room with a single row of chairs pointed toward a dark gray window. Through the window was another room, filled with more of the advanced machines. At the heart of it all was a metal table with arm and leg straps attached to it. Sings-In-The-Night's breath caught, and she backed against the wall.

"That's where they took us," she said. "That's where they . . . did this to me." She looked down at her hideous chicken legs. "That's where they used the lantern on us."

- 176 -

"*The lantern?*" Archie said. "What lantern?"

"It wasn't really a lantern, but that's what they called it. It *looked* like a lantern. It was silver, with dragons all over it."

Archie was so stunned, he sat in one of the chairs. "The Dragon Lantern? They had it? Here?"

"It's what did this to me. Changed me. Gave me these wings, and these legs. It didn't work on everybody. Just some of us. We never understood why. I don't think they did either. All we knew was if it didn't work on you, they took you away. And if it did work on you . . . it hurt."

"What happened to the kids who were taken away?" Archie asked.

"I don't know. But they were the lucky ones," Sings-In-The-Night said. She hurried out of the room. "It worked differently on all of us," she said, looking back down the hall at the rooms with colorful children's drawings taped to the doors. "It turned Twelvetrees into this . . . this minotaur, with the head of a bison. It made Ominotago into some kind of . . . blob thing. We didn't come back to our rooms, after. They had to put us in cages. One girl, it turned her into a fish. A mermaid, like in the storybooks. She suffocated to death. She needed salt water, and they didn't have any this far from the ocean. Never thought they'd need it. My friend Mina, it gave her tentacles. Like an octopus—but more of them. Changed her inside too. Or maybe she had always been that way, and we just never knew it. When they were finished, only seven of us survived."

"Why?" James asked. "I mean, why'd they do it?"

"They told us they were making us into superheroes. That we were going to save the world. They called us the League of Seven."

"No," Archie whispered. "*No.*" Was this how he'd been created? Was this *where* he'd been created? A sudden thought seized him, and he ran down the hall, looking at all the names on the doors. Was his name here? Had he somehow forgotten all this? Blocked it from his memory?

"Master Archie," Mr. Rivets called. "Master Archie, I was there when you were brought to your parents as an infant twelve years ago. I watched you grow up. This facility has been abandoned for nearly twenty-five years. This cannot be where you are from," he said, like he could read Archie's mind.

Still, Archie read the name on every door. But Mr. Rivets was right—when he came to the end, his name wasn't there. He didn't know whether to be relieved or disappointed. But he and this place were connected by the Septemberists and the Dragon Lantern—that much he knew.

"What happened to the lantern?" he asked Sings-In-The-Night.

"I don't know. When they had the seven of us, they stopped using it on kids and started training us to be heroes. But Ominotago, Ivan, Twelvetrees, even Henry—they were all too far gone. They weren't human enough anymore. Henry had no hands. He couldn't even eat without a feed bag. And Ominotago—for Hiawatha's sake, Ominotago was just a brain and eyes floating in ooze. She couldn't handle what had been done to her. None of us could. But they told us we were heroes, and that Mina was our leader. And then they sent us to Beaver Run."

"The village just outside of here," James said. "The ghost town."

"Is that what it is now?" Sings-In-The-Night said. "I expect it is. There was a fire. One of the buildings in town had caught fire, and it was spreading. The Aegyptians, they thought it would be a good test of our team. They took us to Beaver Run and told us to put out the fires and save the townspeople. It went . . . badly. Very badly. The townspeople thought we were monsters and attacked us. Mina turned the League against them, killing everyone, destroying everything. It was like hell—fire everywhere, people screaming, Mina laughing. Henry and I tried to stop her, tried to stop all of them, but they were mad. Insane. We weren't human anymore. None of us were. We were the monsters they all thought we were. The Aegyptians, or whoever they were, the scientists—they moved in with rayguns and killed the rest of them. Ominotago, Twelve-trees, Ivan, Renata. I saw a burning building collapse on Mina."

"How did you survive?" Archie asked.

"I can fly," Sings-In-The-Night said simply. "I grabbed up Henry, and flew us back here."

"Why here? Why not run?" James asked.

"There was a scientist here, Dr. Echohawk. He'd been kind to me. I—I didn't know where else to go. But the Aegyptians who ran this place, they released something into the air, something to kill off everyone who was left. Dr. Echohawk and I had been working on the amber as a way to preserve things—people. So I . . . I ambered Henry and me, to protect us from the toxin."

"You were the scientist," Archie said, realizing that this "Forged" League had even been constructed to have the same roles as a real League of Seven.

"Some scientist," she said. "I'm the only one who survived."

"And they call us inhuman like it's a bad thing," Jesse James said, and he left them to go outside.

Sings-In-The-Night put a hand to one of the pyramid eye logos on the wall. "Whoever the Aegyptians were, I'm glad they're gone," she said.

Archie closed his eyes. There was no way he could keep it a secret from her. Not if he was going to ask her what he wanted to ask her. "They're not all gone," Archie told her. "They're not called the Aegyptians either. They're called the Septemberists, and I'm one of them."

Archie led her back outside, and they walked around Dodge City while he told her everything he knew—about the Septemberists, the Dragon Lantern, the Mangleborn, the ancient Leagues, and the new one he was putting together.

"You want me to become a part of your League?" Sings-In-The-Night asked incredulously. "After what your Septemberists did to me?"

"At least help me get the lantern back," Archie said. "Whatever it did to you—whatever it did to *me*—we can't let it happen to anyone else."

"I need to think about it," Sings-In-The-Night told him, and with a flap of her great wings and a swirl of dust, she shot up into the air. Archie watched her circle as she gained altitude, and then she glided away on the warm evening air. As he watched her go, Archie wondered if he might never see her again.

"Whoa! Was that a flying girl?" Clyde asked, his voice booming through the amplified trumpet inside Buster. The giant steam man hopped after Sings-In-The-Night, barking at her with his whistle, until Clyde got him to heel. Buster bent down close to Archie and opened his mouth, and Archie climbed inside.

"Check it out!" Clyde said, gesturing at the repaired left eye. "The Tik Toks fixed him up! Repaired his eye, put in new pedals for me—said they made some upgrades to his engine room too."

"Yeah. They 'upgraded' Mr. Rivets too," Archie told him.

"So, we ready to make tracks?" Clyde asked. "Like Mrs. DeMarcus says, there's no time like the present, and no present like time."

Archie knew they needed to get underway. The fox girl had a head start on them to Cheyenne—if her airship didn't get caught in a cyclone first. But he wanted Sings-In-The-Night with them. She was supposed to be part of their League. He was sure of it. Even if the League she'd been created for was gone now, even if the way she had been created was awful and horrible and wrong, this was right. This was what she was made for.

It was what Archie was made for too.

⤷⤶

Buster's whistling woke Archie the next morning, and Clyde called him up to the bridge. Sings-In-The-Night was outside, flapping her black wings to stay level with Buster's eyes. Clyde opened one of the windows, and she spoke to them through it.

"I'll come," she said. "I'm not sure I can join your League, not after everything that's happened, but there's no life for me here. And I don't want anyone else hurt by the lantern."

She turned and flew off in the direction of the Moving City of Cheyenne. Archie saw a smudge of black on her shirt and realized she must have spent the night in the burned-out ruins of Beaver Run, surrounded by ghosts.

18

New Orleans was having a party.

All along Canal Street, a row of colorful airship balloons bumped and bobbed into each other. Some of the balloons were shaped into long faces—a crocodile, a jester, a ghost—but most were just decorated in gaudy splashes of purple and green and gold. It was what hung below them that really mattered. In the place of airship capsules and cabins, each balloon carried what parade-goers called "floats"—long, open-topped barges in even more bizarre shapes than the balloons. One, Hachi could see, was made to look like a steamboat. Another was a mermaid with a trumpet, emerging from majestic blue waves. Another, in the shape of a stick with a net at the end, paid tribute to New Orleans's celebrated lacrosse team, the Saints. On the floats stood armies of costumed revelers throwing necklaces and charms to the huge crowds swarming the sidewalks.

"Is this what Mardi Gras is like?" Hachi asked.

"Dis is bigger dan Mardi Gras," Erasmus Trudeau told her. The Pinkerton agent swung their tiny airship around, and Hachi saw the masses of people filling the side streets, all dancing and singing and drinking. "It's dat Baron Samedi. He put everybody in a party mood."

Everyone but Hachi. She was feeling distinctly unparty-like. She had just watched Madame Blavatsky be "ridden" by the loa of Baron Samedi right when she was about to get her hands on her. Now, instead of interrogating Blavatsky in some hidden garret, she was getting ready to drop in on a parade float to give Blavatsky an impromptu haircut.

"A true bokor can welcome a loa as easily as she can expel one," Marie Laveau had told them as they left the palace after the séance. "But Blavatsky is no true bokor. Without the knowledge or the strength to push him out, Samedi can ride her until she dies. And will."

What they needed, Laveau told them, was a voodoo doll of Blavatsky. And to make a voodoo doll of Blavatsky, they needed a lock of her hair.

"We just coming around now, Miss Hachi," Erasmus said.

Hachi clipped a carabiner to the harness she wore and opened the bottom hatch on the little airship.

"You got your barber's shears?" Erasmus asked, laughing.

Hachi patted her knife. "Something like that."

"Den good luck—and good cutting!"

Hachi jumped out of the airship, the rope attached to her harness buzzing as it ran out of the airship's winch. She shot down past a long, tall balloon in the shape of a rampant bull, and as the winch slowed her descent, she swung onto the deck of a float decorated with empty-eyed skeleton skulls. A zombi soldier turned at the sound of her landing, and she kicked him in the chest, knocking him over into the cheering, singing crowd below.

The float was like a long sailing ship, with a wooden plank floor and short walls at the sides. A network of ropes held its balloon in place above, and more ropes stretched from the prow and the stern to the porters on the street below who pulled it along the parade route. All along the low walls, men and women in skeleton costumes threw baubles to the crowd below, ignoring her.

Hachi gave the rope on her harness a quick tug to let Erasmus know she'd landed, and she felt it go slack. Two more tugs, and Erasmus would throw a lever on the winch, whipping her back up.

"Circus, showtime," Hachi said. From her bandolier flew the three remaining wind-up animals her father had built for her before he'd died. Each time she saw them, she was filled with a mix of emotions, ranging from happiness and comfort to sadness and loss. "You know what to do," she told the little gorilla, lion, and giraffe, and they buzzed off into the chaos.

Hachi slipped up behind one of the revelers and put a chloroform rag to her face. "Sorry," she said as the young woman slumped in her arms. One of the other costumed partiers looked over. Hachi smiled and shrugged. "Too much to drink," she said. She pulled the woman away and quickly stole her costume, mask, and basket of charms. Looking just like the rest of the revelers, Hachi made her way toward the front of the float, where Baron Samedi, still riding Helena Blavatsky, waved to the crowd.

Blavatsky had changed. Not like Marie Laveau changed, not physically. She still looked like Madame Blavatsky, but now she wore a black tuxedo, a black top hat, and round black tinted glasses. She smoked a cigar all the time now too—and in her other hand she carried a bottle of rum. Baron Samedi was making up for lost time.

Drink up, Hachi thought. *Playtime's almost over.*

Hachi threw trinkets to the crowd as she moved up the float, pretending to be just another of the revelers. Samedi still had his back turned toward her. Hachi was almost to him when she saw Queen Theodosia sitting in a gilded throne near the prow.

"Your Highness," Hachi whispered. "Your Highness, what are you doing here?"

Queen Theodosia stared straight ahead, as though she was mesmerized. Hachi waved a hand in front of her face and snapped her fingers, but Theodosia didn't budge. Baron Samedi must have put her under some sort of spell. Hachi looked up and was surprised to see the decrepit General Jackson standing behind her. Why hadn't the general defended her against Samedi? Then Hachi remembered: Baron Samedi was the loa of resurrection. No matter who had made them, all zombis answered to Samedi.

Hachi left Theodosia behind. The best way to save her was to get rid of Baron Samedi, and the best way to get rid of *him* was to get a lock of Blavatsky's hair for Laveau's voodoo doll.

Focus, Hachi, she told herself.

She picked up her mantra where she'd left off the last time and creped forward, her knife in her hand.

Hahyah Yechee, the sheriff.
Thomas Stidham, the horse breeder.
Arkon Nichee, friend to many.

One hundred men.

Claiborne Lowe, twelve times a grandfather.
Pompey Yoholo, seventh son of a seventh son.
Woxe Holatha, the banker.

One hundred murdered souls, and only Helena Blavatsky knew why they'd been killed. Hachi brought her knife up to the back of Blavatsky's head and held it there. Blavatsky's white neck called out to her to be cut, and Hachi put a hand to the long scar at her own throat. One pull of the knife, and it would be over—Blavatsky would be dead, and her father would be avenged.

But no—Hachi had to know why she'd done it. And she had to get the names of the others too, the ones who'd been at Chuluota with Blavatsky. Her father and the ninety-nine other men who'd been murdered would never be avenged until the last of their killers rotted six feet underground.

Cursing everything, Hachi took a lock of Blavatsky's hair in her hand and sliced it off with her knife.

Shing! Hachi heard the sound of a blade behind her and spun, yanking twice on her rope. It dangled uselessly in her hand. The other half, still connected to the airship, was held by a stout reveler in a skeleton costume and mask. In the reveler's other hand was the machete that had cut her rope.

The reveler laughed—a deep, booming chuckle—and Hachi knew immediately who it was.

Baron Samedi.

Hachi looked down at the lock of hair she held and saw that her hand was covered with black shoe polish. The hair was somebody else's, painted to look black. Hachi spun the person she'd thought was Blavatsky around and stared into an old, weathered face she recognized from his portrait in the throne room. It was Aaron Burr—Theodosia's father, and the first king of Louisiana— who'd died years ago.

Baron Samedi—the *real* Baron Samedi—laughed again and tore away his skeleton mask.

"Yes, it's King Aaron!" Blavatsky said with Samedi's voice. Blavatsky's face was painted white, with big black circles around the eyes and vertical lines drawn on her lips like the masks on Laveau's assistants. Like the string that sewed the zombi soldiers' mouths shut. "I thought I'd bring the old fool back. A zombi king, for a zombi nation! And he makes a good stand-in for me too, don't you think? Though there's nothing like the original."

Hachi tossed the shoe-blacked hair aside and stood ready for whatever Samedi threw at her.

"Not talkative, eh?" Samedi said. "What's the matter, they cut out your tongue when they slit your throat? Oh—wait. No. I know exactly what happened," Samedi said. He tapped his head with the point of his machete. "It's all right here, in this fool Blavatsky's head! Oh yes. I see what they did. Oho!" He laughed long and hard. "Oh, it's too wonderfully terrible. I'm tempted to tell you, just to see the look on your face. That would take the steam out of you!"

"Why don't you tell me, then," Hachi said.

"Ho-ho! Brave girl. But then you would just kill this body, yes? And I'm not finished with it. No, I think I'll wait—and so will you." He tugged at the rope, and it shot from his hand back up into the air, leaving Hachi stranded with him on the float.

"Now," Samedi said. "I believe you came for a lock of my hair, yes? I thought my new old friend Laveau would be cooking up something like that." Samedi, in Blavatsky's body, crouched low and brandished his machete. "You're a great warrior, Hachi Emartha. But are you good enough to defeat the Loa of Death?"

"No," Hachi said. "But I'm good enough to trick him."

Samedi yowled and clapped a hand to the back of his neck, but he was too late—Jo-Jo, Mr. Lion, and Freckles each had a lock of his hair. He swatted at them, trying to catch them, but they buzzed up and away from him into the air.

"Enjoy the rest of your time in New Orleans," Hachi told Samedi. "It's going to be a short visit."

Hachi grabbed a rope, looped it around her wrist, and leaped off the prow, swinging like a buccaneer over the heads of the porters to the dragon float ahead of them. Behind her, she could hear Baron Samedi howling out a magic incantation.

Hands caught her on the dragon float, and she fell into their embrace.

"You give him a trim?" Fergus asked her.

Hachi smiled up at him as her clockwork menagerie appeared, clumps of Samedi's hair in their little mouths.

"That's my girl," Fergus said.

"Where's Laveau?" Hachi asked.

Fergus pointed to the stern, where a girl about Archie's age leaned over the rail. Hachi looked at Fergus like he had a gear loose, but he shrugged. "Tell me it's not," he said.

The girl turned, and Hachi saw Fergus was right. The girl was the very image of Marie Laveau, only younger still. Instead of the elegant white dress she had worn the night of the séance, she wore a simple white smock and a gold handkerchief tied over her dark hair, which hung down in the back.

"You changed again," Hachi told her.

"Samedi's already seen my older faces," the young Laveau said. "I didn't want him to recognize me too soon."

Hachi collected Samedi's hair from her menagerie and held it out to Laveau. "This enough?"

Laveau's eyebrows went up. "Plenty. But we'd better get out of here, and fast. That spell he just cast—it's to summon the dead."

"You mean all the zombi soldiers?" Fergus asked.

"No. I mean all the dead Blavatsky didn't already raise. He's waking all the dead in New Orleans!"

There was a scream on the edge of the crowd, then another, and the air was filled with panicked cries. Hachi clambered up a rope ladder to get a better view and saw hordes of zombi shambling into the crowd, clawing and biting anyone living.

"Looks like this party just got ugly," she called down.

"It was ugly already!" Fergus said, zapping a zombi off the side of the float with a lektric blast.

Hachi scrambled back down to the deck. "I'll cut the lines!" she said.

"Wait! We can't leave all these people!" Laveau said.

On the streets below, anyone who couldn't get away was penned in, surrounded on all sides by flesh-eating zombi.

Hachi cursed. Nothing was ever easy. "Get into the floats!" she cried, but no one could hear her above the screaming.

Suddenly there was a bright blue-white flash, and all eyes in the crowd turned to Fergus, who stood clinging to a rope on one of the low walls. Lektricity still crackled between his fingers from where he'd generated the flash.

"Everyone who isn't dead already, get into the floats!" he announced, his voice booming down Canal Street through some kind of lektrical amplification. Hachi was impressed despite herself—he'd been experimenting with his powers. He had new tricks even she didn't know about.

The crowd got the message loud and clear, and suddenly their float rocked and sank as people grabbed the sides and climbed on board. Hachi and Laveau helped people onto the float while Fergus ran to the furnace, stoking it for more hot air. When they had all they could carry, they cast off their lines and rose into the air, the other floats not far behind them.

"Now what?" Hachi asked Laveau as they stood together beside the rail.

"Now we have to get Baron Samedi to eat salt," she said.

Below them on the street, the zombi hordes massed around Baron Samedi's float, creating a moat of undead around him. Hachi sighed. They had his hair for Laveau's voodoo doll, for whatever good that would do, but getting to Samedi again to make him eat salt—to make him do *anything*—was going to be even more difficult than before.

Whatever they had to do, Hachi would do it. She knew now it was worth it, no matter what. Blavatsky had the answers she wanted. Samedi had seen them inside her.

But for the first time, she wondered if she really did want to know. What could be so terrible—so much worse than what she already knew—that Samedi had almost told her just to hurt her?

19

The Moving City of Cheyenne was an impressive sight. It was an immense city of gleaming brass, stained wood, and iron girders, level upon level of houses and shops and offices shaped like the teepees the founders' ancestors had lived in long ago when they roamed the Great Plains on horseback. Now the Cheyenne migrated with the buffalo and the seasons in their moving city, built on enormous wheels as tall as Buster. The giant wheels rode on massive steel tracks a half a mile wide, laid by Cheyenne engineers generations before the Romans rediscovered the New World. Driving the city, fueled by the raging furnaces that poured black smoke into the air day and night, was a gargantuan cog wheel called the Wheel of the Sun that eclipsed everything else. It ran down the middle of the city, rising high above even the tallest cone-shaped building like a second sun on the horizon. While the wheel still turned, the City of Cheyenne still lived, or so the saying went, and it was turning now, moving Cheyenne south before winter set in.

Sings-In-The-Night was the first to see it, and she came flying back to Buster with the news. "It's incredible!" she said. "I heard stories, but I never thought—never imagined!" It was as many words as she had said to either of them in the days since they had left Dodge City, but as quickly as she had appeared, she flew away again.

Archie had tried to talk to her on the trip to draw her out. But she was still too scarred by what had happened twenty-five years ago, which for her, frozen in amber all that time, still felt like yesterday. One day she had seen her friends become monsters and watched them kill and be killed; the next she had awakened in Archie's arms, where he'd immediately asked her to join his new League. He cursed himself for being such a flange. The only one she'd spent any real time with was Buster, flying off alone with him each night while he was "getting his wiggles out," as Clyde called it.

"She just needs time," Clyde said, like he could read Archie's mind. Even Clyde, with his smooth tongue and ability to make friends with just about anyone, had failed to get through the wall Sings-In-The-Night had built around herself. "It's like Mrs. DeMarcus always says, time heals all—*whoa!*"

Buster suddenly lurched, and Archie had to grab a brass pipe to steady himself. The levers and pedals bucked under Clyde's hands and feet, like he was having trouble keeping control.

"What is it? What's wrong?" Archie asked.

"It's Buster. I don't know what he's doing, but—Buster! Heel! Heel, Buster! Heel!"

Buster didn't heel. He got down on all fours and bounded toward the City of Cheyenne, which had just become visible in the distance.

The *Moving* City of Cheyenne.

"Clyde—Clyde, he's chasing it!" Archie said. "He's chasing it like he did *Colossus* when he was a dog!"

Buster gave a whistle-bark and ran headlong for the city. He was like a real dog chasing a steam car through town—only this dog was ten stories tall and weighed 100,000 pounds, and the car he was chasing could run over Dodge City and keep going.

"Whoa, Buster! Heel! Heel, boy!" Clyde called out, but it was a lost cause. Buster's greatest love was chasing things, and his instincts took over. The steam man ran up alongside the moving city, whistling and nipping at the thing's wheels. It was so silly that Clyde started laughing, and soon Archie was laughing too.

They stopped laughing when the raycannons started hitting them.

Archie ran to the windows and looked up. "They're shooting at us! They have raycannons mounted all along the wheel wells!"

Clyde wrenched at the controls and managed to drag Buster away from the moving city, and they could see the powerful blue aether beams carving the ground around them. They could also see Cheyenne's legendary Howler-On-The-Hill, the largest raycannon ever built, its barrel as wide as Buster's head, slowly twisting their way from the top of the city.

"We ain't gonna survive that!" Clyde said. "We gotta let them know we come in peace!"

Clyde got on the speaking trumpet, trying to get the attention of one of the lower gunners, and Archie threw open the hatch at the top of Buster's head and hung outside, waving a white handkerchief. But Buster pulled away from Clyde again and ran in at the wheels, biting and barking, and the raycannons peppered them again. The Howler-On-The-Hill began to charge.

Archie scanned the skies for Sings-In-The-Night and flagged her down.

"I need you to fly me up there!" Archie hollered. "If they shoot that thing, Buster's toast!"

Sings-In-The-Night looked doubtful, like she didn't want to get involved, but finally she swooped in, dodged a raycannon blast, and picked Archie up under his arms. With a mighty beat of her wings they were flying. It was all Archie could do not to whoop with joy, and he understood why Sings-In-The-Night spent so much time in the air.

"Drop me up there!" Archie called, pointing to the deck where soldiers with painted faces and elaborate feather headbands were aiming the Howler-On-The-Hill.

Sings-In-The-Night swooped down. Her great black wings beat more quickly as she landed Archie on the deck, as smoothly as if he'd just stepped out of bed. For a moment, the soldiers did nothing but stare incredulously at the girl with bird wings. Then, just as she shot back up into the air, they regained their senses and aimed oscillators at Archie.

"Don't shoot!" he said, raising his arms. "We come in peace!"

The soldiers shot anyway. The rifle blasts burned for a second and torched his clothes, but they did about as much to his body as a stiff breeze. He put a hand up to his face to keep the beams out of his eyes and took a step forward.

The soldiers stopped shooting and stared at him with as much wonder as they had Sings-In-The-Night.

"I said don't shoot! We come in peace," he told them again.

"Then why does your steam man attack our city?" one of them said.

"He's . . . he's like a big dog. He's not attacking. He's *chasing* it. For fun."

The soldiers looked down at Buster, who was still running alongside the city, darting in and out along with the other dogs who chased Cheyenne. While they watched, he bit a brass railing and stripped it away, whipping it around the way he had the rock monsters in the canyon. The soldiers ran back to the Howler-On-The-Hill.

"*Wait wait wait wait!*" Archie cried. "All we have to do is distract him; then my friend can get him back under control. I don't suppose you have a big bone lying around anywhere, do you?"

The soldiers stared at him out from under their feathered headbands.

"Right, no. Of course not," Archie said. His eyes fell on a flagpole at the top of the city, bearing the Cheyenne tribal flag: a bright blue background with a white gear on it. That would do! He snapped the pole off at the base, causing more stares from the soldiers. "Um, sorry," Archie told them. "I'm just going to borrow this."

"Buster!" Archie cried. "Buster! Hey Buster! Fetch!"

Archie was countless stories up—too far for any human being to hear him—but not too far for a dog. Buster looked up at him and whistled, and Archie hurled the flagpole like a stick, sending it hundreds of yards away. Buster suddenly broke off his pursuit of the moving city and sped after the flagpole, and the soldiers on the deck powered down the Howler.

"So hey," Archie said. "My name's Archie Dent. I don't suppose any of you have seen a girl with a fox tail anywhere, have you?"

∽

The strangely dressed warriors were called Dog Soldiers, even though they looked nothing like dogs. They wore brown pants and moccasins and blue shirts, all covered by ceremonial beaded bone armor. Their faces were painted white below their eyes and black above, making their eyes disappear like they were wearing masks, and each wore a feathery headdress that looked like a turkey had exploded on their heads.

The Dog Soldiers were silent as they marched Archie, Clyde, and Mr. Rivets to the council chamber at the heart of the Moving City of Cheyenne. Sings-In-The-Night had apparently had all the public contact she wanted for the week and had decided to stay with Buster, who was sleeping off his big adventure.

All through the city, people stopped and pointed at Archie. Had *everyone* seen him throw the flagpole? Cheyenne was a big place. Word of his strength couldn't have gotten around *that* fast, could it?

The big room where the Cheyenne Council of Forty-Four met was dominated by a table in the shape of an enormous gear, with spaces in between the cogs for forty-four chairs. An elderly Cheyenne introduced himself as Chief Black Kettle and officially welcomed them to Cheyenne.

"We are sorry for firing on your steam man," Black Kettle said.

"I'm the one who should be doing the apologizing, charging your city with a United Nations Steam Man," Clyde said, shaking the chief's hand. "He's got a mind of his own. I gotta get Buster better trained, and that's a fact."

One of the clerks passing through the room stared openly at Archie and whispered to a friend on the way out. Archie frowned.

"You'll have to forgive them, Mr. Dent," Black Kettle said. "You're something of a celebrity."

"Just for throwing a flagpole?" Archie asked.

"Ah, no," the chief said. "For your starring role in the dime novels. They're very popular here. *The League of Seven and the Peril of Standing Peachtree,* and all the others. My grandchildren have read them all. Hachi's their favorite."

Senarens! He was still writing pulp stories about Archie, Hachi, and Fergus. Before he was finished, everybody in North America would know their secrets.

"Yes, you're not exactly keeping a low profile," said a familiar voice.

"Mrs. Moffett!" Archie said. She swept into the room wearing a burgundy dress that once again covered her from top to bottom, billowing out into a bell-like bustle at the bottom.

"When you didn't return right away, I set out for Kansa City, hoping to meet up with you there," she said. "That's when word came from Chief Black Kettle that he needed the Society's help with a little problem they've dug up cutting a tunnel through the mountains for the new Transcontinental Railroad."

Black Kettle frowned. "If you call stumbling onto a Mangleborn a 'little problem.'"

"A Mangleborn?" Clyde said. "One of them big monster things Archie was telling me about?"

"Wait, you know about them?" Archie asked Black Kettle.

"It comes with the job," he told them. "I'm not a Septemberist, but we have people on the council who are. When we blasted our way into that thing's prison, they found me fast enough to tell me what they knew."

"Blasted your way into a Mangleborn prison?" Archie said.

Mrs. Moffett held up a hand. "Our more immediate concern is the Dragon Lantern."

"More immediate than blasting into a Mangleborn prison?" Archie said. "How close is it to Cheyenne?"

"The lantern," Mrs. Moffett said. "I take it you do not have it?"

"No," Archie said. "But we think it's here. The fox girl took an airship from Ton won tonga, and it was headed to the Moving City of Cheyenne."

Mrs. Moffett nodded. "That fits the new information we have: that she is taking it to a criminal overlord in Ametokai, in the Japanese colony of Beikoku. We must find her before she leaves this city."

"But how?" Archie said. "She can make us see things that aren't there."

"The Dog Soldiers," Black Kettle said. "If she uses glamours, as Mrs. Moffett has told me, the Dog Soldiers will be able to see through them. They . . . have ways of seeing things others can't."

Archie didn't see how that was possible, but when Black Kettle called over the leader of the Dog Soldiers, Tall Bull, there was something about the way he looked through Archie that made him shiver.

And that low, rumbling sound—was Tall Bull *growling* at him? He shrank back behind Mrs. Moffett, forgetting for the moment that he was invulnerable.

"We will find this fox girl you speak of," Tall Bull said, his voice a low whisper. "We also offer our services for your dog."

"Our dog?" Mrs. Moffett asked.

"The steam man," Tall Bull said. "We see the dog spirit within him. A little brown dog with a bandana. *Your* bandana," he said to Clyde.

"Y-yeah, that's right," Clyde said. "You can see all that?"

"I told you, the Dog Soldiers see many things we don't see," Black Kettle said. "It's the mushrooms they eat and the pipes they smoke."

"If you could see all that, why'd you attack us with the Howler-On-The-Hill?" Archie asked.

"Dead dogs do not bite," Tall Bull said.

Archie saw anger flash in Clyde's eyes the same way it had when Nahotabi had shot at Buster from *Colossus*. He squared off against the much bigger Dog Soldier like he might take a swing at him. "Buster didn't mean nothing by it! He was just playing! It was just his instincts that took over!"

"Which is why we will help you train your dog, if you wish," Tall Bull said, not reacting to Clyde's aggression.

"Clyde, training Buster is a good idea," Archie said. "He may be a little dog at heart, but he's really a ten-story-tall steam man, and that makes him dangerous if you can't control him."

Clyde calmed down. "Yeah. Okay. Training would be good. Thanks."

"Small Wolf will accompany you," Tall Bull said, and a very tall, very thin Dog Soldier gestured for Clyde to follow him.

"Uh, okay," Clyde said. "So, you're gonna be all right then?" he asked Archie.

"Go," Archie told Clyde. "It's not like you can bring Buster in the city anyway."

"All right," Clyde said. "Just whistle if you need us. I won't hear it, but Buster will!" Clyde gave them a proper army salute and left with Small Wolf.

"We will join you in the search for the fox girl," Mrs. Moffett told Tall Bull.

"No," Archie said. "We should go check out this Mangleborn."

"You are not in charge here, Mr. Dent," Mrs. Moffett said. "We search for the lantern."

"The Dog Soldiers know this city far better than you do," Black Kettle said. "They will find your thief. If this Mangleborn is the threat my advisors say it is, isn't it more important that we protect Cheyenne?"

Mrs. Moffett's frown turned into a radiant smile. "Yes. Of course. We'll go there at once," she said.

Archie was glad she had made the right decision, but as he followed her out the door, he couldn't help feeling that for some reason Mrs. Moffett cared more about the Dragon Lantern than the Moving City of Cheyenne.

The inside of the Mangleborn cave was tall and wide, just like the final room in Malacar Ahasherat's puzzle trap in Florida. But this one was crooked. The walls were set at odd angles, the ceiling sloped from left to right, and the floor slanted from right to left. The cavern was carved out of brown rock, and its walls were decorated with primitive images of dogs. Coyotes. They were all dancing around something bigger, something thin and bent and gangly, in the shape of a coyote but standing like a man—a crooked man. Its arms and legs and neck were all cocked at the wrong angles, like all its bones were broken. Instead of fur, it had needles all over it, like a porcupine, and its crooked arms ended in long black claws.

Archie ran his hand over the carvings and felt a shudder. Whatever this was, it was just beneath their feet, waiting to get out.

Jandal a Haad, something whisper-sang in his head. *Made of stone.*

Archie pulled his hand away.

"What is it?" Mrs. Moffett said. "You can hear it, can't you."

Archie nodded reluctantly. For some reason he shared a link with the Swarm Queen, Malacar Ahasherat, and that made him sensitive to the whispers and songs of the other Mangleborn. It gave him a connection to the very things he was supposed to fight.

"Why was this done to me?" Archie asked. "Who did it?"

"The Dragon Lantern holds the answers," Mr. Moffett said. She stood in the middle of the room, arms crossed. "That's what we should be focused on. Where is this engineer we're supposed to meet?"

"We found a place on the prairie," Archie said. "On the way here. We found a place where Septemberists had used the Dragon Lantern on people. On kids."

Mrs. Moffett paled. "*What?*"

"Sorry to be late!" a Cheyenne man in a black suit and vest called, jogging in. He slowed when he came to the great room with its bizarre images carved into the walls, like he could feel the evil. He took off his wide-brimmed brown hat and walked the rest of the way, watching the pictures on the walls.

"Sorry," he said again as he shook their hands. "Name's Quick Hammer. It was my crew who found this place. At first we thought it might be Ancient Cheyenne, but then we saw the Latin." He nodded to a giant seal on the floor, in which were carved the words DOMVM PRAVA. House . . . crooked? Crooked house. That would explain the walls and floor. *There was a crooked man, who lived in a little crooked house*, Archie thought, remembering one of the nursery rhymes his parents had hammered into him. The nursery rhymes that were the clues to unlocking the puzzle traps where the Mangleborn were kept.

There was more to the crooked man rhyme. Archie had no idea

what any of it meant, how any of the puzzle traps that led to the Crooked Man in his Crooked House were solved. None of it mattered now that the Cheyenne had accidentally blasted their way past all the traps with dynamite.

"Bury it," Mrs. Moffett told him. "Why haven't you already? I saw the crates of dynamite outside."

"We were waiting on you, miss," the engineer said, hat in hand. "And besides, we can't just go blasting away." He nodded at the floor again. "We do it wrong, and we're as like to blow that cover there to pieces as we are to bring down the mountain. We were told that would be bad."

"Yes," Mr. Moffett said. "That would be bad."

Bad was an understatement, thought Archie. If that seal broke, the Mangleborn would get free, and the Moving City of Cheyenne would be destroyed.

"We've been surveying the cave, marking the right places to trigger a collapse," Quick Hammer said. He pointed to painted red Xs all around the cavern. "Once we get it all plotted out, we'll bore holes in the rock for the dynamite and bring her down."

"You should do it as soon as possible," Archie told him. "And don't let anybody else in here."

"Real shame," Quick Hammer said. "We were going to bring the railroad tunnel right through here. We've had to go round. We'll be hard-pressed to make next month's deadline, but we'll do it. Can't have all those important folks standing around outside Salt Lake City with no Transcontinental Railroad to open."

"You seem to have everything well in hand," Mrs. Moffett told him. "Carry on." A Dog Soldier had just come into the cavern, and she glided over to him. Archie didn't think anything would be "well in hand" until this Mangleborn was good and buried, but he left Quick Hammer and hurried to Mrs. Moffett's side.

"The Dog Soldiers have treed our fox," Mrs. Moffett said. "It's time to collect the lantern."

The fox girl wasn't up a tree; she was up a gear—the giant spoked Wheel of the Sun that turned at the heart of the Moving City of Cheyenne. She sat in between two of the cogs like she was riding a Ferris Wheel, and she was almost all the way to the top. On her back was slung the canvas bag with the Dragon Lantern in it. Behind her, in the spaces between cogs farther down the gear, sat pursuing Dog Soldiers.

"Is that safe?" Archie asked.

"Not entirely," Tall Bull said. "But it is a Cheyenne rite of passage to ride it from one side to the other." The gear was like Cheyenne's main street, running right down the middle of the city, and they stood on the wide sidewalk on one side of it. Expensive shops, restaurants, and hotels faced the big turning gear on either side. A tunnel formed by the hollow axle in its hub allowed people to pass from one side to the other. "Lovers, too, like its views at night," Tall Bull added. "And its privacy."

Archie couldn't believe anyone would ride that high and that exposed for fun, but the Dog Soldiers seemed as comfortable on the big wheel as the Illini did on the swaying gangplanks of Cahokia in the Clouds.

The fox girl reached the very top and began her long, slow descent down the other side, where more Dog Soldiers waited for her. But the girl had other plans. She stood and got herself balanced, facing away from them toward a smaller though still enormous gear that turned nearby.

"She's going to jump!" Mrs. Moffett cried. "If she gets over there, she'll be seven levels above us. We'll lose her again!"

Tall Bull dispatched a pack of Dog Soldiers with a hand signal, and they ran for an elevator. But they were going to be too late. As the Wheel of the Sun moved her closer to the other gear, the fox girl got ready to jump.

"Knock her off," Mrs. Moffett told Archie.

"With what?"

"With your fist! Knock her off!"

Archie hesitated, worried about damaging the big wheel, but decided it was bigger than he could smash. He reared back and punched the big brass wheel with all his strength. *THOOM-OOM-OOM-OOM!* it echoed. The blow shook it just enough to throw off the girl's balance as she jumped, and she missed the gear she was aiming for and tumbled through the air, crashing through a canvas teepee roof and disappearing into a building on the other side of the Wheel of the Sun. There were Dog Soldiers on the other side, but not near the building where she had fallen. Tall Bull and his men raced for the tunnel in the center of the wheel.

"They'll never make it in time," Mrs. Moffett said. She backed up, got a running start, and leaped through one of the empty spaces between the Wheel of the Sun's spokes, soaring to the other side. Archie ran to the gap to follow her across, but pulled up short. There was no way he could make that jump. The Wheel of the Sun had to be fifty feet thick. How in the world had Mrs. Moffett been able to do it?

Archie followed Tall Bull and his men through the tunnel. The building the fox girl had fallen into was a clothing shop called "Brook Bros. By-Spoke Tailoring." The Dog Soldiers were almost to the door when suddenly the wooden deck beneath them began to rattle and shake. The air was filled with an incredible wail, like a fire engine siren, and the shaking intensified. Everyone on the sidewalk stopped, trying to stay on their feet, and shoppers up and down the promenade screamed.

"Earthquake!" Archie heard someone yell. An earthquake? Here? In the Moving City of Cheyenne? The shaking got worse, and Archie fell down. Glass windows shattered, wood splintered, and metal groaned. Then, as suddenly as it had started, the wailing and shaking stopped, and the city was still and quiet again but for the rumble of the Wheel of the Sun and the cries of the injured.

Tall Bull helped Archie to his feet.

"Does that happen often?" Archie asked.

"No," Tall Bull said. "Never."

One of the Dog Soldiers cried out, and they turned. The conical roof on top of the clothiers exploded in a burst of flames as a gas line broke, and the second floor of the shop started to go with it. Archie rushed for the front door.

"You can't go in there!" Tall Bull called to him. "It's going to collapse!"

"Mrs. Moffett's in there!" Archie called back. "I have to save her!"

Archie ran inside. Mr. Moffett was hurrying for the door, but the ceiling above her shuddered, shifted, and collapsed. Mrs. Moffett was knocked to the floor, but Archie caught the roof before it could crush her.

"Mrs. Moffett! Mrs. Moffett, are you all right?" Archie yelled.

"Yes—yes. I'm all right," she said, her voice hoarse. "The fox girl—she was here, but she got away. You must—you must go after her!"

Archie held the burning ceiling above him. The fire didn't hurt him, and the weight was nothing, but he knew it could break apart in his hands any second now. "Are there any more people inside?" he asked.

Mrs. Moffett coughed. "I don't know," she said. "Forget them. Get the lantern!"

"Get to the exit!" he told her.

Moffett crawled away, and Archie tossed the burning wreckage into a wall full of men's suits. He would go after the fox girl, but not before he made sure there was no one left in the building. Archie climbed the burning stairs to what was left of the second floor, but he found no one, not even bodies. Fire raged throughout the shop, and he heard the sirens of fire airships. The staircase collapsed as he turned to go, and he jumped out a window into the back-street instead. The boardwalk cracked as he landed, but it held.

Huddled in a doorway across the alley were two men and three women wearing tailors' tape measures around their necks like scarves.

"Were you in there?" Archie asked. "Did you see a girl with a fox tail?"

"No," one of the women said. "But there was a Dog Soldier. He ran upstairs just before the earthquake started. He helped me get out from under a sewing machine that had fallen on me, then got us all out to the fire escape before the gas line exploded. I'd be dead now if it wasn't for him."

Archie knew no Dog Soldiers had been in the building with Mrs. Moffett and the fox girl. That could mean only one thing. "Where'd he go?" Archie asked.

The woman pointed to a spiral staircase down to the next level, and Archie ran for it. It collapsed when he was partway down it, crashing down on itself for three levels before spitting Archie out in a heap of twisted brass and broken wood into a Harley–Dancing Sun monowheel factory. He looked up into the face of the startled fox girl, and she dashed away.

"Wait!" Archie called, but she had already jumped into one of the monowheels. It roared to life, and she tore off through the fac-tory, knocking over tables full of parts as she struggled to steer the thing. Archie chased her until she smashed through a wall. Sun-light spilled inside the factory, and the monowheel went sailing through the air. It slammed down onto the hard ground of the prai-rie, wobbled, balanced itself, and sped away.

Archie ran to one of the railed balconies along the edge of the city, where he watched the monowheel tear off into the distance, trailing dust and smoke behind it. Around the balcony from one end ran Mrs. Moffett; Tall Bull and the Dog Soldiers ran around from the other side, growling menacingly at him. Archie didn't understand—were they mad about him letting the thief get away, or because she had torn up five levels of a city block?

"She's getting away!" Mrs. Moffett cried, and Archie heard the scary anger in her voice he'd heard before at the Cahokia Arms.

"We'll catch her!" Archie said. He put his fingers in his mouth and blew a sharp whistle, and in moments the bald brass head of Buster the steam man appeared in front of them, whistling happily.

"You called?" Clyde's voice boomed from the steam man.

"Clyde! Buster! The fox girl, she's getting away in a monowheel!" Archie pointed at the dust and smoke in the distance.

"We're on it!" Clyde said. "Deploying aeronaut scout!"

The hatch on top of Buster's head flew open, and Sings-In-The-Night climbed out and spread her great black wings.

Beside Archie, Mrs. Moffett gasped. "No—no, it can't be!" she cried. She put her hands up and took a step back like she had seen a ghost.

Sings-In-The-Night froze, staring at Mrs. Moffett. "*Mina?*" she said.

Archie's skin iced over. Mina was the name of the girl Sings-In-The-Night said had been the leader of their Forged League, one of the children the Septemberists had experimented on. The one who had turned on the humans in Beaver Run, killing them all and destroying their town.

Mina.

*Philo*mena *Moffett.*

"But—but I saw you die!" Sings-In-The-Night said.

Archie took a step back toward the Dog Soldiers, and they growled again. But they weren't growling at him, he realized at last. They were growling at Mrs. Moffett.

Mrs. Moffett turned on Archie and the Dog Soldiers, her eyes wide and wild. She wasn't just angry; she was insane. She rose as if lifted by hot air balloon, and that's when Archie saw them—thick, purple-black tentacles, dozens of them, writhing out from under her enormous floor-length bustle. One of them whipped out, wrapped around Archie's neck, and tossed him over the side. Sings-In-The-Night caught him before he hit the ground, and Buster caught the Dog Soldiers as she threw them over the side too, but none of them could do anything to stop her from taking a deep breath and shrieking at the mountains they were passing by. Her scream was an ear-splitting wail like the one Archie had heard during the earthquake, and now he knew where it had come from. Tentacles wrapped around the rail, chest thrust forward, fists clenched at her side, Mina Moffett emitted a howl from her throat that warped the air like waves of heat and ripped up the ground like a steam plow. Her shriek widened, churning up more and more ground until it hit the mountain, shaking rocks loose in an avalanche.

Slowly, dully, Archie understood what she was doing.

"Sings-In-The-Night! Fly me back! We have to stop her!" Archie cried.

But it was too late. The mountain exploded, and the Mangle-born called the Crooked Man crawled up through the rubble and howled.

21

Baron Samedi howled with laughter and smacked a serving girl on the bottom. "More rum!" he cried. "More rum for me and my distinguished guests!"

Samedi's "distinguished guests" were three pretty young women he'd stolen off the streets. They laughed with him and smiled, but there was fear in their eyes, and they kept stealing glances at the zombi guards at the doors. Samedi grabbed one of them by the wrist and pulled her onto his lap.

"Drink!" he said, tipping a goblet of rum to her lips. She choked a little as she swallowed, rum dribbling down her chin, and Samedi bellowed again.

At the other end of the table, watching all this without a hint of emotion, was Queen Theodosia. She sat with her hands in her lap, doing and saying nothing to stop Samedi. She might have been in shock—Hachi couldn't fault her for that—but Hachi still hated her for not protesting, for not fighting back.

Hachi nodded to Fergus, and together, dressed in maid uniforms and bonnets to hide who they were, they wheeled in big serving carts filled with silver-plated dishes. Baron Samedi's palace was crawling with zombi, but the one place he still needed humans was in the kitchen. Zombi didn't make very good cooks; they liked all their food raw.

"Dinner is served, my lord," Hachi said, using a small, frightened voice.

"Aah! At last!" Samedi said. He pushed the girl off him and rubbed his hands together as Hachi set a covered dish in front of him. She lifted the lid and tried to turn away, but Samedi's hand whipped out and caught her.

"Wait," he said. "I smell salt."

Laveau had warned them about this. The taste of salt drove zombi back into their graves, and would make the Lord of the Dead weak enough to push him out of Blavatsky's body. But Samedi knew his own weakness and was crafty. He'd already gotten rid of every grain of salt in the palace and commanded the kitchen staff never to use it, unless they wanted to join his growing zombi army.

Samedi pushed the plate of deep-fried crawfish at one of the girls. "Taste it," he said.

With a frightened glance at Hachi, the girl picked up one of the crawfish and tasted it.

"Is it salted?" Samedi asked.

The girl nodded tearfully, her eyes apologizing to Hachi.

Samedi pulled back Hachi's bonnet and roared with laughter when he saw her face. She struggled to pull away, but he held on tightly to her.

"Oh no, girl. You're not getting away this time! Guards, lock the doors!" He laughed again as she tried and failed to yank her hand away. "I knew you'd try something like this, girl! Old Baron

Samedi, he know all the tricks." He pulled her closer, his face suddenly dark and serious. "But he also know you, Hachi Emartha. He know you never have just one trick."

"You're right," Hachi told him. "But I have to admit, this one was Fergus's idea."

"Who's Fergus?" Samedi asked.

Near the middle of the table, Fergus lifted the lid of a silver platter with a flourish.

"*Et voila!*" Fergus said in a very poor Acadian accent. "Tonight I have prepared for you a meal of sautéed sodium on a bed of finely chopped chlorine."

On the plate was a shiny silver block of metal, a little smaller than a lacrosse ball, nestled in an inch of white powder.

Samedi sniffed. "That's not salt," he said. "And whatever it is, you'll never get me to eat it."

"No, it's not salt. Not yet," Fergus said. "And I don't need you to eat it." Fergus put his finger in a glass of water on the table and flicked one drop onto the block of sodium. It erupted into a ball of fire so big and so bright, it blew all the girls to the floor and sent Fergus spinning away.

Baron Samedi tried to stand, but Hachi wrenched his hands behind his chair and tied them together. "Oh no, Baron. This time it's *you* who's not going anywhere."

Fergus's chemical reaction roared and grew, catching the table on fire. White-black smoke billowed out from it, filling the air, and Hachi could feel it burning the back of her throat, could taste its sting on her tongue. Sodium plus chloride made NaCl—salt. Or in this case, *salt vapor*. Samedi didn't have to eat anything; if they waited long enough, Blavatsky would breathe in enough salt to drive Samedi out of her.

"Guards!" Samedi choked. "Guards! Kill them! Kill them all!"

Fergus ducked behind the chair with Hachi, shielding himself from the massive inferno on the table, and they hastily tied bandanas around their faces to block the salt vapor.

"Nice trick, but you didn't say it was going to explode in a huge fiery ball of death!" Hachi yelled at him.

"Right," Fergus yelled back. "That reminds me. I should warn you, it's going to explode in a huge fiery ball of death."

Samedi tried to call for help again, but Blavatsky's body was racked by a coughing fit. The zombi guards at the door had heard him the first time, though, and were shambling toward them—including General Andrew Jackson, cutlass drawn.

Hachi pushed Laveau's voodoo doll of Blavatsky into Fergus's hands. "Get Baron Samedi out of her," Hachi told him. "I'll take care of the zombi."

To kill a zombi well and good, Laveau had told them, you had to stuff its mouth with salt and sew it shut. Either that or kill the bokor who created it. But zombi didn't breathe, so they weren't getting the mouthful of salt vapor that Samedi was, and Hachi wasn't going to kill Blavatsky—not yet—so she couldn't get rid of them that way either. And because they were dead already, they would keep coming no matter what she did to them.

But that didn't mean she couldn't make it harder for them.

Hachi pulled a machete out of the serving cart and lopped off the head of the first zombi to reach her. The head went bouncing across the floor and thunked against the wall, its dead, empty eyes staring up at the ceiling. Its body didn't die, but without eyes to guide it, it wandered away from the table, arms still groping for her.

Hachi smiled. This was going to be fun.

As she whacked off the zombi heads, she glanced back to make sure everything was going according to plan with the voodoo doll. Laveau—wearing her old body this time—had sewn the voodoo doll together herself, stuffing it full of a strange assortment of ingredients, including a healthy chunk of Blavatsky's hair and a tiny doll made to look like Baron Samedi. Fergus had cut into the thing and was pulling the Baron Samedi doll out of it now. If Laveau was right, the salt in Blavatsky's mouth and the Samedi doll yanked out of her voodoo doll would be enough to knock the Baron off his horse.

Queen Theodosia snatched a knife up from the table and ran at Fergus.

"*Fergus!*" Hachi cried, too far away to protect him.

He looked up too late to blast her. She raised the knife over her head. Fergus flinched and closed his eyes. Theodosia brought the blade down with a vicious stab.

Shunk!

She buried the knife in Blavatsky's chest.

"*NO!*" Hachi cried. No! Blavatsky couldn't die! Not yet! Hachi ran for Blavatsky, but Theodosia twirled her hand in the air, and suddenly there was a storm in the room. Lighting flashed and thunder boomed, and rain and wind put out the fire and blew the salt vapor away. Hachi put an arm across her face to protect herself, and Fergus hobbled over to join her.

"Who is she?" Hachi cried out over the storm. "What's she done?"

"I am Maman Brigitte, this toekay ragpicker's wife!" Theodosia said in a rich, thick voice that wasn't her own. "I come through when he did, and I watch him the whole time while I ride this no-'count 'queen.' Always he come to the real world, and when he come back I ask him, 'You make time with other girls?' And he say, 'No, of course not, Maman Brigitte! I got no other woman but you.' Liar! I catch you out this time! And now Maman Brigitte, she punish you. Now I kill you before they can push you out, and you not come back for a dozen-dozen years! See if you sorry then!"

"No!" Hachi said. She pulled away from Fergus, but too late. All around them, the zombi collapsed to the floor. Their bokor, Helena Blavatsky, was dead.

Maman Brigitte swept up and out the window on a gust of air, cackling, and Hachi ran to Blavatsky. She pulled out the knife and beat on the woman's chest, trying to bring her back to life. Fergus tried to pull her away, but she fought him off.

"I can do better!" he told her.

She backed away and Fergus put his fingers to Blavatsky's chest. *Zap!* Blavatsky's body lurched in the chair, but she didn't wake up. Fergus did it again—*zap!*—and again—*zap!*—but Blavatsky never stirred.

She was well and truly gone, and with her went Hachi's only chance at finding out who else was there at Chuluota, and why her father had been killed.

"I'm sorry," Fergus told her. He took Hachi into his arms, and she let him, glad of the rain that still poured in the room if only because it hid the tears of anguish that streamed down her face.

Escaping airships shot into the air from all over the Moving City of Cheyenne as though someone had just let go of handfuls of balloons at a party. But if this was a party, it was the absolute worst one Archie had ever attended.

The Crooked Man, a hideous, malformed coyote creature standing taller than the city, was climbing its way out of the rubble of its Roman puzzle trap, free once more. Worse, boulders from the smashed mountain had rolled down into the narrow canyon Cheyenne was passing through, blocking the tracks and trapping the city with the monster unless it could back out. The city engineers were trying to bring Cheyenne to a stop, but halting a locomotive the size of a city *quickly* was impossible.

"Mina Moffett is probably getting away on one of those airships," Sings-In-The-Night said, rejoining Archie and Clyde inside Buster.

"If we want to save Cheyenne, we have to let her go. For now," Archie said. "That's why she did it." Archie watched the Mangleborn pulling itself out of the mountain, which sent more rock avalanching into the city's path. "We have to get those tracks clear, at least far enough for the city to stop!"

"We better do something about that big dog too!" Clyde said.

"I think the Dog Soldiers may have the answer to that," Archie said.

High above them, Howler-On-The-Hill, the enormous raycannon, was slowly turning toward the Mangleborn. While it took aim, Buster tossed aside the smaller boulders that lay on the tracks and Archie punched the larger ones into gravel. The giant wheels of the Moving City of Cheyenne crept closer and closer, groaning and squealing as the engineers threw on the brakes.

"We're never gonna make it!" Clyde called down to Archie. He was right—they were making more room, but they would never be able to clear the landslide off the tracks completely. Not before the city ran into it.

"We have to push it!" Archie yelled.

"*Push it?* You mean the *city?* Are you crazy?" Clyde asked.

"Probably," Archie muttered.

Jandal a Haad, a voice boomed in his head, and Archie was staggered by a vision that hit him like a steamhammer. Suddenly it was night, and the Crooked Man stood over the glowing, sparking, lektric wreck of the Moving City of Cheyenne in the distance. Around Archie were six other figures, all much shorter and smaller than he was. Archie recognized one of them: Finn McCool, the Celtic warrior. And another: Robin Hood, the Anglish thief. This was the Medieval League that had risen to put down the Mangleborn a thousand years after the Roman League had beaten the monsters before. But this had to be decades, *centuries* before Europe had "rediscovered" the New World! How were they here then?

"Rabbi Loew," said Sir Galahad, "we have need of our shadow, methinks."

An old man wearing a long white beard, a tall round hat, long black robes, and a white prayer scarf reached high up to Archie's forehead and carved something into his clay skin.

"Destroy the Mangleborn!" Rabbi Loew told him. "Golem, destroy!"

Archie felt his arms and legs come to life, and he lumbered forward, swinging his mighty fists at anyone and anything. Kaveh the Blacksmith turned him away with a vibrating shield, and Finn McCool beat him back with his sword until Rabbi Loew could finally get him pointed at the Crooked Man.

Then Archie was outside himself and saw the golem for what it was: a giant hulking stone man with hollow eyes, no mouth, and metal braces bolted onto its body to keep the cracks in it from splitting wider. This was Rabbi Loew's monster. The League's shadow. A mindless creature made of clay: so simple, so inhuman, that it couldn't even tell its enemies from its friends. This was what the Crooked Man thought Archie was.

Jandal a Haad, the Crooked Man sang-laughed.

No. I am not a mindless monster! I am not a creature made of clay. I am a human being! A boy! Archie cried, but no words came from his mouthless clay face.

"A little help here!" Clyde yelled, and Archie was back in the present, the Crooked Man still freeing itself from its prison and Cheyenne not a smoking wreck but a living, moving city.

A city that needed saving.

Buster had his hands on the outside of the city and was pushing against it, trying to slow it, but Cheyenne was still creeping toward the mountain of rock on its tracks. Archie scrambled up the boulders, grabbed a deck of the city as it inched toward him, and pushed. The metal deck bent in his hands, and the city kept coming, but he could feel it slowing.

"We're doing it! *We're doing it!*" Archie yelled.

Still the deck kept coming, until it pushed Archie over and pinned him to the rocks behind him. It pushed and pushed, crushing him between the rock and the city, but he didn't break, and he didn't die.

Jandal a Haad, a voice whispered inside him, and this time the voice was his own.

"I'm *not* a monster," Archie cried, shoving and punching the city. "I'm not! I'm not a golem! I'm not a stone robot!" He pushed and punched again and again, wrecking the deck and denting the huge iron belly of the city. "I'm not! I'm not! I'll destroy you! I'll destroy you all!"

"Archie—Archie!" a big brass steam man yelled at him. "Archie, we stopped the city, but you're wrecking it! Stop!"

Archie stumbled back among the rocks, losing his footing and falling. That made him madder, and he picked up one of the boulders and hurled it at a bird girl who hovered in the air nearby. She dodged it easily, and Archie picked up another to throw at her, even madder for having missed.

"Archie!" the bird girl cried.

He started to throw the giant rock, but the air crackled and exploded—*HAROOOOOOOOOOO!*—and the Moving City of Cheyenne slammed into him, burying him a hundred yards into the rock pile.

The next thing Archie knew, Buster and Sings-In-The Night were pushing and lifting rocks off him.

"What—what happened?" Archie asked.

"They shot that giant raycannon at Dog Boy," Clyde told him.

"Dog Boy?" Archie said, still dazed.

"That coyote Mangleborn. Turns out that raycannon's got one helluva kick. We better clear out before they shoot it again."

"It didn't take it out?" Archie asked Sings-In-The-Night as she lifted him from the rubble.

"No," she said. There was fear in her eyes, and doubt written all over her face. Archie knew that look: He'd seen it on Hachi's and Fergus's faces after he'd attacked them in Florida.

"I went crazy again, didn't I?" he asked her.

"Yes. I've seen all my friends become monsters, just like that," she told him. "And I don't want to see it happen to another."

"Me either," Archie told her. He had to find a way to control his anger, or he would do worse than become a monster—he would hurt his friends.

HAROOOOOOOOOOO! The Howler-On-The-Hill roared again, and this time Archie watched its massive blue beam of aether hit the Mangleborn square in the chest.

It had absolutely no effect.

"It's not doing a thing to it!" Clyde said.

"But . . . how?" Archie said. A raycannon that big could blow a hole in a mountain.

There wasn't time to figure it out. The Crooked Man tore itself free of the rubble and lurched on its broken, mangled legs toward the trapped city of Cheyenne. They had to come up with some other way of defeating it, and fast. If only Hachi were here! She was so good at coming up with plans.

"The other side of the canyon," Clyde said when they were back inside Buster. "We have to bring it down on him!"

"How?" Sings-In-The-Night asked.

"All that dynamite," Clyde said. "You said they had crates of it."

"Yeah," Archie said. "But what about Cheyenne? It'll be buried too!"

"Not if they turn the Howler on that pile of rocks and get going again," Clyde said. "Sings-In-The Night, we'll need you to set the dynamite up high, on the ridge. I'll help the Dog Soldiers clear the rocks."

The Crooked Man dragged an enormous clawed hand through

the other side of the city, shredding metal and wood. Fire exploded from gas lines, and broken bodies spilled from the city.

"And I suppose I'll keep the Mangleborn busy," Archie said.

Clyde and Sings-In-The-Night had that look on their faces again, like they were amazed by him and scared of him all at the same time, but they didn't argue with him. That's what worried Archie the most.

Sings-In-The-Night flew Archie high above Cheyenne and the Mangleborn. It howled as it tore into the city again.

"You sure about this?" Sings-In-The-Night asked.

"It's what I was made for, however it was I was made," Archie said. "Let's just do it."

Sings-In-The-Night dive-bombed the Crooked Man, letting Archie go at the last second before pulling up and flying away. Archie threw a punch at the Mangleborn's face as he collided with it, knocking the thing back. It howled in pain and fury, and Archie grabbed at its tree-branch-sized porcupine spikes to stop his fall. *THOOM. THOOM. THOOM.* He hammered at the thing's chest, breaking off some of the spines. He was like a flea in the Crooked Man's hair, but he was a flea with a heck of a bite.

The Mangleborn swiped at him with a claw. It missed Archie and tore a gaping purple wound in itself.

Archie laughed. "If you've got an itch, scratch it. I'll bet Mrs. DeMarcus used to say that too."

HAROOOOOOOOOOOO! Archie felt the crackle of the city's giant raycannon before he heard it, but the beam didn't hit him. So Clyde had gotten them working on the rockfall already. Good.

The Crooked Man roared again, but instead of swiping at Archie with its claws, it snapped him up in its huge tooth-filled mouth, shaking him like a rope toy. Archie's head spun, and he thought he might be sick, but otherwise it didn't hurt.

Jandal a Haad! The Crooked Man screamed in his head, no

longer laughing or whispering. *Jandal a Haad, go away!* With a flick of its head, it tossed him into the wall of the canyon. Archie slammed into it, knocking rock loose with him as he fell all the way to the ground with a *thud*.

HAROOOOOOOOOOOO! The Howler-On-The-Hill fired again, and this time Archie heard a cheer go up from the city. The tracks must have been cleared.

High above him, the Mangleborn turned its ugly head toward Cheyenne and took a step toward the city.

Archie dragged himself to his feet. "Wait, Crooked Man. The Jandal a Haad isn't done with you yet."

Archie threaded his fingers together and slammed his fists down on the hard-packed dirt floor of the canyon. *WHAM!* The earth bucked and rippled, and the Mangleborn lost its balance. *THOOM.* It slammed into the ground, knocking Archie to the floor with it.

Archie propped himself up, tired but unbroken, and so did the Mangleborn.

"Ready for Round Three?" Archie said wearily.

But then Clyde and Buster were there, straddling the Mangleborn and punching it with both big brass fists. Right, left, right, left—*WANG! WANG! WANG! WANG!* The Mangleborn swiped at Buster, its claws screeching across his brass chest, but Buster kept on busting.

"Tag, your turn," Archie said. He had just let his head thunk to the ground to rest when something big and black fluttered down over him, blocking out the sun. "Time to go?" Archie asked.

"Only if you don't want to get buried under a mountain of rock," Sings-In-The-Night said. She picked him up and flew past Buster, signaling that it was time to run. Behind them, the dynamite began to explode in a chain, following them up the canyon. *BOOM! BOOM! BOOM! BOOM! BOOM!*

Sings-In-The-Night hovered with Archie just beyond the canyon, but Buster hadn't followed them.

"What's he waiting for?" she said. "He's going to get buried with the monster!"

Clyde and Buster were still sitting on top of the Mangleborn, but they weren't punching it anymore. What was Clyde doing? Was he just trying to keep the Mangleborn down until the last possible second? Surely it couldn't get up in time.

BOOM! BOOM! BOOM! BOOM! Rocks and boulders exploded from the canyon wall beside them, and finally Buster started to move. Stone beat down on them, almost knocking Buster over as he ran, but he cleared the avalanche just in time. With an earth-shaking roar that might have been the Mangleborn and might have been the rockslide, the Crooked Man disappeared under a mountain of stone.

Archie, Sings-In-The-Night, and Clyde watched the rock pile from Buster's bridge to see if the Mangleborn would rise again, but it didn't budge.

"What happened back there?" Archie asked Clyde. "Why'd you wait?"

"It was Buster," Clyde said. He ran a hand along a brass rail, as though comforting a frightened dog. "We were whaling on him, givin' him the old one-two, as Mrs. DeMarcus used to say, and then he just stopped paying attention to me. It's like . . . it's like that big dog thing was mesmerizing him somehow. Talking to him. He locked up, and I couldn't do a thing with him."

"The pictures on the wall, in the Crooked Man's Crooked House. It showed all these little dogs dancing around him," Archie said. "That thing must have some kind of crazy effect on dogs."

"Well, I thought we were goners, but then suddenly Buster was listening to me again, and we got the heck out of there. I think it was all that training with the Dog Soldiers. You're such a good dog, Buster." Clyde patted a console full of gauges. "Good boy!"

Buster whistle-barked, and they hiked around the Crooked Man's new prison to rejoin the Moving City of Cheyenne.

"I can't tell you how grateful we are," Chief Black Kettle told them. He had his hands full coordinating rescue and repair efforts, but he and Tall Bull took the time to meet them at the side rail of the city. "Cheyenne owes you an incredible debt."

"Just promise me you'll go back and pile more rocks on that thing," Archie said.

"We will," Black Kettle told them. "And when we lay new tracks, we will go far, far around it."

"And Mina Moffett? She's gone?" Sings-In-The-Night asked.

Tall Bull nodded. "On one of the airships that fled the city. We know not where."

"I do," Archie said. "Ametokai. The Japanese city in the northwest. If that's where the lantern is headed, that's where she'll go too."

"Be careful there," Black Kettle told them. "Their chief—the daimyo, they call him—rules with an iron fist."

"That's okay," Clyde said, raising Buster's fist. "We got two brass ones."

Black Kettle smiled. "I would say you do. And now we must go to the aid of our city. Be well, my friends. May your wheel ever turn."

Clyde turned Buster northwest. "Well, like Mrs. DeMarcus says, the longest journey begins with the shortest step."

Sings-In-The-Night opened the hatch at the top of Buster's head to go and fly solo again. Before she took off, she looked back at both of them.

"I'm with you," she said.

"You mean you'll come to Ametokai with us?" Archie asked.

"I mean, I will join your team," Sings-In-The-Night said. "We must stop Mina before she hurts anyone else. And we must stop her from getting that lantern."

Buster stepped back as a giant brass sword the size of an oak tree whistled by, scraping his chest. Clyde swung the steam man's huge left fist, but the meka-samurai ducked and slammed the hilt of its sword into Buster's chest, sending the steam man staggering.

"Hey! Whoa!" Clyde said through his speaking tube. "I told you! We're not here to attack you! We want to see the daimyo!"

The pilot of the meka-samurai either didn't understand, or didn't care. He wasn't going to let Buster get anywhere near the Japanese city behind him. Ametokai stood like a mountain on the shore of the Great Western Sea, an emerald-and-ivory jewel sparkling in the late-summer sun. Whitewashed buildings with curved, peaked roofs hid behind tall green pines and firs, rising in a mound that mirrored Mt. Tacoma in the distance. Aerial tramways hung from low, swooping cables that stretched from the peak of the city down to the patchwork of low-lying rice fields around it, and colorful gaslit signs written in the squiggly, brush-stroke language of the Japans hung from shops in the narrow, crowded streets.

Atop the city, like Mt. Tacoma's snowcap, was a tall white castle in the Oriental style, a layer cake of curved roofs and fortified battlements, watching over everything below. Clyde, Archie, and Sings-In-The-Night had traveled for days to get here, but now this meka-samurai threatened to send them packing again.

While Buster was still righting himself, the meka-samurai lowered its massive shoulder and charged. *Clang!* Buster teetered and fell backward into a rice field with a *fwoosh* that sent water over the sides in giant waves, swamping a row of farmers' houses. Archie went tumbling again, crashing around the captain's quarters to which he'd just carried Mr. Rivets.

"Mr. Rivets! Are you all right?" he asked.

"Yes, Master Archie," Mr. Rivets said, picking himself up from the smashed ruins of Custer's writing desk. "And I assume it is pointless to ask you the same question?"

"Unbroken, as usual," Archie said. "Come on. We have to get you to the bridge."

Mr. Rivets had put in a Japanese Language talent card (by himself), and Archie was trying to get him to the speaking trumpet, where he could tell the meka-samurai they weren't an enemy.

Sings-In-The-Night landed on Buster's head as Archie pulled Mr. Rivets onto the bridge.

"It's the fox girl!" she told them. She pointed to the shoulder of the enormous meka-samurai, and there she was, perched like a cat in a tree. Archie almost thought he could see her smiling at them.

The meka-samurai lifted its foot to stomp Buster's head, and Sings-In-The-Night jumped away into the air. Clyde caught the foot in one of Buster's giant hands. Metal sheered and groaned as the meka-samurai pushed them down farther and farther into the mud.

"Hang on!" Clyde yelled. The hand holding the foot disappeared into Buster's enormous forearm, and Archie felt the hair on the back of his neck stand up as the giant raycannon's aggregators charged. BWAAAAT! The meka-samurai went flying backward with the blast, landing in another rice paddy with a booming splash.

Clyde hauled Buster to his feet, water and mud and rice plants sluicing off him. Below them, the green-and-brown meka-samurai lay motionless in the mud. It was two or three stories shorter than Buster, but wider, with an armored chest, wide, flaring shoulder guards that came to points, and a metal "skirt" that covered the top part of its legs. Its head was low and wide too, the steam man's face hidden in a helmet with a large raindrop shape etched into it.

The fox girl was nowhere to be seen.

"Tell it we're not here to attack!" Clyde said.

Mr. Rivets said something in Japanese through the speaking trumpet, and they waited. The meka-samurai slowly rose to its feet and sheathed its sword. Japanese words boomed back, and they waited for Mr. Rivets to translate.

"They say we appeared to be a *daikaiju*, which, roughly translated, means 'giant strange monster.' It was this beast they thought they were fighting. They are quite surprised to learn we are not a *daikaiju* at all, but another steam man like themselves."

"The fox girl," Clyde said. "She must have been making them see something else!"

"A Mangleborn," Archie said. "No wonder they attacked us!"

Mr. Rivets spoke again, and the meka-samurai bowed.

"What'd you say?" Archie asked.

"I told them we could explain, and they have granted us an audience with their leader, the Daimyo."

Clyde had Buster return the bow, and after Sings-In-The-Night rejoined them, the meka-samurai led Buster to its repair yard on the far side of the city. From there, they could see the choppy, dark Great Western Sea and the submarine docks that connected the Japanese colony to its homeland across the ocean.

The daimyo of Ametokai met them in a plain, rectangular room with white paper walls and doors. The floors were carpeted with tightly woven reed mats, and they all sat on cushions on the floor instead of chairs. The only decorations in the room were a black-and-white ink-brush painting of Mt. Tacoma on one of the walls and a vase of white roses on the low table in front of them.

The daimyo was a stern-looking man with light brown skin, a sharp, hawkish nose, and a high, round forehead. He wore a black silk robe, black silk pants, and black socks with reed-and-wood sandals. His jet-black hair was tied up into a tight knot that stuck out the back of his head, and over his eyes he wore a pair of brass glasses with rubber tubes that stuck out the sides, and green lenses that ticked and whirred.

A clockwork woman made to look as though she was wearing a long, loose robe tied tightly around the waist brought a tray with a teakettle and small handleless teacups and set it on the low table between them.

"This fox girl, you say she has the power to make one see whatever she wishes?" the daimyo asked. He spoke Anglish with a thick accent, blurring his *r* and *l* sounds.

"Yeah," Clyde said. He had quickly taken on the role of spokesman for the group, which made Archie both relieved and a little disappointed. "She tricked my whole regiment into thinking we were under attack by the Sioux, just like she made your steam man think we were a Mangleborn."

"A *daikaiju*," Mr. Rivets interpreted.

"Ah. *Hai*. That is why Metal Samurai Gunray was built, along with all the others. To fight the *daikaiju*."

"Others? You mean you got more than one of those samurai steam men?" Clyde asked.

"Not in Ametokai, no," the daimyo said. "But in Nippon, our homeland, each city has its own metal samurai to protect it. Edo, our capital, has seven."

"And, excuse me," Archie said. "These *daikaiju*—what we could call Mangleborn—everybody knows about them?"

"How can they not?" the daimyo said. "They come up from the ground; they climb out of volcanoes; they emerge from the sea. And always they destroy. Our cities burned in their footsteps until we created the metal samurai to protect us."

Archie couldn't believe it. A whole country—a whole *civilization*—aware of the Mangleborn, and able to deal with that knowledge? Better, a whole civilization working together to defend themselves against the Mangleborn! The Septemberist Society had kept the existence of the Mangleborn a secret for centuries so people could live their lives without knowing the horrors that lay just beneath the surface. But what if everyone knew, like they did in the Japans?

"For two hundred years, we closed our borders, fighting off any advance from the *daikaiju*. We held out, but the Cathay Empire on the mainland did not. There, Darkness has fallen. There, the *daikaiju* rule."

"Just like in Europe," Sings-In-The-Night said.

"Nippon is a small island compared to the might of Cathay. We hold, but our resources wear thin. That is why we built the Beikoku colony," the daimyo told them. "Here in the Americas, where there are no *daikaiju*, we grow rice to feed our warriors, and in Ametokai we build more metal samurai and send them across the sea to protect Nippon."

"Oh, they're here all right," Clyde said. "You'll want to keep that Metal Samurai Gunray on duty 24/7, and that's a fact. We just fought one of those monsters at the Moving City of Cheyenne."

"This is most distressing news," the daimyo said. "But it is a fox girl you seek in Ametokai, not a *daikaiju*?"

Clyde told the daimyo all about the girl, and about Mrs. Moffett.

"We need to find this fox girl before Mrs. Moffett does," Archie added.

"Moffett is a monster," Sings-In-The-Night said. The daimyo's green glasses clicked and whirred as he studied her. She had hidden her backward bird legs under a long skirt, but there was no disguising her big black wings, which she kept folded on her back.

"I am learning that the Americas have many more monsters than at first we thought," the daimyo said.

Did he mean Sings-In-The-Night? She looked away, and Archie bristled. He was about to ask the daimyo exactly what he meant when the leader called over one of his human samurai guards.

"If your thief and monster woman are in the city, they are no doubt with the Daimyo Under the City—or will be soon," he said.

"The Daimyo Under the City?" Clyde asked.

"That is what they call the man who rules the Ametokai criminal underworld," the daimyo said. "Though we have tried for years, we have been unable to bring him to justice. But we know some of the establishments in which he operates. Take them to the Pike Place Market," the daimyo told the guard. "Do everything you can to help them find the Daimyo Under the City."

The samurai bowed low, and their audience was at an end. The samurai ushered them out, and he and four other samurai led them out of the castle and down into the winding roads of the city.

"What he said back there, about there being a lot of monsters in the Americas, that was clinker," Archie told Sings-In-The-Night.

"Yeah," Clyde said. "I wanted to give him a big brass knuckle sandwich."

"No," she said. "He's right. I am a monster, just like Moffett."

Archie stopped her. "No. Having bird legs or stone skin doesn't make you a monster. It's not Mrs. Moffett's tentacles that make her evil. It's what you *do* that makes you good or bad. The same thing happened to you that happened to her, but she's using it as an excuse to hurt other people, and you're using it as a way to *help* other people. She's the monster, not you."

"Yeah," said Clyde. "What he said."

Sings-In-The-Night didn't argue, but she didn't look convinced either.

On the way to the market, they passed coffee shop after coffee shop.

"Sheesh, how many coffee shops does one city need?" Clyde asked.

At last they came to a large market, with row after row of steam-wagons filled with fruits and vegetables grown in the countryside and sold in the city. Mixed in among the produce sellers were spice sellers and tinkers, musicians and fishmongers, secondhand Tik Tok sellers and book stalls.

The samurai led them to an indoor coffee house in the market called Queequeg's, which had a green-and-white sign featuring a man with a harpoon. Inside were a number of small wooden tables, three of them occupied by scruffy, bearded sailors nursing steaming black cups of coffee. A strange Asian plinking music played on a phonograph in the corner, and a Japanese woman in a plain gray robe wiped down a counter at the back. One of the samurai nodded toward her as though she was the one they should ask about the fox girl and Mrs. Moffett.

Archie had just stepped up to the bar when he heard the *shing* of swords being drawn behind them. The samurai guards pointed their swords right at him and his friends.

"What's going on?" Clyde asked.

The other customers in the coffee shop got up and hurried out.

"We've been betrayed," Archie said. "*Again.*" He stepped between his friends and the samurai. "I have to warn you right now," he told the guards, "this isn't going to work out so great for you. I'm—"

Before he could say "invulnerable," the floor dropped out from under Archie and he fell into darkness.

24

It was a dark and stormy night.

Fergus watched through the window of Marie Laveau's shop as a hurricane raged over New Orleans. The storm drains were handling the rain so far, but the streets were already little rivers. Soon there would be so much water that the storm drains would back up, and the city would be flooded. And if the levees that held back the Mississippi River or Lake Pontchartrain or the Atlantis Ocean broke . . .

Fergus shook his head. From an engineering point of view, New Orleans seemed like a terrible place to build a city.

"We have to stop Maman Brigitte," Marie Laveau said. She was the middle-aged version of herself again and wore a much simpler white dress with a red-and-gold headscarf. Her two creepy masked assistants hovered in the shadows behind her.

"But how?" Hachi asked. She was pacing the shop, her thoughts, as always, on her ultimate goal. "We can't use Fergus's salt vapor trick again. She'll see it coming a mile away."

"We don't even know where she is," Fergus reminded her.

"Maybe she's sitting on Theodosia's throne. She's riding her body," Hachi said.

Laveau shook her head. "Maman Brigitte, she's not like her husband. She doesn't need to put on a show. We're more likely to find her in a cemetery."

"Then we'll search the cemeteries," Hachi said, heading for the door.

Fergus stepped in front of her. "Let's come up with a bit better plan than slogging through cemeteries at night in the middle of a hurricane looking for a woman with a Manglespawn spirit riding her, eh?" he said.

Hachi frowned, but she gave in. Fergus knew she would rather do something useless than sit around and do nothing, but she was also smart enough not to go spinning off like a loose shackle bolt.

"Look, since we're not rushing off to go kill an invisible beastie at the moment, maybe it's time I gave you something," Fergus told Hachi.

He went to his satchel behind the counter and pulled out a small leather-wrapped gift.

Hachi held it in both hands. "What is it?" she asked.

"Well, the general idea with a present is that you unwrap it, and then you find out what's inside it," he told her.

She frowned at him and pulled loose the knot. The leather fell away, and a little wind-up elephant with wings lay in the palm of her hand.

Hachi choked back a sob and put a hand to her mouth. "Tusker! Tusker—you put him back together!"

"I did better than that," Fergus said. He took the tiny toy from her hand and turned the key that wound its mainspring. The little elephant awoke as if from a nap and took to the air, his little wings beating like a hummingbird's. He trumpeted happily at Hachi and flew circles around her head.

Hachi threw her arms around Fergus and squeezed him tightly. He could feel the warmth of her tears through his shirt. Before he knew what was happening, Hachi was kissing him, and then just as quickly it was over, and she was ducking away to dry her eyes. Fergus felt a tingle from his head to his toes, and only after a minute or two did he realize it had nothing to do with the lektricity he had stored inside him.

"Thank you, Fergus," Hachi said. Tusker landed in her hand, and she hugged him close. "I can't—I don't—"

Fergus put up a hand. "Just remember he got broken because you were so obsessed with revenge you couldn't see anything else—or any*one* else—and promise me you won't ever let that happen again."

Hachi was quiet for a moment. "I promise," she said finally.

The bell over the door trilled, and a dripping-wet Erasmus Trudeau hurried into the shop, followed by an equally large Haitian woman and two little round children.

"I found her!" he announced.

Hachi pulled her knife on the woman behind him.

"Oh! No, *chère*. Dis not Maman Brigitte! Dis my wife, Cassandra, and my two darling daughters, Saraphina and Catheline. I bring them here to protect them."

"I thought you didn't trust Laveau's magical powers," Fergus said.

Erasmus looked chagrined. "Between Madame Laveau's white magic and Maman Brigitte's black magic, Erasmus choose Madame Laveau's white magic."

"Your family is most welcome," Marie Laveau said. She gestured to her two assistants, and they led Erasmus's wife and daughters upstairs.

"But you did find Maman Brigitte? Queen Theodosia?" Hachi asked.

"Oh yes. She on de docks at Lake Pontchartrain, whipping up one helluva nasty storm."

"Why there? What's she doing?" Fergus asked.

"It doesn't matter," Hachi said. "Now that we know where she is, we can take her down. Erasmus, you're amazing!"

The Pinkerton agent smiled modestly and shrugged. "Finding people, dat is what I do. Most of de people, dey have left de city. But dere are some who stay, just like dey always do in de storms. Dey stay wit de Voodoo Queen."

Laveau nodded. "And we have to protect them. But to do that, we have to do the same thing to Maman Brigitte we were trying to do to Baron Samedi. We have to get close enough to get a lock of her hair to make a voodoo doll, and stuff her mouth full of salt."

"How do we do that when she can blow us away with a flick of her wrist?" Fergus asked.

"We have to distract her," Hachi said. She was pacing again, with Tusker still flying around her head. She looked up at the little elephant and watched him circle for a few seconds, and her face lit up. "I've got it!" she said. Hachi hurried to the wall of masks, but it was a hat she pulled down, not a mask.

A black top hat.

"What we need is Baron Samedi back."

❦

The rain blew sideways at the docks on Lake Pontchartrain, making Queen Theodosia's gray hair clump together and wave beside her like she had a head full of snakes. The lake behind her chopped and churned, the brackish water crashing up onto the dock in tall white jets of spray. She stood with her eyes closed, a thick python snake slithering around and between her arms high above her head, entirely focused on creating the hurricane that was drowning New Orleans.

Until Baron Samedi walked up from the city, riding a seventy-year-old Marie Laveau.

He wore his black top hat and a black tuxedo, and had black circles painted around his eyes and black lines like teeth on his lips the way Blavatsky had during the street party. In one hand he carried a bottle of rum, and in his mouth he puffed on a damp cigar.

Baron Samedi's deep, booming laugh broke Maman Brigitte's trance, and the wind and rain slackened as she stared at him in fear and amazement.

"Who are you?" she yelled over the storm. "What is this trick?"

"It is no trick, dearest wife," Laveau said in Samedi's voice. "Don't you recognize your own husband?"

Maman Brigitte staggered back on the dock and dropped her snake. "No—no! I kill you before you free! I send your soul to the Dreamplanes of Leng, where you be imprisoned for a dozen-dozen years!"

"You think you can kill Baron Samedi so easily?" he said. "Baron Samedi is the King of Death! See now my army of the dead, come to kill you!"

Out of the rain and darkness behind Samedi shambled a ragged zombi army, their clothes tattered and torn, their faces pale and gaunt. When Maman Brigitte saw them, her face went white and the heavy rain and wind dropped to a gentle gale.

"Once upon a time, the goose drank wine," Samedi sang, doing a little dance. "The monkey played the fiddle on the sweet potato vine. The vine broke, the monkey choked, and they all went to heaven on a nanny goat."

"No. No!" Maman Brigitte cried. "You dead! I kill you! I kill you once, and I kill you again!"

Maman Brigitte pulled a knife, but up behind her in the dark choppy water loomed an enormous steamboat, the sound of its paddlewheels and steam engines hidden in the storm. It rammed the dock—*crash!*—and the platform exploded, throwing Queen Theodosia's body through the air like a sack of sugar. She hit the ground with a lifeless thud, and the steamboat's drawbridge dropped on top of her, pinning her to the ground.

Hachi ran down the drawbridge, followed by Fergus. Marie Laveau hurried to join them, followed by the hundreds of very alive people from New Orleans they'd recruited to play Baron Samedi's zombi army.

Hachi put two fingers to Theodosia's neck and nodded. "She's still alive."

Hachi shoved a handful of salt into Theodosia's mouth and held it shut while Laveau cut a lock of the queen's hair and pinned it to the doll she had hidden in her hat.

"It worked just like you said it would," Laveau told Hachi. "As soon as she thought Baron Samedi was back, nothing else mattered to her. Even the storm died down."

"Fergus gave me the idea," Hachi said. She glanced up at him. "He reminded me what it is to be so focused on one thing you don't pay attention to anything else around you. Maman Brigitte was so focused on killing Baron Samedi, she didn't hear a steamboat chugging up behind her."

"Nice job playing Samedi," Fergus told Laveau.

"I ought to know him well enough by now," Laveau said. "He and I go way back."

Fergus felt something crawl across his boot and jumped back as Maman Brigitte's python slithered past. He shuddered. "Big snake," he said.

Laveau had just begun to dig the Maman Brigitte doll out of the Theodosia voodoo doll when one of the fake zombi behind them cried out and pointed at the lake. "Li Grande Zombi!"

Out of the choppy black water rose the giant head of a snake, the black slits of its pupils glistening in the lightning from the storm. A forked tongue the size of the steamboat flicked out and licked the air, and with a hiss like a locomotive emptying its boiler, it opened its mouth and bared its glistening white fangs.

The Mangleborn in Lake Pontchartrain had awakened.

"Slag!" Archie cried out before landing with a thunk. The trap-door quickly snapped shut, and he was in total darkness.

"Clyde?" he called. "Sings-In-The-Night?" Above him, he heard the scuffles and thrown furniture of a fight. Archie called his friends' names again, but this time he heard nothing. They had probably been captured without him there to protect them.

Anger rose in Archie, and he spun in the dark, peering hard to try and make out where he was. He felt out blindly until he came to a cold, damp, earthen wall, and he moved along it until he came to bars. A prison. An underground prison.

Archie was getting seriously tired of being underground all the time.

He felt the rest of the way around the room, and as he did, his eyesight got a little better. He was in a small cell, about six feet by six feet wide, with a high ceiling he couldn't reach and a floor made out of dirt.

He wasn't going to be in here for long. Archie pulled his fist back to punch a hole in one of the walls when a voice in the darkness stopped him.

"I wouldn't do that if I were you."

Archie spun. He recognized that voice. He'd heard it before in Cahokia in the Clouds, and again the night of Custer's last stand. It was the fox girl.

"You knock down that wall, and you'll bring the whole place down," she told him.

"Why shouldn't I?"

"Because there are lots of other people trapped down here just like us, and you don't want to kill them."

"Where are you?" Archie asked. He threw his arms out, trying to find her in the darkness.

"I'm not in your cell," the fox girl said. "I'm in the next one over."

She rapped on something metal, and Archie went toward the sound. On one of the walls was a small barred window. He could just see her fox-eared shadow on the other side.

"You expect me to believe you're in prison," Archie said.

"I am," she told him. "I'm a prisoner of the Daimyo Under the City. He makes me steal for him, and when I'm finished, he puts me back here, in a cell."

"Right," said Archie. "He 'makes you' steal. And just how does he do that?"

The fox girl sniffed. "He . . . he has my father. If I don't do whatever he says, he'll kill him."

Archie frowned in the darkness. What she was saying was *possible*. But everything this girl said and did was a lie. Could he really believe what she was telling him?

"Why don't you just trick them, the way you do? Make them

see a bear, or a Blackfoot raiding party, or a swarm of bees or something?"

"The Daimyo Under the City knows all my tricks. He has meka-ninja guards. Tall, thin, black Tik Toks with red eyes and all kinds of weapons and no fail-safes."

"Yeah," Archie said. "I've met one before."

"But it couldn't beat you, could it? I've watched you. You're super strong, and nothing hurts you."

Almost nothing, Archie thought, putting a hand to the crack in his arm. But he didn't say it.

"You'll help me, won't you?" the fox girl asked. "If you do, I'll get that lantern back for you. I don't care anything about it. I don't even know what it is, or why it's so valuable. All it does is shine a bright light."

"You opened it?" Archie asked.

"Of course."

"Did it . . . did it do anything to you?"

"Do anything?" the girl said. "No. It's just a lantern."

"It's not just a lantern," Archie told her. "And I have to get it back."

"I gave it to the Daimyo Under the City. If you help me free my father, I'll help you steal it back. Will you do it?"

A number of colorful curses came to Archie's mind, but he put his fingers through the bars and yanked the metal grate out of the wall for her to climb through.

"I knew you'd help," the fox girl said as she climbed in.

"Just no funny business," he told her. "And you get me the lantern *first*, and then I help you free your dad."

Up close, Archie could see the fox girl pout. "You don't trust me?"

"No," Archie told her.

The fox girl grinned. "Good. You're learning already. My name is Ren."

"Archie," he told her. He pulled the door off the wall of the cell as though it was made of cardboard and set it aside.

"How did you get to be so strong?" Ren asked him.

"How are you able to make people see things that aren't there?" Archie asked.

"I asked you first," she said.

"I don't know," Archie told her. "But it has something to do with that lantern. That's why I want it back. What about you?"

"I was born in the forest and raised by foxes."

"I thought you said you grew up on the streets of Cahokia in the Clouds," Archie said.

Suddenly the fox girl jumped on his back and wrapped her arms and legs around him.

"What are you—*what are you doing?*" Archie cried.

"The floor outside the cells is covered with glass so people can't escape," Ren told him. "I need a ride."

Archie took a tentative step outside and heard the sound of crunching glass.

"Don't you have shoes?" he asked.

"They take them away from you when they throw you in here. Unless you come in through the ceiling like you did."

"What is this place?" Archie asked.

"The Shanghai tunnels," she told him. "They run for miles under the city, connecting all the coffee shops and sake bars and stores and hotels to the submarine docks. At first, it was just to catch people, knock them out, and sell them to sub captains. They call it "Shanghaiing" because most of them are sailing for Shanghai, in Cathay, and no sailors want to go there. Too far, too long. And of course there's the Darkness. But then everything else illegal in Ametokai moved down here too—the slavers, the prostitutes, the gambling halls, the opium dens. The Daimyo Above the City turns a blind eye to it all."

Archie grunted. "Maybe it's time somebody took him down."

"I thought you only fought monsters," Ren said.

"What makes you a monster is what's in your heart," he said, telling her the same thing he'd told Sings-In-The-Night. "Not what you look like."

"Are you saying that for me, or to remind yourself?" Ren asked.

Archie didn't answer. They passed a small room stacked floor to ceiling with wooden shelves that doubled as beds, where a mix of Japanese, First Nations, and Yankees lay smoking opium through hookah tubes. In another room, a man took money from a sailor and pointed him to a woman on a bare mattress on the floor before pulling the curtain closed.

From what Archie could see, there were a lot of monsters in the tunnels beneath Ametokai.

"Turn right here," Ren told him, "then take the second left."

"You know these tunnels awfully well," Archie said.

"I practically grew up down here," she told him.

"So which was it, you grew up here, or in the forest, or in Cahokia?"

"Actually, it was in Don Francisco, in California."

"Everything you say is a lie, isn't it?" Archie said.

"No," Ren said.

"I'll bet *that's* a lie too."

"Do you know the Navajo story of the fox and the scorpion?" she asked. "A scorpion wants to get across a river, so he asks a fox if he can ride across on the fox's back." Ren shifted, climbing higher on Archie's shoulders. "The fox says, 'No way. You'll sting me, and I'll drown.' But the scorpion points out that if he stings the fox, they'll *both* drown. So the fox agrees, and the scorpion climbs on his back. Halfway across the river, the scorpion stings him. As the poison spreads through him, paralyzing him, the fox says to the scorpion, 'Why did you do that? Now we're both going to drown!' 'I know,' says the scorpion. 'I couldn't help it. It's in my nature.'"

Ren pointed to a door on the left. "The lantern's in here," she said.

Archie turned into a dark room. A metal door slammed shut and bolted behind him, and gaslights suddenly came up. The Dragon Lantern was in the room, all right, but that wasn't all. Archie was in a square room exactly like the one where he'd sat with the Daimyo Above the City, but the samurai guards here wore white, not black, and there were just as many black meka-ninjas as there were humans. On a cushion on a raised platform beside the Dragon Lantern was the same man as above too, with the same black hair and same green glasses, but now wearing white robes. The Daimyo Above the City was the same man as the Daimyo Under the City—and Ren had brought Archie right to him.

"Sorry," she said. "It's in my nature."

"Welcome to the city under the city, Mr. Dent," the daimyo said. "I asked Kitsune to bring you here without a fuss so I could speak to you again. She assures me you're quite capable of destroying everyone and everything down here."

"'Kitsune'?" Archie said. She'd told him her name was Ren.

Kitsune shrugged as if to say, "It's in my nature."

"What do you want with the Dragon Lantern?" Archie asked the daimyo.

The daimyo waved a disinterested hand. "It's not what I want, but what I can get for it. Arcane items such as this are highly prized in *kaiju*-ruled Cathay. This one will make me a very rich man."

Archie took an angry step toward the daimyo. A room full of meka-ninjas and samurai guards might have scared everybody else, but not him.

"Ah ah ah," the daimyo said, holding up a finger. "Attack me, and Kitsune's father dies."

A meka-ninja emerged from behind the dais with a ragged, bearded Japanese man in one arm and a short sword in the other.

So—Ren or Kitsune or whatever her name was hadn't been lying about her father, at least. Archie had seen Thomas Edison's meka-ninja kill quickly and efficiently at a single brief command, and he stayed where he was.

"I'm not her father!" the man in the meka-ninja's arms cried.

The daimyo ignored him. "You see, Kitsune and I have an arrangement. She does whatever I ask, and I do not kill her father."

"I'm telling you—I'm not her father!" Kitsune's father said again.

"Now you and I will have the same arrangement," the daimyo told Archie. "You will stay here, as my guest, and do . . . favors for me. Errands. And in return, I will not kill this man."

Kitsune's father struggled in the meka-ninja's grasp. "You're making a mistake! I'm not her father!"

"I'll never work for you," Archie said.

"Then I can kill this man?" the daimyo said.

The meka-ninja raised its sword to Kitsune's father's neck.

Archie's blood boiled. He couldn't let the daimyo control him the way he controlled Kitsune. *Wouldn't* let him. How many lives would he hurt—how many deaths might he cause—just to save the life of one man? But he was a hero. Heroes didn't let innocent people die for any reason.

Hero? a voice whispered inside his head. *You're no hero. You're a monster. Clyde would take that deal—accept a life of slavery and crime just to save the life of one man. But not you. You're the shadow. You're the one who can trade one life for a thousand, and never blink.*

It's in your nature.

"Go ahead," Archie said. He took a step forward. "Kill him. And then I'll kill you, and everybody else down here."

The meka-ninja drew its blade up tighter, and a thin line of red blood rolled down the man's neck.

"I'm telling you! Please! I'm not her father!" the man begged.

"He's right," Kitsune said. She stepped up alongside Archie, and the anger and bloodlust in him subsided as he tried to figure out what she was playing at. "He's not really my father," she said.

"Yes! Yes, I told you!" the man said. "This is what I've been trying to tell you for three years!"

The daimyo stood. "Do not test me, girl. I *will* kill him!"

"Fine," Kitsune said. "His real name is Nori Shizuka. He used to keep children in dark little prisons like yours before selling them into slavery until I stopped him. You wanted to control me, and I wanted a punishment that fit his crime, so I pretended he was my father so you would throw him in your dungeons."

"Yes, yes," Shizuka sobbed. "Finally, the truth. It's all true. I have been a terrible man, and I have paid for my sins."

"Not enough," Kitsune told him.

"But—then—why do my bidding if this is not really your father?" the daimyo asked.

Kitsune smiled. "For fun. But then I found something even more fun to do."

"What?" the daimyo asked.

"Bring this boy and his friends here to destroy you."

"Kill them!" the daimyo commanded, and chaos erupted. At the same moment the samurai and meka-ninjas leaped at them, the roof exploded, half of it caving in, the other half lifted out by a giant brass hand. Sings-In-The-Night dropped through the hole onto a samurai's shoulders and lifted him away. Archie batted one of the meka-ninjas across the room. Kitsune made another samurai swing his sword at a phantom.

Buster's head appeared in the hole in the ceiling, and he whistle-barked.

"Like Mrs. DeMarcus says, better late than never, huh?" Clyde's voice boomed.

Archie stuck his fist through a meka-ninja and ripped out its clockworks. "I thought you were captured!" Archie yelled back.

"Please," Clyde said. "There were only five of them."

Sings-In-The-Night flew by, picking up a meka-ninja and smashing it against the wall. "I'm going after the lantern!" Archie told her. The daimyo had the lantern in his hands, and Archie wasn't going to let him get away.

But the daimyo didn't run. Not at first.

First, he opened up the lantern and flooded the room with its light.

26

Archie ducked away from the Dragon Lantern's light, but it didn't do anything to him but make his skin warm. It did something to some of the samurai guards in the room, though. As the light fell on them, they screamed, their bodies twisting and contorting in ways human bodies weren't supposed to twist and contort. One of them sprouted bat wings and a spiked tail. Another's head grew fur and rabbit ears while his bottom half melted into goo. Spider legs erupted from the stomach of a man beside Archie.

All of them screamed.

Archie had seen enough horrors in his short life to turn his hair white, but this was something else entirely. Most of the samurai were mutating, their bodies breaking and melting under the Dragon Lantern's light. Archie, Kitsune, and Sings-In-The-Night weren't affected.

Maybe because they already had been.

"Clyde! Clyde, stay out of the light!" Archie yelled.

"You don't have to tell me twice!" Clyde said. The light didn't do anything to Buster, of course, who still happily pulled meka-ninjas from the hole he'd dug and whipped them around like string bones, but Archie didn't want to test it on Clyde.

Kitsune stood mesmerized, watching the samurai transform into monsters under the lantern's light.

"So that's what it does," she whispered.

A samurai with a shark's mouth in his stomach came gurgling at her, and Archie snatched her out of the way. As he set Kitsune down again, his hand accidentally came away with a white pearl necklace she wore.

Suddenly Archie's hand was on fire. He waved it to put out the fire, but then there was a snake in his hand. Then it was crawling with bugs. Illusions, he realized. Kitsune was making him see all those things, trying to get him to drop the necklace.

"If you want it back, you could just ask," Archie said.

"Give it back!" she demanded. She grabbed for the necklace, but Archie yanked it away.

"I will, if you make me a promise."

"*What?*" Kitsune said. Another monster samurai came at them, but Buster snatched it away in his giant brass hand.

"Join us. Join the League. It's—I'll explain later. But we're good guys. We do good things. We help people. And so do you. I've seen you. You led me to that abandoned warehouse in Ca-hokia before you blew me up so no one else would get hurt. You saved all those people from the fire in the shop in Cheyenne. And that man—Shizuka. You stopped him from selling children as slaves."

"Fine. Yes!" Kitsune said.

"Yes, you'll join us?"

"Yes," Kitsune said. "Now give it back!" The fight raged around them, but all she cared about was the necklace. It must have really meant something to her.

"One more promise," Archie said, holding it back. "You tell me who you really are, and where you really came from. The truth."

"*Right now!?*"

"No. Later." He held the necklace where she could see it. "Promise."

"I promise," she said.

Archie started to hand her the necklace, then pulled back. "How do I know you're not lying?"

"I may be a liar, but I keep my promises," she told him.

Archie gave her the necklace back, and it disappeared inside her white robe.

"So. What now, boss?" she asked.

"We get that Dragon Lantern back," Archie said. But the daimyo and the lantern were gone! He'd wasted too much time!

"There's a secret passage under the dais," Kitsune said, leaping up onto it. "That's where he went. We just have to find the trigger that opens it."

Archie slammed his fist down through the wooden platform and ripped up the planks, revealing a hidden staircase.

"Or you could just do that," Kitsune said.

"There are people being held prisoner in the tunnels!" Archie called to Clyde and Sings-In-The-Night. "Get them out! We're going after the Dragon Lantern!"

"Who? You and the girl who stole it?" Clyde said.

Kitsune scampered down the stairs, and Archie followed. The staircase led to a lower series of tunnels, and whether Kitsune really grew up there or not, she knew the way well enough to guide them. Archie had to trust that she wasn't lying to him again, but he didn't have any other choice.

"I fell from the sky," Kitsune said as they ran.

"What?"

"You wanted to know where I came from. I fell from the sky."

"Where?"

"The rice fields of Beikoku, near Yakima, in the shadow of Mt. Tacoma. An old farmer and his wife said they saw me fall from the sky, and they rescued me and raised me as their own daughter. They always hid me away, afraid I'd be persecuted as a monster because of my ears and tail, and one day they heard someone coming and sent me to the basement. When they didn't come back for me, I crept back upstairs. They were dead. They'd been killed by Paiute digger pirates, driving one of those big tunneling machines they have. I swore then and there I would use my powers to protect the innocent and punish the wicked."

Archie followed her down another dark corridor.

"Is any of that true?" he asked her.

"I promised I'd tell you the truth, didn't I?" she said.

"Yes," Archie said. "But you didn't say when."

Kitsune gave Archie a sly grin. It was just as he thought—all lies.

They were climbing through a busted-out hole in a brick wall when they heard something metal jangling in the next room. Kitsune put a finger to her lips. The daimyo stood in front of a rusted iron door, running through the keys on a big ring with shaking hands. The lantern sat on the ground at his feet.

"Boss, you need any help?" Kitsune said.

The daimyo wheeled on them, a raygun in his hand. Archie cursed inwardly, sure Kitsune had tricked him all over again. But the daimyo lowered his raygun and relaxed.

"Oh! Taro! It's you," he said, his eyes looking over their heads. Archie looked behind him to see what the daimyo was looking at, but there was nothing there but wooden barrels. *Kitsune,* Archie realized. *She must be making him see us as someone else. His taller samurai guards.*

"Were you followed?" the daimyo asked.

"No," Kitsune said. "Those monsters the lantern made—they took care of the kids."

"Good, good," the daimyo said, clearly still shaken by what he'd seen. "Wait—Taro, you were one of the ones I saw turn into a monster!"

Kitsune looked at Archie with wide eyes and nodded at the daimyo. Archie frowned back. *What?*

"It's you!" the daimyo said, and he shot Archie with the raygun.

"Ow!" Archie said. He grabbed the raygun and crushed it with one hand. With the other, he flicked the daimyo in the face with a finger. The daimyo's head snapped back and slammed into the iron door, and he slumped to the ground, unconscious.

Kitsune did her wide-eyed nod again. "This means *hit him*!"

"Well, I'm sorry!" Archie said. "I don't read fox girl sign language!"

"Once somebody sees through the illusion, I've got to be ready to hit or run. With just me, it's usually run. But with you around, now we can do some hitting."

"So do we haul him back?" Archie asked. "Turn him in to the authorities?"

Kitsune picked up the daimyo's keys. "He *is* the authorities. I've got a better idea. Just let me find the key to this door."

Archie moved her to one side and punched the door off its hinges.

"Or you could just do that," Kitsune said. "Pick him up. I'll carry the lantern."

"Uh-uh," Archie said. "I'll carry them both."

The iron door led to a smaller tunnel that came out in the busy outdoor docks of Ametokai's submarine port. Unlike New Rome, Ametokai wasn't exactly on the ocean. It was a hundred miles inland on Puget Sound, where the water wasn't as choppy and impassable on the surface as the Great Western Sea beyond. Submarines of all sizes and colors bobbed in a long line stretching in either direction, and crowds of Tik Toks and human porters and passengers pushed past each other trying to get to their ships.

"Let me do the talking," Kitsune whispered to Archie. She whistled to catch the attention of a loitering sailor with a tall furry hat and a long clay pipe. He gave a wary look around, then joined them.

"You the boarding master for the *Potemkin* there?" Kitsune asked.

"Might be," the sailor said in a thick Russian accent. Just like the daimyo, he looked over their heads, like he was talking to someone taller. Archie wondered what exactly Kitsune was making him see.

"Where you headed?" she asked.

"Siberia."

"Gone long?"

"Five years."

"Got a volunteer for you." She nodded to Archie. Did she want him to punch the guy? No—her eyes went to the daimyo, and he understood. He handed the daimyo's unconscious body to the boarding master. He hefted him, having more trouble with his weight than Archie did, and started to walk away to his ship.

Kitsune caught him by the arm. "Hold up," she said. The sailor frowned, dug in his pocket, and stuffed a wad of bills into her hand. Kitsune counted it as he left.

"Fifty bucks a head. That's the going rate," she said.

"You're a mean one," Archie said.

"Only to people who deserve it. I think he'll enjoy Siberia. I hear the summer there is beautiful. All four days of it." She nodded at the lantern. "So. I guess now I know why you were so desperate to get hold of that thing."

"Well, I thought I was getting it to bring back to someone, but now I'm trying to keep it from her," Archie said.

"Who?"

"*Me*," Philomena Moffett said.

Archie spun. Mrs. Moffett was right behind him! Her tentacles were hidden under her skirts again, but Archie knew they could whip out at him at any time. He held the lantern tightly in his arms as Mrs. Moffett circled them.

"Oh, you're good," she said. "Can you see it, Archie? She's made you look like two of the daimyo's samurai, down to every last detail. But I know it's you under there. I watched you before she created the glamour."

"How did you find us?" Archie asked.

"It wasn't too hard," Mrs. Moffett said. She looked beyond the submarine docks toward the city, where Buster was trading punches with Ametokai's Metal Samurai Gunray. "So. Are you going to give me the lantern, or do I have to take it from you?"

Archie put the lantern in Kitsune's hands and got ready to fight. "I'd like to see you try."

"*So be it*," Mrs. Moffett said. Her chest swelled, and she clenched her fists at her side and screamed. It was like being hit with a ray-cannon, only it was sound waves, not aether. WOMWOMWOM-WOMWOM! Mrs. Moffett's sonic scream ripped up the wooden docks and sent crates and barrels flying. Kitsune went with them, tumbling end over end until she crashed into a crane and slumped, unconscious, to the ground. Archie held his ground, though, the sound waves pounding him like a giant steam man's brass fists.

Mrs. Moffett's scream died away, and Archie stumbled, trying to keep his balance. All around them, the panicked people on the docks fled.

"Impressive," Mrs. Moffett said, picking up the lantern. "Nothing has ever been able to stand up to my sonic scream. Not mountains, or rivers, or trees, or the armor plating the scientists built to test me at the Forge. Nor the scientists, in the end. But you, Archie Dent, you're different, aren't you? The Boy Made of Stone."

"I know what they did to you was awful," Archie said. "Sings-In-The-Night told me. But that's no reason to—"

Mrs. Moffett screamed again. The sonic waves blasted Archie into the hull of a submarine with a loud *clang*, leaving a dent. Mrs. Moffett's sonic scream was a violent force she wielded like a fire hose, ripping the submarines from their moorings and knocking them into each other. Archie held on to a wooden piling, but felt even that starting to splinter. He was just about to slip off when a giant brass hand slammed down into the dock, knocking Mrs. Moffett off her feet.

Clyde and Buster! And Sings-In-The-Night, flying alongside! Mrs. Moffett turned on them and screamed again—WOMWOMWOMWOMWOM!—staggering the enormous steam man and sending her former friend tumbling through the sky. She kept her scream on the steam man and Buster stumbled backward under the force of it, his brass plating wobbling and groaning. If he didn't get away, Mrs. Moffett's scream would vibrate him to pieces.

Archie grabbed a little one-man work sub that sat on the dock and lifted it like a massive club. He slammed it down on her, but at the last moment she turned the force of her scream on the sub. WOMWOMWOMWOMWOM! The sonic scream held the submarine suspended in the air until it vibrated it to pieces around her.

Mrs. Moffett's scream gave out, and she collapsed to one knee to catch her breath. Buster had backed into a warehouse near the dock and fallen bottom-first into it, and Kitsune and Sings-In-The-Night were nowhere to be seen. Archie picked up another sub.

"I'm not going to let you take the lantern," Archie said. He took a step toward her, and she hit him with another sonic scream. He dropped the sub and stayed on his feet, but he could only move toward her when she backed away.

"It would appear we are at an impasse," Mrs. Moffett said when her scream ran out. "I can't stop you, and you can't stop me. But you can try again in Don Francisco. That's where I'm going, if you're interested. I have one last errand to run before my triumphant return home."

Mrs. Moffett used her sonic scream on a crane, bringing it down on Archie's head. It didn't hurt, but in the time it took Archie to dig his way out from under it, Philomena Moffett was gone.

27

Fergus took a step back. "*Bigger* snake," he said.

Li Grande Zombi's head rose out of Lake Pontchartrain, water sluicing off it like a surfacing submarine, and it rose high into the air and hovered over them like an Apache Air Liner. As Hachi stared up at it, she wondered idly why she was thinking of airships and submarines.

Maybe because I want to run as far away as fast as I can, she thought. That's what the men and women who'd come pretending to be Laveau's zombi army did, screaming as they disappeared into the night.

"He come. Li Grande Zombi, he come to make you pay," Theodosia said in Maman Brigitte's voice, salt spilling from her mouth.

"The hurricane!" Marie Laveau cried. "That's what Maman Brigitte was doing! Li Grande Zombi is just like its loa—put salt in its mouth, and you put it back to sleep. The water in Lake Pontchartrain was just brackish enough, but the hurricane dumped gallons of freshwater into it, diluting the salt water!"

The giant serpent struck like a flash of lightning, snatching up the steamboat in its giant jaws and smashing it to pieces. The steamboat's boiler exploded, and Hachi, Fergus, and Laveau ducked as the docks were showered with wood and metal. When the last of the pieces of the steamboat had fallen from its mouth, Li Grande Zombi gave another hissing roar. The explosion hadn't hurt it at all.

"Crivens," said Fergus. "Where's Archie when you need him?"

"Yeah," said Hachi.

"Your strongman? I told you—you are stronger together than apart," Laveau told them.

"Well, he's not here now," Hachi said. "So what do we do?"

Lightning struck Li Grande Zombi, and it seemed to swell and grow taller. The serpent rose and slid up and out of Lake Pontchartrain toward the city behind them.

"We run!" Laveau said, and she did just that.

Hachi couldn't argue with her. She grabbed Fergus by the arm and pulled him back toward the city. But Fergus was too slow on his dead leg. The serpent would overtake them at any moment, crushing them flat beneath its enormous belly.

Lektricity sparked between Fergus's fingers.

"No, don't," Hachi told him. "You saw it—it feeds on lektricity just like the rest of the Mangleborn."

"I'm not charging up for that," Fergus said. He pulled a rip cord that dangled from his belt, and up from a harness on his back shot a metal rod with four curved blades like a fan.

"Oh no," Hachi said. "Not that thing!"

"Oh aye," Fergus said. "Only mine's better." With a blue spark, the fan blades started whirring so fast Hachi couldn't see them. Fergus grabbed her in his arms, and they shot up out of the way of

Li Grande Zombi just as it crushed the dock where they'd been standing.

"Mine's *lektric*," Fergus said.

Fergus hovered far enough away from the giant serpent that it couldn't get them, and they watched it pass.

"I told you—one day one of my inventions was going to save your life," Fergus said. "And what are you supposed to say?"

"'Fergus, you're a genius,'" Hachi said. "But I thought you weren't supposed to build lektric machines," Hachi said. "That's what wakes the Mangleborn."

"Aye, well, it doesn't much matter now, does it?"

He was right about that. They watched as Li Grande Zombi ripped up a building on the outskirts of the city with its giant jaws. While it chewed, its tail flicked out and destroyed a levee, flooding an entire quarter with canal water.

"That's it!" Fergus said. "I know what to do. How to take it down. We have to drive it back into Lake Pontchartrain."

"Yes, but how?" Hachi asked. "And even if we could, the water isn't salty enough to keep it down."

Fergus flew them higher, out over the heart of the city. In the flashes of lightning, he pointed to the landscape below. "New Orleans sits between Lake Pontchartrain, the Mississippi River, and the Atlantis Ocean. All we have to do is bring the saltwater of the ocean to Lake Pontchartrain. That's how it got salty to begin with."

"And how do we do that?" Hachi asked.

"We destroy the levees holding the ocean back."

"Fergus, if we destroy the levees that hold the ocean back, it'll flood the city."

"Aye. Sweeping Li Grande Zombi back into Lake Pontchartrain, and filling it with saltwater."

"*And flooding the city.*"

"I don't know what else to do, Hachi! Besides, if we don't stop that thing, there isn't going to be much of a city left!"

Below them, Li Grande Zombi was smashing and slithering its way toward the center of New Orleans. Hachi had to admit he was right—and she didn't see any other way. She nodded and Fergus swooped down, landing them on the sea levee near a submarine dock on the other side of the city. All the submarines that hadn't escaped before the hurricane hit were torn from their moorings. Some of them had washed up and over the levee and lay grounded like beached whales; others were still at sea, trashing the dock as they smashed against it again and again in the churning, roaring waves of the Atlantis Ocean.

Fergus pulled the gyrocopter harness off and slipped it over Hachi's shoulders.

"What are you doing?" she asked.

"What's it look like I'm doing? I'm giving you the gyrocopter," he said. "You have to go back and get anybody out who's left. The battery's all charged up."

"And what about you?" Hachi asked.

"I'll figure something out."

"No," Hachi said. "When the levees go, you'll drown. You hate water. And you can't swim. Not without a head in a jar to hold you up."

"Anybody left in the town won't know what's coming," Fergus told her. "You have to get them to high ground." He held her away at arm's length. "Go. You know you have to."

Behind them, they could hear Li Grande Zombi roar as another building was destroyed.

"I hate you," Hachi said.

"I hate you too," Fergus said. He surprised her by kissing her, and while she had her eyes closed he pushed a button on the controls in her hand and she shot into the sky.

It took Hachi a minute to get the hang of the gyrocopter, and by that time she was out over the heart of the city again. The rain came down in sheets, and the wind blew her around like a leaf.

Maman Brigitte! They hadn't made sure she was out of Theodosia before they ran, and she must be back at it again. But never mind. They had bigger problems. *Much* bigger problems. And only destroying the levees would solve them.

Hachi swooped down and buzzed through the empty streets, looking for signs of life in every window. She saw candles flickering in an upstairs room off Rampart Street and flew over, kicking the window open on a startled Creole family.

"Get to the roof! The sea levee's going to burst!" she told them. The momentary shock of a girl on a gyrocopter gone, they hurriedly collected their children and pets and ran for the roof.

Hachi found more holdouts on Bourbon Street, and still more on Dumaine Street. Why were these people still in the city? At least the hundreds who'd seen the Mangleborn rise from Lake Pontchartrain had fled. She flew on through the Seventh Ward, and the Lower Ninth, where she was sure the water would go, and helped anyone too old or too ill up onto their roofs. Why hadn't Fergus blown the levees yet? The only answer was that he was giving her time to save as many people as possible. But behind her, a black silhouette against the almost black sky, Li Grande Zombi slithered near what must be Metairie Road. If Fergus didn't do it soon, it would be too late. The water would sweep the Mangleborn into the Mississippi, not the lake, and they would never get the monster back to sleep.

Hachi was just about to give up and go back for Fergus when she turned a corner and saw a streetcar named *Desire* rattling its way toward the city center.

A streetcar filled with children.

Hachi cursed loudly and swooped down, landing on the back of the streetcar with less grace than she would have liked. She killed the gyrocopter's engine and grabbed the first adult she could find, a woman in a long white dress, gray apron, and white nurse's hat.

"What are you doing?" Hachi cried.

The stunned Haitian woman was still staring at the gyrocopter. Hachi shook her. "*What are you doing?*" she asked again. "Where are you going with all these kids?"

The woman snapped out of it. "I'm Miss Jakande, head of the Gentilly Orphanage on Elysian Fields Avenue. I'm trying to get the children downtown, away from the ocean and the lake."

And toward the giant snake monster destroying the city, Hachi thought. But there were too many little eyes looking up at her for her to say it and scare them.

"The sea levees are going to go any second," Hachi told her. "We have to get these kids to a rooftop!"

"But—but how?" the nurse asked.

"Hang on!" Hachi called to the kids. She pushed the nurse away from the streetcar's controls and threw the brake. The streetcar screeched and squealed as it lurched to a halt, but none of the kids went tumbling out. Hachi grabbed the first one she could reach, fired up the gyrocopter, and lifted off. As she set him on the flat roof of the five-story hotel next door, she heard the first of the explosions.

Fergus was finally blowing up the levee.

There would never be enough time to ferry each of the kids up to the rooftop one by one. "Take the big kids up the stairs!" Hachi told the nurse when she flew back down. They heard another *boom*, and the streetcar shook as another part of the sea levee was destroyed.

"What about the rest of them?" Miss Jakande said.

"Just go! I'll fly them up! They'll slow you down too much!"

Miss Jakande took two of the orphans by the hands. "Fives, Sixes, and Sevens with me!" she called, and hurried toward the front door of the hotel.

Another *boom*. Fergus wasn't playing around.

"Circus! Showtime!" Hachi cried. Four little animals burst from her bandolier this time, not three, and Hachi almost cried for joy at the sight of them. "Mr. Lion, Tusker, follow Miss Jakande. All those boys and girls have to get to the roof. No stragglers!"

The little lion and elephant darted away, not-so-gently herding the slowpokes with nudges in the back. Hachi looked around at the five children who were left—what she guessed were the Fours. *At least there aren't Ones, Twos, and Threes too,* she thought.

Another *boom,* and this time, the distant sound of rushing water.

Hachi grabbed one of the Fours and started the gyrocopter.

"Everybody, this is Freckles and Jo-Jo," she told the other children, who were already delighted by the flying gorilla and giraffe. "They're going to keep you company until I can come back for all of you, all right? Jo-Jo, Freckles, parade! But don't let any of them wander off!"

Hachi's little wind-up animals started a two-animal song-and-dance routine, and Hachi lifted off. One by one, she flew the Fours up to the rooftop, but each time, Hachi could feel the gyrocopter getting slower and weaker.

"Come on, come on," Hachi urged it. "Just a couple more."

On the next-to-last child, Miss Jakande and the other kids were there to take the Four from her without her having to land. She swooped down and grabbed up the last of the children, who was happily applauding Freckles's antics, and hauled her up. One story. Two stories. Three stories . . . The gyrocopter started to flag. Four stories . . . The gyrocopter topped out and started to dip. They weren't going to make it!

And then Jo-Jo and Tusker and Freckles and Mr. Lion were there, grabbing on to her harness and pulling up for all their little wings were worth. The gyrocopter and Hachi's circus lifted her just enough to pass the last Four off to the reaching hands of Miss Jakande and the Sevens, and then she was falling, spiraling down toward the street as the last of the lektricity drained from the gyro-copter's battery with a whine.

Hachi landed with a thunk on the rooftop of the streetcar and looked up to see a giant wave of seawater towering over her. Fergus's invention wasn't going to save her this time.

Nothing was.

Buster sat in a park near the top of Nob Hill in Don Francisco, watching the city's streetcars. Every time one of them clanged, Buster took the bell as an invitation to play chase, and Clyde had to remind him to stay. Thanks to his Dog Soldier training, Buster hadn't gone chasing after a single streetcar. But he longed to.

"Good dog," Clyde told him, petting a rail on the bridge. "That's a good dog. Stay. I know you want to play."

They had been sitting atop the hill in the city by the bay for three straight days now, looking for some sign of Philomena Moffett. While Buster watched the streetcars, Clyde, Archie, and Mr. Rivets watched the rolling hills of the city and the open-air submarine docks for trouble. So far, there hadn't been any. Sings-In-The-Night hadn't seen anything on her daily flights over the city, and Kitsune hadn't found her on the streets. Every morning the fox girl disappeared into Don Francisco, and every evening she came back with sacks full of food. Archie never asked where or how she got it, but he had a guess.

All five of them met up again in Buster's galley, where Mr. Rivets inserted a Chef talent card and made them dinner. Archie looked around the table at his new friends and teammates. They were four of the League of Seven. The hero, the trickster, the scholar, and the shadow. In New Orleans were the tinker and the warrior—five and six—leaving only a seventh to join their League: the lawbringer. Would they find him or her here, in the Republic of California, on the other side of the continent from Septemberist headquarters?

"I don't think she's here," Kitsune said.

"What?" Archie said.

"Mrs. Moffett. I think she tricked us," Kitsune said. "Told us she was going to California to mislead us, then took off for the United Nations."

"It's possible," Clyde said.

"No," Archie told them. "No, she's here. I know it. She told me she was coming here because she wanted me to chase her. She's messing with me. With all of us. She hates me. She hates all of us, and she wants to hurt us."

That made everyone quiet for a while.

"I have an idea how to counteract that sonic scream of hers," Sings-In-The-Night said. "I've been thinking about it during my flights over the city." She spread a large piece of paper filled with scribbles and equations out on the table. "It all has to do with resonant frequencies. If we can find a way to turn Buster into a tuning fork, or maybe install one on him, we might be able to reach an equilibrium with her sonic scream."

"And then Buster wouldn't shake all to pieces?" Clyde asked.

"That's the idea," Sings-In-The-Night said. "I know the theory is sound, if you'll forgive the pun, but I don't know how I could actually *build* it."

"Leave that to Fergus," Archie said. "You guys are going to love working together."

Mr. Rivets was just bringing the food to the table when they all heard it—a piercing alarm ringing out over the city, and a low *womwomwomwomwom* that vibrated in the air.

"*Mrs. Moffett*," Archie said.

He and the others raced to the bridge, leaving Mr. Rivets holding an enormous steaming bowl of fish stew. "I'll just keep this warm for later then, shall I?" he asked the empty room.

Buster was already honed in on the ruckus, and Clyde activated his magnifying eye lens as soon as he was in the driver's seat. The glass panes clicked down, zooming in on an island in the bay near the Golden Gate Bridge.

"That's Alcatraz Island," Sings-In-The-Night said, studying a map at the navigator's station. "It says the Republic of California has a high-security prison there."

"What's she doing there?" Clyde asked.

They watched as a building on the island crumbled. "Whatever it is, it isn't good," Archie said. "But how are we all going to get there?"

"I can fly you and Kitsune over one at a time," Sings-In-The-Night said. "But that doesn't get Clyde and Buster there."

"I know how to get there," Clyde said. "Hold on!" A streetcar was just coming over the crest of Nob Hill, and Clyde pointed Buster at it. "Buster, fetch! Get it, Buster, get it!"

Buster leaped to his feet and charged after the streetcar, whistling happily. The driver of the little red-and-gold trolley looked back over his shoulder and panicked as the ten-story-tall steam man bore down on him. He released the hand brake and the streetcar shot away, but all that did was make Buster happier. Steamcars and horse buggies scattered, and people screamed and dove for shop doors as Buster ran back and forth behind the trolley, nipping at its bumpers.

"Clyde!" Archie cried. "Clyde, what are you doing! We can't ride a streetcar to Alcatraz Island!"

"No, but it gives us a running start!" Clyde said.

The streetcar swerved away, but Clyde kept Buster running straight ahead at full speed toward the bay.

"A running start at *what?*" Archie asked, but he was afraid he knew the answer: the Golden Gate Bridge.

The Golden Gate Bridge was a tall orange suspension bridge that connected the city of Don Francisco to the Marin Headlands on the other side. It had been built millennia ago by some ancient civilization, and from the gold curled corners at the top and the pair of dog-like stone lions that guarded each end, it looked like the same civilization that had made the Dragon Lantern.

Buster ran up the hill to the entrance of the bridge, sending trucks and taxis steaming up the curbs.

"*Clyde,*" Archie said. "*Clyde, what are you doing?*"

"I'm going to jump it!"

"Jump from the bridge to Alcatraz?" Sings-In-The-Night said. "You'll never make it!"

Buster leaped over a bus.

"No—I can make it! The island's closer to the bridge today."

"Wait, what?" Sings-In-The-Night said. "You *do* know islands don't move, don't you?"

"Here we go!" Clyde cried. "Hang on!"

Buster angled toward the low point in the suspension wires and jumped.

Clyde's arms windmilled in his chair like it was he who had jumped. Archie closed his eyes. Sings-In-The-Night shot out the top hatch. Kitsune yelled *"Woohoo!"* It looked like they were going to make it, but then they were dropping too fast, too soon—

KER-SPLASH!

Buster hit the water feetfirst. The impact ripped Archie from the railing he held and threw him into the metal wall between the front windows. Water gushed up in great waves around the steam man, and he bobbed back up before starting to sink. They had landed just short of the island!

"Swim, Buster! Swim!" Clyde yelled, doing a dog paddle in his seat. The giant steam man pawed at the water, pulling himself toward the shore. Archie hauled himself to his feet and looked out the window.

"We're sinking!" he cried.

"As long as the water doesn't put out the furnace, we're okay!" Clyde yelled.

Archie looked down again. More than half of Buster was already underwater. The engineering deck had to be completely submerged! The water had just reached Buster's neck when they felt the lurch of his feet meeting solid ground, and Clyde marched the steam man up out of the water onto Alcatraz Island.

"Made it!" Clyde said. "Told you we would! Good dog!"

Buster shook himself like a dog trying to get dry, spraying the buildings below with bay water and tossing around everything and everyone inside him. Kitsune giggled.

Sings-In-The-Night flew down and hovered in front of them. "Moffett's on a roof near the central courtyard. She's knocked down the walls. It's a prison break!"

Clyde steered Buster to follow her, stepping over a water tower.

"Kitsune, you and I can—" Archie began, but suddenly he was overwhelmed with a vision. He was holding his breath underwater, the sea a murky green all around him. He was naked but for a loincloth at his waist, and his long brown hair flowed around his face like seaweed.

"Enkidu," said a voice. He put a hand to his ear and found a tiny aetherical device there that carried sound. A Cathay woman riding a snakelike dragon swam up, speaking to him through an aetherical mouthpiece connected to the air tanks she wore. "Enkidu— Sun Wukong and Gilgamesh are already in place. Are you ready?"

Archie looked around. Nearby floated a young bearded man wearing a tunic and a monkey-man wearing fitted leather armor and carrying a staff.

Archie shook his head. He wasn't ready. He didn't know who "Enkidu" was or what he was doing here.

An eye opened in the darkness of the water before them: an eye fifty feet tall and glassy black, filled with stars.

Jandal a Haad, it whispered.

Archie felt the crack of a slap across his face, and he awoke from his dream back on the bridge of the steam man. Kitsune stood in front of him holding the lead pipe she'd hit him with.

"Dang, that's a bit much, isn't it?" Clyde asked.

"No," Kitsune said. "This doesn't hurt, does it?" she asked Archie, whacking him over the head with it again and again.

Archie caught the lead pipe. "No," he said, taking it away from her. "But it's really annoying."

"We lost you for a second there," Clyde said.

"Don't worry about it," Archie told him. But Archie was worried. Why was he hearing the song of a Mangleborn here? Now?

"There she is!" Clyde said.

Buster loomed over Mrs. Moffett. She stood on a rooftop with the Dragon Lantern, watching Alcatraz prisoners fight in the courtyard below.

Sings-In-The-Night met Archie and Kitsune in Buster's mouth. "Take Kitsune," Archie told her, and he jumped.

If there was one thing Archie was good at, it was falling.

Archie slammed into the rooftop behind Mrs. Moffett, almost crashing straight through. As he climbed to his feet, Sings-In-The-Night landed next to him with Kitsune.

Mrs. Moffett smiled at them. "So. You've brought friends this time," she said. "Do you really think three children, a giant steam man, and a dozen Dog Soldiers can stop me?"

Archie didn't understand—Dog Soldiers? Kitsune winked at him, and he understood: She was making Mrs. Moffett think they had brought reinforcements.

"Give me the Dragon Lantern," Archie told her.

"I can't just now," Mrs. Moffett said. "I need to use it again. Do you know who those men down there are?" she asked. "They are the worst criminals in the Republic of California. Maybe the worst criminals in all of the North Americas. *Monsters*, just like me. Just like you. And I'm going to take six of them with me. That's what I told them. I'm recruiting, you see. I'm putting together my own league. I call it the 'Shadow League.' Has a nice ring to it, don't you think? That's why they're fighting—to see which of them will get to escape with me." She patted the Dragon Lantern lovingly. "If only they realized what winning meant. Well, Sings-In-The-Night and I understand, don't we?"

"You can't use that on more people, Mina," Sings-In-The-Night said. "How can you, when you know how painful it is. How awful . . . "

"Don't you think someone else should experience that pain, Sings?" Mrs. Moffett asked. "Don't you think everyone should know what we went through?"

"I think they should know, yes. But not like this. These men don't deserve that. Nobody does."

"*Everybody* does," Mrs. Moffett said. "Californians, Cheyenne, Pawnee, Texans, Cherokee, Iroquois, Yankees. *Septemberists*," she said, looking straight at Archie. "Anyone who would trade the lives of children for their own safety and comfort. So I'm going to show them. I'm going to show them what happens when you let children be sacrificed so everyone else can live quiet, happy lives."

"Nobody sacrificed me," Archie said.

Mrs. Moffett laughed. She laughed long and hard. "No. No, they didn't sacrifice *you*, did they, Archie Dent?" She laughed again. "But they didn't use the lantern on you either."

"What do you mean?" Archie said. "You said it was."

"*I lied*," Mrs. Moffett told him. "Your fox girl can appreciate that, I think. The lantern wasn't used to create you; it was used to create *me*. That's why I wanted it back. But you needed that fairy tale to go after it for me."

Archie fumed. "You never knew, did you? You never knew where I came from, or what was done to me."

"Oh, no, I know all of those things," Mrs. Moffett told him. "It was all in the Septemberists' records. The ones you only get to see when you become the society's chief. It made for fascinating reading."

"Tell me," Archie said.

"Join me, and I'll tell you."

"*What?*"

"Join my Shadow League! The Darkness is in you. It has been all along. They *speak* to you. You *hear* the Mangleborn. Do you know how rare that is? But you fight it. You reject this amazing gift you have. Join me, and you'll never have to deny it ever again. You're the shadow, after all, aren't you? Given how *they made you*, I should think you're the darkest shadow of all."

"She's lying," Kitsune said. "She doesn't really know where you come from. She's trying to trick you."

"The invitation's open to you too," Mrs. Moffett said to Kitsune. "You'd be a wonderful addition. And you, Sings-In-The-Night."

"No," the flying girl said.

"But this is what we were made for, you and me," Mrs. Moffett said. "Look at us!" she said, rising up on her tentacles. "We're monsters, both of us! They *made* us this way—and I was made to be a *leader!*"

Mrs. Moffett opened the Dragon Lantern on the men who were left standing in the courtyard below, and they began to shriek.

"No!" Archie cried. He charged at Mrs. Moffett, but she turned and screamed. WOMWOMWOMWOMWOM! The roof collapsed under Archie's feet. Sings-In-The-Night snatched up Kitsune and took off, but Archie fell again. He crashed down through empty prison cells and was buried in broken bricks and twisted metal.

JANDAL A HAAD, a voice sang in his head. The same voice from before.

"No!" Archie cried. He spat dust and flailed with his arms and legs, knocking debris away from him. "No! My name is Archie Dent!"

ENKIDU. HERACLES. ARCHIE DENT. ALWAYS DIFFERENT, BUT ALWAYS THE SAME, the voice sang, and Archie's head was flooded with images of the League's other shadows, all mindlessly, furiously breaking and smashing and thumping things, and always hurting the ones they loved. Who was doing this to him? Mrs. Moffett? Kitsune? Only Mangleborn had been able to get inside his head like this, but there weren't any Mangleborn around. And still the visions came. Rayguns, lektricity, Manglespawn—none of them hurt like this hurt, the agony filling him, making him want to tear his own skin off to get it out. He was Heracles killing his own children. He was Enkidu howling naked in the forest. He was Archie Dent attacking Hachi and Fergus with a metal club in the prison of Malacar Ahasherat. The visions tormented him with pain and sorrow, and he pounded on his own head, trying to drive them away.

A giant brass hand brushed away the rest of the rubble on top of him, and Buster tried to pick Archie up. But the visions still filled him with rage. Archie batted the big brass hand away and punched at what was left of the prison wall, blowing it apart. Above him, Mrs. Moffett clung to a piece of the wall with her tentacles, the Dragon Lantern still turned on the mutating horrors just beyond him.

"Tell me!" Archie cried, pounding on the brick wall. "Tell me how I was made! Tell me where I come from!" The wall crumbled and fell on him, and he kicked and swatted at the bricks like they were a swarm of gnats. "Get off me! I hate you! Get off me!"

Above him, Mrs. Moffett sent Buster staggering with another sonic scream, then turned it on the other steam man that had arrived. There wasn't another steam man—it was another one of Kitsune's illusions—but it bought Buster time to get away from the sonic wave.

BE STILL, JANDAL A HAAD, the dream voice sang, knocking Archie to his knees.

One of the horrors Mrs. Moffett had created jumped on Archie, its lava skin hissing, and Archie tore it off and used it to beat down what was left of the building's walls.

"Archie! She's getting away!" Sings-In-The-Night called as she flew by. Archie didn't care. He picked up a twisted prison cell door and hurled it at her to make the bird girl leave him alone.

JANDAL A HAAD, BE STILL, the voice in his head said again.

"Who is that?" Archie cried, spinning around. "Who are you? Where are you?"

I AM GONG GONG, JANDAL A HAAD, the voice said. WHY DO YOU WAKE ME?

"My. Name. Is. Archie. Dent!" Archie cried, pounding the rubble at his feet with his fists with every word.

And then the earth underneath him moved.

Buster staggered, trying to keep his footing. The water tower crumpled. Cracks appeared in the buildings that hadn't fallen.

"Earthquake!" someone yelled. But this was no earthquake, and it wasn't Mrs. Moffett's screams again. The island was turning over in the water, and as it did, an enormous fin emerged on the side that was rising.

Alcatraz Prison was built on the back of a Mangleborn.

"Well, I didn't see that coming," Mrs. Moffett said.

Archie slid on the tilting ground and slammed into the wall of one of the buildings. As the island turned, the buildings leaned and then started to collapse. Buster scrambled up them like a mountain climber, trying to stay away from the water.

"Archie!" Clyde called. "Archie, we have to get out of here! The island's alive!"

Archie didn't care. Still angry, he ran across the face of one of the sideways buildings and threw himself at Mrs. Moffett. He hit her before she could scream, knocking the Dragon Lantern from her hands. Somewhere in the back of his mind, Archie knew he should dive after it, that the Dragon Lantern was what really mattered, but he was consumed by rage. Mrs. Moffett had lied to him. The Mangleborn beneath them was driving him crazy. The world was falling apart around him. He brought his fists together and smashed them down on the sideways building he and Mrs.

Moffett stood on. It collapsed, and they tumbled into a labyrinth of crumbling prison cells.

Mrs. Moffett scrabbled up out of the rubble, trying to keep her balance as the world turned. She ran the back of her hand across her mouth and came away with blood, and she smiled.

"I told you you were a monster," she said to Archie. "This is who you are. This is why you were created. To *destroy*."

Archie picked up a broken toilet and hurled it at her with a roar. She moved faster than any real person could, her tentacles pulling her sideways across the shattered building, and the toilet exploded where she'd been standing. The Dragon Lantern clattered down through the broken building, and she slithered after it.

JANDAL A HAAD, Gong Gong murmured inside Archie's head. *JANDAL A HAAD, LET ME SLEEP.*

Archie swung his fists at the floor. He swung his fists at the falling bricks. He saw Mrs. Moffett through his fury, clambering toward where the Dragon Lantern lay half buried in the wreckage. She was almost to it when Sings-In-The-Night swooped down and snatched it away.

"Archie! I've got it! I've got the lantern!" she called.

A thick tentacle whipped out from the writhing mass under Mrs. Moffett and caught Sings-In-The-Night by the leg.

"And I've got you!" Mrs. Moffett crowed.

It took the Jandal a Haad a long moment to process what was happening. Through the red-rimmed haze of his all-consuming rage, he watched as the bird girl fluttered in Mrs. Moffett's grasp, trying to break free. The bird girl called to him for help. The stone boy panted, fists still balled, anger still coursing through his veins, the voice in his head telling him to pick up a rock and throw it, kill them both; but the bird girl called out to him again, her words finally penetrating his madness.

"Archie!" Sings-In-The-Night cried. "Archie, help me!"

Archie. That was him. *His* name was Archie. Not Jandal a Haad.

He was a person, not a monster. He had a name. He had a family. He had friends. And Sings-In-The-Night was one of them. Sings-In-The-Night was his friend, and she needed help. Archie fought down the fury inside him, still breathing hard. He had to focus. Remember who he was. He had to stop Philomena Moffett. He had to save Sings-In-The-Night. Slowly, with difficulty, Archie's rage ebbed, only to be replaced by horror.

Mrs. Moffett had Sings-In-The-Night, and Archie was too far away to help her.

"Hold on! I'm coming!" Archie cried, his voice ragged from screaming. Archie tried climbing across the crumpled iron bars toward her, but they gave way and he fell. He clung desperately to a disintegrating wall and tried to pull himself back up.

Sings-In-The-Night's wings tore at the air, trying to pull her free, but Mrs. Moffett's tentacles anchored them like roots to the rubble. She pulled Sings-In-The Night down, a tentacle coiling up around the bird girl's leg while another slipped up around her neck. Sings-In-The-Night let out a choking gasp.

"Clyde! Kitsune! Help!" Archie called as bricks rained down on him. He could feel the wall he clung to collapsing.

"They created me to be a leader," Mrs. Moffett told Archie, her voice quiet and calm in the crashing chaos around them. She took the Dragon Lantern from Sings-In-The-Night, and the bird girl put her hands to the tentacle around her throat and tried uselessly to pull it loose. "But I was always a shadow," Mrs. Moffett said. "We all were. Monsters. Just like you, Archie. And you know what monsters do, Archie Dent. They destroy everything they love."

Crack. Mrs. Moffett's tentacle snapped Sings-In-The-Night's neck, and the bird girl's body went limp.

"*Nooooo!*" Archie cried.

The wall he was holding gave way, and he fell like a stone into the cold, dark sea.

30

Seawater swallowed Hachi, tumbling her like a shell on the beach. Water filled her eyes, her ears, and her mouth. She reached out blindly, grabbing the brass railing along the top of the streetcar before she was swept away. The water beat her like fists, trying to rip her loose, and with a searing pain that made her cry out underwater Hachi felt her shoulder dislocate. She gulped water, choking, and let go of the streetcar as the water pushed it over. She tumbled again and didn't know which way was up in the dark, churning water, until she struck a tree and wrapped herself around it.

The brunt of the wave finally passed, and the flood waters settled in. Hachi pulled herself up with her one good arm, branch by branch, until her head was above water. She gasped and coughed, sucking in air through the water in her throat. Her shoulder screaming in pain, she tried to climb higher in the tree.

The street was a river. Only the tops of streetlights and trees stood up out of the water, which poured into the second-story windows of the shops and homes all around her. The hotel she'd put the orphans on was so far away now she couldn't see it anymore, and when she cried out for help no one appeared in the windows and rooftops around her. With only one good arm, she was trapped here until the floodwaters receded, which could be days.

Or until someone came along in a submarine.

She saw the little two-person worker tug sail around the corner moments later, its periscope swinging this way and that as it searched for survivors.

"Here!" Hachi cried. She waved as much as she could while still holding on with her one good hand, and yelled out again. "Over here! Hey!"

The submarine turned like it was going down a side street, and Hachi panicked that it hadn't seen her. She tried to climb higher, but her dislocated shoulder shrieked in agony, and she slid even lower, her face buried against the tree bark in pain.

Ding-ding! Hachi looked up as the little sub rang its bell and pulled alongside her, anchoring itself to the tree with the claws it used to grab onto tankers and push them out to sea. The hatch on the top flipped open, and Fergus's head popped out wearing a white sailor cap.

Hachi laughed through her tears.

"Hello there, ma'am," Fergus said. "Looks like you could use a handsome sailor to rescue you."

"I could," Hachi said. "But you'll do."

"Sorry—had to steer around a streetcar under the water. Wouldn't know anything about that, would you?"

"It was in perfect condition when I got on board."

Fergus helped her into the sub, and she settled into the copilot's seat.

- 276 -

"My shoulder's dislocated," she told Fergus. "I'm going to reset it."

Fergus looked horrified. "Shouldn't a doctor do that?"

"Do you see any doctors around?"

"Well, no, but—do you even know *how* to do that?"

"Yes. I've done it before. Lots of times."

"Of course you have. All right. What do you need me to do?" Fergus asked.

"Nothing. I just wanted to let you know so you don't freak out."

Hachi slowly lifted her dislocated arm up over her shoulder, sucking in air as she fought the pain, and reached behind her head for her other shoulder. *Pop!* Her shoulder shifted back into position and relief washed over her. Her shoulder still hurt, but not nearly as badly.

"Oh, crivens," Fergus said, looking pale. "Telling me about that in advance did *not* help."

"Do you think it worked? Flooding the city?" Hachi asked.

"Well, there's no giant beastie tearing up the city anymore, so at a guess, I'd say yes."

Hachi nodded. "Thanks for giving me time to get people to safety. I needed it."

"At MacFerguson Demolition Services, safety is job one. Where to now, miss?"

Hachi had Fergus take them back to Marie Laveau's store. Laveau had been able to make her way back there before the flood and was sitting up on the rooftop with her two masked assistants and Erasmus Trudeau and his family. Dark clouds still rumbled over the city and rain still fell, but the hurricane winds and constant lightning were gone.

"We see it," Erasmus told them. "De water hit dat big snake monster and dragged it down, and it never come up again."

"Let's hope it's sitting at the bottom of Lake Pontchartrain again, sleeping off its adventure in the big city," Fergus said.

"I—I'm sorry I ran," Laveau said. She looked even older than her seventy years now, her drenched Baron Samedi tuxedo clinging to her frail body.

"You should have," Hachi told her. "We never expected you to fight that thing."

"But *you* did," Erasmus's wife said. "And for dat, we thank you."

"All part of the service," Fergus said, tipping his sailor cap.

"Will you get rid of that stupid thing?" Hachi said. She snatched it off his head and tossed it over the side of the building past Queen Theodosia, who hung in the air.

Everyone gasped. Trudeau hid his family behind him.

"Maman Brigitte!" Laveau said.

The lightning picked up around the rooftop again, making everybody but Fergus flinch.

"You put salt in my mouth," Maman Brigitte said, landing on the rooftop. "You try to kill me, Baron. But I live. And now I kill *you*."

Hachi put herself between Maman Brigitte and the others. "She's not Samedi, Maman. It was a trick. She's just Marie Laveau."

"Maybe Maman Brigitte believe you, maybe she don't," she said. The wind began to swirl again, though still not with the force of a hurricane. "Maybe Maman Brigitte kill her anyway, just to be sure. Maybe Maman Brigitte, she kill you *all* just to be sure."

Maman Brigitte raised her hands, and the storm intensified.

"I still have the voodoo doll!" Laveau said, pulling it out of her jacket.

"But where you get the salt?" Maman Brigitte said.

"The water!" Fergus said. "The floodwater is all seawater!"

Hachi dove for Maman Brigitte, driving her back to the edge of the rooftop. Fifteen feet below them, the floodwaters surged. Hachi pulled her knife.

"You kill me, you kill your queen!" Maman Brigitte said.

"I'm not going to kill you," Hachi said, her injured shoulder burning. "I'm just going to hurt you!"

Hachi stuck her knife in Maman Brigitte's arm, and the loa howled. Lightning flashed and thundered right on top of them, making Hachi flinch, and Maman Brigitte kicked her off. Another bolt exploded in the air above them again, and Hachi saw Fergus absorb it like a lightning rod through his outstretched hand. Laveau, her assistants, and Trudeau and his family cowered at the far side of the roof.

"I got the lightning!" Fergus yelled. "Get her into the water!"

Hachi went for Maman Brigitte again, and they grappled by the edge of the roof.

"You drive me out, girl, and you never find out what happened to your daddy!" Maman Brigitte said.

"What do you know about it?" Hachi said. Her shoulder throbbed with pain as she deflected an attack from the loa.

"Maman Brigitte don't know nothing," Maman Brigitte said. "But that body Samedi was riding, she know. And Maman Brigitte, she have the same power her husband does to make the zombi." Hachi jabbed her knife at Theodosia's other arm, but the loa caught Hachi's wrist and leaned in close where no one else could hear. "You let Maman Brigitte go, and she bring that woman back and make that woman tell you her secrets. You drive Maman Brigitte away, you never *ever* find out."

Hachi paused. Bring Blavatsky back as a zombi? Could Maman Brigitte really do that? If she could—if she did—the secret of Chuluota didn't have to die with the bokor. Hachi could finally learn what Blavatsky was doing there, and who else was with her.

That moment of indecision was all it took. Maman Brigitte wrenched the knife from her hand and plunged it into Hachi's stomach.

Hachi sank to her knees.

"*No!*" Fergus cried.

Maman Brigitte smiled and turned to the rest of the people on the rooftop.

Bwaaaat. A purple raygun beam lanced out, hitting Maman Brigitte square in the chest. Queen Theodosia's dead body toppled over the side of the roof and into the water below.

Erasmus Trudeau lowered his aether pistol. "Dat loa not going to hurt my family. She not going to hurt nobody no more."

Fergus rushed to Hachi and put his hand to her bleeding stomach. Marie Laveau and her assistants were close behind.

Hachi grabbed Fergus's arm, her hand slick with her own blood. "She told me—she told me she could bring Blavatsky back. Get answers. And for a moment, I—just for a moment, I—"

"Hush," Fergus told her. "You've just been stabbed."

"Been stabbed before," Hachi said. "Lots of times."

"Of course you have," said Fergus.

Laveau pulled back Hachi's shirt to examine the wound. "I can open her up when we get back downstairs," Laveau said, "see if anything has been damaged. But we must stop this bleeding."

"I'm going to cauterize your wound," Fergus told Hachi. "I just wanted to let you know so you don't freak out."

Lektricity crackled between Fergus's thumb and forefinger, and he held it to the inch-and-a-half cut on Hachi's stomach. She arched her back as the lektricity coursed through her, and Fergus yanked his hand away.

"Telling me . . . didn't help," Hachi gasped.

Laveau examined the wound. "The bleeding's stopped." She turned to her assistants. "Go back downstairs. See if the water's gone from the second floor. We need my medical things."

"Last chance," Hachi murmured, slowly losing consciousness. "Last chance to find out . . . what Blavatsky was doing in Chuluota. . . ."

Marie Laveau took off her jacket and folded it into a pillow for Hachi's head. "Oh, my dear *chère*, but of course it isn't."

31

Everything moved in slow motion for Archie.

The dark, cold seawater swallowed him, air bubbles hanging suspended right before his eyes. Sunlight glistened off the top of the water, like the light filtering down through the quartz ceiling in the Great Bear's cave in Nova Scotia. The chaos of a few seconds before was gone, and everything was quiet and still.

Then Archie sank.

He flailed his arms and legs, trying to get back to the surface, but he dropped like a rock. Because he *was* a rock. A rock in the shape of a boy. Archie stopped struggling, but his hands still reached for the surface, still reached for Clyde and Buster and Kitsune and Mr. Rivets.

And Sings-In-The-Night.

Archie bumped to a rest among plants and corals. He put a hand to the seafloor to right himself, but it wasn't sandy. It was soft and squishy. Slick, like sharkskin. The whole floor of the sea was made of the stuff. He poked a finger into it, and it bounced back.

Beside him, a giant eye opened. Just a crack. It was glassy and black and twenty feet tall and full of stars, just like in his dream of Enkidu.

JANDAL A HAAD, Gong Gong's deep voice-song murmured in Archie's head. *JANDAL A HAAD, LET ME SLEEP.*

The seafloor tilted, and Archie tumbled slowly down it through the rough coral and slimy plants. He came to the edge of the tilting reef and fell off, barnacles scraping at him. He sank another few feet and hit bottom again—a sandy bottom this time, barren and dark. Above him, the giant fin he'd thought was the ocean floor settled again, and the giant eye closed. Gong Gong the Mangleborn wanted to sleep, and Archie was more than happy to let him.

Archie looked around, trying to make out shapes in the darkness. He panicked—how long had he been holding his breath? He was going to drown! Then he realized: He hadn't been holding his breath at all. He'd forgotten to as he sank, maybe because he hadn't needed to. Archie put a hand to his throat. He wasn't breathing in water. He just . . . wasn't breathing at all. He was so inhuman he didn't even need air. Maybe he really was indestructible. Archie didn't understand how that was possible, but nothing about who he was or what he was made sense to him. He should be dead, again, but he wasn't. Again.

Unlike Sings-In-The-Night, who shouldn't be dead, but was. Sings-In-The-Night, who'd been a part of the League of Seven for barely a week. *His* League of Seven! Archie sat on the cold, dark ocean floor and watched it all replay in his mind. Philomena Moffett catching her, Archie trying and failing to get to her, Mrs. Moffett snapping Sings-In-The-Night's neck. *No. No no no no no.* It was all Archie's fault. He'd messed everything up. He'd led his friends to Alcatraz Island without a plan, and then he'd lost control. Lost himself. Kitsune and Clyde might even be dead, for all he knew. He'd abandoned them in his rage. He hadn't been there to fight alongside them. To protect them. And now Sings-In-The-Night was dead, and Mrs. Moffett had the lantern.

Archie put his head in his hands and wished Hachi and Fergus were here. They would understand. They could help him. But they weren't here. He wouldn't see them again until Houston. And maybe not even then, if he couldn't swim out of the bay.

Archie stood, the sand of the seafloor swirling around him. Even though he was indestructible, it was scary down here. He wanted to get back on land. He jumped off the sand, kicking and waving his arms, but he quickly sank right back to the bottom of the bay.

He was made of stone, and stones didn't float.

Panic seized him. What if he spent the rest of his life down here? And how long *was* the life of a boy made out of stone? Archie had never thought about it before, but now he wondered if he would live forever. If maybe he would be stuck here, on the ocean floor, forever. He spun around in the water, sand kicking up around him again, and he flinched as a giant crab worked its way up out of the sand and scurried away on its gnarled crab legs.

Stop freaking out, you blinking flange, Archie told himself. *Even if you can't swim, you can still walk.* He tried to calm himself. Like the crab, he could walk along the ocean floor. But which direction? The last thing he wanted to do was walk out of the bay into the ocean and come up a year later in the Japans.

The ocean is down; Don Francisco is up, he told himself. He walked in a broad circle until he could get his bearings, and then started up the sloping sands toward the city. After what seemed like an eternity, he saw the enormous round pilings that supported the city's wharf growing out of the sand. A big metal cage filled with Dungeness crabs stirred and began to rise from the floor of the bay, and Archie climbed on top of it, riding it like an elevator. He stepped off as it came up to Fisherman's Wharf in downtown Don Francisco, much to the wonder and amazement of the tattooed Ohlone fishermen working the winch.

They were even more surprised when the giant brass steam man came loping and whistling at them down the pier. The fishermen scattered and ran as Buster barked and danced around Archie, knocking barrels and crab cages into the sea.

"Okay, okay!" Archie said, trying not to get knocked back into the ocean himself. "Hello, Buster. Hello. Clyde? Are you in there?"

He wasn't. Buster picked Archie up in his mouth and ran with him back along the wharf, depositing him near a group of Don Francisco police and ambulance workers who all stood talking with Clyde.

Clyde saw him and hurried over to shake his hand. "We thought we'd lost you," he told Archie. "But I told them you were . . . pretty indestructible."

"Yeah," Archie said. "I fell into the bay and had to walk back. How did you get Buster back?"

"Hitched a ride with a whale oil tanker," Clyde said.

Buster left them to go sit at the far end of the pier, smokestack wagging, where he watched Alcatraz Island floating in the distance.

"He's been sitting there ever since we got back," Clyde said. "Waiting for you and Sings-In-The-Night."

"Could she be—?" Archie asked.

"No," Clyde said. "I saw her die. Kitsune saw it too."

Archie closed his eyes. He'd seen it too, but he'd hoped that somehow maybe he'd been wrong.

"Where is she? Kitsune, I mean."

Clyde led Archie to a small beach at the end of Fisherman's Wharf, where Kitsune had arranged thousands of little white seashells on the wet sand in the shape of a bird, its wings spread wide.

"I robbed an Illini chief's tomb near Shikaakwa once," she said, laying the last shells in her design. "He was lying on a bed of sea-shell beads in the shape of a giant bird. Figured she deserved a hero's burial too."

"When the tide comes in, all that's just going to get swept away," Archie said.

"Good," Kitsune said, rubbing the sand off her hands. "Then they can fly to her in the sea."

They were all quiet for a moment. All Archie could see was Mrs. Moffett breaking Sings-In-The-Night's neck and dropping her into the ocean while he hung there helpless and watched.

"You went crazy," Kitsune said at last.

Archie flushed. "I'm sorry. I kind of—I kind of do that sometimes."

"You threw a prison door at Sings-In-The-Night," Kitsune said. "You threw things and smashed things while Sings-In-The-Night went for the Dragon Lantern, and Mrs. Moffett killed her for it."

Archie closed his eyes and hung his head. "I'm sorry. When I get like that, I can't think," Archie told them. "I lose my mind, and I become . . . I become a monster. I've been trying to control it. My friend Hachi, she's been teaching me to focus. But they get inside my head. Start telling me things. Make me mad."

Neither Clyde nor Kitsune had anything to say to that.

"Everything on Alcatraz was destroyed," Clyde said finally. "Most of it ended up in the harbor as the island turned."

"Because it wasn't an island," Archie said. "It was a Mangleborn. That's what was making me crazy."

"So what do we do now, boss?" Kitsune asked Archie.

Archie didn't know. Everything was lost. Sings-In-The-Night, Mrs. Moffett, the Dragon Lantern.

"We go east," Clyde answered. The League's leader, leading. "That's the direction Mrs. Moffett went."

"Back to New Rome?" Archie asked.

"No. Paiute country," Clyde said. "Where they're bringing the Transcontinental Railroad together next week. Kitsune followed her to the train station. She bought a ticket for it, special."

"Why? What's she want to do there?"

"Make trouble," Kitsune said.

"What about the men she turned into monsters?" Archie asked. "Her 'Shadow League'?"

"They didn't go with her," Kitsune said. "She left alone."

"The rest of them disappeared into the countryside," Clyde said. "They've got police out looking for them. With Buster's help, we could probably get them all rounded up in a couple of weeks."

Archie shook his head. "No. You're right. We have to stop Mrs. Moffett. She's got the lantern."

If they *could* stop Mrs. Moffett. She'd beaten them too easily at Alcatraz, and it was mostly Archie's fault.

"What about that thing underneath the prison?" Clyde asked.

"It's not going to rise. Not now, at least," Archie said. "It just wants to sleep. It . . . it told me."

Kitsune cocked her head as though looking at Archie in a new way, and Clyde searched the sand at his feet like there might be some answers there to the questions in his frown.

"I'll explain everything about how I hear them when we're on the way," Archie promised. "As much as I understand it, anyway. I just—I just want you to know, I'm not one of them. I'm not a monster. I really am your friend."

"I'm glad," said Clyde. "'Cause I'd hate to have you for an enemy, and that's a fact."

The tide began to come in, pulling away the first shells in Kitsune's memorial to Sings-In-The-Night.

"Come on," Clyde said. "I gotta go tell Buster his bird friend ain't coming back."

32

The sun glinted over the white-capped mountains on the horizon, and waves of heat rose over the broad, dry salt flats of Paiute country as Buster steamed into Salt Lake City. A crowd was gathered around the railroad just south of town where the two ends of the Transcontinental Railroad finally met—one built east from Don Francisco, the other built west from Cahokia on the Plains. A newly built platform for official speeches bore the flags and banners of the various nations crossed by the rail line, and the salt flats all around it were full of steamcars, airships, and Tik Tok attendants.

Buster immediately drew a huge crowd of his own, including a nervous contingent of Paiute soldiers there to guard the ceremony. Clyde changed into his cleanest UN Steam Cavalry uniform and descended to introduce himself, telling everyone he had been sent as an official representative of the United Nations. Clyde shook hands and showed off Buster while Archie, Kitsune, and Mr. Rivets searched the crowd for Mrs. Moffett.

"She might have gone on back east," Kitsune said.

"No. I think she's here," Archie said. "She loves an audience. And what better audience is there than this?"

Besides the crowd, there were reporters and photographers from all the continent's major newspapers—*The New Rome Times, The Houston Chronicle, The Don Francisco Examiner, The Shikaakwa Sun, The Cahokia Post-Dispatch, The Standing Peachtree Journal*— and tribal chiefs and VIPs from coast to coast. As soon as the last ceremonial spike was hammered in, news reports would fly away from Salt Lake City by pneumatic post, announcing the opening of the railroad that finally connected one side of the continent to the other. Mrs. Moffett would be here, Archie was sure. She wouldn't miss the chance to announce her intentions to the world.

"Then if I were her," Kitsune said, "I'd be hiding in plain sight. That's the best place to hide."

"I would take Miss Kitsune's word as authoritative on that score," Mr. Rivets said.

Kitsune bowed. "Thank you, Mr. Rivets. It's always nice to have one's skills respected. Sorry about the eyes, by the way."

"Nothing that couldn't be repaired, miss," Mr. Rivets said, indefatigable as always. "In fact, it prompted something of an upgrade." Mr. Rivets gave the wind-up key on his chest a turn.

"Let's spread out. If you see her, yell," Archie said.

Archie moved among the adults. The men wore black three-piece suits and top hats, and the women wore big pastel hoop skirts and fancy bonnets. One woman wore a hat that looked like a bird's nest, with fake birds hovering over it on wobbly wires. For the millionth time since they'd left Don Francisco, Archie saw Sings-In-The-Night struggle to fly away, saw the tentacle coil up around her, heard the *crack* as her neck broke. No matter what he did, he couldn't stop thinking about it. Every little thing reminded him of it. Sings-In-The-Night's death would haunt him for the rest of his life.

"If I could have your attention, please," someone announced from the podium. "If all our special guests would assemble around the Golden Spike, we'd like to take a photo to commemorate this august occasion."

Men and women from various tribes gathered where the railroad came together, and Cheyenne engineers drove two locomotives face-to-face with each other behind them to symbolize the meeting of East and West. A little Navajo man with a porkpie hat ran around telling the VIPs to squeeze closer together for the photograph, and Archie scanned their faces, looking for Mrs. Moffett. She wasn't among them. Where was she? Was she already on her way back to the East Coast, to turn the Dragon Lantern on New Rome, or Tethis, or Philadelphia? No, he couldn't believe it. She had to be here! He scoured the crowd for her face, but he still didn't see her.

"Yes, just there, please," the little Navajo man said. "Just there. And in back? If you could move in a little closer, please?"

A red raygun beam sliced through the air above the crowd—then another—and there were screams. Archie caught Kitsune's eyes in the crowd and saw Clyde running for Buster. This was it! Mrs. Moffett was making her move! Archie pushed through the tall adults all around him, ready for a fight, but it wasn't Mrs. Moffett shooting a raygun. It was Jesse James!

The FreeTok bandit rode up with his gang in their modified steamtruck, whooping and hollering and firing into the air with their rayguns. If there was one person who loved a show more than Mrs. Moffett, it was Jesse James.

Archie ran out to meet him as he climbed out of the truck. "No! You can't be here! Not now," Archie said.

"And miss liberating all this wonderful machinery?" James said.

A Paiute guard raised his oscillator to shoot, but one of the James

Gang was faster. A ruby red aether beam lanced out and knocked the Paiute guard to the ground. People screamed.

"All right!" James yelled, stepping around Archie. "Let's not have any more heroes, and everyone will walk away from this in one piece! This here's a holdup! You have the honor of being robbed by the one and only Jesse James, outlaw FreeTok. This is a story you'll tell your children, and your children will tell it to *their* children, and they'll tell it to *their* children. You'll have reporters knocking down your doors to hear your tale of the day you were robbed by the great Jesse James, and your names'll be in papers from coast to coast. Maybe even a dime novel or two. And all it'll cost you are your machine men and your steamcars."

A woman in the crowd cried out, and some of the men yelled their objections. Jesse James silenced them all with a shot from one of the raypistols he wore at his belt.

"Now, now. I think that's a small price to pay for being famous, don't you?" he said.

Clyde steamed up in Buster, ready to fight, but Archie signaled for him to wait and grabbed James by the arm. "Jesse, don't do this. Philomena Moffett's here somewhere—one of the kids they experimented on at Dodge City. The one who killed everyone in Beaver Run. She killed Sings-In-The-Night in Don Francisco!"

That gave James pause, but he shook his head and leaned in close. "Listen, kid. I like you. You're not like all these other meatbags who wouldn't wind their Tik Toks unless they needed a cup of tea. And I know there's nothing I could do to stop you from tossing me into the next territory. But this doesn't concern you. You let me take care of my business here, and nobody gets hurt. You interfere, and my boys'll start shooting innocent people."

Archie let Jesse James go and found Kitsune in the crowd. Her eyes asked him if they were going to fight the FreeToks. Archie frowned and shook his head. What were they supposed to do? He couldn't let people get hurt—not when all James really wanted was to steal their machinery.

James motioned to his FreeTok gang, and they spilled off the truck and ran for the Tik Toks and steamcars. Two of them climbed into the parked locomotives. James stayed behind to work the crowd.

"Now," he said, "I understand we have members of the press on hand for today's heist. I'm afraid I don't have time for an interview, but I'll gladly pose for photos, gents!" James spotted the men and women set up in front of the locomotives. "And lookit here— we've already got one all lined up!" he said. "Move aside," he told a woman in the middle. "Squeeze over so I've got room."

The woman hurried away, but the rest of the VIPs stayed frozen where they were, afraid James would shoot them if they moved.

"Archie, you want in on this?" James asked, offering him a place by his side. Archie just frowned at him. "Suit yourself," James said. "All right. Where's the photographer at? I'm ready for my publicity photo!"

"All ready, Mr. James," called a voice Archie had heard before. Kitsune and Clyde recognized it too, and they all three turned their heads to where Philomena Moffett stood, one hand on the shutter release of a big accordion camera, the other on the Dragon Lantern, sitting high on a pole like a camera flash.

"Say cheese," Mrs. Moffett said, and she opened the lantern wide.

Hachi and Fergus bowed to Marie Laveau as she came into the room. "Your Majesty," Hachi said.

"Stop it," Laveau said. "Nobody bows to me."

"But you're the queen now," Fergus told her. "Not just the Voodoo Queen, but the queen of Louisiana."

When Theodosia died and Aaron Burr's short family line ended, Louisiana needed a new leader. And there had been no question who it would be. As the storm cleared and the waters receded, the people of New Orleans had come by the hundreds to Marie Laveau's door begging her to be Louisiana's queen, and at last she had accepted. But she had refused to sit on the throne in the palace the Burrs had built, choosing instead to rule from behind the counter in her shop, where she and her masked assistants met them now.

Whether or not she wanted the job, Fergus thought, Marie La-veau looked every inch a queen. She wore her beautiful middle-aged body, and over that she wore an elegant white dress and a sparkling pearl necklace. On her head, instead of a crown, she wore a blue tignon with yellow fleur-de-lis on the fabric, the headscarf twisted and pinched up into knots like the spikes of a proper crown.

"I am a voodoo queen, for a voodoo nation," Laveau said. "I will govern how the power of Li Grande Zombi in the lake is used—and I will teach my people all about the Mangleborn, so no one makes the same mistake again. There will be no more secrets."

An entire nation who knew about the Mangleborn! Fergus won-dered if that was wise, then wondered why it wouldn't be. The Sep-temberists worked so hard to keep the existence of the Mangleborn a secret, but that meant some people discovered them accidentally, without understanding what they were doing. Like he had tinkered with lektricity without realizing the consequences. Could every-one know about the Mangleborn without it scaring them to death or driving them mad? Well, if there was one place in the Ameri-cas where they could understand the Mangleborn, it was New Or-leans, where the dead sometimes walked the streets.

"Will you even teach them the secret to your long life?" Hachi asked, like she was sharing a joke with Laveau. Hachi's right arm was in a sling, and Fergus knew her stomach was bound tightly with a corset of bandages where Laveau, wearing her older body, had operated on her. But even weak from her injuries, Hachi had been in a good mood ever since Laveau had told her there was another way to get answers from the dead Helena Blavatsky.

"No," Laveau said coyly. "That is perhaps one secret that I will keep for myself. Shall we begin the séance?"

Laveau gestured toward the stairs to the second floor, where Erasmus Trudeau stood beaming at them. He bowed low to Fer-gus and Hachi as he unlatched the chain that kept customers down-stairs.

"Miss Hachi," he said. "Master Fungus."

"*Fergus.*"

Erasmus gave him a big white smile.

Laveau had set up a round table in a small room on the second floor with five chairs. Erasmus pulled one out for Laveau, and Fergus did the same for Hachi. Laveau thanked Erasmus; Hachi frowned at Fergus. When Erasmus was finished, he took a place by the door.

"You're not joining us?" Fergus asked.

"Oh no. Erasmus, he agree to be de queen's personal bodyguard. But I tell her already, dat voodoo magic stuff not part of the deal."

"Then who are the other two chairs for?" Fergus asked.

Hachi smiled. "Will your mother and daughter be joining us?" she asked the queen.

"*Her mother and daughter?*" Fergus asked.

Hachi glanced at Erasmus by the door, but Laveau smiled. "He knows. I thought I'd better share my secret with my bodyguard, at least. He'd be bound to figure it out."

"Figure what out?" Fergus asked. "What are you talking about?"

"We're talking about how Marie Laveau knew that first night why Blavatsky's spell to give Theodosia eternal youth wasn't going to work. Because there *is* no spell that gives you eternal youth."

Laveau put a hand to her cheek. "Oh, but if only there were," she said.

"But—we've seen you change!" Fergus said.

"No," Hachi said. "You've seen Marie Laveau, Marie Laveau the Second, and Marie Laveau the Third."

Laveau's two assistants pulled off their masks. Underneath were the seventy-year-old Laveau and the ten-year-old Laveau. They smiled mischievously at Fergus's stunned look.

"Mother, daughter, granddaughter," Hachi said, "all named Marie Laveau. They pretend to be assistants when they're not being the official Laveau so they can listen in on conversations and know what people are talking about later when it's their turn."

"You—but—I thought—how . . . ?" Fergus spluttered. He turned to Hachi. "You knew? For how long?"

"I guessed the minute I saw the new Marie Laveau that first night at the palace, and I kept an eye on them all after that," she said.

"I'm an idiot," Fergus said.

Queen Laveau laughed. "No. But luckily the people of New Orleans are as willing to believe the impossible as you are. Together with the daughter I hope my own daughter has one day, and her daughter, and her daughter on down the line, we will forever be Marie Laveau, the eternally young queen of Louisiana."

"Long live the queen," Fergus muttered.

"I promise we won't tell," Hachi said.

"We know you won't," the older Marie Laveau said, taking a place at the table. The youngest Marie Laveau sat down beside her. "And now, *chère*," the old Laveau said, "let us ask Helena Blavatsky what she knows about your past."

A man right beside Archie screamed as his skin erupted in porcupine spikes. A woman near him melted into a puddle of mucus. Another man grew a duck bill, shaggy yak hair, and a lion's tail. The lantern didn't affect everyone—just half the crowd, maybe less—but the resulting chaos was immediate. Some of the Manglespawn created by the lantern were like Sings-In-The-Night: They weren't evil, just frightened and confused by their mutations. They ran away screaming. Archie knew they would have to be rounded up later, but for now they weren't a threat. The rest became inhuman animals. Monsters. Those turned on anything that moved—human or monster or Tik Tok—biting and clawing and oozing. The air was filled with roars and shrieks and wailing, and it was impossible to tell which was human and which was Manglespawn.

Archie kicked a slathering snail-thing away from a screeching woman who wouldn't get up off her knees. Archie had to pick her up to haul her to safety. "Get the people separated from the monsters!" Archie yelled to Kitsune.

Kitsune shook off her momentary horror at the things the people around her had turned into and began working her illusions on the humans, herding them toward the edges of the crowd. High above them, Clyde didn't need any guidance—Buster was already wading into the crowd, stomping on monsters and hurling others into the distance.

Archie found Jesse James blasting away at a mob of creatures that had once been VIPs posing for a photograph.

"*What in the name of the Emartha Machine Man Company is going on?*" he cried.

"It's Mrs. Moffett! I told you! One of the experiments from Dodge City!" he told the FreeTok. "She used the thing they used on her on all these people!" Archie pulled a coiling vine-creature off James and tossed it away. "I need you and your gang to help me protect all the people who weren't turned!"

James blasted a writhing mass of snakes right in what Archie guessed was its face. "Protect the meatbags?" James said. "Forget it. We're grabbing the Tik Toks and the locomotives and getting out of here."

Archie grabbed James by the shoulders and spun him around to face him. "They treat you like soulless automatons because that's what they think you are," Archie told him. "This is your chance to prove to them you're not."

Jesse James stared back at him through his glass-and-metal eyes, then cursed. "Cole! Clell! Robert!" he called, amplifying his voice. "You and the other boys, form a circle around that locomotive! We're getting these people out of here!"

One of them started to argue, but James cut him off. "Just do it!" He turned to Archie. "We better get some good press for this," he said.

"The best," Archie promised. "I know a dime novelist." He ran back into the fight, slugging a cross between a bear and a bird. "Get the people to the trains!" he called to Clyde, Kitsune, and Mr. Rivets. "Jesse James is going to get them out of here!"

Buster plucked a woman up and put her inside the protective circle the James Gang had made, and Archie saw Kitsune chasing a terrified man in that direction. Archie almost hated to wonder what she was making him see.

WOMWOMWOMWOMWOM! A sonic wave hit Archie, knocking him head over heels through the crowd. Monsters and people went flying with him. When he'd finally tumbled out of the wave's reach, he picked himself up and found Mrs. Moffett in the crowd. It was easy; she was coming right for him.

Mrs. Moffett clenched her fists at her sides and screamed again—*WOMWOMWOMWOMWOM!*—but this time Archie was ready for it. He dug his heels in the hard-packed salt flat and leaned into the pounding sound. It beat against him like the waves of the Don Francisco Bay.

Mrs. Moffett kept coming at him. The sound waves got stronger, harder to fight, but then she ran out of breath and had to stop, taking in huge gulps of air. Archie staggered toward her, his ears ringing, and threw a wild punch at her. She danced out of the way on her octopus legs.

"You should be honored," Mrs. Moffett told him, still sucking in deep breaths. "You're witnessing history. The start of the Monster War."

A dog-creature leaped for a cowering woman nearby, but Buster was there to swat it away. Mrs. Moffett screamed at the steam man, and Buster staggered, knocked sideways under the oscillating sound waves.

"Don't get close!" Archie yelled. He charged Mrs. Moffett, but she turned her sonic scream on him again. Without his feet planted, he flew through the air and slammed into the ground.

Mrs. Moffett glided over to him on her tentacles. "The way the Dragon Lantern works," she said, "is by activating latent Mangleborn DNA in humans. It's there, in some of us, after millennia of interbreeding. Hideous, horrible interbreeding between Mangle-spawn and humans. And sometimes Mangleborn and humans. Or maybe we're related, somewhere back in the mists of time. Maybe we're *all* monsters of one kind or another."

Archie wasn't on his feet yet, and Mrs. Moffett was taking another deep breath to scream again. He thumped his fist on the salt flat, knocking everyone around them off their feet. Everyone except Mrs. Moffett. She was thrown back, but her swarming mass of tentacles caught her and righted her before she could fall.

"Oh, good," Mrs. Moffett said. "Primitive, but good. I suppose my weapon isn't much more sophisticated."

Mrs. Moffett screamed. Archie dug in just in time, throwing his arms up in front of his face to avoid the beating the scream gave him. The ground ripped up and flew away all around him and his white hair whipped into his eyes, but he stood his ground.

Mrs. Moffett's scream died, and Archie lurched toward her, trying to catch her with a punch again. But Mrs. Moffett was still too fast for him.

"Stalemate, Archie Dent. They made us both too well," Mrs. Moffett said. "Not all of us have it, mind you. Mangleborn DNA. Only about forty percent. That's what Dr. Echohawk and the others at the Forge discovered. That's why the lantern only worked on some of these people. And that's why it only worked on some of the children at the Forge. *Just the lucky ones.* It doesn't work on your fox-tailed friend because her Mangleborn DNA was already activated. She was born a monster." Mrs. Moffett looked up at Buster saving another person from the Manglespawn. "I wonder if it would work on your other friend? We'll find out when I pry open that tin can he's driving."

Archie wiped salty dirt from his mouth. "You're trying to make me mad," Archie said. "You can't beat me, so you're trying to make me lose control. But I'm not going to let it happen again," he told her. "Not after what happened to Sings-In-The-Night."

"You think so?" Mrs. Moffett said sweetly. "You think nothing can make you that angry again? Oh! I have a *wonderful* idea! What if I told you where you come from, Archie Dent? How you were made? I thought it was more torture for you not to know, but now I think the truth may just do the trick. I think knowing how you were born might just make you mad enough to lose control. *Forever.*"

⟲

A cold breeze swirled in the little room above Marie Laveau's shop, flickering the candles on the table where the five of them held hands—Fergus, Hachi, Marie Laveau, and her daughter and granddaughter.

"Papa Legba, I beseech you," the oldest Laveau said. "Open the door to the afterlife, that we may speak once more with one you have taken past the crossroads. Papa Legba, bring to us the unsettled spirit of Helena Blavatsky, dark bokor of Russia, so that she can make right in death the wrongs she did in life, and find rest for her soul."

Fergus felt Hachi's hand tighten in his own as she looked up sharply. "Find rest? You mean by telling us what she knows, she'll earn a better afterlife?" Hachi asked.

"She may," the elder Laveau said. "In voodoo, good deeds are rewarded."

"But I want her to suffer."

"Then say so, and I will bring this séance to an end," Laveau told her.

Hachi looked imploringly at Fergus.

"You came here to find out what this woman knows about how your father died, about why they killed all the men in your village," Fergus told her. "You can't go home without that. Not after all this. She may not find rest if you don't ask her, but neither will you."

Hachi squeezed his hand. "I guess dead is dead, after all."

"Well, not so much here in New Orleans," Fergus muttered.

"Shall I continue?" Laveau asked, and Hachi nodded.

"Helena Blavatsky, bokor of Russia, I call thee to our table," Laveau said. "Speak to us, witch. Speak to us from beyond the grave."

The smoke from the candles swirled over the table and hung there, gaining form, until Fergus saw the head and shoulders of Blavatsky take shape. He heard Hachi suck in a sharp breath beside him.

"I am here," the smoke Blavatsky said.

Laveau nodded to Hachi, who for the first time in her life seemed afraid.

"Blavatsky," she said, her voice hoarse and shaking. "Tell me what happened eleven years ago at Chuluota. Tell me why my father and ninety-nine other men were killed."

The smoke Blavatsky raised her hands. "Oh, no. Don't ask me that," she begged. "It's too awful."

"Tell her, and your soul may at last find rest," Laveau said.

The smoke Blavatsky cried, which surprised Fergus. Real tears dropped into the candles, making them hiss and splutter.

"Forgive me. Forgive me!" Blavatsky sobbed.

"Not until you tell me what you did," Hachi said.

Blavatsky nodded. "I will tell you. May the Hidden Masters have mercy on my soul, I will tell you. Where shall I begin?"

"Tell me who else was there. The names of the other men and women, the strangers who came to Chuluota that night and killed the hundred and anyone else who got in their way."

"There were seven of us," Blavatsky said. "I will tell you our names."

"Do you want me to write this down?" Fergus whispered to Hachi.

"No," Hachi said, her voice hard and cold. "I'll remember."

34

"I don't care," Archie said. He took a swing at Mrs. Moffett, but she danced out of the way. "I don't want to know where I come from."

"Of course you want to know!" Mrs. Moffett crowed. "That's how I got you to abandon your friends and go after the Dragon Lantern in the first place. Because you *had* to know."

Archie could feel himself getting angrier. He could feel himself losing control. But no—he wouldn't. He *couldn't*. Not after what he'd let happen when he lost control the last time. Archie clapped his hands, making a sonic boom of his own. It knocked Mrs. Moffett back off her octopus legs before she could catch herself. Archie rushed her and tried to jump her, but she caught him in her swirling mass of tentacles and held him helplessly up off the ground.

"Last chance, Archie Dent," Mrs. Moffett said. "Join me, and I promise I *won't* tell you where you come from."

"No," Archie said. "No! I'm not a monster." He wriggled in her grasp, trying to get free.

"Oh, but you are a monster, Archie Dent. I told you they used the Dragon Lantern on you when you were a baby, but that was a lie. They never used the Dragon Lantern on you. They couldn't. *Because you were never human*," Mrs. Moffett said, her eyes bright with excitement.

Archie's blood was boiling. He had to get away before he heard any more, but he couldn't get any kind of power to his punches and kicks with Mrs. Moffett holding him. Instead he pulled his hands toward each other and yanked away the tentacles coiled around each wrist. More of Mrs. Moffett's tentacles grabbed for him, but he punched her in the head.

Mrs. Moffett howled and rolled away, her human hands holding her face. Her tentacles had kept him from throwing a full punch, or she'd be dead. Instead she wiped a thin line of blood from her mouth and smiled a wolfish smile.

"Still not angry?" she asked.

WOMWOMWOMWOMWOM! She hit him with another blast of her sonic scream, and he went tumbling again, slamming into one of the locomotives. It tipped over and crashed onto its side with a thundering clangor of metal and wood. As the sonic waves petered out again, Archie caught sight of the second train, running backward away from the fray. Jesse James and his gang were escaping with the humans who had survived the Dragon Lantern and its hideous creations.

Mrs. Moffett glided over to him. "You're not human, Archie Dent. *I'm* more human now than you *ever* were," she said.

Archie struggled to his feet. "That's not true," he said. He reached into the wreckage of the locomotive and grabbed it, lifting it high over his shoulder like it was a lacrosse stick and Mrs. Moffett was the ball.

"Oh, but it is," Mrs. Moffett told him, unperturbed. "Blavatsky and the others made you out of clay."

Archie froze. Clyde and Buster stomping on Manglespawn, Kitsune jumping from podium to table to chair—everything around him slowed to a stop like it was frozen in ice. He shuddered in the chill.

"What did you say?" he asked with a voice that came from someplace far, far away.

"I said, *Helena Blavatsky made you out of clay,*" Mrs. Moffett said, and she blasted Archie with another sonic scream.

∽

"Why?" Hachi asked when Blavatsky had told her the names of the others who'd been with her at Chuluota. "Why were you there? Why did you kill all those men? Why did you kill my father?"

"To create the Jandal a Haad," Blavatsky said.

Fergus got a sick feeling in the pit of his stomach. "But—but that's what the Mangleborn call Archie, isn't it?" he asked.

Fergus felt Hachi's hand go slack in his. Whatever it was he didn't understand yet, she did.

∽

"*The Boy Made of Stone,*" Mrs. Moffett said. She hit Archie with another sonic scream, and he went rolling. "Blavatsky read how to do it in an ancient manuscript she found in Siberia, written by the First Men," she said, following Archie. "The First Men were as cold and heartless as your Septemberists at the Forge. They had no problem sacrificing people to destroy the giant monsters in the world. What are a few human lives to save an entire race? So they carved you from stone, put you on an altar over the closest Mangleborn they could find, stirred up some lektricity, and said the magic words.

- 304 -

But they needed one more thing," Mrs. Moffett told him. "One more very precious thing."

∽

"Blood," Blavatsky said. "We needed human blood. The blood of a hundred men to make a single boy with the strength of those hundred men."

Hachi shot to her feet, her chair clattering to the floor behind her. "No!" she cried.

∽

"*Yes*," Mrs. Moffett said, standing over Archie. He lay covered in dirt, curled up into a little ball. "Now you understand why you're truly a monster," Mrs. Moffett told him. "Why you're more a monster than any of these Lanternspawn. More a monster than *me*. You exist only because Blavatsky and her friends murdered *one hundred men* to make you."

"Where?" Archie asked, his face to the ground. But he already knew the answer.

"Does it matter?" Mrs. Moffett said. "Somewhere in Florida."

It mattered, Archie knew. He closed his eyes. It was bad enough that a hundred men had been killed to create him, but one of them mattered to Archie even more than the rest.

"Hachi . . . ," he said, sobbing into the salty dust. "Oh Hachi, I'm so sorry."

∽

"I'm so sorry," Blavatsky sobbed. She reached out for Hachi, but Hachi ran past Erasmus out of the room.

"Please, be merciful. You have to forgive me. I thought we were creating a champion, a servant of the Hidden Masters," she said, her voice small. "And after all we did, after that awful night, it didn't work. The child didn't live."

"It did," Fergus said. "*He* did. His name is Archie Dent."

"The Jandal a Haad—it survived? But it was lifeless when the Septemberists took it from us! We thought we had eluded them, but they caught us. They stole the homunculus and drove us apart. But you say we did it? We brought forth the Jandal a Haad? Glorious!"

"At the cost of a hundred lives," Fergus reminded her.

"Wouldn't you trade the lives of a hundred men for the greatest hero the world has ever seen?" Blavatsky asked.

"I think the question is, would *he?*" Fergus said.

Blavatsky's face fell.

"Be gone, spirit," Laveau said. "Papa Legba, take this wretched soul back to whence she came."

"Forgive me," Blavatsky said again, and she disappeared as her tears put out the candles that gave her form.

"This information, what Blavatsky had to say, it means something to you and Hachi?" Queen Laveau asked.

"Aye," said Fergus. "It means everything."

∞

Mrs. Moffett cackled, hitting Archie again with her sonic scream. He did nothing but lie on the ground and take it.

"I thought you would be mad. I thought you would lose control, and I could loose you on the rest of the continent with my monster army. But all you do is whimper and cry!" Mrs. Moffett crowed. "If I had known it would do this to you, I would have told you where you came from sooner!" She hit him again, and again, and again. Maybe if she blasted him enough, he thought, he would finally break apart and die.

Death would be better than living with the truth.

Archie waited for another blast from Mrs. Moffett's sonic scream, but she cried out instead.

"No—no! It can't be!"

Archie looked up to see Sings-In-The-Night swooping down out of the sky, the high bright Paiute sun glinting off her beautiful black wings. Sings-In-The-Night wasn't dead. She was alive! Archie felt his heart glow as Sings-In-The-Night descended like some glorious savior from on high, a heavenly creature come to grant him forgiveness and wipe away the sins done in his name.

"No—no, I killed you!" Mrs. Moffett cried, backing away.

Sings-In-The-Night hit Mrs. Moffett feetfirst, knocking her to the ground. She perched on top of Mrs. Moffett, wings wide, while her old friend tried to scrabble away in horror.

Archie reached for her. "Sings . . . ," he said, his throat dusty and sore.

And then Archie was being picked up, lifted by a great brass hand. Buster! The steam man stuffed Archie into his mouth and turned to run away.

"No," Archie said, thrown around the captain's quarters. "No—no, wait!" He scrambled up the ladder to the bridge and grabbed Clyde's arm. "No, we have to go back!"

"Are you crazy?" Clyde said. One of Mrs. Moffett's sonic screams caught them, and Buster lurched forward, almost falling over. Clyde steered Buster out of its path, running as fast as he could.

"Clyde, we have to go back! Sings-In-The-Night was there! She's alive! I saw her!" Archie pulled on Buster's controls, wrenching them back.

"Archie—Archie! It was Kitsune!" Clyde said. "It was just an illusion to distract Mrs. Moffett so we could get you out of there. It was just Kitsune!"

Clyde pointed, and Archie saw Kitsune hopping up the length of Buster's arm to climb into the top hatch.

Clyde grabbed Archie's arm and shook it. "She's dead, Archie," Clyde told him. "I'm sorry, but Sings-In-The-Night really is dead."

Archie sank to the floor. Of course she was. And all Archie wanted was to be dead with her.

35

Clyde banged on something with a wrench, his blue-and-yellow UN Steam Cavalry pants and black boots sticking out from under a bundle of hissing pipes in Buster's belly. Kitsune perched high up on top of a water tank, studying a map.

Archie sat in the shadows, where he belonged.

Archie had been carved out of stone and soaked in blood, and now he had the strength of a hundred men. A hundred men who had been killed to create him. A hundred men, including Hachi's father, Hololkee Emartha. No matter what he did with his life, no matter what kind of hero he became, he could never repay that sacrifice.

"Twisted pistons!" Clyde called. "I can't get this thingamajig to go back in the whatchamadoodle. Unless it goes in this doohickey . . ."

"Sounds very technical," Kitsune said.

"Perhaps a break is in order, Master Clyde," Mr. Rivets said. He came into the tight engineering space bearing a military-grade tea service and three metal mugs. Kitsune hung upside down from a pipe to grab her cup, and Clyde wormed his way out and took his, mopping his brow with a yellow handkerchief.

"Thanks, Mr. R. This hits the spot," Clyde said.

Mr. Rivets offered Archie a cup. "Master Archie?"

Archie shook his head.

"You have to have something to eat and drink sometime," Mr. Rivets said.

"No, I *don't*," Archie said. "That's the point, isn't it? I don't need air to breathe, and I don't need food to eat or water to drink. *I'm not a real boy.* I never was. I really *am* a shadow. I'm a dark, crooked thing that looks like a person, that moves like a person, but when you put your hand out to touch it, there's nothing really there."

"Well," said Clyde, "Mrs. DeMarcus used to say you can't have a shadow without a little light."

"*Will you shut up about Mrs. DeMarcus?*" Archie spat.

Clyde folded his arms and looked down at the metal gangplank at their feet, and Archie immediately regretted his words. But slag it, this wasn't something he could just whitewash with one of Clyde's homilies. He was a *monster.* An honest-to-goodness horror. He saw now why he could never be the leader of the League of Seven— not with a history like his. When he came right down to it, Archie wasn't sure he could even be the League's shadow anymore. He was too awful even for that.

"Master Archie," Mr. Rivets said. "There's no reason to be rude."

There was every reason to be rude. To everyone. Forever. But Archie couldn't disappoint Mr. Rivets. "I'm sorry," he told Clyde. "I just—I don't think there's anything you could say that would help."

"If you don't want to hear it from Mrs. DeMarcus, then hea

from me, Archie," Clyde told him. "We need you. I know all this business about how you were made is awful—I ain't saying it isn't. I don't know if I could deal with it myself, and that's a fact. But the bigger fact is that you're the only one of us who can go toe-to-toe with Philomena Moffett, and she's brewing up a mess of trouble. Without you, she beats all the rest of us put together—me, Buster, Kitsune, your two friends back in Houston—and she makes monsters out of half the continent. You got powers, Archie. *Super*powers. And you gotta use them to stop her."

"But I'm not even strong enough to beat her!" Archie said. "We fought to a standstill every time!"

"Which is why you've got the rest of us," Clyde said. "The people of the United Nations—of all the nations—they need somebody out there protecting them from Mrs. Moffett and the Mangleborn, and me and Buster are volunteering for duty. We can stop her, but we gotta have all hands on deck. The whole team. What about you, Kitsune?"

"*I'm* not volunteering. But I'm in," Kitsune said. She put a hand to her pearl necklace and glanced at Archie. "I got shanghaied."

"All right," Clyde said. He stuffed his handkerchief in his back pocket. "Buster needs repairs. Repairs I can't do. I'm a soldier, not an engineer, dang it. I wish we had your tinker friend here right now, but we don't. So I gotta put in someplace with a machine shop. You got me a place yet?" he asked Kitsune.

She handed the map down to him. "Ute town called Wasatch. I've been there. It's nice. The bank backs right up onto the railroad tracks. Makes for an easy getaway."

"Well, we'll be coming and going through the front door this time," Clyde said.

Kitsune shrugged and grinned, wrapping her fox tail around her ₃s.

"So here's the plan," Clyde said. "Me and Kitsune will take

Buster to Wasatch for repairs. Archie, you and Mr. R. will catch a train south to Houston. Find your friends."

Archie opened his mouth to say something, but let it go. He had to admit, Clyde really was a natural-born leader. Archie wanted nothing more than to crawl into a corner and hide there for the rest of his life, but he couldn't say no to Clyde. To the League.

"Me and Kitsune will be right on your heels," Clyde said. "Once we're all together, we'll go after Mrs. Moffett as a team. Stop her before she destroys the United Nations. There's only five of us, not seven, but that'll have to do."

The engine room rocked, and something slammed against the hull. *Clang-clang-clang-clang!*

Clyde rapped on one of the pipes with his wrench. "Stop scratching, you big oaf!" he yelled at the steam man. "You don't have fleas anymore! You're made of metal!"

Buster whistled happily to hear Clyde's voice, and Clyde shook his head. "Dumb thing. Doesn't even realize he's not a dog anymore."

And that was it, Archie realized. He was Buster. He was a golem who was pretending to be human, just like Buster was a steam man pretending to be a dog. No, not pretending—fooling themselves. Everyone else could see what they really were on the outside. He and the dog were ghosts in the machine, but that's all they really were—machines.

"I'm going up top," Clyde said. "Get us going to Wasatch." Kitsune hopped down off the water tank to join him. "You coming?" Clyde asked Archie.

"In a minute," Archie told him.

Clyde nodded. He climbed halfway up a ladder and stopped. "For what it's worth, Archie, I've seen what kind of monsters there really are out there, and you're not nearly the worst of them."

Clyde and Kitsune left Archie and Mr. Rivets alone in the engine room. Within minutes, the machinery around them came to life as Buster steamed south, toward Wasatch. Toward Hachi and Fergus.

Hachi and Fergus. Archie buried his head in his hands. "I know I have to do this, Mr. Rivets. I know I have to find Hachi and Fergus, go after Mrs. Moffett. But how am I going to tell them? What am I going to say? How are they still going to be my friends when I tell them where I came from? How I was made?"

Mr. Rivets put a hand on Archie's shoulder. "They can hardly blame you, sir. You had nothing to do with it."

"But it had everything to do with me, Mr. Rivets."

"I'm sure Master Fergus will understand," Mr. Rivets told him.

"And Hachi?"

"Miss Hachi will be all right too," Mr. Rivets said.

Archie stared up at him.

" . . . in time," Mr. Rivets added.

"I will never be all right, ever again," Hachi said.

Fergus crossed Hachi's hotel room to the bed, where she was hastily stuffing her clothes into a satchel.

"Okay," Fergus said. "So 'Are you all right?' wasn't the smartest question I've ever asked. Of course you're not. But you can't just go steaming out of here without telling me where you're going."

"You know where I'm going," Hachi told him. "I have a list. People to track down. Erasmus has already sent out pneumatigrams to Pinkerton agencies across the continent. I'm going to track down the other people who were with Blavatsky that night, and I'm going to kill them. As slowly and as painfully as I can."

Fergus put a hand to her shoulder and she flinched, batting it away with one hand and drawing her knife with the other. Fergus put his hands up in surrender, and she sheepishly put the knife back away.

"You're going to have to deal with this eventually," Fergus told her.

"I am dealing with it," she said. "I told you—I'm going to track them down and kill them—"

"That's not what I mean, and you know it."

Hachi stared at her bag. "Not yet," she said.

"Then when?" Fergus said. "We told him we'd meet him—"

"No."

"He's still our friend," Fergus said. "It's not his fault he—"

"*No*," Hachi said. She zipped up the bag, threw it over her shoulder, and turned toward the door. Fergus put a hand to her arm again, but this time she didn't flinch. Instead she just closed her eyes.

"I'll come with you, then," Fergus said.

"No."

"Why not?"

"The things I'm going to do—the things I *have* to do—I don't want you to see them."

"What? Crivens. I'm a big boy, Hachi. I can handle—"

"No," Hachi said. "You don't understand. I don't want you to see *me* do them."

Fergus hadn't expected her to say that. Hachi prided herself on her toughness. She wore it like a raygun on her hip, for everyone to be afraid of.

"Hachi, I love you," Fergus said.

She batted his hand away. "I don't want you to love me! I have a job to do, and I don't have a place in my life for anything else! I have to kill the people who killed my father. Who killed ninety-nine other men at Chuluota. All so that—all so that—"

Fergus pulled her into a hug, and she sobbed into his shoulder.

"I know," he said softly. "I know." He let her cry until she had cried herself out, and still Fergus knew it wouldn't be enough. She had had eleven years to cry every last tear she had for her father and the other ninety-nine men who died at Chuluota, but she was just getting started crying over Archie.

"Go on without me, then," Fergus said. "I slipped one of those beeping homing beacon things I hate so much in your bandolier. When you're . . . when you're finished, you turn that on, and I'll find you. We'll find each other."

Hachi nodded into Fergus's chest, gave him a quick kiss on the cheek, and was gone out the door.

∽

The little Cheyenne steamburb of Medicine Bow had stopped at the junction depot it shared with the Transcontinental Railroad and was just settling in for the night. Gaslights glowed in the teepee-shaped houses up and down its seven stories like jars full of fireflies stacked on shelves. Nearby, the herds of buffalo the town tended slept in great brown-black piles against one another.

The sound of a train in the distance was so familiar, neither herd nor town stirred. Only the stationmaster, frowning at the railroad timetable that listed no trains due to arrive until early the next morning, was there to meet the locomotive as it pulled into the station. The train hauled but one passenger car, and even more mysteriously, no porters or engineers or passengers climbed out when it stopped.

"Hello in there!" the stationmaster called, raising his lantern to see into the cab. A dark figure moved away from the light. "Hello?" the stationmaster tried again.

The locomotive blew its steam whistle, making the stationmaster jump. Then it blew again, and again, and again. The Cheyenne and their buffalo were used to train whistles too, but not one that blew over and over again. A train whistle blown like that—*any* whistle blown like that—meant trouble, and the people of Medicine Bow came out to the rails of their moving village to see what was wrong.

The stationmaster saw someone climb to the top of the passenger car—no, not climb, he thought, more like glide—with what looked like a lantern in hand.

"Hello, dear friends," said a woman's voice, loud and clear in the prairie night. "For too long, you have lived in darkness. Let me show you the light!"

The woman opened her lantern, and as the light fell on the people of Medicine Bow, they screamed. They screamed so loudly they didn't hear the army of monsters that shambled up the tracks behind the locomotive, hooting and howling, following their shadowy leader across the continent to the United Nations of America.

ARCHIE

HACHI

WHO WILL BE
THE NEXT
TO JOIN

FERGUS

The League
of Seven

CLYDE

KITSUNE

?

?

ACKNOWLEDGMENTS

Thank you to everyone at Tor/Starscape who has helped to make this book and this series a success: to my wonderful editor, Susan Chang, whose continual enthusiasm for these books makes me keep trying to outdo myself; to Ali Fisher, publishing coordinator, for answering all my crazy requests with such speed and grace; to Leah Withers, publicist extraordinaire, for arranging my first-ever book tour; to Deanna Hoak, copy editor, for reminding me how I spelled all those crazy words in the first book; and of course to Kathleen Doherty, publisher, who took a chance on *The League of Seven* to begin with. I would be remiss not to thank illustrator Brett Helquist, whose amazing art graces the front cover and chapter headers. Everywhere I go, people tell me they picked up my book because of his awesome illustrations! Thanks too to Linda Marie Barrett and everyone at Malaprop's Bookstore/Cafe in Asheville, North Carolina, for their continuing support of the series, and to all the students, teachers, librarians, and booksellers I met on tour for book one. Thank you to Bob, and to my friends at Bat Cave and Blue Heaven. And last but not least, thanks again to Wendi and Jo. You're the aether in my aggregator.

Read on for a preview of
THE MONSTER WAR,
Book Three of The League of Seven

Archie Dent sat in the shadows in the corner of his hotel room in Houston. This was where he belonged. This was what he was, after all. A shadow. The darkest shadow of them all.

Mr. Rivets, Archie's clockwork manservant, tutor, and constant companion, ticked into the room and threw the curtains wide. Archie squinted and threw an arm over his eyes as the bright Texian sun streamed into the room.

"Don't!"

"It is time you roused yourself, Master Archie. Cleaned yourself up. Had some food. You haven't eaten in days."

"Why should I?" Archie asked. "I don't need to. I can't die. I don't even need to breathe. I could sit here forever if I wanted to."

"Which would be an incredible waste, sir. It is time you rejoined the world of the living," Mr. Rivets told him.

"No," Archie said. He'd told Mr. Rivets the same thing every day for a week now, ever since they'd arrived in Houston. Ever since he'd learned the horrible truth about how he'd been brought to life. "Close the curtains. I don't want the light."

"There are matters you must attend to, Master Archie. If I were not now self-winding, I would have run down long ago. And you promised Miss Hachi and Master Fergus you would meet them here in Houston. They may be somewhere in the city as we speak, and we must warn them about Philomena Moffett and her Monster Army."

"I don't care. I don't want to see them. I don't want to see anyone ever again. I'm done. With everything."

"There is something else, Master Archie. Something I have uncovered in my own search for Master Fergus and Miss Hachi. Homeless children are being taken from Houston's streets."

Archie lifted his head. "What?"

"By masked men with steamwagons," Mr. Rivets said. "They take the children in broad daylight. I interrupted one such kidnapping only this morning, and alerted the local authorities to the problem. But they are too taxed with the annual Livestock Exhibition and Rodeo currently being held in the Astral Dome. Nor, I think, do they much care about children without families to miss them."

"The . . . *what?*" Archie shook his head. "No. I don't care either. It's not my problem."

"I see," said Mr. Rivets. "I apologize, Master Archie." His clockworks ticked softly as he considered his young charge. "There is one small matter at least that must be attended to. Your parents have sent us funds via pneumatic post, and the post office requires you be there in person to sign for it."

"I don't care," Archie said.

"May I remind you, Master Archie, that without these funds we shall be turned out of the hotel and onto Houston's streets, where, I can assure you, it is far brighter and hotter than your corner."

Archie huffed. Fine. He'd go to the post office and sign for the money. But he wasn't taking a bath, and he wasn't eating or drinking anything. He was through pretending to be human.

Houston was hot and dusty, just like every other part of the Republic of Texas Archie had seen. Mr. Rivets led him along a sweltering wooden sidewalk past saloons, general stores, and steam horse stables. The brown-skinned, black-haired people of Houston kept turning to stare at Archie's pale white skin and white hair, and he heard one or two whisper his name. Senarens and his clacking League of Seven dime novels were more popular than ever! Archie slipped his brass goggles down over his eyes and dragged Mr. Rivets across to the dark side of the street, where he hoped he'd be less conspicuous, and cooler too. A Wel-suh Fargo steamwagon almost ran over them, but Archie still didn't care. It would have done more damage to the steamwagon than to him.

After a few blocks, Mr. Rivets turned off San Jacinto Street and led Archie into a maze of side streets, where at last they came to a narrow, rutted lane squeezed in between two wooden warehouses. A dozen or so half-naked Texian children were playing some kind of game where they tried to bounce a rubber ball through barrel rings they'd nailed to the wall. Farther down the alley, two dogs fought over a scrap one of them had dug out of an overturned trash can, and a pile of empty wooden crates looked as though someone might be living in them. Archie didn't understand. Where was the post office?

"I would advise you not to fight at this juncture," Mr. Rivets told Archie. "You should allow yourself to be captured instead. That way you'll be taken to the ringleaders of the operation."

"What are you talking about?" Archie asked. Had Mr. Rivets slipped a cog?

The ground rumbled as two steamwagons backed into the lane, one from each direction. Texian men in brown leather pants, denim shirts, and white cowboy hats leaped from the covered beds on the wagons, rayguns in hand and bandanas covering their faces. *Kazaaack!* An orange beam from one of the pistols blew up the rubber ball, and the children screamed. They tried to run, but both ends of the street were blocked by the men and their steamwagons.

"Mr. Rivets, what's going on?" Archie asked, but when he turned around the machine man was gone. "Mr. Rivets?"

Archie heard the blast of another raygun and ducked instinctively.

"All right, *chamacos*!" one of the banditos called. "No messing around now! Into the trucks nice and easy, and nobody gets hurt."

The banditos circled the kids. A boy tried to escape by crawling under one of the steamwagons, but a bandito caught him by the heel and dragged him back. *Whack!* The bandito cracked him over the head with the butt of his raygun, and the boy went down in the dirt. After that, nobody tried to run.

Archie was steaming. First he'd been tricked out of his hotel room by Mr. Rivets, and now these kidnappers were hitting defenseless kids. Slag it all—he wasn't even supposed to be here! His fists clenched and he started for the bandito who'd knocked the boy down when he felt something hard poke him in the back. It was another of the banditos with a raygun.

"Hey, *mano!*" the bandito called. "What about this one? He's a Yankee."

"Are you kidding, *güey?*" said the bandito who'd hit the kid. "They pay double for *gabachos!*"

The raygun in Archie's back poked at him, nudging him toward the other children. Archie was tempted to turn around and crush the raygun in his fist and punch the bandito through the wall. A raygun blast couldn't hurt Archie. It wouldn't even knock him down. He could send all six of these banditos into the next alley before they knew what hit them. But Mr. Rivets was right: That wouldn't stop whoever was behind this. Cursing Mr. Rivets with names the machine man would have scolded him for, Archie let himself be loaded onto one of the two steamwagons with the other children.

A few of the children cried as the banditos went through the covered wagon and shackled them, but most looked resigned to their fate. Archie wanted to tell them everything was going to be all right, but he didn't want to draw attention from the banditos. Not yet.

The steamwagon shuddered as they got underway. A bandito shackled Archie's right leg to the left leg of the boy sitting beside him. Archie wasn't worried about the chain—he could rip it off whenever he wanted to—but the boy he was shackled to looked frightened. He was a Texian about Archie's age, and just as small, with light brown skin and black hair. He was grubby like he lived on the streets, but, unlike the other children, at least had blue denim pants, a cowboy shirt that used to be white, and a well-worn pair of brown leather boots. The boy stared straight forward, his eyes distant like so many of the others'.

"Everything's going to be okay," Archie and the boy told each other at the same time.

Archie blinked. This homeless kid was telling *him* everything was going to be okay?

"My name's Gonzalo," the boy said, still staring straight forward. "What's yours?"

Archie didn't want to tell the kid his real name. He might have read one of Senarens's dime novels and start talking. "It's, um, George," Archie lied.

Gonzalo turned his head at that, almost like he didn't believe him, but he didn't say anything. "Where you from, George?" Gonzalo asked.

"Philadelphia," Archie said, telling the truth this time.

"You're a long way from home."

"What about you?" Archie asked.

"Austin, originally," Gonzalo said. "Now kind of all over. Where are your parents?"

The couple who'd raised Archie, Dalton and Agatha Dent, lived just outside Philadelphia, in Powhatan territory. He'd thought of them as his parents for the first twelve years of his life, but technically he didn't have parents, because he wasn't human. The thought chilled him all over again, and he longed for the seclusion of his dark corner in the hotel.

"I . . . I don't have any parents," Archie told him, which was true and wasn't true.

"Me either," Gonzalo said.

"So you've been living on the streets?" Archie asked.

Gonzalo nodded, still staring straight ahead.

Archie looked around at the other children. They probably all had similar stories. It was bad enough that they were orphans with no place to go, no clothes to wear, and no food to eat. Now they were being rounded up by kidnappers and hauled off to who-knows-where, to do who-knows-what.

As to what, Archie had a guess. In his experience, it always came down to the Mangleborn, the giant prehistoric creatures that stirred every few hundred years to drive humanity mad and destroy everything they'd built. Some Mangleborn-worshipping cultists needed children's blood for sacrifices, or wanted to turn them into hideous half-human/half-animal Manglespawn, or meant to feed them to a Mangleborn or Manglespawn. Archie shook his head. Whatever it was, he would stop it, and then he was done. For good. And nothing Mr. Rivets could say or do would change his mind.

Archie heard a roar outside the steamwagon as it slowed to a stop. *Here we go,* Archie thought. *A Manglespawn with a bat's wings and a bear's body. Or maybe a Mangleborn with a thousand snakes for arms and rooster legs for feet.* Archie popped his neck and got ready to fight.

"Sounds like a crowd," Gonzalo said. "A big arena. The Astral Dome, maybe."

Archie blinked. Now that Gonzalo mentioned it, it *did* sound like the roar of a crowd.

The bandits hooked a cattle ramp with covered sides to the back of the wagon and shooed the children out, two by two. As they passed from the steamwagon, Archie briefly saw the round, silver top of the Astral Dome, one of the Seven Wonders of the New World. The ancient coliseum dominated Houston's skyline.

"You're right," Archie whispered. "They're taking us into the basement of the Astral Dome!" He shook his head again. "Underground. It's always underground."

"What is?" Gonzalo asked.

"Nothing," Archie said. No reason to scare him until he saw whatever monster it was these guys worshipped. That would be enough scare for a lifetime.

The roar of the crowd above was louder now, and came every

few minutes. It was like they were right underneath the arena floor. Something thudded above them, shaking the stone ceiling and the walls, and the crowd roared again. What exactly did people *do* in a rodeo? The pens they passed in the hallways under the arena were filled with steam horses and mechanical bulls. Did they race them? Fight them? Archie had no idea. There weren't a lot of rodeos in Philadelphia.

It took Archie a few minutes to notice that the lights in the passageways weren't gas. They glowed bluish-yellow from behind small orbs set into the walls.

"Are the lights . . . *lektric?*" he whispered.

"You mean like lightning? No, I don't think so," Gonzalo said, his eyes still straight ahead. "I'm told they glow the same way fireflies do. That's why they call this the Astral Dome. The roof is covered with them, like stars. It's ancient technology. Older even than the Romans. It's never dark inside the Astral Dome. Never hot, either."

Gonzalo was right—it *wasn't* hot in here! Archie felt a cold breeze coming out of a metal vent, cooling the underground passage. "But how—?"

"Air-conditioning," Gonzalo said. "Legend says the ancients had a way to cool the entire arena without ice, but no one knows how to do that anymore. Instead, they pack the bottom levels with ice and blow air over it and through the air ducts the ancients built."

So. Some kind of ice monster then, Archie thought. *Something living in the frozen depths of the Astral Dome. Or maybe it's the ice itself—a kind of living ice that gets inside you, turns you into a killer snowman.*

"In here, *chamacos,*" a bandito told them, pointing to a dark chamber deep inside the passageways underneath the arena.

Here we go, thought Archie. *Now we meet the monster.*

The chamber was lined with more of the mechanical bull pens Archie had seen earlier, but these pens were full of children. Mostly Texian, like Gonzalo, and all dirty and thin and ragged. Archie looked around for some sign of Mangleborn or Manglespawn, but there was nothing. Nothing but shabby, crying children, and smiling banditos.

"A good haul today, *jefe*," one of their captors said. He gave Archie a push, and Gonzalo stumbled forward with him on their chain. "We even got a *gringo*!"

A redheaded mestizo man with a bushy red beard, black suit, and brown bow tie crossed the room to them. "So I see! He'll fetch a good price in New Spain." He lifted Gonzalo's chin to look at his teeth. "They all will! Put them in the pens."

"Procopio Murietta," Gonzalo muttered.

"You know this guy?" Archie asked.

Gonzalo nodded. "He's wanted for murder, bank robbery, and cattle rustling from Texas to the California Republic, and everywhere in between. And now, apparently, child slavery."

Was that really all this was? Banditos rounding up children off of Houston's streets and selling them as slaves to ranchers across the border in New Spain who couldn't afford Tik Toks? Not that it wasn't awful and didn't need to be stopped. It was, and it did. But Archie had been so sure there would be some Mangleborn connection to it all. He couldn't believe it was just good old-fashioned bad guys.

Archie planned out his attack. He could knock down any jail cell door they put him behind, but it would be better to move now, before they locked him away. Better to keep the other kids safe until he was finished with the banditos.

"We should make our move before they lock us up," Gonzalo whispered.

Archie stopped in surprise, bringing Gonzalo up short on the chain that connected them. "Who, you and me?" Archie asked.

"No," Gonzalo said. "I was talking to—"

Something big and wild roared deeper down in the Astral Dome's sublevels, shaking the ground like an earthquake.

"*Órale!* What was that?" said Gonzalo.

Archie was afraid he knew.

"The *cucuy* is hungry," Procopio announced. "We need tributes."

The prisoners in the pens cried out and retreated into the darkness.

"What's a *cucuy*?" Archie whispered.

"It's a kind of bogeyman Texian parents scare their kids with," Gonzalo said. "A monster."

"Right. Of course," Archie said. No matter what, things *always* came back to the Mangleborn.

Gonzalo looked at the floor. "Is this one of those creatures you were talking about?" he asked. "The ones causing all the trouble?"

Archie frowned. "I didn't say anything about monsters." He'd been thinking it, but he hadn't said anything about the Mangleborn. Before he could ask what Gonzalo meant, the redheaded bandito started rounding up children.

"Take these, and these, and these," Procopio said, skipping Archie and Gonzalo, "and feed them to the *cucuy*."

"Wait! Take me instead!"

Archie and Gonzalo turned to stare at each other. They'd both yelled exactly the same thing at the same time.

Reading & Activity Guide

THE DRAGON LANTERN
A LEAGUE OF SEVEN NOVEL

by Alan Gratz

Grades 4–8, ages 9–13

About This Guide

The questions and activities that follow are intended to enhance your reading of *The Dragon Lantern*. Please feel free to adapt this content to suit the needs and interests of your students or reading-group participants.

BEFORE READING THE BOOK:
Writing & Discussion Activities

The pre-reading activities below correlate to the following Common Core State Standards: W.4–8.3; SL.4–8.1, 3

1. Ask each student to reflect on a skill or talent they possess. Are they proud of this ability? Why or why not? How does this ability affect the student's daily life, friendships, future plans, and dreams? After reflection, ask each student to write a short essay describing a quality or talent he or she would like to have and why.

2. Invite students to define the word "hero." Do they know any heroes in their school or community? Can they list some heroes from history, fiction, film and/or television? What qualities make these people heroes? Are heroes all good or all bad? What kinds of heroes does the world need today?

Discussion Questions

The discussion questions below correlate to the following Common Core State Standards: SL.4–8.1, 3, 4; SL.6–8.2, 3; RL.4–8.1, 2, 3; RH.4–8.6

1. The first words of *The Dragon Lantern* are "Archie Dent dangled from a rope . . ." What ideas or images does this line bring to your mind? In what ways is Archie dangling both physically and emotionally?

2. What is the relationship between Fergus and Hachi? How does Archie feel about this relationship?

3. Who is the Cahokia Man? What is a Mangleborn? Who or what are "Mangleborn," "Manglespawn," the "Septemberist Society," and the "League of Seven" and how do these groups relate to each other?

4. Throughout the novel, Archie is struggling to adjust to some difficult truths about his identity. What are these truths? How does this make him feel less connected to Fergus and Hachi and, possibly, more empathetic toward the Cahokia Man?

5. Early in the novel, Archie reflects on the story of the Cahokia Man, noting "The story of course, like most stories . . . had been rewritten over the centuries, in part because people forgot, and in part because people *wanted* to forget." (p. 33) Why do people want to forget? Have you ever had an experience you wanted to forget? Do you think it is right to try to do so? Explain your answer.

6. On page 78, Custer gives Archie some advice about being different: "Whatever it is you're embarrassed about, whatever it is you wish was normal, embrace it. *Own it.* Because that's what makes you special. And being special is way better than being normal, no matter what the cost." What does it mean to be special? Do you agree or disagree with Custer's statement? Why or why not?

7. Why does Archie part ways with Hachi and Fergus? Do you think this is a good decision? Is it a necessary decision?

8. Compare Archie's main objective with Hachi's. In what ways are these objectives similar? What are both characters really seeking?

9. Describe the voodoo world Hachi and Fergus encounter in Louisiana. How is this similar to, and different from, the wild West?

10. What is a "gris-gris"? How does Marie Laveau react when Fergus declines to call his building abilities magic?

11. Name at least three ways in which it is important that Hachi is now head of the Emartha Machine Man Company.

12. What is a FreeTok? What changes does Archie see in Mr. Rivets when they are reunited in Chapter Sixteen? Do you think the outlaw FreeTok Jesse James is right to compare the lives of Tik Toks to slavery? Explain your answer.

13. What roles does "lektricity" play in the story?

14. What does Sings-In-The-Night, the bird girl, reveal about the use of the Dragon Lantern? About the League of Seven? Whose frightening true identity does she reveal in Chapter Twenty?

15. As the dangers mount, in what ways do Archie, Hachi, and Fergus wish they were still together as a team? How do they defeat their foes nonetheless?

16. On page 228, Sings-In-The-Night bemoans her strange body and Archie comforts her, saying, "Having bird legs or stone skin doesn't make you a monster . . . It's what you *do* that makes you good or bad." How does Archie struggle to believe his own statement as he continues his quest for the Dragon Lantern?

17. In Chapter Twenty-Nine, what persuasions does Mrs. Moffett use to convince Archie and his friends to join her Shadow League? How does Archie feel the darkness to which Mrs.

Moffett refers as the Mangleborn beneath Alcatraz awakens? How do Clyde and Kitsune react to Archie's behavior?

18. What is the relationship between the Daimyo of Ametokai and the Daimyo Under the City? Compare this relationship to the relationship between Archie and the Jandal a Haad.

19. How does the Dragon Lantern work? Should it ever be used?

20. How was Archie made? How does this connect Mrs. Moffett to Madame Blavatsky? What do these discoveries lead Hachi and Archie to realize? In the final chapters of the novel, what characters ask for forgiveness? What characters need or want forgiveness? Explain your answers.

21. What is a human being?

22. Can *The Dragon Lantern* be read as a story about how people face the reality of who they really are—and how they can separate their history and origins from the person they are today? If so, what lessons might this novel offer readers about identity?

Research & Writing Activities

The research and writing activities below correlate to the following Common Core State Standards: L.4-8.4; RL.5–8.4, RL.5–6.5, RL.6–8.6, RL.4–8.7; SL.4–8.1, 3; W.4–8.2, 7; WHST 6–8.6

1. Go to the library or online to learn more about the literary subgenre of *steampunk*. Find at least three sources for your information. Use your research to create an informative poster that includes a definition of steampunk, a short history of the origin of the genre, and a list of some famous steampunk novels and/or movies.

2. In steampunk novels, famous historical figures often interact with fictional characters. *The Dragon Lantern* features General George Custer. Learn more about Custer's life and times, then write a short essay explaining why you think author Alan

Gratz chose to use this character to tell the story of Archie and his friends' pursuit of the Dragon Lantern.

3. Several Native American tribes are referenced in the novel, as they are in the first League of Seven book. In real American history, these tribes had tragic relocation experiences as the American government set them on the "Trail of Tears." Research the Trail of Tears then create an annotated map (with dates) showing how at least five tribes were affected by the Trail of Tears.

4. A. Go to the library or online to find a definition of "colossus." Learn about things that have been named Colossus through history, such as the Colossus of Rhodes, the Colossus computer, or the Colossus character in the Marvel Comics universe. Use PowerPoint or other multi-media software to create a presentation entitled, "Colussus: Ideas, Images, and History" to share with friends or classmates.

   B. Using pencils, pen-and-ink, or even 3-dimensional arts media, create a drawing or model of *Colossus* based on details found in the novel.

5. A. Many characters whom Hachi and Fergus meet in Louisiana are true figures from history. Go to the library or online and use research skills to identify at least three characters from the Louisiana-based chapters of the novel who were not simply invented by the author. If desired, continue your search for real historical figures in the story. Keep track of them in a notebook.

   B. Use your research as the base for a card game: Write each character name on a separate index card. On the reverse side write "F" for fictional or "R" for real historical figure along with 2–3 facts about this individual. Take turns holding up cards to see if friends or classmates can tell the fictional from the real and what they know about the real people.

6. In the character of Sings-In-The-Night, write at least four journal entries, including one recounting your transformation into a bird girl, one explaining your complicated behavior toward Archie and his friends, one describing your decision to join forces with Archie, and one exploring your feelings toward Mrs. Moffett and what you may understand about her that the other League members do not.

7. Create a chart comparing Buster, Mr. Rivets, Philomena Moffett, and Kitsune in terms of their machine, human, spirit, and animal qualities. Based on your chart, write a MANIFES-TO (a declaration of your guidelines and goals) explaining how all creatures of the earth should be treated. Read your manifesto aloud to friends or classmates.

8. Create an illustrated booklet entitled, "A Reader's Guide to the Heroes of the League of Seven." Make a page for each League member, noting his or her physical appearance, what you know of their history and powers, and how they contribute to the group. Leave two blank pages for future League members to be discovered in novels to come!

9. Role-play a conversation between Archie, Hachi, Fergus, Clyde, and Kitsune in which each discusses why he or she agreed to be part of the League of Seven and their feelings about the group.

10. Help Archie and his friends find their next League member by creating an early chapter for the next League of Seven novel. Select your favorite historical time and place and research at least two real people, events, or important objects from this time to include in your chapter. Invent and name a new fictional League member and decide what abilities he or she will have. Write a 3–6 page chapter in which Archie or Hachi meets this new League member.

11. In the last century, philosopher and essayist George Santayana (1863–1952) wrote: "Those who cannot remember

the past are condemned to repeat it." How does this relate to Archie's observation that people sometimes "want to forget" horrible experiences? Is forgetting dangerous? Write an essay explaining how Santayana's quotation can be understood in terms of the novel.

JOIN THE
SEPTEMBERIST
SOCIETY!

www.septemberistsociety.com

ABOUT THE AUTHOR

Alan Gratz is the author of *Samurai Shortstop*, an ALA 2007 Top Ten Book for Young Adults. He began writing *The League of Seven* by listing all the things that ten-year-old Alan would have thought were awesome, including brass goggles, airships, tentacle monsters, brains in jars, windup robots, secret societies, and superpowers. (In fact, he still thinks all those things are awesome.) When he's not writing books like *The League of Seven*, *Samurai Shortstop*, *The Brooklyn Nine*, and *Prisoner B-3087*, he's usually reading other people's books or creating an awesome new costume for science fiction/fantasy conventions. Visit his website at www.alangratz.com.